"I'm quite capable of finding
my own way, thank you."

She began walking toward the house, and with one long step, he caught up with her and matched his stride to hers.

"How unseemly of you, my dear," he said mockingly, "to go unescorted. Remember that it's my privilege, and pleasure, to accompany you henceforth."

Miss Stuart stopped short. Green eyes blazed up at him, and he had to remind himself that blue eyes were better than green, and it was a foolish, regrettable kiss that had stolen from him his safe, predictable future. If she hadn't been so tempting, everything would be perfect right now.

"If you really think I'm going to marry you, you're wrong!" she said with a distinct snarl in her voice. "I'd rather be a scullery maid in the nearest inn!" Then she whirled and ran into the house, the hem of her white dress (which, stubbornly, he still considered quite ravishing, no matter what his grandmother might say) fluttering behind her.

Let her go, Gabriel thought to himself. One last, small gesture of freedom before they were both ensnared forever.

By Lisa Berne

The Penhallow Dynasty
You May Kiss the Bride

Coming Soon
The Laird Takes a Bride

LISA BERNE

YOU MAY KISS THE BRIDE

The Penhallow Dynasty

AVONBOOKS

An Imprint of HarperCollinsPublishers

HarperCollins
PUBLISHERS
Since 1817

This is a work of fiction. Names, characters, places, and incidents are products of the author's imagination or are used fictitiously and are not to be construed as real. Any resemblance to actual events, locales, organizations, or persons, living or dead, is entirely coincidental.

Excerpt from *The Laird Takes a Bride* copyright © 2017 by Lisa Berne.

First Avon Books mass market printing: April 2017

ISBN 978-06-245178-1

Avon Trademark Reg. U.S. Pat. Off. and in Other Countries, Marca Registrada, Hecho en U.S.A.
Avon, Avon Books, and the Avon logo are trademarks of HarperCollins Publishers.
HarperCollins® is a registered trademark of HarperCollins Publishers.

17 18 19 20 21   QGM   10 9 8 7 6 5 4 3 2 1

For Cheryl Pientka

Chapter 1

Wiltshire County, England
1811

This was dangerous. If she bit her lip any harder, thought Livia Stuart, it would probably begin to bleed, sending a bright red rivulet dripping down her chin, and end up staining—in a spectacularly uncouth way—the bodice of her gown.

The bodice of the gown which, Cecily had casually mentioned, was hers from two years ago.

"And you've altered it so cleverly, I scarcely recognized it." Cecily's voice was soft and friendly, but in her pretty blue eyes there was, unmistakably, the gleam of cruel mischief. "I knew, of course, from the color, which is no longer *quite* in fashion."

Short of telling Cecily to stuff it, there didn't really seem anything Livia could say, but she was spared the necessity of trying to think up something polite when Lady Glanville, Cecily's mother, turned her gaze to Livia and subjected her person to a comprehensive scrutiny.

"Indeed," her ladyship finally said, with the gravity of one considering a matter of deep existential import. "That particular shade of rose was very popular. Princess Charlotte, I believe, favored it highly. I'm not at all certain, however, that it's suitable for one of your coloring, Livia dear. It complements fair hair, such as Cecily's, as well as a pale complexion, like hers. I'm sorry to say that you are rather brown."

"She *would* be out of doors so much," Aunt Bella interpolated in her vague, melancholy way. "I've told her repeatedly how injurious it is to both health and appearance, but I do not think Livia attends to me." She sighed gustily, sending the faded ribbons of her cap a-fluttering. "I do not think anyone attends to me. I do not think I am listened to by—"

"Far be it from me to pontificate," said Lady Glanville, "but one ought not to dwell on oneself, you know. We must always think of others. As Cecily does, for example. She *could* give her cast-off gowns to her maids, as most other young ladies do, but instead she insists that dear little Livia have them. It's quite touching, really."

"Your Uncle Charles doesn't give you a dress allowance, does he, Livia?" Cecily's tone was sympathetic. *Too* sympathetic. "But then, you don't go anywhere, so perhaps it doesn't matter a great deal."

"No," Livia answered flatly. "No, it doesn't matter at all."

Now it was Lady Glanville who audibly sighed as she glanced around the large drawing-room with its dated, shabby furniture, the wallpaper from a generation ago pockmarked with ghostly rectangles where valuable paintings had once hung but had since been sold. "It's dreadfully lowering," she said, "to see a gentleman's family so reduced. Why, it was only ten years ago that we met nearly as equals."

Livia felt her teeth grit. She'd been forced to participate in these occasional morning visits from Cecily—the *Honorable* Miss Orr—and her mother—the *Right Honorable* Viscountess Glanville—for years. Because they were wealthy and highborn, apparently their arrogance and rudeness were to be endured. Livia clenched her hands tightly in the folds of her gown.

Cecily's gown.

"Well, there's no use in dwelling on what can't be changed," went on Lady Glanville. "I am afraid that life simply isn't fair. A disagreeable fact, but what can one do? Now, do stop frowning, Livia dear, for I'm delighted to tell you we've come for the express purpose of offering a little treat."

"I'm all ears, ma'am," replied Livia with what had to be obvious sarcasm, but Lady Glanville only said, with her arctic smile:

"We are hosting a ball next week. It shall be a kind of *début* for Cecily. In addition—"

"Mr. Gabriel Penhallow and his grandmother, Mrs. Penhallow, come to visit us!" Cecily said breathlessly. "The *Penhallows!* Of Surmont Hall! We met Mrs. Penhallow in Bath a few months ago. She wrote us a letter. He's going to—"

"My dear Cecily, pray refrain from interrupting. It is most unbecoming," said her ladyship. "As you know, Bella, earlier in the summer I insisted that Lord Glanville go to Bath in order to drink from the waters. His gout, unfortunately, had been paining him a great deal. The nobleman's affliction! And I thought Cecily might benefit from mixing in a wider society, for it is sadly limited in this neighborhood. There are, alas, so few families of our caliber. As both the daughter of an earl and as a viscountess, I fear I cannot but be aware of how limited our acquaintance must necessarily be. Yet one must, in these rackety modern times, sometimes unbend, and here we are."

"Too, too kind," Aunt Bella murmured, evidently with real, if muzzy, gratitude. She took a sip from the delicate crystal glass on the little table at her elbow. In it was her cordial which, Livia knew, was heavily laced with laudanum.

Lady Glanville nodded serenely, and the peacock feathers in her elaborate silk turban waved gently, as if in agreement. "While in Bath, we had occasion to observe Mrs. Penhallow in the Pump Room. I distinctly noticed her looking at Cecily but, naturally, would not have dreamed of encroaching upon her. An earl's daughter is as nothing compared to *her*. The Penhallows came to England with the Conqueror, you know, and it's said that the Conqueror bowed to *them*. Thus, imagine our gratification when she sent the Master of Ceremonies to us, so that he could escort us to her and perform the introduction."

"My knees were positively *shaking!*" Cecily put in. "But I curtsied quite well, didn't I, Mama?"

"Creditably so. I had no occasion to blush. I must plume myself on my foresight in having you practice curtsying before we left for Bath. An hour a day works wonders. But I digress. Mrs. Penhallow and I spoke for some fifteen minutes, and at the risk of seeming boastful I must say that she was condescension itself! We discussed the weather and the dreadful state of the roads. I happened to mention Lord Glanville's gout, and she recommended a treatment which—"

Her ladyship went on to recount further details of her conversation with the redoubtable Mrs. Penhallow, a personage of whom Livia knew nothing and cared less. Bored, she stopped listening and instead she looked at the rapt, lovely face of Cecily as she hung on her mother's every word.

Not for the first time, Livia thought how uncannily Cecily resembled the china shepherdesses Aunt Bella had once collected—it was that shining hair of hers, the color of new straw, those cornflower-blue eyes, that pale, creamy skin. Today she wore an exquisite long-sleeved gown of the finest, whitest cambric, which set off her willowy figure to perfection; from underneath its lacy appliquéd hem peeped dainty kid slippers with pretty little pink rosettes. Livia resisted the urge to glare at her own slippers, very old, very run-down.

Instead she looked over at Aunt Bella (*her* slippers weren't much better), who kept her sleepy gaze fixed on Lady Glanville as she droned on, occasionally murmuring "Indeed" and "How delightful." She lay half-reclining on her sofa, draped in innumerable shawls, some of which puddled forgotten on the floor. Aunt Bella suffered from an extensive variety of ailments, none of which she ever openly discussed, all of which she treated with her cordial which she described, nebulously, as a superior medicinal. She spent a good deal of her time dozing in this room, with only a cage of small birds to keep her company.

Livia glanced at them now, huddling on their perches. Their cage was set near the window, but because Aunt Bella had an aversion to sunlight at all times, the heavy greenish-black drapes were drawn as was her custom and the drawing-room was gloomy and dim. It felt like she was underwater, Livia thought. Drowning. At least she would escape this room, for eventually this epically awful morning-call would end, but those little birds were trapped.

Quietly she stood and went to them. They looked at her without moving, their eyes dark, soft, pitifully dull. Livia inched the drapes apart and a welcome beam of sunlight illuminated the cage.

"—and after kindly informing me that my color was

a trifle high, Mrs. Penhallow advised a diet of dry toast with a small quantity of pickled onions to stimulate the juices of digestion, for which she very generously divulged the receipt."

"How delightful," said Aunt Bella. "Livia, close those drapes at once."

Sulkily Livia obeyed and returned to her seat.

"In short, it was a most gratifying exchange," said Lady Glanville, "and concluded with Mrs. Penhallow actually offering two fingers to shake. I don't know when I've been more pleased! You may therefore envision with what transports I received a letter from Mrs. Penhallow just a few days ago."

She withdrew from her large beaded reticule a folded sheet. "My dear Bella, rejoice with us! Mrs. Penhallow writes that her grandson, Gabriel Penhallow, is in London, having returned from several years abroad. 'He and I agree that it is high time that he marry and ensure the succession,'" Lady Glanville read aloud. She took a deep breath, causing her already prominent bosom to swell prodigiously.

"Only listen! 'Your daughter, Cecily, seems to me to be a most suitable candidate. Her demeanor is ladylike and her movements graceful. I perceived, too, that her teeth are good. Following our propitious meeting at the Pump Room, I of course had my man of business thoroughly examine your situation in life and your family lines. Your fortune is sufficient and, aside from a slight taint of trade arising from mercantile activities during the time of Queen Elizabeth, I find your ancestry to be acceptable.'"

Lady Glanville cleared her throat. "I need hardly say that those activities occurred on Lord Glanville's side of the family."

"Indeed," Aunt Bella murmured.

"So they are coming here!" burst out Cecily excitedly. "So that Mr. Penhallow can meet me!"

"It is an honor quite overwhelming," said her ladyship. "We've entirely put off our plans for Cecily's Season. Naturally Mrs. Penhallow most specifically states that no promises have been tendered, but she makes it very clear that should Mr. Penhallow find Cecily agreeable, we may expect to promptly receive an offer of marriage."

"They say he's one of the most eligible men on the Marriage Mart!" Cecily said happily, her blue eyes sparkling. "He is so wealthy, too! Only think of my jewels and carriages! I shall move in quite the highest, most fashionable circles!"

Remarkably, Livia thought, Cecily had no objection to being inspected as if she were some sort of prize heifer. And if the fabled Mr. Penhallow were to deem Cecily an acceptable wife, why, what a perfect match it would be. So perfectly, terribly romantic. She felt her lip curling in a sneer she just barely managed to repress.

Cecily now smiled at Livia with that same kindly air. "And I won't be too grand to forget *you,* Livia dear. Your future must be thought of, too. I don't suppose I'll be able to arrange a match for you—that would be reaching a little *too* high—but perhaps I could ask among my new acquaintance if they might need a governess. That, I daresay, would suit you admirably. Not *quite* belowstairs, but elevated above the other servants." Then she lifted her delicate blond eyebrows. "Oh, dear, no, it would be impossible, wouldn't it? You've had no training. But perhaps I can find *something* for you by and by, once I'm Mrs. Penhallow. Perhaps even in my own household. Wouldn't that be jolly?"

"Well, well," Lady Glanville said indulgently, "let's not get ahead of ourselves, my dear. You are not Mrs. Penhallow *yet.* Although I doubt that Mr. Penhallow will meet with a prettier girl anywhere, here *or* abroad." She folded the letter and with conspicuous care put it back into her reticule. "We must be on our way. There's a vast deal yet to do, for the Penhallows arrive the day after tomorrow. Our ball will be, I may say without false modesty, exceptional. All the neighborhood gentry are to come."

"And you," Cecily said, still smiling sweetly at Livia, "are invited too. And dear Mrs. Stuart, of course."

"Too, too kind." Livia could tell her face was getting red with the effort of remaining civil.

"I know you do not dance, not having had the benefit of a master," Lady Glanville told her, "but you must come, find yourself a quiet little corner, and enjoy the decorations. We are doing up the ballroom in the Egyptian style. Quite a hundred pounds have been spent on potted palms alone."

"How delightful." The hot flush was spreading down her neck.

"Yes, yes, delightful," Aunt Bella said to Lady Glanville, struggling feebly to sit a little more upright, "but you know I don't go out. Charles must take her."

Her ladyship smiled archly. "I knew such would be the case. Lord Glanville sent a message to that effect. He is bringing up from the cellar some Spanish port and trusts Charles will share it with him."

"Oh, he'll go then," answered Aunt Bella, visibly relieved and sinking back onto her cushions. "How nice for you, Livia."

"Yes, and we brought some more of my old gowns for you," added Cecily. "My maid has them in the hall. Perhaps one of them might suit you for the ball. Though you *are* wider than I am."

"My Cecily is quite the soul of benevolence, is she not, dear Bella? Well, Livia, you must be anxious to see your new dresses. Why don't you run along, and retrieve them from Cecily's maid. What fun you shall have."

She had been dismissed. Livia rose and after dipping the briefest of curtsies in Lady Glanville's direction, went to the door with long strides, so angry that she felt she had to get out of there or explode. Behind her she heard Aunt Bella saying in a soft little bleat, "Livia! No word of gratitude! Pray come back!" Instead, she closed the door with exaggerated gentleness and leaned against it for a moment.

By the bannister stood a maidservant with an armful of gowns. With a muttered sentence of thanks Livia took them and hurried upstairs to her room where with savage satisfaction she flung the gowns against the wall, leaving them to lie in a crumpled heap on the floor. She paced back and forth, back and forth, until the red haze of rage subsided. Then she went to her bed and dropped full-length upon it with unladylike abandon, causing the old wood frame to creak alarmingly.

It was stupid of her, she knew, to react like that to the Orrs. But it was hard, so hard, when Cecily had everything and she had so very little. No parents, no brothers or sisters; no money, no education, no prospects.

Your future must be thought of, too.

It was strange, now that she considered it, how little time she *had* spent thinking about her future. Possibly because there was no point to it. In her existence here she was like a great hoary tree, deeply, immovably, rooted into the earth.

She couldn't even hang on to the morbid hope of inheriting anything from Uncle Charles when he died. He'd run through most of Aunt Bella's money ages ago, and year by year everything had slowly declined, dwindled, faded away. Now there wasn't much left; the estate barely brought in enough for Aunt Bella to pay for her cordial, and for Uncle Charles to spend his days hunting, drinking, and eating. Speaking of romantic marriages.

Well, it could be worse. At least she didn't have a mother like that revolting Lady Glanville. Imagine having *her* breathing down one's neck all day.

Still, this was only a small consolation.

A very small consolation.

Livia thought about Cecily's beautiful white gown and those elegant kid slippers with the dainty pink rosettes.

It was those rosettes that did it.

Envy, like a nasty little knife slipping easily into soft flesh, seemed to pierce her very soul.

Abruptly Livia twisted onto her side and stared at nothing.

She would *not* cry.

Crying never helped anything.

There came to her, suddenly, the memory of the first time she had met Cecily, some twelve years ago; they'd both been around six. Cecily and her mother had come to call. Livia, recently arrived from faraway India, desperately lonely, was so anxious to be friends with the lovely, beautifully dressed girl with the long shining curls. Shyly she had approached, trying to smile, and Cecily had responded by saying in a clear, carrying voice:

"Oh, you're the little orfin girl. Your papa was sent away from here and he died. And your grandpapa was a runaway and he drownded. And your mama drownded, too. Why is your skin so brown? Are you *dirty?*" And she had backed away, to hide behind the skirts of her mother Lady Glanville, who had said to her, with that same cold smile that never reached her eyes, "Poor little Livia isn't a native, my dear, she's every bit as English as you and I. The sun shines quite fiercely in India, and she had no mama or papa to make sure she stayed under her parasol. Do you see?"

Livia had never forgotten the burning sense of shame from that day. Nor had Cecily made it any easier, for from time to time she would laughingly recall the occasion of their first meeting and how she had thought Livia to be unwashed, as if it was the funniest anecdote in all the world.

Livia did not like to remember, even if only hazily, how when she was four, the monsoon season struck Kanpur with devastating onslaughts of rain. Both her widowed mother and her grandfather had died in a great flood, and it was with grudging reluctance that Uncle Charles had sent money for his niece's passage to England.

Upon arriving in Wiltshire, Livia was not so much welcomed into the home—if such the ancient, rambling domicile known as Ealdor Abbey could be so termed—of Uncle Charles and Aunt Bella, as absorbed. Aside from grumbling within earshot about the expense of feeding her, Uncle Charles barely noticed her. Aunt Bella, childless, somnolent, always unwell, with interest in neither Society nor useful occupation, accepted Livia's presence without a blink but also without care or concern for the little girl for whom she was, ostensibly, responsible.

Oh, you're the little orfin girl.

Livia smiled without humor.

Yes indeed, Cecily certainly had a knack for getting to the heart of things.

Gabriel Penhallow rode alongside the large, old-fashioned, perfectly sprung coach in which sat his grandmother and her companion Miss Cott. Its stately black panels as always were polished to a blinding gleam. Behind the coach, at a respectful distance, followed the light carriage bearing her dresser and maidservant as well as his valet, along with an astonishing quantity of his grandmother's luggage.

He turned his head to look inside and saw his grandmother dozing, sitting bolt upright and her mouth firmly closed. Even in her sleep she was indomitable, he thought with a flicker of amusement. Miss Cott, slim and short, sat opposite Grandmama, gray hair tucked neatly inside her serviceable bonnet and holding in her lap her employer's enormous jewelry case. She was gazing out the window, away from Gabriel, her expression calm and remote.

He had known Miss Cott nearly all his life, and never once had he seen her shaken from her pleasant equanimity, no matter how extreme were Grandmama's outbursts of impatience or anger. Or how frequent her orders to move a sofa cushion, freshen her pot of tea, fetch a stepstool, ring for a maidservant, write a dozen letters, rearrange flowers in a vase, summon the doctor, even put on a different shawl not so distasteful to her employer.

In point of fact, his grandmother was not an easy person to be around. Both his parents having died in the typhus epidemic of 1791 that swept through Somerset, Grandmama had been his guardian since he was seven, and he remembered being secretly glad to have been sent away to Eton, and even gladder as a young man, after a few obligatory years spent in Society, to have seized the opportunity to travel across Europe as a member of the Diplomatic Corps. Between Grandmama's relentless pressure to marry, and the brazen machinations of ambitious mothers and their wily daughters, he'd had enough of the so-called gentler sex. Experience among the *ton* had taught him that women were, evidently, crafty and manipulative creatures, vain, shallow, their heads full only of dresses, parties, gossip, intrigues, conquests.

All in all, a dead bore.

He had been happy to seek his pleasures elsewhere, sensibly, in the arms of well-paid courtesans, with whom there was no need to pretend he was interested in Lady Jersey's latest *on-dits* about who had been dampening their petticoats, or how much the Regent (then still the Prince of Wales) had spent on new boots, and so on.

When finally the government had summoned him back to England, and released him from service with thanks, he'd been forced to admit that Grandmama was right—about one thing, at least. He was nearly thirty years old and he could no longer ignore the obligations of his station. He needed to marry and produce offspring. There was a nursery, long empty, at Surmont Hall.

Not that he had any particular intention of returning to the Hall. It was merely a place where he'd lived for a few years of his childhood. What would he *do* there, anyway? For a man used to active occupation, to utilizing his intellect each and every day, life in the country was bound to be unutterably dull. Besides, the bailiff—what was his name? Edwards? Eckers? No: Eccles. Eccles ran the place quite competently.

It all came down to one thing.

Choice.

He could certainly choose where he lived, but he couldn't choose not to marry.

There *had* been a time, in his early twenties, after he'd nearly been maneuvered right into the proverbial ball and shackle . . . Good Lord, that fiendish Lady Washbourne, so mind-bogglingly determined that the world would have been an infinitely better place had she deployed her talents in the pursuit of something useful, like a cure for cholera. Her daughter, a beautiful half-wit, somehow ending up in his carriage made more than a little drunk and obediently prepared to yield up her virtue to him: It had been rather startling to discover in this way her ladyship's estimation of his character, her assumption that he was so animalistic in his desires that he'd cheerfully ravish an innocent girl— one, moreover, who couldn't even sit up straight on her own—and then, of course, marry her at once. What a tangle *that* had been, getting her safely returned home and himself neatly extricated from an absurd and awkward situation. He knew that any hint of scandal would enrage his grandmother; he didn't fear her outbursts, but he owed her, at least, the courtesy of an unsullied reputation.

After that charming little debacle, he'd toyed with the idea of remaining unwed, and allowing the Hall to eventually pass into the hands of his cousin Hugo Penhallow. He was a nice young chap, good-tempered, poor as a church mouse, Army-mad. As soon as Gabriel had come into his inheritance he'd set up Hugo with an allowance and purchased his commission. The lad was now roiling about the so-called United States, happy as a lark.

But there was no certainty that madcap Hugo would return alive and whole, leaving open the ominous possibility of the heir being his distant Scottish cousin Alasdair Penhallow who, if the rumors were correct, was a most unsavory fellow as well as being irremediably stupid.

Before long, he'd come to accept his fate. The

Penhallows had been arranging dynastic marriages for decades—centuries, really. He would wed and do his duty, but aside from the congress necessary to create progeny, he and his wife would lead separate lives. It was the Penhallow way, and he'd yet to hear anyone complain about it. Besides, he wasn't in any danger of giving way to maudlin sentimentality about his lot in life. Generally speaking, he was a fortunate man, blessed with intelligence, good health, and a substantial fortune; too, he wasn't some callow lad, pining away in the quest for some kind of grand idealized love.

No, he had business to transact.

And luckily, Grandmama had spared him the tedium of having to search for a bride.

Some months ago she had left Bath—where she'd been ensconced for many years—and made her way to London. There she had taken occupancy of the family townhouse in Berkeley Square and proceeded to spend the Season looking for a worthy young lady. Invited everywhere and universally fawned upon, she attended breakfasts, teas, dinner parties, assemblies, balls, Almack's; indefatigably had she searched, interviewed, investigated. Her letters came to him bristling with detailed reports.

Angrily, she wrote that *this* earl's daughter was already affianced, and *that* duke's girl had just gotten married; their available sisters were too young, or too old, or had a squint, or teeth that made one blench. The girls of a fine old family from the North *would* have been considered if not for their abject lack of fortune. One otherwise promising young lady, Grandmama had learned to her fury, had been concealing the ugly fact of an uncle in the fishmongering trade. The granddaughter of an old friend, whom she had long thought to be a possibility, looked decidedly consumptive. Another girl who had seemed likely at first came from a family in which the women were notoriously poor breeders. And, naturally, there were whole swathes of young ladies who could be ignored—no matter how wealthy or pleasing in appearance—as their bloodlines were pitifully inferior.

On and on it went, until at last the Season had come to an end, and Grandmama returned to Bath in defeat.

Then she had met the Orrs.

Not long after he arrived in London had come the jubilant letter with the news that she had finally met the perfect young lady for him: the Honorable Cecily Orr was from a noble family, wealthy, exceedingly good-looking, elegant, fashionable, and graceful.

It was all arranged.

He was to come to Bath immediately, whereupon they would together set out for Wiltshire so that he could meet his prospective bride. She had no doubt that he would approve her choice.

He'd been slightly annoyed by her peremptory tone, but, after all, business was business. He might as well get it over with, and the sooner the better.

So off he had gone to Grandmama's palatial residence in Upper Camden Place where she had—over a distinctly odd supper—declared her intention to leave at dawn the next morning. But it had taken several hours until the carriages had been loaded to her satisfaction. In the meantime, two footmen had nearly been dismissed. The cook, castigated for the inappropriate nature of the muffins she had baked and tenderly packed in a basket, wept. Miss Cott had trotted up and down the steps with an apparently infinite number of band-boxes, cases, and shawls. And when finally they had set out, the pace of the massive coach was so ponderously slow that Gabriel felt like they were on a royal progress of yore. He half-expected the people they passed on the road to wave and offer posies.

Once underway, Grandmama's spirits had brightened considerably. At their halts she spoke ceaselessly of the wedding, the brilliancy of the guests, the beauty of the bride-to-be and the handsomeness of the Penhallow sons she would produce; he listened politely and thought of other, more interesting things. He was thankful to be riding outside, as at least she did not shout to him through the carriage window, and confined her seemingly endless flow of remarks to the more receptive Miss Cott.

Livia looked balefully at the rumpled heap of expensive, fragile gowns lying on the floor. So Cecily thought one of her old cast-offs might suit her for the ball? And Lady Glanville thought that she'd be thrilled, *grateful*, to peek out from behind a potted palm to enjoy a glimpse of luxury?

Well, they were wrong.

Dead wrong.

Livia jumped to her feet and went over to the gowns. She snatched them up and shoved them onto a low shelf of her armoire.

She was *not* going to the ball. Uncle Charles might if he wished—and let him drink port until he had to be carried out by the servants. It certainly wouldn't be the first time.

Gabriel walked rapidly to the Orrs' stables, conscious only of an overpowering desire to escape the house and each and every one of its occupants. A day (not even a *full* day) here had stretched his patience to the limit—not to mention how his grandmother had, within an hour of their arrival, managed to entirely overset the household. The sheets in her bedchamber hadn't been properly aired, the wood in the fireplace looked wormy, the chairs were inconveniently placed, Miss Cott's accommodations were too far away, she required better candles, and the cook was to prepare her special dishes according to exacting specifications. Oh, and dinner needed to be served forty-five minutes earlier.

Lord and Lady Glanville had scrambled to meet these demands, and servants had scuttled about under a dizzying array of orders. He'd had only a brief opportunity to meet their daughter, the Honorable Miss Orr, who was indeed as beautiful as he'd been led to expect. She had smiled and swept into a graceful curtsy while Grandmama looked meaningfully at him. Later, Miss Orr had been quiet during dinner, her eyes cast down in maidenly modesty; it wasn't until he and Lord Glanville and his gawky lout of a son Tom, after a vapid interval over some very good port, had rejoined the ladies that he realized, without surprise, that Miss Orr was like every other young female he had met among the *haut monde*. She talked about the roads, she chatted about the weather; she complained about the servants, and casually let fall the fascinating fact that her gown for the ball had cost thirty-eight pounds.

"But what about yourself, Mr. Penhallow? You have recently been in Town, I believe? Tell me—" And here she leaned forward, her blue eyes shining in the candlelight. "—have you met Mr. Brummell? Is he as diverting as they say? And is it true that he wears coats made of *pink silk*?"

Grandmama stopped short in her elucidation to Lady Glanville regarding the most efficacious methods of polishing silver, as she had noticed (she did not scruple to divulge) a certain dullness in the implements set out at dinner. "Brummell? An upstart grandson of a valet and a dreadful *égotiste*, whose so-called charm I find to be entirely overrated." She fixed her gaze sharply on Miss Orr. "How on earth do you know about his absurd pink coats?"

Quailing slightly, Miss Orr answered, "I only happened to read about Mr. Brummell in one of Mama's magazines."

"Magazines." Grandmama sniffed, managing in a single audible inhalation to convey a rather ominous disapproval.

"Of course, dear Cecily doesn't make a habit of reading magazines," Lady Glanville interpolated hastily. "She's far too busy visiting the poor. Why, just the other day she gave away quite a number of her old gowns to a deserving orphan."

"Very laudable," Grandmama had said, unbending, and deigned to accept from Miss Orr a cup of tea.

The conversation then meandered again to the weather, Lady Glanville expressing at length the hope that it might be fine for the ball. Tom stared into space and Lord Glanville snored quietly on a sofa. Miss Orr expertly played for them several songs on the pianoforte. Grandmama nodded off but did not snore. Lady Glanville came to sit next to Gabriel and in a low, confidential tone regaled him with details concerning the extremely costly carpet they had recently laid in the drawing-room—the very one upon which his feet now rested. Miss Orr joined them and animatedly described to him the distinguished people to whom she had been introduced while in Bath. "Mrs. Penhallow being first among them, to be sure," she had concluded with a pretty smile.

"Without doubt," her ladyship added punctiliously. "But Cecily was quite an acknowledged favorite, Mr. Penhallow, I assure you. Why, the cards we received were beyond counting."

"I can easily believe it, ma'am," he said, his boredom by now so acute that he wished *he* could take a nap too.

Miss Orr had blushed and at that moment Grandmama snapped awake. "A charming performance on the pianoforte, my dear," she said graciously. "Most refreshing."

When later he had escorted his grandmother to her rooms she pronounced the evening to be an unalloyed success, aside from the unpalatable food served at dinner and the draughts roaring throughout the drawing-room. "And I could see how taken you were with Miss Orr," she said, with what in a lesser person would have been termed smugness. "Shall we announce the engagement at the ball?"

Gabriel felt a cynical smile curving his mouth. Although he had certainly exerted himself not to let it show, he was not particularly taken with the beautiful and accomplished Miss Orr. Not that it mattered. She was, in fact, an entirely suitable choice. And it had been made very plain to him how satisfied she would be to accept his offer. For all she knew he was the worst sort of monster imaginable, but he *was* a Penhallow, with his limbs intact and a full head of hair, and that was clearly good enough. Miss Orr had spent well over twenty minutes inquiring in the minutest detail as to the particulars of the Penhallow townhouse in fashionable, exclusive Berkeley Square, while her mother sat by, nodding approvingly.

"Perhaps," he had suggested to his grandmother, irony in his tone, "I ought to propose first."

Airily she waved a bejeweled hand in the air. "Fine."

He *had* planned to speak to Miss Orr the next day, but found himself at breakfast being eyed by Lady Glanville and Miss Orr as if he were a juicy first-rate carcass hanging in a butcher's shop. And when her ladyship made a blatant attempt to hustle him and Miss Orr out into the garden for a private stroll, a flash of intense irritation overrode his good intentions—how he *loathed* being manipulated!—and he only said, standing:

"If you'll excuse me, ladies? My horse is in need of exercise."

"But—" Miss Orr glanced toward the window. "But it looks as if it might rain, Mr. Penhallow."

"Then perhaps," he said, pleasantly, "it would have been a mistake to walk in the garden. Your gown would most certainly have been spoiled. Good day."

At the stables he had his horse Primus saddled, and rode away toward the woods. Already he was a little sorry for giving in to his annoyance; he really should have gone out into the garden and gotten it over with. When he got back to the house, he'd do it. A few polished phrases, perhaps a quick obligatory kiss, and then everything would be nicely settled to everyone's satisfaction.

Cheered by a comfortable sense of resolve, Gabriel rode on.

Chapter 2

"**N**ot go to the ball?" Aunt Bella said, for what was possibly the twentieth time. "But Livia, whyever not? Such a delightful treat for you, I'm sure, and your Uncle Charles so thoughtful as to take you. Come away from those drapes. It will rain, I feel it in my very bones, and I do not care to see it. What on earth are you wearing? You look a positive ragamuffin. Your ankles are showing! Surely it's not one of the gowns which Cecily so generously gave you?"

"No." Today was one of those days when Livia couldn't bear to put on yet another of Cecily's things, and so she'd worn an old dress of Aunt Bella's which she hadn't even bothered to alter. What did she care that it was too short and an ugly puce color and looked ghastly on her? As Cecily had pointed out with that barbed sweetness of hers, she didn't go anywhere anyway.

Briefly vivified by Livia's dreadfully off appearance, Aunt Bella now lost interest in the subject. "My head is aching," she said fretfully. "I need a little more cordial. Ring for someone to bring it to me. And do go. Your pacing about is making my head worse."

"Certainly, Aunt." Livia pulled violently on the bell cord and without ceremony left the drawing-room. She went quickly to her bedchamber where she exchanged her slippers for a pair of sturdy old boots and flung round her shoulders another of Aunt Bella's discards—a large and hideous gray shawl, stretched in places and shriveled in others. Then she ran downstairs and out a little-used side door. She couldn't bear the stifling atmosphere for one more minute.

Outside.

She needed to be outside.

Livia walked rapidly along the damp, soft path that led her to the woods and into their quiet refuge. With a deep sense of relief, she breathed in the rich, wild scent of earth, plants, seemingly even the sky itself. How beautiful it was. She had spent so much time here, walking and wandering, it seemed that every tree, every shrub, every stone was known to her. Rain began to fall, and a cool wind whipped playfully around the tops of her boots and fluttered at loose tendrils of hair that had escaped her careless braid.

She had forgotten to wear a bonnet, but there was no one to see her and besides, she was hardly some delicate little miss to melt away in a little rain: she had no fear of succumbing to illness. A good thing, she thought sardonically, for who would tend to her if she did? Not Aunt Bella, who could barely get herself out of bed each day, nor any of the harassed, unhappy servants who went sullenly, sloppily, about their duties.

Livia could feel her boots sinking deliciously into the mud, then kicked at some sodden clumps of leaves, scattering them. She wished she never had to go home.

Not that Ealdor Abbey had ever *really* felt like home.

Fighting back a sharp, sudden pang of loneliness, Livia found herself walking quietly now, along a faint and twisting track that led to the old woodsman's cottage she had discovered long ago. Here it was, a simple little dwelling formed from crudely fashioned logs, abandoned and decrepit, entirely covered with vines, with only a gaping space where once a door had been and the doorway itself rotted away. In her fancy it had been an elven home, or a mystical chapel where fairy weddings took place beneath the green canopy that the roof had become. All at once a slight movement within stopped her. She caught her breath in wonder, and stared, for inside the cottage, twenty feet away, stood a young doe, unmoving, gazing back at her with dark liquid eyes.

And then: a tawny form to her left, among the trees; it shifted, stamped a hoof, and she saw a great stag, its head lifted proudly. The doe's mate?

Livia stood absolutely still, as if frozen in time, half-expecting some fantastical minister—part human? part beast?—to show himself and perform the sacred rites of marriage.

Instead there came the unmistakable sound of hoof-beats. The doe darted in one direction, the stag another, directly across the path where a rider had come and startling his immense black horse, which reared in alarm, deadly sharp hooves flying out, and was promptly reined in, in a display of strength and finesse that Livia watched with a kind of fascinated alarm. She wanted to run away—the horse looked horribly fierce—but wondered, panicked, if it would come after her. It was just the sort of situation in which she would be running, trip over an exposed tree root, and immediately be trampled. For all she knew, the horse and rider would simply go on and leave her to die an ignominious death in the mud. Things like that happened all the time. Her life was far from perfect, but neither did she have any interest in meeting her Maker today. So, willing her erratic breathing to slow down, she stayed right where she was.

It was almost as if she were rooted to the ground.

Five minutes before, Gabriel had muttered out loud:

"Oh, bloody *hell*."

It was time to face the truth. He was lost, completely lost, in these infernal woods. He'd tried going in different directions, but it was useless. Finally he pulled Primus to a halt and looked around, scowling. No path in sight. Nobody and nothing.

Except—

He squinted. Yes, there *was* somebody. He urged his horse forward only to see, in a sudden blur of movement, a stag bolting past, close enough that he might almost have touched its immense antlers. Primus reared and if not for his own quick reaction might have unseated him, but by pulling sharply on the reins he'd brought him back under control.

Now Gabriel rode forward.

That somebody was a shabbily dressed girl. Excellent— a servant from a local manor, surely able to give him directions. He noticed that there was quite a bit of mud on her cheek. And on her decrepit shawl, and the revealingly short hem of her gown. Even on the thick untidy auburn braid which lay draped forward over her shoulder.

Then he noticed that her eyes were green—not the hard, overbright green of emeralds, but the deeper color of pine, oak leaf, laurel—and quite pretty.

Really, if one were prone to imaginative flights, one might almost think of a nymph, or a wood sprite, or a sylph from Arthurian legend.

He looked again into those big green eyes.

Which might have been a mistake. A single word floated across his mind:

Entrancing.

For a brief, crazy moment Gabriel felt that he could happily drown in their deep green depths.

No, more than that.

Much more.

Desire surged through him, raw and primal, and as if in a sudden fever-dream he felt that he could with enormous pleasure slide from his horse, take her in his arms, press her against him, and have her—possess her—up against the nearest tree, here in the cold rain, bury himself in the warmth of this living nymph, stay lost with her in this insanely confusing forest forever.

Then he gave himself a mental shake. What in God's name was he thinking? Within hours he was going to be affianced to the exquisite, the appropriate, the ideal Penhallow bride Miss Orr, and here he was lustfully eyeing this girl like she was his last meal on earth.

Besides, he wasn't one of those men who viewed comely servant girls as prey.

"Don't be a fool," he muttered under his breath, as if giving himself instructions. Water droplets dripped gaily from the brim of his hat, and suddenly he wanted more than anything to be back at the Glanville home, that large and ludicrously overfurnished manse, where his perfectly mapped-out future awaited him. But to accomplish that, he needed this girl's help. And he'd reward her for it, of course.

Gabriel reached into his pocket and pulled from it a coin, which he held out for her to see. "Hello," he said. "Can you tell me how to return to the Glanville estate?"

She only gazed up at him, her expression startled.

Oh God, no. Just his luck. A pretty girl, but a simpleton. The way things were going, he'd take the wrong path and end up in Scotland, bumping into his idiot cousin Alasdair, and wouldn't *that* be fun. If she would just *point*. That could be enough. Perhaps he could galvanize her into speech—or a lifted finger, north or south—

He reached for another coin and tossed them both to her which she caught adeptly.

"Tell me how to return to the Glanville estate," he repeated, enunciating with extra care as well as increased volume.

Livia frankly stared. Heavens, but he was good-looking. He sat his horse with effortless, athletic grace (rendering her odds of being trampled reassuringly low), and it was easy to see the strength of his broad shoulders and long, powerful legs. It was nice to see someone so well put together. And she liked his hair, too: it was brown, neither dark nor light, and thick, straight, rather long. His eyes were also brown, intense and piercing, set off by dark brows. Long sideburns framed aristocratic cheekbones; his nose was straight, proud. And his mouth. He had a thin upper lip which, when you looked at it, and compared it to the fuller lower lip, would seem to be unattractive, but it wasn't. Somehow they just went beautifully together. It was surprising, really.

"Can you assist me?" he said. "I must return to the Glanville estate, where I am a guest."

Livia snapped out of it. His tone now struck her as being unpleasantly loud and patronizing. He was a guest of the Orrs? Could it be he was the celebrated Mr. Penhallow, Cecily's soon-to-be betrothed?

He *had* to be. Of *course* he was. You only had to look at him—and why was he frowning at her?—to see the arrogance practically dripping off of him.

All at once she realized the implication of the coins she'd foolishly accepted. Why, he thought she was some lowly country bumpkin to whom you'd offer a *gratuity* in exchange for a little help!

For a few seconds she felt hurt. Humiliated. Then she felt angry.

Very, very angry.

She wished, violently and with all her heart, that she could slap that superior expression right off his handsome face. It being an impractical option, instead she bent her knees in a deep, deliberately clumsy curtsy.

And at last she spoke.

In precisely the way a lowly country bumpkin would.

"Oh, sir," she breathed, "ye're stayin' with them Orrs? Why, they be the finest family of these parts! I do hear they dine off plates made of *solid gold!*"

"No, no, that's not—"

"And that Miss Cecily! She's said to be the prettiest young lady in the land! And her the granddaughter of a real earl! Oh, sir, ye've had the honor of *meetin'* her and all? Myself, I'd be all a-tremble!"

His scowl deepened, and now he looked quite fierce. Not that she cared. He said:

"Now see here, girl—"

She rolled right over him.

"They say that ball comin' this week is to be all done up like them Ejip-shins did use to live! Mam says it's heathenish, but I'd give anythin' to be goin'! Why, I could just stand in a corner somewhere and be as happy as the day is long!"

"I hardly think you would be invited," he replied, icily. Somewhere in the back of his mind, he was amazed at how he sounded just like his grandmother at her least pleasant. But he couldn't seem to stop himself. *Don't fall into her eyes, you fool.* "Now, do you know the way or don't you? You've your money, so—"

"Oh, indeed I do, sir, indeed I do! 'Twill feed my family for nigh on a month, sir, so generous have ye been! And my poor old granny is ailin' so—now we can buy her a blanket, sir, for she has none. Ye're a fine, fine gentleman, sir, if ye'll forgive my familiarity in sayin' so, and—"

"*Do you know the way?*"

From fifteen feet away, Livia could see his long, strong fingers tightening around the handle of his riding crop.

He was, in fact, an easy twenty-minute ride from the Glanville estate. Livia knew the path well. Instead, still in that breathless, subservient voice, she gave him elaborate directions so convoluted that she doubted he would make it there in less than two hours. When she was finally done, he gave her a hard stare from underneath those dark brows, then wheeled his horse and galloped off.

Livia watched him go. Horrible, horrible man! On his great, horrible horse! She flung down the two coins, then ground them into the mud with her boot. It was a silly gesture, given that she was literally penniless, but it was, nonetheless, deeply satisfying.

She turned and began to walk back toward the Abbey.

In her mind, over and over again, rang his dismissive words: *I hardly think you would be invited.*

What did *he* know? What did *any* of them know about her? She was only *poor little Livia.*

Your Uncle Charles doesn't give you a dress allowance, does he, Livia? But then, you don't go anywhere, so perhaps it doesn't matter a great deal.

Do stop frowning, Livia dear, for I'm delighted to tell you we've come for the express purpose of offering a little treat.

Oh, you're the little orfin girl.

Her fury grew with every step she took. By the time she arrived at the Abbey, Livia was consumed by a single idea.

Revenge.

She practically flew up the steps to her room, where she went at once to her armoire and pulled out the gowns Cecily had given her. She sat on her bed and spread them around her. Muslin, silk, satin, crepe, gauze, velvet . . .

Her brain worked furiously, envisioning, planning, designing. She brought out her shears, tape, pins, and thread. It wasn't long before her needle was flashing rapidly, in and out of a length of pale gold satin, like a tiny little dagger she'd enjoy plunging into certain people.

By the time Gabriel finally returned to the Glanville estate, he was not a happy man. Either that girl really was a simpleton, or she had tricked him. Either way, he was soaked to the skin and half-frozen. But he was not to be deterred. He bathed, he changed into dry clothes, and he went in search of Miss Orr.

He found only Lady Glanville. And his grandmother. Sitting in a drawing-room and both of them looking well-satisfied.

"Oh, my dear Mr. Penhallow, we were just speaking of you," said her ladyship, with a ponderous sort of lilt to her voice that might have passed for humor.

He bowed slightly. "You flatter me, ma'am."

"We missed you at nuncheon. Such a long ride. I do hope you didn't meet with any difficulties?"

"Not at all. It was delightful. I trust my absence wasn't an inconvenience?"

"By no means. And you weren't the only one absent. Dear Cecily, I fear, has developed—you will forgive my candid speech, but we are, after all, such good friends!—that is to say, Cecily has suddenly developed a spot on her cheek. It's unfortunate, but naturally she must remain in seclusion until the treatments have succeeded in eliminating it. And the ball only the day after tomorrow! But have no fear. Your grandmother was gracious enough to mention a superior protocol involving the cooked yolk of duck eggs and just a dab of aged lard. My own maid is preparing it as we speak. I'm certain it will be most efficacious."

An expression of complete seriousness had settled onto her ladyship's heavy features and earnestly she leaned forward. "I assure you, Mr. Penhallow, that Cecily only *rarely* breaks out in spots. You mustn't think she's one of those young ladies who are constantly disfigured by them. And you will be glad to know that she cleans her teeth regularly. I inspect them every day."

Well, this was a great deal of information he would just as soon not know. All Gabriel could think to do was to bow again, and resign himself to waiting until Miss Orr was released.

But, apparently, lard and duck eggs weren't all that effective, or perhaps they worked at cross purposes with whatever other treatments were deployed (he didn't care to learn what they were), and it was not until two days later, at the dinner preceding the ball, that he saw Miss Orr—now spot-free—again. He had no opportunity to speak privately with her then, but balls were another thing entirely.

There was always the chance to slip away.

Livia sat wrapped in a shawl while Uncle Charles, sprawled across from her, sipped steadily from his flask. As the old ill-sprung carriage bumped its way along the moonlit road, neither of them spoke. Livia was too used to this kind of leaden silence to expect anything different, and besides, she was feeling just a little uneasy and would have found conversation arduous. How was this evening going to unfold, anyway?

She had no idea.

Energizing anger had propelled her forward since meeting that dreadful man in the woods, and she had sewed boldly and ceaselessly. But now, she was . . .

A little uneasy?

Actually, she was very uneasy.

Lady Glanville had suggested she find herself a little corner from which to enjoy the sights, and now she was almost tempted to do exactly that. And she hoped she didn't run into that arrogant coin-tossing man again. Oh, she'd hate that.

They turned off the road and the carriage rolled slowly toward the lofty portico of the Glanville home, one of many vehicles crowding the wide lane. Every window of its enormous facade, it seemed, was illuminated, and Livia fancied she could already hear the music of the orchestra. Her hands were shaking a little. *You can do this*, she told herself firmly. *It's only a silly ball.*

However, twenty minutes later, as she inched her way behind Uncle Charles toward the receiving line, she didn't feel so brave. She had left her shawl in the cloakroom and now she felt terribly exposed. Why had she created a gown cut so low? Would the long panels of delicate white crepe—carefully stitched into the back of the original ivory silk dress, to allow for her more rounded form—seem stupid? As for the pale gold satin slip underneath, it had seemed like such a clever idea when she'd first thought of it, but perhaps it was simply, painfully, wrong. And what about the gold ribbon she had woven through her upswept hair: did she appear garish? People were staring, and whispering—she was sure of it.

Now at last she came up to Lady Glanville, who took one look at her and stiffened. "Why, Livia," she said in a freezing tone. "Here you are. In quite the *ensemble*."

Her expression was so forbidding, her entire attitude so disapproving, that all at once Livia was consumed by a childish, gleeful, and wholly inappropriate desire to laugh. Her courage came roaring back. She lifted her chin and looked her ladyship in the eye.

"Yes, ma'am. Here I am."

Cecily's pretty blue eyes widened rather comically as she took in Livia's appearance. With an artificial smile pasted on her face, she hissed: "Where on *earth* did you get that gown?"

Livia smiled back, just as falsely. "It's yours."

Tom, the Glanville heir, only goggled at her, and tried to hold on to her hand for too long. Livia grinned at him, showing all her teeth, and pulled her fingers away.

And then she had passed through the receiving line. Now what?

Uncle Charles had vanished. Off to find that Spanish port, no doubt. Feeling all too conspicuous, Livia smoothed a nonexistent crease from her gown. Aside from the Orrs and her uncle, she didn't know a soul here. *Keep moving*, she thought. *One foot in front of the other. And when I see some of those expensive potted palms, maybe I'll kick one over.* She set her jaw, and walked on.

Leaving Grandmama established on an ornate gold chair (embellished with dubious hieroglyphics) in the massive, gaudily decorated ballroom, surrounded by a bevy of elderly ladies who sycophantically agreed with every word she let fall from her lips, Gabriel walked away with relief. How could she endure those toadies? Also, he was more than a little annoyed with her. Just before they'd gone down to dinner, she had summoned him to her rooms to triumphantly show him the large stack of letters she'd written—no, that Miss Cott had written—announcing his engagement. She was, she said, looking forward to hearing the announcement at the interval.

You don't think you're being just a trifle premature? he had said, coolly.

There's no time like the present, she'd replied with equal sangfroid. *Besides, we've dawdled here long enough. I've had enough of the so-called food and the draughts and the fireplaces that smoke. My bed, I'm quite sure, is stuffed with chicken feathers and emits a most peculiar odor. I have already set my maid to packing.*

It was time to do his duty. He and Miss Orr were to open the ball. Briefly, he wondered what it was going to be like making love to her. She struck him as the type of woman who would find it all rather messy and, worse, harmful to her coiffure. Oh well. Offspring. Offspring. He repeated the word in his head, almost like a cadence, as he made his way along a corridor, through the throng; he could hear the orchestra's first strains. Offspring, offspring, he told himself, and as he turned a corner he nearly ran into one of the guests.

"I beg your pardon," he began, and then the little smile of automatic courtesy quickly faded as he realized in stunned disbelief that the guest was none other than the disheveled little maid he'd encountered in the woods a few days before. Only . . . now she was wearing a striking gown, simple white over gold, revealing a graceful, womanly figure. Her rich auburn hair was twisted in a shining knot on her head, bound with a gold ribbon, with a few strands let tantalizingly loose to frame a face that was—

Unforgettable.

Those luminous eyes, set off by dark lashes, stared up at him and for a moment he had that same irrational desire to lose himself within their forest-green depths. Her skin was flawless, a warm sun-kissed shade . . . Skin, he realized with growing indignation, without a spot of mud anywhere.

She *had* played him for a fool.

His brows snapped together and he said to her in a harsh undertone: "What the devil are you doing here?"

"Oh, sir," she promptly answered, "I can't hardly believe it myself! The vasty kindness of them Orrs! Their charity to a poor orfin like me! Why, 'tis a dream come true!"

"Orphan? You mentioned your mother before," he said before he could help himself, as if victoriously proving a point, then just as quickly realized how ridiculous he sounded. He took a hasty step toward her. "Why, you little—" He hardly knew what he intended to do, but just then a possessive hand slid around his arm and the girl in white cast him a mocking glance and disappeared into the crowd.

"Mr. Penhallow." It was Miss Orr, smiling up at him. Her willowy form was clad in cream-colored spider gauze, lavishly embroidered with tiny silver flowers that glimmered in the candlelight, as did her artfully curled flaxen hair. The perfect lady from head to toe. "I believe this is our dance."

"Yes," Gabriel answered mechanically. "To be sure." He accompanied her to the ballroom, unable to vanquish a lingering impression of that annoying little baggage who'd so audaciously taunted him.

They began the quadrille, Miss Orr executing the elaborate steps with grace and confidence. They talked, they moved, they twisted, they turned, yet Gabriel couldn't help but notice the girl in white and gold sitting by herself, with empty chairs all around her. He also noticed a lot of young men staring at her, and how their mothers, with an appalling obviousness, steered them away. Her expression was composed, as if she was unaware of being ostracized. Grudging admiration for her courage rose within him and he said casually to Miss Orr:

"Who is the young lady over there, without a partner?"

She followed his glance. "Oh, that's poor little Livia Stuart. An orphan, quite destitute, you know."

"She wears, however, a very elegant gown."

"I gave it to her," Miss Orr quickly said.

"Indeed? Your—ah—dimensions are quite dissimilar."

"Livia is very handy with a needle," answered Miss Orr sweetly. "It's the poor girl's only accomplishment."

"Your brother Tom seems very taken with her. He's been staring at her for some time."

"Of course he is staring," she responded, still in that sweet, soft voice. "Livia is dressed so outlandishly. If her hope was to attract the attention of eligible men, I'm afraid it's impossible. Without money, without important connections, she is, unfortunately, destined for spinsterhood. It's all so dreadfully sad, isn't it? And you needn't worry about Tom, I assure you! Mama has other plans for him. Do you see the young lady standing next to the replica of Cleopatra's barge? That is Miss Gillingham. Her father is a baronet and she is to receive a dowry of twenty thousand pounds."

"Does Tom know he is to marry her?" he asked sardonically.

"Indeed I do not know if Mama happened to mention it. I am sure he will do what is expected of him."

"Duty above all, of course." That word again.

Speaking of which, he wondered how many times he'd have to perform the marital duty with Miss Orr. It wasn't exactly a stimulating thought, but . . . offspring. Offspring. Involuntarily he flicked his gaze to the girl who sat alone, a living goddess, warmth and vitality fairly crackling from her.

"Of course." Miss Orr smiled as if pleased with the perfect understanding they had achieved, then went on to comment about the number of couples in the dance, how delightfully the weather had cooperated, the cost of the orchestra's hire.

Gabriel replied courteously, in exactly the right places. He must have been a little distracted, though, because when the dance ended and he was about to sweep her off, by the time he'd opened his mouth to tender the invitation, another man had borne her away on his arm. So he went on to his next partner.

He danced with a succession of the neighborhood's young ladies as etiquette dictated he ought, as an honored guest of the Orrs, but somehow they all combined to make an unmemorable blur. Only a few images stood out in his mind. His grandmother, watching him with hawklike attention . . . Miss Orr, now partnered by other men, moving gracefully through the steps and, no doubt, discussing how mild it was tonight and how expensive the music . . . Tom Orr, casting furtive glances around him, slowly edging his way closer to the girl in white and gold, and from across the room his mother Lady Glanville's poorly concealed look of alarm.

Livia sat very straight in her chair. Not only she had failed to kick over a potted palm, this ball was otherwise turning out to be a very bad experience. Not a single person had asked her to dance. She would have had to say no, of course, not knowing how, but still. It would have been nice to be asked. Who had made up the rule that men had to do the asking, anyway? It was a thoroughly stupid rule. Also stupid was the fact that she'd had to watch Cecily Orr dancing (perfectly, she had to admit) with *him*. Mr. Penhallow. And *he* was more good-looking than anyone had a right to be.

Livia wished she'd had those two coins right now, so that she could toss them right in his arrogant face.

A very small, slight sigh escaped her.

Lady Glanville was right.

Life certainly wasn't fair.

She gazed around the crowded ballroom as if she didn't have a care in the world, and thought:

This evening cannot last forever. It will end. It must end. And then life will go back to what it was before.

"Miss Stuart," a voice said hoarsely.

Startled, Livia looked up to see Tom Orr standing before her. He was a big, bulky young man, with lank straw-colored hair and protuberant blue eyes. His hands were massive.

"Mr. Orr," she answered blankly.

He shifted on large feet and as he tugged at his neck-cloth, Livia saw that he was copiously perspiring. "May I have the honor of the next dance?" he asked, then looked uneasily over his shoulder.

Behind him, Livia saw Lady Glanville, horrified disapproval radiating from every pore, struggling to make her way toward them. Her progress was hindered not only by the sheer press of bodies but by how often her guests drew her into conversation. Livia felt the corners of her lips quirk up in a smile as that same spirit of defiant mischief took hold of her.

She looked up at Tom again. "I don't dance, Mr. Orr—"

"Good," he interrupted in relief. "Can't stand all that jiggling about."

"But," she went on, confidingly, "I'm in danger of overheating, for the room is so warm."

"Ain't it though? I'm in the same boat. Hot as blazes in here."

There was a brief silence, and Livia could see that more of a hint was needed. "Do you suppose there's somewhere cooler we might go? Into the garden, perhaps?"

He nodded vigorously. "Aye, it *would* be cooler out there. I wonder how we could manage it?"

"Perhaps through the French doors just over there."

His big round face lit up. "By Jupiter, a capital idea! But . . . do you think we ought to? Never know what's right and what's not! My mother's always after me but damn if I can remember her infernal rules! And there I just said 'damn'! *Damn* it all!"

Suppressing a strong impulse to laugh—a loud and wicked laugh—Livia rose to her feet and slid her hand around his arm with the same confidence she'd seen Cecily display toward Mr. Penhallow. Tugging slightly, she propelled him forward, and once he saw that the French doors were ajar, he took to the idea with alacrity and nearly pulled her off her feet as he hurried toward them.

Together they fled into the welcome coolness of the night.

From halfway across the ballroom, Gabriel watched them go. What the hell was that foolish girl thinking, to let Tom Orr whisk her away? Didn't she realize how scandalously she was behaving? Not only that, Tom was an oaf and twice her size. He could easily overpower her. And it was obvious to anyone with eyes that he'd been struck by her alluring appearance. The girl—that irritating ninny!—had willingly put herself into a dangerous situation.

He thought about Lady Washbourne's poor innocent brainless daughter. And *this* girl, Miss Orr had said, was an orphan. Who was looking out for her?

The remaining minutes of the quadrille passed with tortuous slowness. When finally it was over, he politely thanked his partner, whose name he had already forgotten; intent on rescuing the girl in white from Tom's clammy embrace (and then shaking her so hard her head rattled), he utilized his superior height and breadth of shoulder to cleave his way through the masses of people milling about.

As it turned out, his exit through the French doors was not unobserved. If he'd been a little less focused, he might even have realized it.

Chapter 3

Livia stifled a yawn. It hadn't taken much encouragement for Tom Orr to embark on his favorite subject: snuff. He was going on and on about Petersham's Blend, the Prince's Mixture, and Brummel's Sort. He might as well have been speaking a foreign language.

Still, it was nice to be out of that hot, crowded ballroom, where there was nobody gawking at her in that awful way, and here in the midst of a beautiful garden. They had found an inviting stone seat along a wide gravel pathway flanked by shrubs that looked as if they'd been shaped by a mathematician's hand, such were their precise edges. Too, it was pleasant to imagine Lady Glanville's horror when she realized that her precious son was gone, and in danger of being contaminated by the presence of *poor little Livia*.

"—and as for Vigo Prize Snuff, why, that's the dandy! 'Twas the first real snuff I ever tried, and I sneezed so hard my waistcoat could never be made clean again."

"Dear me," Livia murmured. "Do go on."

"Well, there was nothing for it but to practice, you know, and to keep a good supply of handkerchiefs at the ready. Must have gone through hundreds till I got it right. You've got to hold your wrist just so, and inhale so you don't sneeze. I say—" Tom Orr suddenly broke off and grabbed earnestly at her hand. "You *do* listen so well to a chap. Whyever haven't we met before?"

"Oh, Mr. Orr, I—" Livia began, when suddenly a firm step was heard on the gravel path and Mr. Penhallow himself appeared, looking so tall and scowling so darkly that he had all the appearance of an avenging angel. And she had to admit—now that she had the opportunity to look at him more closely—that he was quite dashing in his dark long-tailed jacket and satin knee breeches. But what on earth was he doing here? Had he somehow misplaced Cecily, Miss Perfect?

Tom Orr snatched away his hand, and even in the dimness of the shrubbery Livia could see that he was flushing a bright, embarrassed red. "Oh! Sir! How— how d'you do?" he stammered, quickly getting to his feet. "I was just—just explaining to Miss Stuart here all about . . . about . . ."

"Snuff," Livia put in helpfully.

Mr. Penhallow looked like he could cheerfully strangle both of them, one with each hand. "Snuff."

"Yes, snuff, sir, I'm awfully fond of it, and as I was explaining to Miss Stuart, it takes a—a good deal of practice. So I . . . you see, I . . ." Visibly wilting under the withering gaze of the older man, Tom Orr trailed off and looked miserably at Livia. "Well . . . goodbye," he muttered, and keeping his gaze fixed on the ground, scuttled in a very cowardly way past Mr. Penhallow back toward the ballroom.

"You little fool!" he snapped at her.

He was clearly furious, and so naturally she *had* to say, with an exaggerated simper: "Oh, sir, but why? To sit *that close* to an Orr! Me! I declare, I was near about to *faint* with excitement an' all! To think there was so, so much to learn about snuff, sir! Do *ye* take it? Mr. Tom says he sneezed quite a bit at first, but I'm sure *ye* never did, sir, for ye're far, far too fine a gentleman."

"Not *that* fine," he said in a low growl. In three long strides he was before her. Roughly he lifted her up and the next thing Livia knew, she was being held against a hard, muscled chest—the elegant fabric of his waistcoat and shirt did little to conceal *that*—and being ruthlessly kissed.

How *dare* he!

Horrible, terrible man!

Furious, Livia pushed against his shoulders with all her strength—which didn't seem to deter him in the slightest—and then, abruptly, the grip of her hands loosened as her mind, her being, was flooded with new and vivid impressions.

The shock of his intimate proximity.

Being held by strong arms with bold confidence.

The scent and the feel and—good heavens!—the *taste* of him.

It was some mysterious, intoxicating blend of wine and chocolate . . . and pure masculinity. Could that even *have* a taste? If so, the horrid Mr. Penhallow did. He angled his mouth more firmly over hers.

Yes, a most masculine taste.

It was delicious, really.

Absolutely delicious.

Livia knew what she *ought* to do—scream at the very least, like a proper young lady—but then, swiftly and sweetly, came the startling realization that she *liked* how it felt. Liked feeling the hardness of his body against her own yielding softness, and liked the feeling of his tongue within her, warm, wet, blindingly sensuous: her thoughts melted away even as her body seemed to—well, honestly, it felt as if she'd caught on fire, like a piece of paper tossed into a flame. She was happily going up in smoke. Burnt into pure sensation.

More.

She wanted more.

With a small sound of satisfaction, she slid her hands around the back of his neck and allowed her fingers to glide slowly, so slowly, along the warm skin there. Goodness, how *exciting* a man could feel, and how marvelous it was when he gathered her even more closely to him, his hands big and strong upon her, seeming to send their possessive warmth radiating into her, the thin material of her gown no barrier at all.

Rocked off his balance by her responsiveness, Gabriel grasped the silky thickness of that auburn hair and deepened his kiss into the lush sweetness of her mouth. This was wrong. He knew it was wrong. She was an annoying, impertinent girl and he knew almost nothing about her except for the fact that she made him angry and she made him feel alive.

Had he been angry with her just a few minutes before? Why? He couldn't recall. Rather, he only knew he never wanted this kiss to end. Never wanted to release her, this bewitching nymph of the woods. But then an all too familiar voice came floating from across the shrubbery with piercing clarity:

"I *knew*, dear Mr. Stuart, that you'd wish to be made aware of this regrettably shocking situation. Poor little Livia should not have crept off with Tom. *He,* of course, is equally to blame, but I thought it would be best for you to see it with your own eyes."

It was Miss Orr, sounding more than a little officious. She sounded, in fact, rather pleased with herself.

"Indeed, indeed," rumbled a deeper voice in reply, and before Gabriel could do more than release Livia Stuart, Miss Orr and a red-faced man of middling height had together rounded a shrub and were upon them.

Explosively the man said, "Damn it, Livia, what's this?" just as Miss Orr, her mouth hanging open in astonishment, burst out: "Mr. *Penhallow!* What are *you* doing here?"

Gabriel repressed the urge to tug his waistcoat into place or to check if the lapels of his jacket had been crushed. What ridiculous madness had possessed him? His behavior had been rash and wrong and unforgivable. And he didn't even *like* the girl!

He glanced at Livia Stuart and saw—oh God, no—that her glorious, shining hair was tumbled and one of the delicate white sleeves of her gown had slid down to reveal a bare shoulder. Despite himself, he badly wanted to touch his lips to that smooth, pale skin and it was only with a strong effort of will that he looked away.

"As you see," he replied coolly, with a deliberate (and slightly desperate) understatement, "I am with Miss Stuart."

There was a hurried rustle on the gravel path and with an agitated swish of purple satin skirts, Lady Glanville swept into view. "Where," she demanded, scowling at Miss Stuart, "is my son? What have you done with him?"

"More to the point," said the red-faced man belligerently, pointing rudely, "what's *he* done with my niece?"

All eyes turned to Miss Stuart. For the life of him, Gabriel couldn't tell what she was thinking, so still was she and so blank her expression. Then she opened her mouth to speak, but before she could get a word out there was yet another rustle of skirts on the path.

Now what? he thought. *How could this possibly get worse?*

It did.

Here was his grandmother, not a silvery-white curl out of place, her back ramrod-straight. If she didn't exactly skid to a stop, she certainly halted rather abruptly. On her still-handsome face was a look so fierce that it

irresistibly summoned for Gabriel the image of Medusa
turning her hapless victims to stone.

Appropriately enough, no one moved a muscle.

"Well!" Grandmama exclaimed, her patrician voice
vibrating with fury. "I daresay *someone* will explain to
me the meaning of this shocking tableau!"

There was dead silence.

Rapidly Gabriel pulled himself together and began
framing in his mind a reply that was rational and sooth-
ing, one that would defuse this ghastly tinderbox of a
situation and allow everyone to disperse with both civility and dignity. It could be done; he knew it. He'd
gotten himself out of tight fixes before.

And then—

Then Miss Stuart giggled.

And all hell broke loose.

Livia had never been to a display of waxworks, but
surely it would have resembled the scene of moments
ago, with human forms stiffly displayed in a variety
of attitudes ranging from arrogant imperturbability
(Mr. Penhallow) to horror (Cecily) to outraged hostility (Uncle Charles, Lady Glanville, and the slim, imperious, beautifully dressed elderly lady who had frozen
them all into immobility).

What, she wondered, was her own expression like?
She probably looked exactly like a dazed little country bumpkin, thrust into the wrong place at the wrong
time. Well, hopefully she was at least disguising what
she was actually feeling. Mostly she was angry. No, she
was *furious* that she'd allowed herself to be kissed by
that awful Mr. Penhallow, and then wilted meekly into
his embrace. And how could she have—even if only
briefly—*enjoyed* it?

Obviously she was a dreadful person. And how mortifying to have all these people hanging about. Still, seeing them standing as if paralyzed struck her all at once as so comical that she managed to choke down a rush of hysterical laughter with only partial success.

Her giggle had, at least, the benefit of breaking free the curious impasse.

"That fellow—what's his name? Pinbarrow?—has compromised my niece, that's what has happened!" Uncle Charles said angrily, even as Lady Glanville overrode him with another icy demand to know the whereabouts of her son and Cecily said in a manner perilously close to a screech: "Mr. *Penhallow!*"

"Be quiet, all of you!" said the elderly lady acidly, and such was her commanding air that silence once again descended upon the group. She fixed her piercing blue eyes on Uncle Charles. "And who might you be?" she asked haughtily, as if forced to address a talking bug.

"Why, I'm that girl's uncle *and* guardian," he answered, with stubborn, uncouth bluster. "Charles Stuart, *Esquire*. And who might *you* be, I'd like to know?"

"I am Mrs. Penhallow. I am the grandmother of that *fellow*, as you so eloquently put it. Perhaps you might enlighten me as to why your niece looks as if she has been dragged backwards through the shrubbery."

"Isn't it obvious your nephew has been dallying with her? He's compromised her—we're all witnesses to it!— and he'll have to pay the piper."

Scornfully the old lady said: "If you are suggesting financial remuneration—"

"Dallying?" Cecily cried. "Oh, Mr. *Penhallow!*"

"Money, ma'am?" Uncle Charles's face was a livid scarlet. "He's got to do the honorable thing and marry her! I won't have the family reputation besmirched!"

"*Marry* her?" Cecily grabbed at Uncle Charles's sleeve as might a drowning person reach for ballast. "Oh, no, no, no!"

"Cecily, *do* stop repeating everything you hear," said Lady Glanville. "And pray release Mr. Stuart's sleeve; recall that you are the granddaughter of an earl." She turned to Mrs. Penhallow with ponderous graciousness. "The situation is, to be sure, a trifle awkward, my dear ma'am, but I am confident that between us we can smooth over any rough edges—"

Mrs. Penhallow ignored her. "Well, Gabriel?" she said sharply to her grandson. "Is it true what this Mr. Stuart says?"

Not only had Livia had never seen a waxworks display, she'd never been to a play either, but it certainly felt like she was watching one now. She looked from one person to the next, fascinated. What would happen after this? Fisticuffs, fainting, someone running off, pursued by a bear?

Lady Glanville was smiling her usual cool smile, but Livia could see on her face a waxy sheen of perspiration; Cecily's eyes were as round as saucers and she was gripping her fingers together so tightly that her gold rings had to be hurting her. As for Uncle Charles, he looked as if he were actually *swelling* (reminding her quite a bit of a toad), and how funny that he seemed to think that she and the horrible Mr. Penhallow should marry! That sort of thing only happened in old stories, with noble heroes and evil villains and outraged guardians, and everything very exaggerated and amusing.

When, however, Livia glanced at Mr. Penhallow, she couldn't help but notice that he didn't seem to think it the slightest bit humorous.

"One way or another, I will do my duty, ma'am," he said evenly to his grandmother.

Her scowl deepened. "That is not an answer," she began, when Cecily blurted out in a shrill voice:

"Livia, you low, odious girl! You shan't steal him from me! I won't let you! Oh, I always knew you were despicable!"

Immediately Livia pushed aside the fact that she had, only moments ago, been chastising herself with words not unlike those Cecily was hurling at her. Still immersed in a curious dreamlike state in which everything seemed funny and unreal, she couldn't resist the temptation to get the better of Cecily for once, and so recklessly she tossed another straw onto the camel's back. "Oh, it was only a kiss!" she said breezily. "You can't steal someone with a kiss."

Cecily let out an anguished moan and her knees buckled, prompting her mother to snatch her about the waist, and next to Livia Mr. Penhallow groaned under his breath. "You addle-pated ninny!" he said very quietly.

"Pooh!" she responded saucily, tossing her head, and felt a rather thick tendril of hair, loosed from its clasp, settle against her neck. It was only at this sudden sensation that the first stirrings of true uneasiness prickled in Livia's mind. Cautiously she felt at her hair and realized that it wasn't just that one tendril, but several that had come free. Worse still, she now saw that her gown had slid off her shoulder in a most improper way. Oh dear . . .

She grabbed at her sleeve and tugged it into place and wondered nervously just how disarrayed she really was. Was that ghastly Mrs. Penhallow correct? *Did* she look as bad as all that? And *was* she foolish for having mentioned the kiss? A burning flush heated up her face and throat, and she shot an anxious look at the old lady, who was eyeing her with a distinctly malevolent expression.

"So you think this is some kind of game, do you, missy?" she said unpleasantly. "You'll soon find out that tangling with the Penhallows lands you in very deep water!" The old lady turned to her grandson. "You immediately will set us straight," she said in her commanding way. "I assume this pert young lady is attempting some kind of blackmail."

Mr. Penhallow was silent.

He looked at Livia and she looked back at him, trying to puzzle out the expression on his face. He was very composed, but she got the distinct impression that there was a great deal he could say if he chose. Cold, cutting things. That could slice a person into a million little pieces. Was he the villain of this piece, or the hero? Another hysterical laugh rose within her, but this time she managed to choke it back. She waited for him to end this ridiculous play. She was more than ready for it to be over.

Instead he said, with a kind of steely calmness:

"No, Grandmama, she is not. I take full responsibility for my actions."

"Well then!" Uncle Charles exclaimed triumphantly. "It's settled! You'll marry the girl, and we'll wrap this up all nice and tidy!"

"Yes," said Mr. Penhallow evenly.

"No!" cried Cecily, even as Livia, disbelievingly, croaked:

"*What?*"

For the first time visibly shaken, old Mrs. Penhallow glared at Mr. Penhallow. "We had an agreement!"

"We did, Grandmama, but circumstances have—ah—intervened."

"He was *mine!*" Cecily cried, still held firmly within the circle of Lady Glanville's supporting arm. "Mama, Livia *took* him from me!"

With stunning speed, Livia had passed from wax-works to a play to—well, she hardly knew what *this* was, but things certainly weren't funny now. Get married for such a stupid little reason? Absurd! "Well, take him back then!" she told Cecily fiercely. "I don't want him!"

"Not want him?" Mrs. Penhallow nearly shouted, quivering with affronted loathing. "Not want to marry into the *Penhallow* family? I've never heard of anything so outrageous!"

"You be quiet, Livia!" Uncle Charles ordered furiously. "That fellow did you wrong and he's going to make it right, and that's that! But don't expect a dowry," he added pugnaciously, "because she ain't got one. Been living off my charity for years."

Mrs. Penhallow glared with even greater ferocity, and it seemed to Livia that her saying *I don't want him* was even worse, more offensive, to the old lady than the fact of her grandson being caught in a compromising position.

"Naturally he'll make it right, sir," Mrs. Penhallow said icily. "That is, after all, the Penhallow way. He shall discuss with you the terms at his earliest opportunity." To Lady Glanville she went on: "You had better go, with that girl of yours. I may trust to your discretion in this distasteful matter, of course."

Livia couldn't repress a tiny flicker of glee at seeing her ladyship dismissed so peremptorily, and watched as she managed a cool nod in reply, then drew Cecily away, saying, "Come, we'll go up the backstairs to your bedchamber, so that no one will see you like this."

Over her shoulder Cecily spat at Livia, "I *hate* you!"

Then she and her mother were gone.

"Well, isn't this jolly." Now that he had achieved his ends, a great deal of Uncle Charles's bluster had faded away and he gave the appearance of a man very much in need of a drink. "If you'll excuse me," he said, and began moving toward the house, walking sideways, crablike, as if to conceal the fact of his retreat.

"By all means," Mrs. Penhallow said coldly. "I will serve as chaperone to this most unfortunate couple." Ordinarily Livia heartily disliked even being in the same room with Uncle Charles, but now she was sorry to see him go. She didn't wish in the least to be left alone with the Penhallows. It was two against one, and somehow, they both seemed to take up so much *space*. Still scowling, Mrs. Penhallow stalked over to the stone bench and seated herself like a queen—an angry, angry queen—taking possession of a throne, while Mr. Penhallow, meanwhile, stood there looking as calm as if he'd just agreed to buy a new neckcloth. Or carriage. Or whatever. Some *thing*.

So what if he was terribly good-looking, with those fine dark eyes, and a proud nose and a sensuous mouth, and gleaming hair with a single lock that brushed his forehead in a rather dashing way, and broad shoulders, and—

Livia actually pinched the skin of her forearm, as if to clear her mind of these silly thoughts. Determinedly she faced them both. "This has all been a misunderstanding. Can't we simply forget it ever happened?"

The old lady gave a bark of bitter laughter. "Obviously you have no idea who the Penhallows are. For hundreds of years the family crest has displayed the words *Et honorem, et gloriam*. Do you even know what those words mean?"

Livia lifted her chin. "No."

"How unsurprising. They mean 'Honor and pride,' and we're not about to abandon them because of *you*. If my grandson says he must marry you, marry you he will!"

Livia looked over at Mr. Penhallow, who said coolly: "I've already made known my intentions."

Oh, good heavens, he actually meant it. He really and truly meant it. Livia took a step backwards. "This," she said firmly, "is insane. You don't want to marry me, and I certainly don't want to marry *you!*"

He only shrugged, and Livia felt dislike rising in her. "Well, I won't do it! Not if you were the last man in England!" She spun on her heel and was just about to march away when he reached out, took her arm in an ungentle grip, and turned her around, literally bringing her back into the conversation.

"Not so fast, Miss Stuart," he said, with that same steely composure. "Once given, my word is law. Besides, do you really think your uncle isn't at this moment telling anyone within earshot about our engagement? You're not backing out now. I don't care to be made a laughingstock."

Livia's heart sank. It was anybody's guess as to whether Cecily and Lady Glanville would keep their silence, but as soon as Uncle Charles had downed a few—or several—glasses of whatever spirit happened to be at hand, he'd be talking to his fellow guests, the servants, the *furniture*.

She looked up at him, and Gabriel could see in her expression a reluctant acknowledgement of what he'd said. Quickly he released her arm. Good God, what an unholy mess he'd made of things. Everything had been going so well—until he'd gone off like some misguided chivalrous idiot to rescue her from Tom Orr.

Tom Orr, the most easily managed man in existence.

Now there was irony for you.

And so here he was, engaged to Miss Livia Stuart.

As neatly snared as a rabbit in a trap.

And speaking of irony, wouldn't dear old Lady Washbourne appreciate the situation?

"Look at her," his grandmother said gloomily. "A provincial nobody. And that red hair! There hasn't been such a common shade in the line since Sir Everard Penhallow married into the Yorks three centuries ago." She sniffed derisively. "A bad lot, those Yorks. *I* would have told him to stay away! Well, girl, let me see your teeth."

Gabriel watched as Miss Stuart turned uncomprehendingly toward Grandmama. "I beg your pardon, ma'am?"

"Your teeth," said Grandmama impatiently. "The Penhallows are famed for the superiority of their teeth. *Ours* don't fall out! If yours are deficient they'll have to be corrected."

Miss Stuart clamped her lips together, opening them only wide enough to say in a grim mutter, "I am not a horse."

"Well, you're certainly as stubborn as a mule." Grandmama sighed heavily. "I don't suppose you're related to the *royal* Stuarts?"

"Not that I know of."

"What is your education? What has your governess taught you?"

"I had no governess. I'm sure my uncle would have thought it a waste of his money."

"No education, then. No French, no Italian, no use of the globes. Is it too much to hope that you have any accomplishments? Singing, dancing, drawing? A musical instrument?"

"I can sew, a little."

Grandmama glowered at her. "I daresay that garishly immodest gown is your own creation."

"Yes, it is."

"Put it directly into the fire the moment you return home. Well, Gabriel, it's been quite an evening's work. All my hopes are dashed, and now we're to bring this ignorant little nonentity into the family. Tomorrow morning you shall call on that vulgar uncle of hers and discuss the details. Never let it be said that a Penhallow failed to perform a necessary act, no matter how distasteful. And now I shall sleep on chicken feathers for yet another night, as we can't possibly depart in the morning, and be forced to breathe in a most *peculiar* odor emanating from my mattress. My maid will have to unpack everything, and send orders to the kitchen for a special tisane, for drink that execrable beverage they call tea here one more time I shall not. Perhaps an egg, carefully boiled, but who can say? Miss Cott will have to convey my particular receipt directly to the cook. Take Miss Stuart to her uncle, if you please. I've had quite enough of her."

Gabriel bowed to his grandmother, then turned to Livia Stuart and with cool courtesy offered her his arm. She ignored it. "I'm quite capable of finding my own way, thank you." She began walking toward the house and with one long step he caught up with her and matched his stride to hers.

"How unseemly of you, my dear," he said mockingly, "to go unescorted. Remember that it's my privilege, and pleasure, to accompany you henceforth."

Miss Stuart stopped short. Green eyes blazed up at him, and he had to remind himself that blue eyes were better than green, and it was a foolish, regrettable kiss that had stolen from him his safe and predictable future. If she hadn't been so tempting, everything would be perfect right now.

"If you really think I'm going to marry you, you're wrong!" she said with a distinct snarl in her voice. "I'd rather be a scullery maid in the nearest inn!" Then she whirled and ran into the house, the hem of her white dress—which, stubbornly, he thought rather pretty, no matter what his grandmother might say—fluttering behind her.

He watched her go.

It was rash and unladylike to run, of course, but still, he couldn't help but admire her defiant little gesture in the face of the inevitable.

Livia paced the floor of her room, still wearing the white gown. Throw it in the fire? Why, that rude, high-handed old lady—and as for her grandson, he was even *more* arrogant and detestable. Treating her like a *thing*. Calling her *my dear* in that insufferable way!

After she'd left him in the garden, she'd gone back into the house where she had, without surprise, found Uncle Charles on a sofa in the card room, a drink in his hand and being vociferously congratulated on his niece's most fortunate betrothal. (On the way she had caught a glimpse of Tom Orr, seated under—yes—a potted palm and peacefully eating the most enormous dish of ices she'd ever seen, and how she'd wished she could hide there with him, even if it meant having to listen to him talk about snuff.)

Livia now completed another rapid lap around her room. It was well past midnight, but she wasn't the least bit tired. She couldn't erase from her mind the image of tall, broad-shouldered Gabriel Penhallow looking down his finely chiseled nose at her. His incredible certainty that she was going through with this charade!

Livia's brain moved at lightning speed as she started on yet another circuit. Well, she'd show him!

She had a plan.

It was a crazy, impetuous plan, and how she would have liked to see his face tomorrow—no, later on today—when he arrived.

But she wouldn't be here.

How angry he would be.

How deliciously, wonderfully, *splendidly* angry.

Chapter 4

After a long night of tossing and turning, during which Gabriel wondered if Grandmama's suspicion about chicken feathers was actually correct, he in due course made his way to the Stuart mansion, where he was greeted by a lachrymose, shabbily dressed butler and conducted at a funereal pace to the dark, cavernous study of Mr. Charles Stuart, from whom emanated a strong scent of brandy as he sat slumped behind his cluttered mahogany desk.

Twenty minutes later, Gabriel rose to his feet, thus signaling an end to an irritating, not to mention tedious, discussion with Mr. Stuart concerning the marriage of his niece Livia. She was to receive no money, no trousseau, no wedding dress, no jewels—nothing.

"My wife's in no condition to plan *or* host anything," Mr. Stuart had said in his blunt, blustering way, "nor a fancy breakfast, and I'm damned if I'll spend another penny on that chit." Rubbing his beard-stubbled chin, he'd added sourly, "Nuisance. Should never have let her come here. Better to have saved my money and left her where she was."

Gabriel had repressed a quick, unbidden pang of sympathy for Livia. Why should he feel sorry for her?

After all, she was the one who had made a mess of his life. Of course, he *had* kissed her. On the other hand, she *had* provoked him. Why in God's name had he allowed her to get under his skin? What was the matter with him? And what was the matter with *her*, turning him down like that? Just who did she think she was?

Gabriel broke off this frustrating, hopelessly unproductive train of thought, successfully fighting down the urge to bang his head against the nearest wall. "Thank you for your time," he now said coolly. "Good day."

"What? Don't you want to see her? Settle things?"

"Things *are* settled." Last night, in the intervals during which he lay awake glumly ruminating, he'd decided to leave immediately following his interview with the Stuart fellow. It would give Miss Livia Stuart her own little taste of the Penhallow way.

He knew it was petty, yet still it gave him a small sense of control in a situation which had spun wildly into chaos. "You may inform Miss Stuart that we'll come for her tomorrow morning. We go to Bath, where she is to reside with my grandmother and be taught all that she needs to know to properly enter Society as the future Mrs. Penhallow. And you need not worry, sir," Gabriel concluded with a slight, ironic smile. "The proprieties are to be observed. Naturally I shall be elsewhere."

And with that, conscious of an ignoble feeling of triumph as he pictured Livia Stuart's mortification (having put on her best day-dress, no doubt, and carefully done up her hair), he returned to the Glanville mansion, where it would have been difficult to imagine a scene of greater awkwardness.

Lady Glanville and Miss Orr were pointedly cloistered in their bedchambers; Lord Glanville anxiously skittered in and out of any room Gabriel happened to be occupying; harried servants hastened to fulfill the multitudinous demands of his grandmother as she orchestrated the herculean effort of preparing for tomorrow's journey.

Only Tom Orr seemed oblivious to the strained atmosphere, slavishly following Gabriel around like an overgrown puppy, inviting him to take snuff—*snuff,* for God's sake—and wondering out loud if he had a chance with that dashed attractive Miss Stuart, he'd had the most delightful chat with her last night, didn't Mr. Penhallow find her wondrous agreeable?

Gritting his teeth, Gabriel thought to himself that since evidently nobody had bothered to inform Tom that Miss Stuart was affianced elsewhere, it certainly wasn't any of *his* business. He endured Tom's presence for as long as he could until, after the umpteenth encomium on Miss Stuart's manifold charms and feeling increasingly certain there was a real possibility that he would end up throttling the Glanville heir before the day was out, he retreated to the library, predicting—accurately—that young Tom would find proximity to all those books repugnant.

Perusing the shelves in peaceful solitude, he saw that their contents seemed mostly to date to previous centuries, an impression which aligned completely with his assessment of the current Lord Glanville's intellectual attainment.

Some hours later Gabriel was sitting in a leather armchair, deep into a volume of Francis Bacon's *Novum Organicum,* when there came the sound of tapping on the door, followed by a servant girl cautiously entering, dipping a curtsy, and handing him a folded note.

It was a curt missive from Charles Stuart informing him that his niece was nowhere to be found and that not a soul on the place could remember seeing her that day. *Had the servants searching every nook and cranny and all the fuss is going to make my dinner late. Well, she's your burden now!* the note concluded. *You needn't think you can back out now, for I've had your word on it as a gentleman.*

Gabriel crumpled the note and softly uttered an oath, his mind racing.

"Sir?" the servant girl said timidly. "Is there a reply?"

He stood and tossed the book aside. "Where is the inn nearest here?"

She goggled at him confusedly. "Sir?"

"The nearest inn. Where is it?"

"Why—why, 'tis the Spotted Hare, sir, but 'tis ever so far away! I had to walk there once to retrieve a package for the master, and it took me nigh on the whole day! Master was *that* angry with me and I did quake in my shoes, sir, for fear he'd let me go. But Cook said, 'Oh, never mind about *him,* young Jenny, 'tis the *mistress* ye've got to steer clear of, and that Miss Cecily, who'd as soon claw yer eyes out than say a pleasant word to the staff!' 'Tis true, sir, for last Michaelmas poor Mavis dropped the ash-pan in Miss Cecily's room—'twas an accident, sir, poor Mavis swore upon her mam's grave it was!—and *she* said to poor Mavis—"

"That is enough, thank you." Gabriel held on to his temper with an effort, despite being forced to recall all over again how impertinently Miss Stuart had deceived him with her flawless impersonation of a country maid's accent. He would get directions from the butler, and tell him to lay one less setting for the evening meal, for clearly, he was going to be elsewhere.

Within half an hour he was riding rapidly along a muddy lane, Miss Stuart's hostile retort from last night echoing in his head: *If you really think I'm going to marry you, you're wrong! I'd rather be a scullery maid in the nearest inn!*

Had he been angry with her before? It was as nothing compared to the icy rage he now felt. The little fool! Did she *really* believe she could outmaneuver him? Involuntarily his fingers tightened on the reins and his horse Primus danced nervously. He soothed him with a word and rode on.

Livia pushed a damp hank of hair off her face and plunged another food-encrusted pot into the massive pan of scalding water set in front of her. Her hands were red and raw, and it seemed that for every item she cleaned, three more dirty ones were plopped down. Was this even mathematically possible?

It had been mere minutes following her reckless decision to make good her threat of becoming a scullery maid that she'd packed a small bag, crept from the house, and begun walking. For quite a long time she was gleefully buoyed at how she'd trounced Gabriel Penhallow. How she enjoyed picturing the look of dismay on that smug, handsome face when he realized she'd slipped from his grasp! And it hadn't been difficult to persuade the flustered proprietor of the Spotted Hare to take her on, for he had just lost his kitchen helper to—strangely enough—a runaway marriage.

Nonetheless, it *had* been a rather long day. She was tired and sleep-deprived, her back and her feet and her hands hurt, and she was hungry, too. Her initial euphoria had long since faded, and she'd had plenty of time to think as she washed dish after dish. Had plenty of time to uneasily contemplate the fact that she'd never known she was capable of this much hotheaded impulsiveness. This went way beyond angrily grinding coins under one's boot. She thought she knew herself fairly well, but she'd really astonished herself this time. What other rash things might she do?

She scrubbed the pot, her mind busy.

She thought more about that sense of uneasiness.

It felt a bit like she'd somehow upset the delicate balance of the universe.

In some odd way, it could all be traced back to the intersection of her life with that of the Orrs. If Tom Orr hadn't asked her to dance . . .

If she hadn't wanted to upset Lady Glanville by disappearing into the garden with Tom . . .

If Cecily hadn't been so nasty toward her all these years, she might never have made the fatal remark to taunt her: *It was only a kiss.*

It would be easy, now, to blame everything on Cecily.

Why did she have to be so spiteful and unpleasant, anyway? She already had *everything* in life, didn't she?

And she'd almost had Gabriel Penhallow.

Livia thought back to Cecily's happy words in Aunt Bella's drawing-room.

They say he's one of the most eligible men on the Marriage Mart! He is so wealthy, too! Only think of my jewels and carriages! I shall move in quite the highest, most fashionable circles!

Into Livia's head flashed the image of Cecily's beautiful kid slippers, and those pink rosettes she'd envied. Cecily's fashionable gowns, Cecily's exquisite slippers and gloves, Cecily's elegant bonnets.

Cecily moving in the highest, most illustrious circles, a wealthy, cosseted bride.

Suddenly there was a crash, and Livia jumped.

The Spotted Hare's cook had dropped a just-cleaned plate, and she released an interesting volley of words, none of which Livia had ever heard before. Probably if she were more ladylike, she would have plugged her ears, but she didn't. Instead she pulled her hands out of the dishpan, dried them on the none-too-clean apron she'd been given, and said calmly:

"I'll pick up the pieces."

"Oh, would ye, love? I got these puddings to tend to!" answered the cook, and hastily turned back to her stove.

Livia crouched down and with her fingers swept the chipped pieces of china into a little pile. All at once she stopped. An idea of staggering audacity had occurred to her. Did she *dare* . . . ?

The door to the kitchen swung open and in sauntered Timothy, the waiter, who slipped up behind the cook and pinched her backside. She yelped and bawled some more incomprehensible things, swinging at him with her big wooden spoon. Nimbly Timothy dodged the spoon and then came purposefully toward Livia.

"Touch me and I'll stab you with a shard of china," she said, not bothering to look up at him. Ten long hours in his company had given her an all-too-clear understanding of his temperament.

He laughed. "Oh, you're a funny one."

"Yes, as funny as a tourniquet."

"Here now, Timothy, get along with ye!" said the cook scoldingly. "I got three plates here a-waitin' to be served, and they ain't gettin' any warmer, is they?"

"But *she's* such a joy to watch, old Cookie." Timothy leaned against the wall as if he had all the time in the world. He didn't even move when Mr. Bagshawe came hurrying into the kitchen.

"I heard a noise—Cook, where *are* those puddings?—another customer's in the courtyard and I've no one to hold his horse—Timothy, I'm not paying you to stand around, am I?—go help him and I'll bring out the puddings. What have you done to my fine plate, girl? It *will* cost you!—Timothy, out! Cook! *Puddings!*"

Fine plate? Ha. Livia placed several bits of china onto a larger piece. Goodness, but her hands were red. And just then her stomach rumbled loudly with hunger. No, this certainly wasn't how she had envisioned her glorious dash for freedom. If Cecily could see her now— how she would laugh!

It was then, imagining Cecily's annoying tinkling laughter, that Livia made up her mind. She was going to do it after all. She'd just finish up here and then—

The kitchen door swung open again.

As Livia reached for another shard, into her lowered line of vision came a pair of exquisitely crafted, shining black topboots, looking extremely out of place on the dull, grubby floor of the Spotted Hare's kitchen.

"Sir!" exclaimed Mr. Bagshawe. "We don't let customers into the kitchen!"

"I can see why. Else they'd never eat your food."

Well. What perfect timing.

Livia took a deep breath, and looked up at Gabriel Penhallow, her gaze traveling up from the black boots, up long muscular legs clad in soft yellow buckskin, an elegant ivory-colored waistcoat, and an intricately tied white neckcloth, still immaculate despite the distance he would have ridden: all visible between the open folds of his heavy greatcoat.

He looked impossibly tall, his face set in cold implacability. My, she thought, wasn't he clever to have found her. He grasped her arm and a little roughly brought her upright. Brown eyes, hard and framed rather attractively by black lashes, met her own.

She cleared her throat and in a voice that was only a *little* shaky said:

"Good evening, Mr. Penhallow."

"It is *not* a good evening, Miss Stuart," he replied in a freezing tone. "Let us leave this kitchen at once. I do not in the least care to step on mouse droppings."

"Come now, sir!" puffed Bagshawe, outraged. "I'm sure I never—"

"Mouse droppings. I trust this inn has a private parlor?"

"Yes, but—but it's occupied, sir!"

Mr. Penhallow flicked a coin onto the table where Livia had been laboring. "Clear it at once."

"Yes, sir, right away!" Bagshawe scooped up the coin and hurried off.

Mr. Penhallow looked at her for a long moment. Livia lifted her chin and gazed back. It was then she noticed that *his* chin had a small dimple in it. How nicely it set off the firmness of his jaw. And what a delightful addition to his smile it would be. Had she ever seen him smile? Oh yes, last night at the ball, when he'd come around the corner and nearly bumped into her. (Was it really only yesterday? The ball seemed to have taken place *years* ago.) But that had been a superficial smile, a social smile, when he came upon her; it hadn't reached his eyes. She wondered what his face would look like if he were *really* smiling. He would be even more devastatingly good-looking, that was for certain.

"If you'd care to accompany me, Miss Stuart?" he said coolly.

Livia blinked. How formal he was, how correct; that same dreadful imp of mischief goaded her to say: "Oh, but sir, I haven't finished cleaning these dishes!"

Dark sleek brows drew together, and Mr. Penhallow took hold of her upper arm again. "Come," he said in a low, tight voice, and led her out of the kitchen, across a dim gloomy passage where half a dozen disgruntled guests were making their way into the public taproom, and into an empty parlor where Bagshawe was obsequiously wielding a dirty napkin to dust off two chairs set close to the fire.

"All yours, sir. Shall I bring you some ale, then? Spotted Hare's finest!"

"No. Have you a carriage?"

"No, sir. A pony trap, sir, though it's been put away and the horse is stabled."

"I'll want it in half an hour." Gabriel tossed another coin onto the low table near where he stood. "Find a competent driver, and have my horse readied as well. Now leave us. And see that we're not disturbed."

"Yes, sir!" Bagshawe snatched up the coin and swiftly left the parlor, closing the door with punctilious care, though to Livia the soft click seemed very loud in the suddenly quiet room. Perhaps even too loud. She watched Mr. Penhallow as slowly he turned to her.

I am master of myself, Gabriel thought. *I am master of this situation. I am in control. I am a Penhallow. She is nothing to me—only a duty I must fulfill.*

With deliberate insolence, he looked her up and down. She was positively unkempt. Her boots were soggy and their leather cracked, her apron filthy, the hem of her dowdy gray gown was torn and muddy, and her hair hopelessly bedraggled.

Yet . . .

Boots were only boots, a gown was only a gown.

Messy hair could be made tidy.

There was something about her.

That dangerous word came to him again.

Entrancing.

He saw the generous curve of breasts that narrowed into a slim waist, then flared again, creating a sublimely feminine form that could render a man helpless with desire. He saw, in the warm glow of firelight, that her tumbled hair wasn't a single auburn shade but was formed from a variety of colors—red, brown, chestnut, even gold. How pleasing it was. He had never seen such thick, shining, lovely hair. How might it feel against his naked body? Like living silk?

Stop it, he commanded himself. Sternly he dismissed the too-tempting image of her—of him—together—from his mind.

I am master of myself.

I am master of this situation.

I am a Penhallow.

But it took all his willpower to summon again the cold rage he'd been nursing all the way here. It felt safer, much safer, to be angry, icy, in control.

He met her eyes.

And spoke.

"Your face is dirty."

She reeled back a step, almost as if he had struck her. But then she seemed to gather herself.

"Yes, I'm sure it is. Does this mean our engagement is off?"

"Of course not. What's done is done."

"Good."

He stared at her. "You've changed your mind? You've decided that being a scullery maid *is* worse than being married to me?"

"Well, at least being a scullery maid is honest work. You're only marrying me because of your reputation. Your honor." She sniffed, in a very credible imitation of his grandmother.

"You have no idea how the world works."

"I'm learning. You've engaged yourself to a complete stranger—me—because you grabbed at me in the garden and got caught. *My* feelings don't matter to you at all. *I* don't matter to you. Well then, if this is the way of the world, I accept your offer. You won't matter to me, either."

He was silent for a few seconds. "My God," he then said, slowly. "I thought you were different."

"Different from Cecily Orr, you mean? No, I'm going to be just like her. I'm going to work hard at it, too. You ought to be glad, don't you think? Isn't Cecily Orr what you wanted in the first place?"

She smiled at him, but there was no warmth in her beautiful green eyes, only determination. Christ, she was using him. She *was* like all those other women. He was shocked to feel a jolt of sorrow rushing through him, but then he caught hold of himself.

I am master here.

I am in control.

I am a Penhallow.

Gabriel smiled back at her, but thinly. "Thank you for enlightening me, Miss Stuart. You'll be pleased to hear, then, that tomorrow we leave for Bath—you, my grandmother, Miss Cott, and me. You'll receive your education under my grandmother's *aegis*. The humble caterpillar is to be transformed."

He saw the quick rise and fall of her chest, as if she was assimilating this news. But aloud she said only:

"Fine. I'm going to be a very expensive butterfly, I'm afraid. You already know that I have nothing to wear."

"And you, I'm sure, already know that money is no object for the Penhallows." An idea came to him then, one of staggering audacity. He was too angry, too confused, to pause to analyze it, but it was definitely a way to seize control, and that was good enough for him. So he added:

"But there's one more thing you should know." With that same deliberate insolence, he moved toward her. Her eyes wide, reflections from the firelight flickering

in their green depths, she took another step backwards.
And another, as he continued to approach. It was like
a strange, silent dance, coming to an abrupt halt only
when her back met the wall and he stopped mere inches
from her.

It wasn't a proper distance between a lady and a gentleman. That at least she knew. Livia looked up into his
face. His expression was so distant, so cold, but from
his body seemed to come a bewitching sort of energy
that suffused her with that same delicious warmth
she'd felt last night, seeming to flow through her limbs
and making them feel heavy and peculiar—a fiery sensation, giddy and exciting. It was as if he exerted some
peculiar magnetism over her, for without even touching her he seemed to embrace her, to enter into herself, drawing her inexorably toward him. Livia felt her
lips part and in a willing sort of half-swoon she tilted
toward him, blindly wanting whatever came next from
him. Perhaps another kiss, like that other one, only
longer, longer—

"This marriage of ours," he said, in a voice devoid
of all emotion, "will be in name only. You'll not share
my bed."

His breath was warm on her face, his mouth so close
to her own, but his words were like a bucket of half-
frozen water dumped over her. Livia jerked backwards
and her head came hard against the wall. The shock
seemed to wake her from an all too pleasant dream.

She'd been dismissed. Rejected. Again. Was this
going to be the story of her life? Pride made her lift her
chin, to say in a voice that surprised her in its steadi-
ness, "And once given, your word is law, isn't it?"

"That's right."

"I'm *glad*. You'll go your way, I'll go mine."

"Yes, Miss Stuart, the Penhallow way," he answered evenly. "You're learning fast. I'll leave the damned estate to my cousin Hugo if I have to, or that rustic buffoon in Scotland. These are the terms, and I expect you to conduct yourself with poise and dignity at all times. Is that clear?"

Livia swallowed. It felt like a door was shutting behind her, a door that could never be opened again. But then she squared her shoulders. This was her *chance*, after all. She'd be an idiot not to take it. "Yes."

"Excellent. I'm taking you home now, Miss Stuart. I trust you won't regale my grandmother with the tale of your charming adventure here at the Spotted Hare. It would hardly be an auspicious beginning."

"I'll make sure she doesn't see my work-roughened hands," answered Livia, matching his ironic tone with sarcasm. "Otherwise she might need recourse to smelling-salts."

He smiled that thin smile again. "Know, Miss Stuart, that if you aren't ready by eleven o'clock tomorrow morning, or if you change your mind and decide to run from me again, I'll come after you. I'll find you, and you won't enjoy the consequences."

"You needn't threaten me, you great bully. I'll be there."

He stepped away from her at last, and she was annoyed to find she felt a little sorry.

"That," he said coldly, "remains to be seen. Shall we go?"

"One moment." Livia went briskly to the door and opened it, only to see Mr. Bagshawe loitering in the dim passageway. She almost laughed at the expression on his face; clearly he didn't know whether to bow low before her, or order her back into the kitchen. She untied the dirty apron and gave it to him.

"There was a plate," she said. "A broken plate."

"Ah—yes—one of my best pieces—"

"You can apply my wages toward its cost. They should suffice."

"As to that, I don't think so—an expensive item, it was—an heirloom—"

Livia felt, rather than saw, Mr. Penhallow coming up behind her. And then Mr. Bagshawe did bow.

His nose practically scraped the ground.

"Yes, miss," he said. "Thank you, miss."

Livia nodded. Regally, *just* like that ghastly old Mrs. Penhallow would. Oh yes: her new life was already beginning.

Chapter 5

Livia stood on the uneven stone steps leading up to the Abbey—or away from it, depending on one's perspective—gripping in her hand a battered brown leather portmanteau. Stamped on one side in peeling gilt were the letters JS. It had been her father's bag, and then hers on that sad, seemingly interminable journey from India so long ago. As she had packed her few possessions late, very late, last night, Livia had felt like crying.

But didn't.

Crying never helped.

Besides, she had nothing to cry about.

Everything was going to be fine.

No, better than fine. It was going to be *wonderful*.

Into the portmanteau had gone nothing that had once belonged to Cecily Orr, and this morning she was wearing a faded blue gown of figured muslin (yes, she *knew* the hem was too short), a dark blue pelisse, and an antiquated bonnet in the French style, with a blue satin ribbon that matched absolutely nothing. Ugh. It was the best she could do. But what did it matter? She wasn't going to worry about a thing.

She certainly wasn't going to be concerned that her

face was as white as snow, save for heavy dark circles under her eyes, from lack of sleep; a final glance at the little mirror in her bedchamber had shown her that. She had firmly tied the bonnet ribbon under her chin, then had gone to say her farewells.

Aunt Bella had still been in bed, and woke from a deep sleep too fuddled to comprehend what was happening. "Stop crashing about, Livia, do," she murmured petulantly, "and ring for my cordial as you go."

Livia found Uncle Charles at the breakfast table. "So you're off?" he had said, and took a large bite of kidney pie. "Well, be sure you mind your manners," he went on, speaking through a mouthful of pie, "and don't be expecting any blunt from me. Old Mrs. Moneybags is paying the shot from now on. Aren't you the lucky girl?"

"Oh yes, I'm a very lucky girl, Uncle."

"Indeed you are! And don't think you can come back, for I won't have you. On your own now."

Livia had bitten her lip against the angry rush of words that wanted to tumble out: *Goodbye and good riddance! I'd rather die than rot here another day!*

Now she shivered a little in the cool morning breeze and gripped her portmanteau more tightly. To her ears came the sound of carriage wheels and sure enough, lumbering—no, *gliding*—her way was a coach. The biggest, blackest, shiniest coach she'd ever seen. Riding alongside was Gabriel Penhallow on his big black horse, looking obnoxiously well-rested. His composure was once more absolute.

"Good morning, Miss Stuart. You're very punctual. A delightful quality."

She gave him a hostile glance but said nothing. A footman (much better dressed than she was) had jumped down from the coach and now he took her portmanteau, put down the steps, and opened the door for her.

Livia caught a glimpse of luxurious crimson silk panels, the forbidding countenance of old Mrs. Penhallow, and another face, that of a short, slender, gray-haired lady she'd never seen before.

Livia took a deep breath, and put one foot on the steps. But something tugged at her, pulled at her—

"Pray make haste, Miss Stuart," Mrs. Penhallow said sharply. "I don't care to be kept waiting."

"What, afraid?" said Gabriel Penhallow, mockingly. "I don't think my grandmother will bite you. Or will you, Grandmama?"

"Don't be impertinent! Why you seem to find this situation humorous, Gabriel, is beyond my capacity to understand."

"You mistake me. I am as serious as the grave."

The old lady's still vivid blue eyes were flashing angrily. "I am not sure you are. Miss Stuart, if you do not get in immediately I shall instruct the footman to *push* you in here."

Livia barely heard the old lady, for suddenly she realized why she'd been hesitating. "Just a moment!" she said, and quickly she turned—ignoring the loud affronted puff from Mrs. Penhallow—and ran back into the house, up the stairs, and into Aunt Bella's large, dim drawing-room. As usual the heavy greenish-black drapes were drawn, and near them stood the elaborate birdcage.

Even though the day was well advanced, none of the maids had bothered to remove the green baize cloth covering it. Tenderly, Livia slid the cloth away. Huddled unmoving on their wood perches were the half-dozen small birds, their dark eyes dull. Feeling as though her heart would burst from both pity and excitement, carefully Livia removed the cage from its hook and, indifferent to the astonished looks of the servants loitering in the hall, carried it outside and set it gently on the ground. She undid the latch, opening the little door as wide as possible, and stood aside.

"What on earth is that peculiar girl doing?" came the irritated voice of the old lady from within the coach. There was a soft murmured reply from the other woman and Mrs. Penhallow only sniffed.

Livia glanced up at Gabriel Penhallow. He said nothing, his expression unreadable, but she was grateful that his horse stood still. She looked back at the little birds, who seemed frozen on their perches. "Go, go," she whispered in encouragement. One bird cocked its head, then took a tentative step toward the opening. Livia remained motionless, holding her breath.

Cautiously, the bird took a few more steps, paused before the little gate, and seemed to look straight at Livia; then it took flight, dark wings shimmering before it disappeared toward the woods clustering thickly behind the Abbey. It was only a moment before the other birds followed suit, the last one emitting a joyous trill of notes as effortlessly it soared up into the blue sky, joining its companions, and then they were gone.

Livia let out her breath with a deep sense of satisfaction and stepped into the coach. She settled onto a comfortable, cushioned seat opposite the old lady, who glared at her and said:

"My word! What a perfectly strange thing to do. Ride on, ride on!" she cried, and the coach, with a gentle jerk, began to move.

Next to Livia was the petite gray-haired lady, holding on her lap an enormous, beautifully chased leather case, the lid clasped shut by a large brass lock. She smiled slightly and said in a pleasant voice, "We have not yet met, Miss Stuart. I am Miss Cott, companion to Mrs. Penhallow. How do you do?"

At least Miss Cott didn't seem as if she wanted to either kick her into a ditch or laugh at her. How

refreshing, Livia thought, and answered politely: "I'm
pleased to make your acquaintance, ma'am."

"And I you. I trust the brick at your feet is still warm?"

"Yes. Thank you." It was a luxury unfamiliar to her,
and Livia set her thin slippers more comfortably upon
the welcome warmth. Then there was silence within the
coach. Livia felt no desire to make conversation with
Mrs. Penhallow, who stared balefully at her from underneath beetled silver brows, and occupied herself instead
by looking out the window. The exquisitely smooth rolling motion of the coach was lulling. Exhausted from too
little sleep, Livia felt her eyelids drifting shut, her head
nodding heavily, and then she knew no more.

"How very rude!" muttered Mrs. Penhallow. Five
minutes later, her eyes closed too, and the harsh lines of
her face relaxed in sleep.

Only Miss Cott remained awake, holding the jewelry case securely in her gloved hands. Could Livia and
Mrs. Penhallow have known it, she looked at both of
them with a calm, steady, mild gaze that was both interested and kind.

Livia stood in her expensively furnished bedchamber
in the Inn of the Gilded Lance, staring at the doorknob.
During the journey today in Mrs. Penhallow's enormous black coach she had slept deeply for some three or
four hours and now, even though it was past midnight,
she was still awake.

Tentatively she reached out and put her hand on
the doorknob. She half-expected it to be locked from
the outside, but it turned freely. It occurred to her to
wonder, then, if they would all be glad if she took advantage of the unlocked door and disappeared forever.

She opened the door and glanced out into the

darkened corridor. There was no one there, and so, not bothering to button up her old pelisse, quietly she left her room, padded downstairs, slipped past the still-busy common-parlor, and went outside into the dimly illuminated courtyard, which she had all to herself.

Or so she thought.

She took a few steps, enjoying the cool night air, and then her progress was abruptly halted when her arm was taken in an iron grip.

Livia's breath caught in her throat and reflexively she tried to wrench her arm free, but without success.

"Going somewhere, Miss Stuart?"

She was forcefully turned about, and, her heart thumping hard within her, looked up into the grim handsome face of Mr. Penhallow.

"What are you *doing* here?" she demanded, a little breathlessly.

Gabriel, in turn, answered, "I might ask the same of you." All at once he noticed that the hand that he'd wrapped around her upper arm felt hot, as if he'd grasped fire, and swiftly he released her.

"I needed to be outside," she said reluctantly. "After being cooped up in that carriage all day, and then being bundled in a shawl and hustled up into my room as if I were a prisoner, with supper sent to me on a tray!"

"Your—ah—*ensemble* not being quite up to snuff, according to my grandmother."

"That's tactful of you. She told me I looked like the daughter of a rag-and-bone man."

"Did she? Once," he said reflectively, "when I was seventeen, she told me that my fashionable new waistcoat made me look like a circus performer. I'd been so proud of it, too."

Her expression softened. "How crushing."

"I must admit it seemed so at the time."

"Your grandmother seems to me a person of strong opinions."

"That's one way of putting it." He looked at her more closely. "You're not wearing the shawl she gave you."

"Gave me? You mean *forced* upon me. No, I left it in my room."

"So you just came out for a breath of fresh air," he said, his skepticism renewed. "Not to—oh, take a turn about charming Bradford-on-Avon?"

"In the middle of the night?" she retorted. "In a strange town? Just how stupid do you think I am?"

"You're the one who last night ran away to be a scullery maid, so perhaps I might be forgiven if I'm a little dubious."

Her eyes narrowed. "Have you been out here waiting for me all this time?"

There was no way he'd reveal the truth, that he'd been out here for hours, expecting exactly this scenario. He only said, blandly, "I like fresh air also."

She took this in, then said, "I suppose you think me very impulsive."

"Aren't you?"

"I think *you* are. You're supposed to be marrying in order to—how did your grandmother put it in her letter to Lady Glanville?—oh yes, to ensure the succession. How will you do that now, I wonder?"

He took his time responding, for he was analyzing her tone. It wasn't one he heard often. It was—impudence. Brazen impudence. If he had hackles, he thought, they'd be rising right now. Coolly he said, "That's my problem, isn't it, Miss Stuart? Not yours."

"Aren't you afraid I'll reveal your horrid little secret to Mrs. Penhallow?"

Gabriel shrugged. "Go ahead. What do you think she'd do then?"

She was silent, and he could almost hear the wheels in her head turning. Then, slowly, she answered.

"One way or another, she'd end the engagement."

"And you'd be back where you started, wouldn't you, Miss Stuart? A denizen of that delightful old abbey of yours."

"I'll never go back there, *never!*"

He was startled by her vehemence. But in that same cool voice he replied, "Then perhaps it's in your best interest to be discreet."

Her eyes were huge in the moonlight as she stared up at him. "Don't you *care* about the succession? Your estate? Surmont Hall, isn't that what it's called?"

"Yes, Surmont Hall. And no, I don't really care about it. It's just a house and some land."

"I don't think your grandmother would like to hear you talking about it that way."

"Why would it matter to her? She hasn't been there in many years. She never talks about it. Besides, she doesn't own me. Despite, perhaps, her beliefs to the contrary."

"How proud you both are," she said, wonderingly. "How you like to have your own way. As if it's your right."

"Isn't it?" He smiled mockingly down at her, and she frowned.

"Apparently it is! After all, the Conqueror bowed to you Penhallows, didn't he?"

"So it's said."

He watched as she crossed her arms over her chest. That rather delectable chest.

"Well," she went on, "if you don't care about having an heir, what *do* you care about?"

His smile faded. "I care about my own agency. I don't enjoy being a pawn on someone else's chessboard."

"I understand that. Aren't I a pawn on *your* chess-board?"

"Yes. But if you make the right moves, you'll be a queen someday, won't you? Isn't that what you care about, Miss Stuart?"

"Yes," she answered firmly. "That's all I care about. Will you excuse me, please? I'm going back to my room."

"Allow me to escort you."

"How thoughtful you are," she said, ironically, and when he held open the door for her she swept past him with her head held extremely high, although the over-all effect was ruined when she barreled into someone coming out of the common-parlor, reeled back and bumped into *him*, hastily apologized to both of them, and with her dignity less than intact went on to the staircase and so up to her bedchamber.

At her door she paused. "Go ahead, say it!" she said in what he could only think of as a loud whisper. Even in the dimness of the corridor he could see her eyes snapping with hostility.

"Say what?"

"That I'm a clumsy country yokel!"

He smiled, just a little. "I," he said, rather lazily, "would never contradict a lady. Good *ton* forbids it. I trust you'll pass a peaceful night, Miss Stuart."

She scowled and whisked herself into her room, clos-ing the door very gently. He could tell—oh, he could tell for sure—that she wished she could have slammed it in his face instead.

The coach drew up to an imposing townhouse in a very elegant street—Upper Camden Place, the old lady had called it. They were in Bath. Livia stared, but had no time to think more about it in the bustle of arrival, as steps were let down, she and Mrs. Penhallow and Miss Cott were solicitously handed out by a footman, servants had emerged from the townhouse, the carriage with that incredible quantity of luggage pulled up, horses were neighing, and the old lady was already giving orders to, evidently, everyone, including the horses. A sharp wind seemed to be resisting their every movement and Livia kept a hand on the ribbons of her bonnet, although if it did fly off her head and float off—toward France, say—she would have been glad to see it go. The dreadful ugly thing.

Gabriel Penhallow had dismounted and stood as if immune to the chaos. How did *his* tall low-brimmed hat stay so securely on his head? No doubt through sheer force of will, she thought resentfully.

She watched as he handed the reins of his horse to the footman, then went unhurriedly to his grandmother and said a few words. She waved a hand, impatiently, and composedly he bowed slightly, then came to Livia and said:

"Goodbye."

"Goodbye?" she echoed, startled and, strangely, ridiculously, dismayed. "Aren't you staying here?"

"That would hardly be proper."

"Oh. Of course. Where are you going, then?"

"To the York House."

"Where is that?"

"Here in Bath."

"Oh. When will you—"

"Miss Stuart!" It was the old lady, already at the top of the steps and on the stoop, looking down at Livia as if she were an unruly pigeon, desecrating the pavement. "*Do* stop loitering about in that aimless way. Come up at once!"

"Well," Livia said to Mr. Penhallow, "goodbye then,"

and dutifully went up the steps, despite herself feeling that he had callously abandoned her to the less than tender mercies of his grandmother, who, as Livia crossed the threshold, looked up toward the ceiling as if silently requesting celestial assistance for the monumental, possibly hopeless task awaiting her.

Livia started awake as into her consciousness came the noise of a door whispering open.

Where am I?

She stared up in bewilderment at the unfamiliar canopy overhead. She was in a big four-poster bed draped with sumptuous burgundy silk. How on earth did *this* happen? Then, as she saw in the dimness the quiet white-aproned figure of a housemaid, lighting a fire in the hearth, she remembered.

She was in Bath.

She had been here eleven—no, twelve days now.

She kept track, in order to remind herself that it was all real.

That *she* was real.

In the twinkling of an eye, her life had been turned upside down. No more Ealdor Abbey, no more vacuous Aunt Bella, no more caustic Uncle Charles. No more excruciating visits from the Orrs, and wasn't it all a nice change. Sometimes she had to remind herself that it wasn't a dream.

A bizarre, overwhelming dream that overtook her waking hours.

At first, she could barely sleep. To someone who had spent most of her life in the countryside, often outside and solitary in the quiet of the woods, Bath initially seemed raucously, intolerably noisy.

During the day came the ceaseless rattle, jingle, clink,

clop of horses and carriages; through an open window one might see an endless promenade of strangers. (And how curious to see the elderly and infirm carried along in sedan chairs, some of them so extravagantly fitted out they looked like tiny portable palaces.) Even the night hours were regularly punctuated by the sonorous calls of the watchmen, or by bursts of talk and laughter among the link-boys.

All this was observed only from within the perimeters of Mrs. Penhallow's enormous residence in Upper Camden Place, for Livia had been declared by the old lady unfit to be seen in public.

She was therefore confined to the house, and only occasionally could she escape to its small, high-walled garden in the back where she could pace along the pretty graveled path and tilt her face up to the sun. If it rained—as it often did—she would sometimes seek a few moments of refuge in the large, beautifully furnished bedchamber that had been assigned to her, so sharply contrasting with her former dingy room at the Abbey that she sometimes sat on the edge of the bed, looked around her, and simply stared. At the handsome striped wallpaper in softest ivory and white; at the broad oak dressing-table, on it placed an embossed silver tray holding a comb and brush so lovely she was at first hesitant to use them; at, underfoot, warm carpets in a floral pattern whose colors matched with pleasing harmony the hangings on her bed.

But there wasn't much opportunity for such modest leisure, as Mrs. Penhallow had constructed for her a schedule that kept her occupied from early morning until well into the evening.

Like a powerful wizard waving a wand, her hostess summoned hordes of dressmakers, milliners, corsetieres, and shoemakers to Upper Camden Place, where they were conducted upstairs to a capacious chamber that had been set aside for them.

There they consulted in exhaustive detail with Mrs. Penhallow, who sat regally in the best chair, while Livia was measured, surveyed, scrutinized, assessed, appraised, evaluated, analyzed, and (by Mrs. Penhallow) criticized; made to sit, stand, walk, twirl, and curtsy; held up to her were lengths of satin, muslin, silk, cambric, crepe, lace, net, and the softest wool, in delicious shades of green, blue, violet, yellow; lavender, cream, apricot, silver, gold; and white, a great deal of white, most suitable for an unmarried young lady, the sublime simplicity of which complemented Livia's vivid coloring and sent even Madame Lévêque, the most exclusive and supercilious of Bath's numerous modistes, into ecstasies of praise.

These beautiful fabrics fascinated and delighted Livia, but the moment she ran a speculative finger along a length of sleek satin or delicate lace, the old lady would snap with maddening perceptiveness:

"You need not indulge yourself with flights of fancy! We'll have no repeats of that earlier monstrosity of yours!" Or, after what felt to Livia like hours—like eons—of being made to stand absolutely still while a hem was adjusted or a sleeve set or a sash remade (and discouraged from offering any sort of opinion whatsoever), Mrs. Penhallow might say impatiently, "Do stop fidgeting! Most uncouth!"

Day dresses, walking dresses, and carriage dresses were ordered, along with evening dresses and ball-gowns, and of course reticules, fans, stockings, shawls, gloves, and embroidered handkerchiefs by the dozen. Then there were muffs, tippets, cloaks, pelisses, and spencers; slippers and half-boots; parasols, extremely fragile but charmingly designed and so very, very pretty.

Spangles, feathers, ribbons, tassels, ruffles, lappets; hats, caps, bonnets, in a kaleidoscopic riot of styles, shapes, fabrics, colors, and embellishments.

Each and every garment, accessory, and shoe was subject to the approval of old Mrs. Penhallow, whose taste was exquisite and unerring: with consummate judgment she rejected anything with the slightest taint of inelegance or excess. Even Livia, whose ignorance of *les habillement à la mode* was extreme, could see that she was in the presence of a savant. Madame Lévêque herself acknowledged it with humility.

One morning, after several new items had arrived (including, to Livia's intense gratification, a pair of kid slippers with ravishing pink rosettes), she said impulsively to Mrs. Penhallow:

"All this, ma'am, for me? I must thank you."

The old lady had somehow managed despite her inferior height to look down her nose at Livia. "It is not for, or about, you, young lady," she replied with her usual hauteur. "Never think that for a moment. It is merely that you are to represent the Penhallows, and standards must be upheld."

Temporarily cowed by this frigid set-down, Livia submitted to successive applications of Lotion of Ladies of Denmark, Milk of Almonds, and the distilled water from green pineapples, her complexion having been pronounced shockingly brown, and also to the rose oil and white wax for lips deemed repulsively dry and chapped.

She balked only at the hairdresser who, with a martial light in his eye, came at her with scissors and hot tongs, but she did permit her new dresser—a laconic, efficient, middle-aged woman she was to address only by her surname, Flye—to employ a little pomade and create a rich, shining coronet of braids that even Mrs. Penhallow admitted was both flattering and fashionable.

A dancing master came three times a week. In the long, light-filled drawing-room, with his assistant at the pianoforte, Monsieur Voclaine taught her the country-dance, the cotillion, and the quadrille under the sharp, watchful gaze of Mrs. Penhallow and the milder one of the ever-present Miss Cott.

At first, Livia found the complicated steps horribly confusing, nor did it help to overhear Mrs. Penhallow commenting complacently to Miss Cott, "I was universally considered quite the best dancer in London; even Richard said so, the first time we met."

Miss Cott smiled and nodded, but even as she did a stiff mask seemed to swiftly descend upon the old lady's features and she called out in a cold voice, "If *that* is how you perform the *glissade,* Miss Stuart, you shall never be ready to appear in Polite Society."

"Again, *s'il vous plaît, mademoiselle,*" coaxed Monsieur Voclaine. "If you will slide the foot, thusly . . ."

Livia clenched her jaw and tried again. And again. Both she and Monsieur Voclaine were sweating by the time Mrs. Penhallow pronounced her *glissade* to be passable. "But you are visibly damp, Miss Stuart, and that is simply not done. Change your gown and we will continue."

"Yes, ma'am," Livia muttered grimly and made for the door, while Monsieur Voclaine turned away and discreetly mopped his brow.

"And *do not* do it yourself!" Mrs. Penhallow called after her. "That is the purview of your dresser! You have not always summoned her and this behavior must stop. It displays an abhorrent lack of refinement."

"Yes, ma'am," Livia repeated, trying not to sound surly, and whisked herself out of the drawing-room. How did the old lady *know* these things?

Then there was the matter of her education, both academic and social. Every afternoon, while Mrs.

Penhallow napped, Livia met Miss Cott in the library which, like every other room she had seen in this enormous, high-ceilinged house, was furnished and decorated with impeccable good taste. It contained hundreds of books, lined up neatly on burnished mahogany shelves, as well as inviting armchairs, a merry little fire always burning for their comfort, and plenty of light.

The first time Livia had entered, she looked around it in wonder: it was so different from Uncle Charles's study, which was dark, untidy, odorous, and lacking in reading matter other than a few old tomes about horse-breeding.

"How lovely!" she'd exclaimed unguardedly.

"Yes." Miss Cott had smiled her soft, slight smile. "This was one of Mrs. Penhallow's favorite rooms, for she was a great reader."

"Was?"

"Her eyesight for close work is not what it used to be. Shall we sit down?"

It was clear to Livia within minutes just how intelligent, how widely educated, how *kind* Miss Cott was. Under the older woman's patient tutelage she was exposed to literature, geography, mathematics, history, music, even a smattering of French and Italian. She was given newspapers to read, globes to study. She devoured it all, painfully conscious of her ignorance, and eager to learn. In the evenings Mrs. Penhallow quizzed her, made her read out loud, and ruthlessly corrected her many stumbles and mistakes.

There were lessons, too, in deportment, manners, propriety, and address. How to enter a crowded assembly room; acceptable topics of conversation; the intricacies of the peerage. Who to acknowledge and who to cut. At table, the precise arrangement of plates, glasses, forks, knives, spoons. How best to drape a shawl, utilize a fan, settle one's skirts. Morning calls and leaving one's card; the best times to drink the waters; the critical importance of safeguarding one's reputation at all times (she had, in fact, learned this the hard way); and never, ever accepting anything more potent than lemonade while at a ball.

These lessons Livia found less interesting, and quite often pointless and silly, but at them she labored diligently. This was, as she frequently reminded herself, her chance. She could hardly wait to show herself off to Gabriel Penhallow, and flaunt her metamorphosis in his face. *Much* better than throwing coins into the mud!

But for this pleasure she had to wait. Two, then three weeks went by, and still he absented himself from his grandmother's home. Mrs. Penhallow grumbled about his undutiful attitude, then in the very next breath added that it was just as well, for she would, she announced, forbid his presence anyway, until Miss Stuart was no longer a half-savage, unlettered, ill-spoken, maladroit, freckled tatterdemalion.

"I'm not freckled, ma'am," was all Livia could think to answer, and then promptly felt like a fool.

"Not freckled, you say? You are free to delude yourself, Miss Stuart, if you choose," frostily replied Mrs. Penhallow. "The Penhallows never have freckles. Have Flye apply the Milk of Almonds twice today. Now! Suppose you have just been introduced to—let us say—the Duke of Egremont. How do you greet him?"

In his private parlor at the York House, Gabriel lounged in a comfortable wing chair, opening a letter. A little fire crackled cozily in the hearth nearby, and a glass of burgundy, seeming to glow a deep rich red, was on a table at his elbow.

Dear Coz,

I send you greetings from the wilds near the Saint Lawrence River. Tremendous fishing to be had, if only one wasn't so busy engaging in jolly skirmishes! Lord, how we laughed when my cap got blown off by a Frenchy and I tumbled backwards into a briar patch. Looked like I'd been mauled by a tiger and have been ribbed about it ever since. I'm such an ass.

I know you detest being thanked, having told me so in the most vehement terms for these many ages, but coz, can never truly express my gratitude at your setting me up so splendidly. The Army suits me to a T—never a dull moment—although I do think quite often of the dear ones back in Whitehaven. In the mater's latest billet she reports you sent a very generous cheque for which I must add my thanks. Did she tell you about young Bertram's recent exploit? Apparently he blew up one of the attics. All in the name of science, the mater says. He is going to be a Great Man someday, if only he survives to adulthood. A dreadful scamp, you know, but I love him dearly.

What are you doing with yourself now that the Diplomatic Corps have let you go? Cutting a dash among the ladies, no doubt. Trust one day you'll find one who doesn't turn your stomach as they all seem to do. How they swan about you! A wonder you haven't yet developed a head the size of a frigate.

Yours ever,
Hugo

Gabriel smiled slightly, then folded the letter and placed it on the table. Hugo was a good lad, and a plucky one. Although the military held no particular appeal for Gabriel, at this moment he envied his young cousin his active life. Even the idea of nearly getting his head blown off by a French sharpshooter was beginning to sound appealing.

Here he was, cooling his heels in what had to be the most insipid city in the world. Shops filled with feminine fripperies, the Pump Room, the Russian Vapour Baths, the Harmonic Society which sang *glees*—good Lord! And everywhere the infamous Bath tabbies, whose chief interest in life was apparently that of spying on everybody else, and then nattering about it. How could his grandmother stand this place?

He'd wanted to leave Bath after dutifully accompanying the ladies here, but the mere mention of it had provoked such a firestorm of recrimination from Grandmama that he honestly expected her to drop dead from an apoplexy in the middle of it.

Preemptive guilt. What an effective means by which to keep him tethered here. Still, he was damned if he was going to call at his grandmother's residence. Let her—them—make the first move: he'd wait forever if necessary.

And here he was, he reflected wryly. Still grappling for the upper hand.

Well, there were worse things than boredom.

Gabriel stretched out his legs, took a sip of the York's excellent burgundy, and reached for Niebuhr's *Roman History*.

Livia stared dismally at her plate. On it was a mashed turnip cake, three limp mushrooms over which had been spooned a lumpy gray sauce, and half a raw artichoke bottom. Not only did Mrs. Penhallow follow a

most peculiar culinary regimen, so were she and Miss
Cott forced to endure it as well. It was all because of
that repulsive Dr. Wendeburgen, one of Bath's most
eminent physicians and a particular favorite of Mrs.
Penhallow.

No meat, no fish, no poultry, no milk, no cream, no
butter, no eggs, no bread, declared Dr. Wendeburgen.
Above all, no desserts! What could be more injurious to
the human alimentary tract? He and his medicaments—
murky tinctures in small amber bottles, red-painted
little caskets filled with tiny round pills covered in black
beeswax, long linen cloths steeped in pungent vinegar
infusions (to be wrapped around the feet for exactly
one hour)—were in great demand among the elderly
ladies of Bath, to whom he ministered with absolute
authority, and received their enthusiastic expressions of
admiration as if they were no less than his due.

Livia, on the other hand, would have liked to wrap
one of those smelly cloths about the great doctor's neck
until his eyes bugged out. She frowned at her turnip
cake. What were those dark specks? She was so hungry
she would almost rather have gnawed on the elegant
linen napkin spread neatly across her lap. A deep sigh
escaped her and gloomily she reached for a fork.

Opposite her, Miss Cott coughed discreetly and
picked up the fork on the extreme far left of her own
plate. Quickly Livia followed suit, but not before Mrs.
Penhallow sniffed—in that annoyingly audible way she
had—and said to Miss Cott:

"After luncheon, do review with Miss Stuart proper
manners at table. They seem to present quite a challenge."

"Certainly, ma'am," replied Miss Cott with her usual
calm affability.

Livia wrinkled her brow but said nothing and took a

small, careful bite of her artichoke. Why did it have to be raw? Grimly she began to chew.

"I understand from Madame Lévêque that yesterday while I had absented myself from the room," the old lady said in a chilly tone, "you refused to be fitted for a riding-habit. This is nonsensical. All the Penhallows are superior equestrians. Why, I was on my first pony before I was three, although I may say that I was unusually advanced for my age. Indeed, I was jumping fences at four. When Madame Lévêque returns, I expect no further displays of inexplicable obstinacy."

She looked sternly at Livia, obviously waiting for a response, but Livia was still chewing. There was no doubt in her mind that she looked exactly like a cow working on an especially dense cud. It was yet a full minute before she was able to safely swallow. The old lady could order her around in very nearly every other aspect of her life, but here was where Livia was going to make her stand. She had just opened her mouth when Mrs. Penhallow, losing patience, went on talking about horses for the rest of the so-called meal and all the way up the stairs and into the drawing-room, and for the next fifteen or twenty minutes.

Livia, sitting in her chair and watching Mrs. Penhallow, had stopped listening quite some time ago, but marveled all over again at the sheer force of the old lady's personality. It was a shame, she thought, that women weren't allowed in Parliament, because Mrs. Penhallow could have talked all those men down in a single afternoon. And, probably, make them pass a law which exempted Penhallows from being forced into marriage with nobodies.

"Tomorrow, Miss Stuart, you are—I beg your pardon," the old lady said awfully, "have I been boring you?"

"By no means, ma'am." There, Livia congratulated herself, you're learning to lie quite beautifully! "You said something about tomorrow, I believe."

"Yes. Tomorrow. You are to make your *début*. It seems wisest to me to begin in a very small way, so we shall visit the Pump Room. I've sent a note round to Gabriel requesting his presence as well. Restrict your remarks to the weather and inquiries as to the state of others' health. Leave the rest to me. There shan't be the slightest public indication that I am anything other than pleased with your imminent entrance into the family."

"It's very good of you, ma'am," said Livia, so meekly that the old lady's gaze sharpened suspiciously. What she might have retorted remained unsaid when there was a soft knock on the door and Crenshaw, the butler—who alarmed Livia with his seemingly inhuman unflappability—entered the drawing-room and spoke in his measured, sonorous voice.

"I beg your pardon, ma'am. Dr. Wendeburgen has arrived, and has indicated his desire to be admitted at once."

"In matters of health, one can't be too diligent," said Mrs. Penhallow. "Bring him in, Crenshaw."

"Certainly, ma'am."

It was but a few minutes before the doctor bounced into the drawing-room. Livia eyed him with distaste. He looked like a tawdry advertisement in a magazine, with his wavy corn-colored hair, elaborately curled mustachios and little pointed beard (a *different* shade of yellow), round blue eyes, round red cheeks, round stomach. How on earth could he be plump if he followed his own dietary recommendations?

"*Guten Morgen*, dear ladies, *guten Morgen*," he greeted them jovially.

"Good morning, *herr doktor*," replied Mrs. Penhallow. It would not have been accurate to say that her face was wreathed in smiles, but she was, Livia had observed, at her most gracious when Dr. Wendeburgen was around. She herself gave him only a small, cold bow, exactly the sort—if memory served her—one would offer a coxcomb whose pretensions one wished to dampen.

Talking volubly of liver imbalances, skin discoloration, phlegm, and the dangers of a swelling tongue, Dr. Wendeburgen swept Mrs. Penhallow off to be bled without delay, Miss Cott placidly in tow in order to hold the bowl.

Left, unusually, to her own devices, Livia hesitated for a few moments, then quickly rose to her feet and made her way downstairs and toward the kitchen. Never having been there, she made a few false turns and ended up in an empty closet and on the stairwell to the cellar. Retreating, she caught a glimpse of one of the maids hurrying along a corridor and followed hopefully. As she did, she reflected that one good thing about Uncle Charles—quite possibly the *only* good thing—was that he did ensure a palatable table was laid for meals.

Her stomach rumbling wistfully, she passed through a doorway and found herself in the kitchen at last. It was a large, high-ceilinged room, and a quick glance around showed her that it was immaculately clean. It also revealed to her a scene of melancholy. The staff, seated on either side of a long wooden table, were either gazing morosely at their plates or chewing like—she had to admit it—sad cows.

At her entrance they all promptly stood up and looked expectantly at her. Taken aback, Livia wiped her suddenly sweaty palms on the front of her gown, stopped herself from doing it again, and turned her head with relief when her dresser Flye inquired politely:

"Was there anything you was wishful for, miss?"

Livia said, rather shyly, "Well, I was . . . I was wondering what you were eating."

There was a puzzled silence.

Finally a woman in a long white apron stepped forward, dipped a curtsy, and, in the same tone in which one might announce *All my family has recently perished in a fire,* said: "Turnip cakes, miss."

"With artichoke bottoms?" asked Livia, hope beginning to fade.

"Yes, miss," the woman replied, then suddenly burst out: "With mushrooms, and a sauce I'd be ashamed to serve to a *dog!* It's that horrid foreign doctor, miss, and his strange notions! For nigh on a year the mistress has made us all eat like this!" She sobbed, wiped at her damp eyes with her apron, and added: "I'm sorry, miss, it's just the hunger talking! Once when poor Sally over there was sick with an ague, I brought in a bit of pork to make a nice restorative jelly, but when the mistress found it in the accounts, she nearly took my head off!"

Livia nodded. She knew the feeling. "You're the cook?"

"Yes, miss."

She had a fresh, open countenance and under normal circumstances, would, Livia guessed, be a cheerful sort, but it was impossible not to notice that her cheeks were sagging and the bones underneath them sharp. Livia thought of rotund Dr. Wendeburgen and felt a flash of anger. Impulsively she said:

"I think it was very brave of you, Cook, to not conceal the purchase of the pork."

"As to that, we're a good lot here, miss, no finer could be found elsewhere. It's just that—well, do you know what we do on our afternoons off? We go and eat, miss, we eat till we're about to burst!"

I'll go with you, Livia was tempted to say, but instead she responded, thinking out loud, "If you spend your wages on food, how can you put anything aside for—for needful things, or for an emergency?"

"We can't, miss, and that's a fact," Cook said bleakly.

Livia looked around at all the unhappy faces. Gaunt faces. She took a deep breath. And said the only thing that *could* be said.

"I'll see what I can do."

But Mrs. Penhallow was so irritable and snappish for the rest of the day, and in the morning, too, that Livia's courage failed her. What, she wondered, was her next move? She had to do something.

Standing next to Mrs. Penhallow in the Pump Room, Livia looked at her in astonishment. Had the old lady *really* just said, with every sign of complaisance, "Dear Miss Stuart is such a pleasure, and how gratifying to think of the nursery at Surmont Hall filled once more"?

Yes, she had.

How very, very strange life had become.

Murmurs of "Delightful," "Splendid," "The sooner the better, to be sure" filled the air, and to her exasperation Livia found herself blushing furiously. Initially, while accepting the cascade of congratulations on her grandson's engagement, Mrs. Penhallow had seemed just a trifle stiff, then had gradually warmed to her own recitation—"Yes, it was all quite unexpected, but when two young people form such a decided attachment, we must simply rejoice with them" and "Miss Stuart's is a fine old family in Wiltshire" and "I expect I shall be *quite* the doting grandmother"—until Livia could feel her mouth dropping open. Why, Mrs. Penhallow seemed actually to believe her own little fairy tale!

Her plump, discreetly rouged friend Lady Enchwood, swathed in an expensive silk shawl of a size sufficient to entirely drape a barouche, interposed with something between a simper and a cackle, "It's all so romantic! I vow, Miss Stuart, you're the most fortunate young lady alive!"

Romantic? thought Livia. *It isn't the least bit romantic. It's a farce, actually. One in which I am a willing participant.* Aloud she said only, mindful of her instructions from Mrs. Penhallow and ready to master yet another new lesson in the social niceties: "Yes, ma'am."

"I believe this is your first time in Bath, Miss Stuart?" Lady Enchwood went on. "What is your impression thus far?"

"It's . . . it's very healthful, ma'am."

"Indeed it is! You *must* take a course of the farina cataplasms! Most restorative! Dr. Wendeburgen assures me that after six more months, my veinous palpitations will be a thing of the past!" Her ladyship described the innumerable benefits to be gained from this popular treatment until Livia was actively queasy and the gorge had begun to rise in her throat. "—and as for bilious extrusions, of which I am sorry to say I have four—or is it five?—in rather indelicate places—oh! Here comes your betrothed, Miss Stuart! I declare he is the most distinguished gentleman in the room!"

Chapter 6

Livia turned to follow Lady Enchwood's admiring gaze, and for a startled moment the crowded Pump Room faded away and she saw only Gabriel Penhallow. How tall he was. And he *was* distinguished-looking, there wasn't any doubt about it. He was impeccably dressed in pale yellow pantaloons and a dark blue coat that fitted his broad shoulders without a crease. His thick, straight brown hair just touched his collar in a very dashing way.

It seemed like years since she had last seen him. Was it possible she'd actually forgotten just how attractive he was, and how he carried himself with an arrogant assurance that made one feel a little weak in the knees?

For the past few weeks he'd become more of an *idea* to her, something rather abstract, but to see him once again in the flesh—solid, real, intensely masculine— well, that was an entirely different thing, and Livia was shocked to feel a giddy rush of pride that he was *hers*.

And had to sternly remind herself that she was only playing a game.

A game for her own benefit.

And yet, unbidden, into her mind came a vision of a grand nursery. She hadn't lived in the country nearly all her life without learning how nurseries were filled: and another fiery blush was promptly suffusing her face. She could have cheerfully kicked herself for her mooning idiocy *and* for looking like a human beet. The Penhallow nursery would remain empty.

"Good morning, Grandmama," Mr. Penhallow said, at his coolest and most urbane. He greeted the effusive clutch of elderly ladies gathered round and then turned to Livia, bowing slightly. "My dear Miss Stuart."

The old ladies fluttered in a way that struck Livia as shameless, and angrily she dipped a little curtsy. "Sir," she replied, trying hard to match his coolness.

"I trust I find you well?"

"Very well, sir, thank you."

"How are you enjoying Bath?"

"It is delightful."

"Indeed. However, the weather looks rather inclement today, I fear."

"Yes. It's a bit overcast." Livia eyed him closely. Was that a mocking glint in those fine brown eyes? Was he *testing* her? Well then. She would be the perfect young lady or die trying. "I shouldn't wonder if it will rain."

"It does so frequently."

"So I understand. Perhaps," she went on, "it will be fine tomorrow."

"Perhaps. Of course, it may rain."

Oh dear. She was already running out of things to say. Then, a little desperately: "One is grateful for umbrellas."

"Very grateful. Grandmama, ladies, will you excuse us? Miss Stuart looks a trifle overwarm. No doubt she'll benefit from a sip of the waters."

There was an instant chorus of fluttery agreement, and as Mr. Penhallow took her arm and bore her away, Livia felt as if she was being wafted along a wave of sentimental goodwill. "Why, he positively *dotes* on her," came a trill from behind her, and Livia resisted the impulse to snatch her arm away.

The Pump Room water tasted like—well, Livia had never drunk from the puddles standing around dankly at Ealdor Abbey for days on end, but if she had, she would guess that it might even be better than the vile stuff in the glass Mr. Penhallow had, with irritating ceremony, handed to her.

She managed to keep from gagging. "Thank you, that is sufficient."

"Are you certain? Surely you need more."

"Why?" she asked suspiciously.

"While you are delightfully arrayed and coiffed, Miss Stuart—I extend my felicitations on your newly acquired polish!—I can't help but observe that you're noticeably thinner than when last we met. Is town life not agreeing with you?"

His voice was bland, his face—that too dangerously appealing face—unreadable, and altogether there seemed to be such a total lack of real concern in his question that despite her intention to remain just as dispassionate as he was, Livia's temper flared. She leaned in and said in a choked undervoice:

"Oh, I'm thinner, am I? Well, it's because your grandmother is starving me to death!"

Now he was at last shaken from his calm imperturbability. "Starving you to death? What the devil are you talking about?"

"She serves barley gruel! Currants soaked in vinegar! Oatmeal soup with corn husks! Potatoes pickled in lemon water! Carrot pudding! And *turnip cakes!*"

Taken aback, Mr. Penhallow said defensively, "Carrot pudding doesn't sound so bad."

"With sea-kelp and purslane roots?" she hissed.

Just then Mrs. Penhallow sailed by with her satellites in tow, pausing only to whisper fiercely in Livia's direction, "Miss Stuart! Pray refrain from brangling in the Pump Room! A little more countenance, if you please!"

Obediently Livia plastered a smile on her face, but as soon as the old ladies had completely passed by, she continued in the same furious undertone. "And what's worse, that's what the staff must eat as well! The poor things *are* starving."

He stared at her. "How do you know that's what the staff eats?"

"Because I went into the kitchen and they told me."

"You went into the kitchen?" he repeated incredulously.

"Yes, and the cook actually cried. I told them—"

"Are you telling me you went into the kitchen?"

"Aren't you listening to me?"

"My dear girl, I'm quite sure they can fend for themselves. What could possibly compel you to commune with the kitchen staff?"

Livia leaned in even closer, feeling as if she might bite off one of the elegant amber buttons on his waistcoat and spit it high into the air, simply to cause the vulgar scene Mrs. Penhallow had warned against. "I'm *not* your dear girl, and I went there because I was *hungry*, you cruel, dreadful beast!"

He looked at her for a very long moment, and then he took her arm again and began to lead her away. The only words he spoke were to a footman, requesting that he inform Mrs. Penhallow that her grandson and his fiancée would return shortly.

Gabriel sat in the Phelps Tea Room and watched without comment as Miss Stuart, in a very genteel but

methodical way, consumed eight dainty ham sandwiches, three devilled eggs, and most of a plate of pas-
tries. When finally she paused, and took a sip of her tea,
he held out the plate.

"Would you care for another raspberry tart, Miss
Stuart?"

"Oh, no, I couldn't," she sighed, sounding very happy.

Gabriel was startled at the transformation from the
tense, tightly strung young lady he had met in the Pump
Room to this . . . this relaxed, almost languorous girl
who looked like she would at any moment begin to purr
with satisfaction. It was difficult to believe that half an
hour ago she was practically snarling at him and calling
him a beast.

In his long experience with females, he'd never before
had that epithet tossed at him. Usually it was *handsome, charming, debonair, nonpareil, desirable, irre-
sistible, distinguished* (yes, he'd heard Lady Enchwood;
her voice had quite a carrying quality), *prize of the
Marriage Mart, top of the trees, rich as Croesus,* and
so on and so forth, *ad nauseum.* Thoughtfully, he took
one of the tarts and bit into it. Both sweet and tart, its
deep red juices flooded his mouth.

It was delicious.

He took another bite.

Perhaps he *had* been a little insensitive.

He signaled to the waiter for another pot of tea.
"Quite a nice little establishment here."

"Yes, I think so too."

"Are you sure you don't want this last sandwich,
Miss Stuart?"

"Quite sure, thank you."

"I can order another plateful."

"I assure you it's not necessary, sir. Unless you want
more?"

"No, I don't think so." Gabriel finished the tart, then helped himself to that ham sandwich. And gazed at her appraisingly while he ate it.

"My compliment in the Pump Room was not insincere," he said. "You're not that rather feral-looking girl I met in the woods."

"I'm not feral anymore? That's hardly complimentary."

He smiled slightly. "Let us say, then, that you were—ah—unconventional."

"And now?"

"And now you have quite the fashionable air about you."

"I told you I was going to work hard."

"It shows."

"Thank you."

"Oh, and that bonnet you're wearing is very smart."

"Your grandmother picked it out."

"She has very good taste."

"In bonnets. Not in food. Let's talk about the kitchen staff."

"Fine." Feeling remarkably mellow, Gabriel said with kindly patience, "Allow me to set you straight, Miss Stuart. A lady of Quality doesn't lower herself by visiting the kitchen area."

"How is that lowering herself?"

"There's a chain of command. Surely you must know that."

"Yes, but how else does a lady talk with the staff?"

"The cook, or the housekeeper, meets with her elsewhere, in a parlor somewhere. Do you see? They go to her, and not the other way around."

"Wouldn't she want to know what's going on in her own kitchen?"

"I'm confident my grandmother hasn't set foot there in years. If ever. I'm sure the same was true of my mother."

She frowned at him. "It seems silly. How can you know what's going on unless you see it with your own eyes? Isn't the mistress of the house responsible for the welfare of her servants?"

He was now feeling decidedly less mellow. "I take it you frequently visited the kitchen in your former abode?"

"Well, no," she admitted, flushing.

"May I ask, then, why this sudden crusade on your part?"

"Well, I . . . I wasn't the mistress there. And—and this feels . . . different somehow."

"Different in what way?"

"I . . . I don't know. I suppose it's because I somehow feel responsible for them."

"Yes, of course, as one should. But you'll make a smoother transition into your future role if you abide by the established rules. And spare yourself a good deal of embarrassment as a consequence."

"Embarrassment? What does that have to do with it? Your grandmother has allowed herself to come under the sway of that ridiculous Dr. Wendeburgen, and so the servants must suffer because of it?"

He frowned back at her. "What my grandmother chooses to do under her own roof is entirely her own business. It's hardly a concern of mine."

"You refuse to get involved?"

"Why should I?"

"Why, you arrogant, high-handed . . ." She seemed to be searching for a suitable pejorative.

"Beast?" he supplied icily.

"Yes! Beast! Do you know what the servants are forced to do? They spend their wages on food! It's dreadful! Why don't you care?"

He saw that her green eyes, no longer languorous,

were instead sparkling with indignation. Her chin was firmly set, and he also noticed that she had just a few tart crumbs on the bodice of her otherwise immaculate spencer, a handsome white silk, and for a rash, irrelevant few seconds he found himself wanting to brush them away, and possibly even allow his hand to linger on the soft curves there.

Oh, for God's sake, you dolt, he told himself, *look somewhere else. This is to be a marriage in name only.* Out loud he said, "Speaking of kitchens, I have good news for you."

She narrowed those sparkling eyes. "Are you changing the subject?"

"When one is bored, one often does."

"*Bored?* You're impossible! Do you know that? Do you have any idea just how genuinely impossible you are?"

He leaned forward. "And that, Miss Stuart, is precisely why everything is going to work out so well between us. You won't be forced to endure my noxious presence. You see, I've decided that you, in due course, are going to be sent to Surmont Hall, where you'll be its mistress and can spend all bloody day in the kitchen if you like."

"Sent to Surmont Hall? Alone?"

"Yes, and I'm wondering why I'm not hearing a note of gratitude in your voice, either. It's infinitely superior to that ramshackle Abbey of yours, and you'll have plenty of pin-money to spend as you like."

"I see," she answered stonily. "Obviously you've got it all worked out. And your grandmother?"

"She'll continue on in Bath, naturally."

"Where will you be, may I ask?"

"Oh," he said offhandedly, "I'll live in London. Visit friends on their estates. Who knows? It's certainly not your concern." There. It was all out in the open; the future was now laid out to a nicety. And there wasn't any point, of course, in discussing the indelicate subject of sexual needs; one had them, and they could easily be satisfied outside the marriage-bond, just as he'd been doing for quite some time as a bachelor. He certainly wouldn't be the first husband among the *ton* to find his satisfactions elsewhere.

And everyone would be happy.

Perfectly happy.

And even as he was restored to a comfortable sense of his own control, he noticed that several people in the Phelps Tea Room were looking at them with a kind of interested avarice. Christ, he thought, bloody nosy Bath!

"You," he said coolly to Livia, "must return to my grandmother." He rose to his feet and looked down at her from his superior height. Her face was by now a fiery red. It clashed with her auburn hair, but nobly he refrained from pointing this out. "Shall we?"

But when he was alone, a little while later, without Livia near to confuse him, that comforting feeling of sureness was abruptly replaced by the realization that she was right. Completely right. While his grandmother certainly was entitled to eat however she liked, her staff deserved better. If he hadn't been so determined to get the upper hand with Livia . . .

Five minutes later he was on his way to Upper Camden Place, where he asked the butler Crenshaw to conduct him into the presence of his grandmother. She was, fortunately, alone. He did not expect this to be a cordial interview, and he was proven correct. Half an hour later, having gained his point, he left the town-house with the old saying floating through his mind:

Sticks and stones will break my bones, but words will never harm me.

A good thing, too, he thought ruefully, otherwise he'd be hobbling out of there a broken man.

And then he thought of Livia, and the pleasant surprise that would soon await her.

And he smiled.

Livia looked with amazement at the plate in front of her. On it was a fragrant slice of roasted chicken, a wedge of pheasant pie, and a generous serving of peas, lovely and green and shimmery with a rich buttery sauce.

Quickly she glanced at Miss Cott's plate and saw the same thing, then flicked her gaze to Mrs. Penhallow's and saw only her usual cuisine. If that was even the right word for it. What *were* those odd-looking cutlets?

"Yes, you may well gape, Miss Stuart," said the old lady acidly. "No doubt at your instigation, my grandson had the impertinence to interfere with my domestic arrangements. I trust you are well satisfied with your officious efforts."

Livia could feel the saliva gathering in her mouth. Oh, she was, she *was* satisfied, but saying so seemed dangerous. So she only made a soft, vaguely agreeable sound and picked up her fork—the correct one—and knife. The roasted chicken proved to be just as delicious as it looked. A few minutes later she accepted a second slice from the footman, and it wasn't until she had moved on to the pheasant pie that it struck her: Gabriel *had* bestirred himself!

An almost physical sense of surprise rushed through her, followed by—goodness gracious, was it happiness? Had he done this for her?

Clearly, there was more to that exasperating man than only stubborn arrogance. Livia began to feel regretful at parting from him two days ago in the Pump Room with what she had to now admit was outright churlishness. But he had bowed over her hand with such cool remoteness, and had given no indication as to his plans.

Oh, she must, and would, thank him as soon as next she saw him! She would be very proper and aloof, of course, but gracious. Not unlike an empress acknowledging a worthy gesture from a subordinate. *That* would be the ideal note to strike. And she would not, absolutely would not, lose her temper.

Caught up in this beguiling vision of herself, Livia jumped when Mrs. Penhallow rapped her knuckles on the table, and turned startled eyes to her hostess.

"I daresay you had a very good reason for ignoring me," said the old lady with withering sarcasm. "Perhaps you were wondering what the dessert course will be?"

She hadn't, but now she was, although clearly it would be unwise to ask. "I beg your pardon, ma'am."

"I was merely observing that by eating in that indulgent way you risk degrading your pancreas into a cataplectic state. And you can certainly expect your blood to run high and induce *Magenverstimmung,* as Dr. Wendeburgen so eloquently puts it. You'll doubtless need to be bled, but don't think you can come running to me for it. *Must* you take yet another slice of chicken?"

"It would be uncouth to give it back, wouldn't it, ma'am?" Livia asked in the tone of one humbly seeking guidance. This simple question inspired Mrs. Penhallow to discourse at some length not only on table manners but also on the perils of overeating, particularly in the evening, and to quote freely from Dr. Wendeburgen's apparently infinite stock of nutritive precepts. It also enabled Livia to peacefully enjoy the rest of her meal. A surreptitious glance across the table revealed that Miss Cott—with the quiet precision of a little, unnoticed mouse—also cleaned her plate.

But Mrs. Penhallow was, after all, to have the last laugh on them both. With awful civility she said to Miss Cott: *"Et tu, Brute?"* and then turned to Livia. "I had a note from Gabriel informing me he has found a horse for you, Miss Stuart. Your riding lessons will therefore commence tomorrow."

"Oh, but I have no habit," said Livia quickly.

Mrs. Penhallow smiled triumphantly. "Naturally it pains me to contradict you, but Madame Lévêque was able to expedite its completion. I am informed that Flye is even now pressing it out for you."

Sure enough, when Livia went upstairs to her room, there was her new habit, laid tenderly over a chair for her inspection. So what if it was dazzlingly stylish, made of beautiful soft bottle-green wool and with exquisite black embroidery on the cuffs and hem? Or if there were adorable black half-boots to go with it, all laced and fringed with matching green?

She interrupted her scowling survey to ask Flye if belowstairs they too were eating actual food again.

"Yes, Miss Livia, and we're ever so much obliged to you," came the quiet reply.

"It's Mr. Penhallow you ought to thank," Livia said, a little gruffly, then sat down at her dressing-table so that Flye could unpin her hair. She angled herself so that the habit was out of her line of vision.

They can't force me onto a horse. It will never, ever happen.

An enormous nose, with the biggest nostrils Livia had ever seen, loomed in her direction and she stepped back in alarm. *I will not scream, I will not scream.* She did let out a strangled gasp, however, before she stiffened her spine and looked up at Gabriel, who stood very tall and cool, holding the reins of that monster—that horse—with a casualness that seemed almost to insult her.

"You're wasting your time," she told him bluntly. All her pious intentions of gracious condescension had fled, and only pride kept her from turning on her smart little heel and running away in shameful panic.

He looked down at her and said calmly: "Miss Stuart, Grandmama has made it abundantly clear that you, as a dutiful Penhallow-to-be, are to ride. There's nothing more to discuss. Come here."

"I shan't!" she said defiantly, taking refuge in false bravado and uncaring that a pair of interested grooms stood nearby, one grasping the reins of Gabriel's horribly large and lively black horse Primus. "And you can't make me!"

"Can't I?" He thrust the horse's reins into the hands of the other groom, and with a single stride he was before her. Before she quite knew what he was about, his own hands were clasping her waist and with effortless strength he lifted her and placed her onto the saddle.

For a brief, giddy moment Livia registered how delicious it felt to be held in those strong hands of his, and then pure terror took over. Not only did her perch feel horrifyingly precarious and about a mile off the ground, but the horse actually shifted a little beneath her, no doubt in preparation to rear up and dash her brains out on the nearest cobblestone.

Livia squeaked and flung herself off the saddle at

Gabriel's arms, clinging to him shamelessly. Later, she couldn't be sure if she felt his arms tighten about her, but then he said, with that familiar mocking tone in his deep voice:

"My dear girl, I didn't know you cared."

"I *don't* care!" she said hotly, immediately pushing away from him, but once again his hands were inexorably about her waist, lifting her, and she was in the saddle. She wanted to clutch at those powerful shoulders, temptingly close, but instead she grabbed at the pommel.

"There," he said, so soothingly that she would have tried to hit him if she hadn't been afraid to release the pommel. "That wasn't so bad, was it?"

"It's very bad."

"How can it be bad? I've found you the most docile horse in Bath. Possibly in England."

"I don't care. I want to get off."

"The worst part is over."

"No, it's not. We're not even moving yet." She could feel herself sweating. No—perspiring, that's what she should call it, shouldn't she? But somehow, "perspiring" didn't quite convey the full meaning of what was happening to her. She felt damp and clammy all over.

"Let's just try it, shall we?"

"Don't say 'we' in that condescending way."

"Just five minutes."

"I want to get off."

"I'll go slowly, I promise."

"I'm warning you," Livia said, a little unsteadily.

"Nonsense. Stiff upper lip, my dear girl."

"I'm not your dear girl."

"You're sagging. Straighten up."

"I can't."

"Of course you can. Try harder."

"You're just mean." Her voice was wobbly now, and if she weren't hanging on to the pommel so tightly, she'd have wiped away the rivulets of sweat dripping into her eyes. And *then* smacked him.

"You look like a sack of potatoes up there."

"Very, very mean."

"Oh, for God's sake, Livia. I'm not going to stand around all day like this." To the groom Gabriel said, "Give me the reins, please," and when the groom complied, he began to lead the horse slowly forward.

Beneath her the saddle seemed to roll and sway in a highly concerning manner and Livia started to feel dizzy. "This *is* worse."

"Sit up straight."

"Can't."

"Can't, or won't?"

"Same thing," she gasped.

"No, don't close your eyes," she heard Gabriel command, as if from a great distance, and then she was listing to one side in a strangely boneless way, everything was getting all shadowy, and all at once, she and the horse had parted ways.

Chapter 7

Gradually the world brightened again.

Livia realized that she was being held in muscular arms, against a muscular chest, on muscular thighs.

And feeling much safer.

Thank heavens.

Gabriel had seated himself—seated them—on a bench, apparently, which was a *much* better distance from the ground. He had one arm cradling her back, and the other arm around the back of her knees. How cozy. And his face was quite near her own. It seemed to swim a little. Wasn't that odd. His eyes were *such* a lovely color, brown with topaz flecks in them (she hadn't noticed that before), and she *did* like his nose as well. So magnificently straight. Also, it was neither too large nor too small. It was, in fact, just right.

Goodness, but she could stay like this for a while, studying him. He had quite a pleasing face. And wasn't it nice the way his hair was a little long. Such an attractive shade of brown, and so glossy, too. It would feel wonderfully smooth to the touch, she was sure of it. She was just about to lift her hand, to verify this, but stopped abruptly when one of the grooms asked, "Sir? Is the lady ill? Shall I send for a doctor?"

Those brown topaz-flecked eyes were fixed on her. "Are you ill, Livia?" Gabriel asked gravely.

"Ill?" Livia thought about it. To her regret, that lovely limp swimming sensation was already fading away. "No. I fainted. For the first time in my life." She laughed. "An accomplishment! Your grandmother will be proud."

He didn't smile. "Why did you faint?"

The thought of old Mrs. Penhallow had, unfortunately, well and fully intruded. "Which reminds me. She'd be horrified if she saw us like this." Livia struggled free of Gabriel's arms and—not as gracefully as she would have liked—seated herself on the bench at a respectable distance from him, hastily settling her skirts and very sure that she had revealed far more of her ankles than she should have.

"It's nothing," she said, and primly straightened her bonnet.

"Walk them a little," Gabriel told the grooms, who promptly obeyed. He watched them for a few moments, then turned his dark gaze to Livia. "I ask you again. What was that all about?"

Those delightful brown eyes could certainly be piercing. Livia looked down at her gloved hands, and began plucking at one of the cuffs. "I—I don't know what you mean," she said lamely. Stubbornly.

"I think you do. It's a little unusual for someone to pass out when set upon a horse."

"I told you I didn't want to ride. But you didn't listen to me."

"Why don't you want to ride?"

"It's none of your business."

"It certainly is my business. Here we are, you and I, and a horse for each of us."

"So what? There's no *rule* that a Penhallow must ride a horse!"

"My dear girl, it's what is done."

"Stop calling me that, you horrid stuffy man!" Livia snapped, sounding goaded, and then, to Gabriel's astonishment, she let out a wrenching sob and clapped both hands over her mouth.

Good Lord, what had he done? Had he actually driven her to tears? *Was* he as bad as all that?

She certainly had seemed, only a few minutes ago, very relaxed in his arms, all firm and soft and womanly and delectable, and through him had rushed again a hot aching desire. (An unwelcome and unprofitable reaction, incidentally, given that he was going to ship her off—alone—to Surmont Hall as soon as possible.)

Still, that was no reason to be cruel to her about her fainting episode. Despite her accusations, he wasn't a mean person.

Was he?

And *was* he stuffy?

"I'm sorry," he now said, softly. "Won't you tell me what's bothering you?"

"Much you care."

He'd never heard that tone in her voice before. It sounded like—bitterness. For a moment he wanted to put a comforting arm around her, but hesitated. She seemed fully capable of rounding on him, and they'd already been seen in public behaving scandalously.

Good Lord, he really *was* stuffy to be thinking about such things. If he hadn't caught her as she toppled off the horse, she might have hurt herself badly.

He said:

"I'd like to hear what you have to say."

She looked over at him, then slowly let her hands drop into her lap. "I—I am afraid of horses. It's stupid of me, I know, but when I was a girl, my uncle—he— well, I was walking past the stables and he nearly ran me down on one of his hunters. To avoid him, I fell back against a post and—and injured my back rather badly. It took a long time for me to walk normally again."

"Are you saying that Stuart did it on purpose?"

Livia shrugged. "He was drunk."

"You are well shut of him, then. The bloody bastard. I'd like to run *him* against a post." Gabriel realized there was a growl in his voice, and softened it as he added: "May I suggest that you reexamine your opinion of horses? Generally speaking, they are as well-behaved as their riders."

She drew a long, shuddering breath. "I'll think about it. That's all I can promise you."

"Fair enough."

"And now I want to go home."

Bewildered, he said, "To your uncle's?"

"No!" she said quickly. "Back to your grandmother's."

Gabriel brushed aside an unnerving feeling of relief, then dismissed the grooms so they could stable the horses again; he hailed a hack, and escorted Livia back to Upper Camden Place. Not a word was exchanged between them, and yet somehow, it wasn't as awkward as he thought it would be. He helped her down from the hack, and there was Grandmama just emerging from her townhouse, solicitously ushered onto the stoop by her butler Crenshaw, with Miss Cott as always in tow.

"What are you doing here?" she said crisply by way of greeting, as he and Livia went up the steps. "I wasn't expecting you back for quite some time. How did the lesson go?"

Livia shot him a swift, anxious look and so he hedged, "We are proceeding slowly."

Grandmama frowned. "Slowly? What does that mean? Did she ride at all?"

He was silent.

"The truth, if you please!"

Well, he'd just have to lie. He was mean, stuffy, *and* a liar, evidently. But Livia said quietly:

"No, ma'am."

"Unacceptable!" Grandmama said sternly. "Go back at once!"

"Tomorrow, perhaps," he said, and she looked hard at them both.

"What ails the child? She's positively drooping! Gabriel, what have you done to her?" said his irascible grandparent, instantly reducing him to the status of a six-year-old miscreant caught pulling the braids of a hapless little girl. "Doubtless you're wasting away from lack of food," Grandmama added sardonically to Livia. "You must be revived with some at once. I'm sure that Cook—your devoted adherent—would be happy to prepare something repellently hearty."

"I *am* a little hungry," Livia admitted.

"Of course you are. You seem to have the appetite of a farm laborer. That you manage to avoid a commensurate *avoirdupois* is a source of continual amazement. Miss Cott and I were just on our way to attend a lecture on the Music of the Spheres, offered by a very learned astronomer from Italy, but we shall, naturally, remain behind as chaperones."

She led the way to the sunny, elegantly furnished dining-parlor. For someone whose wishes in the matter of horseback-riding had been flouted, she was remarkably sanguine. Halfway through the hastily assembled meal she said:

"I am, Miss Stuart, somewhat satisfied with your progress, and so—you're taking *more* roast beef? You'll be dead before you're thirty, I assure you!—where was I? Oh yes, I'm *somewhat* satisfied with your progress, though you have a long way to go."

"Thank you, ma'am," Livia said, accepting the

mustard pot from a footman and also hoping the report of her disgraceful tumble into Gabriel's arms wouldn't reach the old lady's ears.

"I've therefore accepted an invitation for us—Gabriel, you, and myself—to dine with Lord and Lady Gibbs-Smythe and to go afterwards with them to the Upper Rooms, in their party. The following evening there's a cotillion-ball in the New Rooms. The day after, a driving expedition to Wells, where you'll certainly benefit from the elevating experience of viewing the cathedral. And after that—"

Horses were not even mentioned, except for one penultimate comment which had everyone at the table looking at her in surprise.

"It's my hope, Miss Stuart, that you will soon continue your lessons with Gabriel. Riding is a highly desirable activity for any lady of Quality as well as a suitable form of exercise for a young person. It is also a great pleasure. I wish I could still ride." She glanced at Livia and Gabriel, smiling a very slight smile. "Yes, believe it or not, I haven't always been superannuated. There was a time—" And then she paused abruptly, her smile fading. "Well, that is ancient history indeed, and of no interest to anyone. And now I'm going to take my nap. No, Evangeline, don't follow me up. I wish to be alone."

After leaving his grandmother's townhouse, Gabriel had abstractedly begun walking, at first almost aimlessly, but somehow his feet took him to a certain shop in Beaufort Square, where he purchased maps of both North and South America. Once back in his private parlor at the York House, he spread them out upon a table and looked at them for a very long time.

He had a plan, he reminded himself. He was not

to be manipulated, entangled, caged. Penhallows rose above all that. And Penhallows always got their way.

"**H**er name," said Gabriel, "is Daisy. Give her this."

With one hand holding the reins, he held something out to Livia. Gingerly she took it. A lump of sugar. She closed her fingers around it and he said:

"No. Like this." Gently he uncurled her fingers. "Keep your palm flat."

Pleasure at his touch—his unexpected gentleness— shivered through Livia, and bravely she extended her palm toward the monster whose attributes she'd been cataloging in a rather panicky way. *Big nose, big eyes, long neck, broad back, giant rump, skinny legs, sharp hooves, horribly sharp hooves* . . . And a whiskery, tickly mouth, daintily accepting the sugar lump, without biting her hand off at the wrist with those enormous teeth.

How nice to still have *both* her hands.

"Well done, Livia," Gabriel said, and all at once she felt ridiculously proud of herself. She smiled up at him.

"Ready to try again?" he asked.

"Can I get off whenever I want to?"

"Yes."

"I'll do my best, then."

"That's all one can do. May I?"

"Yes," she said, and felt that same shivery pleasure as his hands went round her waist, lifting her easily into the saddle.

"Here's a nice, level path," he said. "I'll lead Daisy, as slow as you like. All right?"

"Y-yes."

They walked back and forth for a little while, and

Livia gradually relaxed her death-grip on the pommel. She was sure she didn't make an impressive figure, but at least she managed to retain consciousness the whole time.

"Not so bad, Livia?"

"Not *so* bad—" Livia began to cautiously answer, but just then Daisy vigorously shook her big milky-white head as a bee got too close, and she gave a little shriek and grabbed again at the pommel.

"Steady," Gabriel said, and just for a moment his hand was on her waist. Then it was gone, and as soon as her heart had stopped pounding quite so hard—because of the bee and Daisy shaking her head, of course—Livia looked down at him curiously.

"What's the matter with you today?" she asked.

"Nothing's the matter."

"Yes, there is. You haven't snapped at me once, or criticized me, or mocked me."

He glanced up at her, and she saw, in the cool remoteness of his expression, fresh confirmation of what she'd just said. Despite his pleasant manner, he looked as if he were mentally a thousand miles away.

"Then you should be glad that I'm being less awful than usual." His voice was even.

"You're not *always* awful," Livia said. One must, after all, be fair. "You were wonderful to talk to your grandmother about changing her menus. Not just for me, but for Miss Cott and the staff, too."

"A brief aberration, no doubt."

"Surely not," she answered, and wondered why on earth she was defending him from himself.

"Fortunately, it doesn't matter what you think of me, or I of you."

Oh, that was dismissive. And hurtful. And how stupid of her to feel that way. But feelings were such uncontrollable things, and now, vehemently, she wanted to hurt him in return. "I'm reassured," she retorted. "You're back to being mean and lofty. The perfect Penhallow."

He only shrugged. "It's the truth about our situation, isn't it?"

"That's right. I'm just a *thing* to you. And speaking of things, I'm done with this lesson. I want to go back to your grandmother's. A great many new items are coming for me today—some very expensive gowns and shawls and slippers—and I want to go wallow in them, like a pig in slops."

"A delightful analogy."

"Well, that's what ladies here do, I've learned. If they're not talking about phlegm, cataplasms, or bilious extrusions."

"Kindly spare me the details. Here we are at the stables. Allow me to help you down."

"I can get down by myself," Livia said angrily, and swung her knee over the pommel, but in her haste not very skillfully, unfortunately, and might have ended up dangling upside down by one leg if not for Gabriel seizing her, freeing her foot from the stirrup, and setting her upright. His hands were set firmly around her shoulders, and he was so close that she caught the subtle scent of him, soap and leather and pure masculinity.

How tall and solid he was.

How warm and strong were his hands upon her.

She was sweating again, but in a very agreeable way, and Livia felt her entire body heat up. Her stupid, willful, treacherous body . . . As if beyond her own volition, she looked into Gabriel's eyes and tilted her chin just slightly upwards.

Oh, mercy, she was tilting her chin in *invitation*.

She was *not* a proper young lady at all.

How could she be, when her body was clamoring so? It simply wouldn't be denied.

"Gabriel," she said, her voice soft and husky, but just then a big white head thrust itself between them, and was snuffling round Gabriel's pockets for sugar, and a large pointed ear very nearly poked her in the eye.

She leapt away, and the moment—whatever it was, whatever it might have been—passed. Livia stumbled back, came against an old tree stump, sat down hard upon it, and in short order realized it was damp. She would have an embarrassing dark patch on the back of her beautiful habit the moment she stood up again.

Oh, how perfect.

What a perfectly bad day it was turning out to be.

Livia had been placed between her hostess, Lady Gibbs-Smythe, and Mr. Adolphus Olivet. Gabriel was sitting several seats away, on the opposite side, and Mrs. Penhallow even further, both of them actually seeming to recede into the distance. Livia had never seen a dining-table so long, and every inch of it crowded with tall gilded candelabra, ornate arrangements of hothouse flowers in fragile porcelain vases, an elaborate variety of crystal glasses and gold-rimmed plates and what might have been, quite recently, an intimidating array of forks, knives, and spoons.

She drew a deep breath of quiet excitement.

Of triumph.

If Cecily Orr could only see her now.

Not so very long ago, she had been merely *poor little Livia,* in her dowdy cast-off clothes.

And here she was at an elegant dinner-party among the *haut ton,* accepted among them without a blink.

And she was ready: although she had been adjured once again by Mrs. Penhallow to stick to topics appropriate for a young unmarried lady, she'd still been poring diligently over the newspapers and making her way through a tall stack of books. She wanted to be prepared, when the opportunity arose, for lively, well-informed conversation.

For example, only a few months past, in June, the Prince Regent had held an extravagant fête at his fabulous London residence, Carlton House, celebrating his assumption of political power. His poor father, the King, showed absolutely no signs of returning to sanity, and was said to shout the most awful things at all hours of the day and night. One felt so dreadfully for him, and for the poor Queen, too. Meanwhile, the Duke of Wellington had won an impressive battle at Fuentes de Oñoro (oh dear, where *was* that? Was it in Spain, or in Portugal?). The celebrated writer Richard Cumberland had recently died. She and Miss Cott had been making their way through Walter Scott's wildly popular *The Lady of the Lake.* Also—

A shallow plate of soup *à la Reine,* redolent of chicken broth and mace, was set before Livia by a solemn be-wigged footman, and casually, with secret pride, she reached for the correct spoon.

"I say, Miss Stuart," Mr. Olivet remarked, "dashed fine weather we've having, don't you think?"

He was a gentleman in his late twenties, adorned, Livia gathered, in the height of fashion. He wore the correct dark knee-smalls and swallow-tailed coat, as did Gabriel, but there the sartorial resemblance ended. Mr. Olivet's fantastically starched shirt-points were so high and so stiff as to necessitate swiveling in Livia's direction in order to address her. His neckcloth had been tied with a stunning whorl of knots and falls, and his hair gallantly swept into a Caesar, with choppy bits of pomaded locks brushed forward and now immovable. A gold-framed quizzing glass hung suspended from his neck and no less than four ornamental fobs dangled from a gold chain at his waist.

"Yes," Livia agreed, "very fine weather, Mr. Olivet. I thought—"

"I understand you're new to Bath?"

"Yes, I—"

"How were the roads on your journey here?"

"They were quite dry, and—"

"Not too dusty?"

"Perhaps a little, but—"

"Still, better than muddy roads, don't you think?"

"Oh, yes, although—"

"Mighty fine place, Bath."

"Yes indeed. In fact—"

"Been round to all the shops?"

"Not yet. But I—"

"I highly recommend the South Parade."

"Indeed. What—"

"Done the baths?"

"No, but—"

"Everyone does. Dashed healthy town, Bath."

"So I'm told." A yawn threatened, and quickly Livia swallowed it with a sip of lemonade. Was Mr. Olivet boring her on purpose? Surely this wasn't how everyone in Bath talked at dinner-parties. Maybe she could improve matters by introducing a perfectly unexceptional change in topic. But what might that be? Her brain skittered wildly. Then something came to her. "I hope," she said, "to soon visit Godwin's Circulating Library—"

"Whatever for?"

"Why, to take out a book or two, about—"

"A book?" He scrutinized her more closely. "Not a bluestocking, are you?"

"Hardly. But—"

"Oppressive females, bluestockings, and not the thing. Wouldn't wish any of *my* sisters to stuff their heads with learning. Men don't like it. I say, here's the fellow with some fish—stewed trout, is it?—excellent! Well, well, Miss Stuart, what do you think? Rain tomorrow?"

Defiantly Livia rejected the trout and accepted boiled capon, thinly sliced, and served with a delicate saffron sauce.

Lady Gibbs-Smythe turned to Livia and smiled benignly. "Did I hear you mention Godwin's, Miss Stuart?"

"Yes, your ladyship. I hope to visit there very soon."

"I am a great reader myself. Last year—or was it the year before? Yes, to be sure it was the year before, when I was staying in Kent with the Duke and Duchess of Wetherby—are you acquainted with them? The most affable couple in the *ton*. I vow I am devoted to them both! Her brother and my brother, you know, were at Eton together. You *must* meet the duchess's brother, Carlton. He is the dearest man in the world, and such a jokester! Always putting frogs in the beds! Oh, no, not *Carlton*—how silly of me! His name is Theodore. But of course, everyone calls him Theo. Do you know him?"

"No, ma'am."

"Oh, you ought to! At any rate, one afternoon it rained, and also I had slightly twisted my ankle the day before. No, no, *two* days before. Running down the stairs like the veriest girl! And I a grandmother. I wonder if you might know my youngest daughter, Miss Sarah Dauncey that was? She was at Miss Bassenstoke's Select Academy in Kensington. You are quite of an age. Or perhaps you are younger? I *must* introduce you. The most delightful girl in England, I assure you. She married de Cheuvre—the dearest fellow!—and now has two children of her own. Or is it three?"

Her ladyship looked at Livia as if *she* would know, but before Livia could do more than helplessly open her mouth, Lady Gibbs-Smythe plunged gaily on.

"So there I was, simply dashing down the stairs, and it was on the next to last step that my ankle turned quite underneath me. Or perhaps the step before that. I was wearing the sweetest little slippers, sky blue, with white ribbons. Although now I come to think on it, they may have been silver. How Lord Gibbs-Smythe teased me afterwards! Insisting that I was inebriated! He has *such* an engaging sense of humor, and is forever sending me off into absolute *gales* of laughter."

"Indeed," Livia murmured, hating the way she sounded exactly like Aunt Bella, and also the fact that she was so bored right now that she'd gladly take a swig of Aunt Bella's cordial.

"Yes, gales! Having positively *limped* into the drawing-room—or was it one of the saloons? Yes, it was one of the saloons, for I distinctly recall the charming wallpaper. It was mauve, in the French style. Or was it yellow? And I quite *devoured* that novel—oh dear, what was it called? Wonderfully Gothic, and the story was simply riveting! *The Romance of the Grove*? *Dangers in the Forest*? I was there all the afternoon, and finished three chapters entirely. So you see," her ladyship finished victoriously, "I am quite the reader."

Now that she thought about it, Livia mused balefully, it would be better to pour a large dose of Aunt Bella's cordial into Lady Gibbes-Smythe's glass instead. Lady *Gabs*-Smythe was more like it. Why had she even bothered reading all those books and newspapers?

Her ladyship had turned once more to the gentleman on her left, and Livia looked down the table again, to Gabriel. He was tonight utterly the cool, elegant, imperious-looking gentleman. She watched as he responded with courteous reserve to a remark from his own neighbor, a rotund dowager sporting an immense spangled turban festooned on one side with a long, broad ribbon, the gaily fringed end of which seemed likely to end up in her plate at any moment.

She wondered what Gabriel was saying.

Was he bored also?

He seemed infinitely far away from her.

Mr. Olivet began to talk about the wind possibly rising later that evening, and Livia simply stopped listening. Instead she rehearsed in her mind all the steps Monsieur Voclaine had been teaching her.

In due course their party proceeded to the Upper Rooms, where Livia's hand was promptly claimed. As a Mr. Tenneson—approved by Mrs. Penhallow as the nephew of one of her cronies—led her out onto the floor for the first quadrille, Livia felt again an exhilarating surge of triumph. She'd done it. She'd reinvented herself. And spectacularly, too: she was dressed in the height of fashion, in an enchanting dress of snow-white crepe over a white satin slip and on her feet the most cunningly pretty white satin sandal-slippers embellished with dozens of little sparkly brilliants.

She glanced around at the other couples assembling on the shimmering wooden floor beneath massive crystal chandeliers. They all looked so assured, so confident, so perfectly a part of this elegant world. And *she* was part of this world now.

All at once she wanted to know where Gabriel was. Ah: he was leading out a pretty girl in a Roman tunic of Sardinian blue, but—very properly—he did not look her way. And there was old Mrs. Penhallow, sitting perfectly upright among the row of high-backed chairs lining the wall and flanked by her usual crowd of friends and hangers-on. She wasn't looking at Livia, either.

Still, that was no reason to suddenly feel so alone. She had it all. She had everything. She was *happy*.

So she smiled at Mr. Tenneson.

The orchestra launched into "La Rosalinde."

And they began to dance.

Oh yes, she was very happy.

Gabriel came to Livia for the country dance preceding the interval. As their hands met, he tried to ignore an odd fiery sensation that—palm to palm—seemed to connect them in some mysterious way. If he'd had his choice, he wouldn't have danced with her at all tonight. It brought him too close. But—inexorably, inevitably—duty called. Politely he said:

"You're making a sensation this evening."

"The right sort, I hope."

"Of course. Congratulations."

"Thank you."

"Are you having a good time?"

"Why would you even ask that?" she said, rather quickly. "Of course I am."

He lifted his brows. "It was merely a routine inquiry."

"Oh. I see. Are *you* having a good time?"

"How could I not? I've been besieged with congratulations on my engagement. Haven't you?"

"Yes." She sounded a little defiant. "From dozens of people. It's been delightful."

"You don't feel a trifle—ah—hypocritical?"

"Not at all. I'm enjoying every minute of it." Her big green eyes were sparkling militantly.

"How splendid for you."

"Yes. Extremely splendid. Let's change the subject."

"By all means," he answered. "What would you like to talk about?"

"Well, at dinner Mr. Olivet pretty well thrashed out the subject of the weather, and Lady Gibbs-Smythe covered literature in five minutes or less. Do you know who Humphry Davy is?"

"Of course. The scientist."

She nodded. "I've been reading about him. I don't think I'll ever fully grasp what he means by Galvanism, electrolyzing, and the voltaic pile—it sounds like a nasty device Dr. Wendeburgen would use—but I *am* interested in his scientific method."

He found himself staring at her. No other woman he knew would dare to talk about such things at a ball. He supposed he ought to mention it. How predictably stuffy of him. So instead he asked, "Why?"

"Because of how he gains knowledge through experiments. Some succeed, some fail."

"And so?"

"So I've been conducting an experiment of my own lately."

"What kind of experiment?"

"Why, I've been experimenting at being the person you and your grandmother want me to be. The docile, well-bred young lady Society assumes I am."

She was smiling, and her voice was light, yet he thought he heard a faint brittle tone beneath it.

"And?"

"Why, now that I've more or less mastered the rules of etiquette, it's wonderfully easy, I find. Very little, in fact, is expected of me. A few monosyllables here and here, a laugh, a smile, and I am one of you. As long as I stick to the rules."

"Does this mean your experiment is a success or a failure?"

She blinked, as if for a moment she'd forgotten he was even there. "Oh, a success, of course!" she said, and gave a little silvery laugh which reminded him unpleasantly of Miss Cecily Orr. "How stupid of me to be droning on about scientists and experiments! Who could possibly care about such dry things? Do forgive me! Oh dear, our dance is over. I've enjoyed it so much! And here is Mr. Tenneson, to take me in to tea. You know each other, of course? Yes. Well then. *Au revoir.*" She spoke as if Gabriel were a stranger to her—or at best a mere acquaintance—and lightly went off with her escort, looking as if she were the most contented woman on earth.

Chapter 8

It was exactly one week after her discussion with Gabriel about the scientific method that late one night, alone in her magnificent bedchamber, Livia lay in bed with her eyes wide open.

She should have been tired; she ought to have been sleeping. For the past seven days she'd been whisked from one glittering affair to the next, and more were scheduled for tomorrow.

But she had done something, earlier in the evening, which had shocked her. Made her deeply ashamed of herself. And frightened her.

In the Upper Rooms, while waiting for the concert to begin, she'd been chatting with a little group of young ladies. To one of them she had sweetly said, *Your gown is so charming, it has such a delightful old-fashioned quality.*

Oh, thank you, Miss Stuart, the young lady had submissively replied.

Hard upon that, another young lady had felicitated her upon her engagement, and she'd smiled and said, *Yes, and only think of my jewels and carriages! I'll be moving in quite the highest, most fashionable circles, you know. After all, the Penhallows came to England with the Conqueror, and it's said that the Conqueror bowed to them.*

And that young lady had smiled fawningly back.

In the dimness of her bedchamber, Livia pulled the covers higher around her. She thought again about her conversation with Gabriel. Her experiment *was* a success, but in a horrible way.

She really had become Cecily Orr.

It seemed she was going to marry Gabriel Penhallow and continue to take, take, take, without giving anything in return.

Not that he wanted anything from her. He'd made it clear they would live with the complete and total absence of affection.

Did she care about that?

Her mind stretched back to those long, lonely years at Ealdor Abbey. She'd gotten used to the lack of love.

Now, its absence was only magnified amidst the clatter and noise and endless activity in which she found herself.

She'd thought she was capable of coldly, calculatingly marrying Gabriel because of what he was, not who he was. Marrying him because he could give her *things*. In short, for his money.

And there was a name, a detestable name, for women who sold themselves to men for money.

A heavy weight seemed to come upon her now, and she struggled to fill her lungs with air.

She imagined herself at the altar, the vows spoken, and Gabriel turning to kiss her.

It would be the emptiest, most meaningless kiss in the world.

Was she really going to go through with this preposterous engagement?

The ladies sat at breakfast, Mrs. Penhallow sorting through a pile of notes, letters, advertisements, and, of course, the gilt-edged cards of invitation which poured daily into the house.

"Hmm," she said, "hmm. An evening party at the Courtenays'. A driving expedition to Stanton Drew, to view the Great Circle of Druidical monuments. Possibly. Hmm! Lady Enchwood invites us to dine Tuesday next, and to join their party at the theatre. A new production of *Macbeth* is being mounted. Not, perhaps, my favorite among the Bard's tragedies, but nonetheless a worthy treatise on the dangers of overweening ambition. Most instructional. We'll say yes. What's this—why, I haven't heard from Sarah Douglass in an age. A distant connection, whom I met in London decades ago," she explained to Livia.

She broke the wafer, unfolded the missive, and rapidly scanned it. "She says the sheep are doing very well, save for a touch of bloody scours and rupturing blisters . . . Dear me, life in Scotland! It's always about the sheep, isn't it? Two daughters wed, both of them increasing, and she's just married off the youngest. Still no luck with the eldest."

The old lady's silvery brows drew together in a sudden frown. "She feels I ought to know that Alasdair Penhallow is, according to common report, continuing to engage in disgraceful behavior—consuming spirits to excess, presiding over debaucheries, and in general scandalizing the Eight Clans of Kilally. I wonder what she thinks *I* can do to influence that young scapegrace? I can only be grateful that he's at such a vast remove I'm spared more frequent knowledge of his shocking way of life."

Livia pulled herself out of her abstraction. "Who is Alasdair Penhallow, ma'am?"

Mrs. Penhallow laid down the letter with a sniff. "He is Gabriel's cousin, and the head of the Scottish branch of the Penhallows—we here in England have nothing to do with them as they are a backwards, uncouth lot. This Alasdair is evidently an utter wastrel and is known, among our own intimate circle, as the black sheep of the family. A highly appropriate term, given the Clans' apparent obsession with their sheep. For myself, I have never cared for mutton, but Dr. Wendeburgen says under extreme circumstances, such as a fit of sneezing that lasts more than an hour, consuming it in pureed form is of the utmost urgency."

"My father was considered the black sheep of my family," Livia said pensively, "but for the wrong reasons."

"A very decided observation. What were those reasons?"

"Papa was the younger son, ma'am, and was sent, much against his inclination and talents, to India. He wished to become a scholar, you see, but was instead supposed to become a great nabob. But once in Kanpur, he couldn't go through with it. He became a school-teacher, and it was there he met my mother, the daughter of an Englishman, whose school it was."

"Kanpur? You said this Englishman ran a school? Was his name Samuel Espenson?"

Livia stared at her in astonishment. "Yes, it was, ma'am! How did you know that?"

The old lady's expression was shuttered, as if in her mind's eye she was fixed on something very far away. "I knew the family. Samuel Espenson was, like your father, also a younger son—his father was Viscount Ormsby. Samuel rejected the young woman who had been selected for him as a wife, as he had clandestinely engaged himself to the daughter of a clergyman. They ran off together, quite literally to the ends of the earth, and almost nothing was ever heard from them again, except that he had formed a small school in Kanpur, and that his wife died in childbirth, leaving behind a daughter."

"The daughter, Georgiana, became my mother," breathed Livia. "She and Papa fell in love when he came to teach at Grandpapa's school. Papa died not long after I was born, and Mama when I was four, but I know that they loved each other very much."

Mrs. Penhallow looked at her for a long moment, and abruptly, as if waking from a troubling dream, said cuttingly: "Enough talk of black sheep, and the past, and foolish marriages! When I was a girl, our parents made the matches, and they were based on rank and bloodlines and property, just as they should be! I'm sick to death of all this namby-pamby twittering about love, as if it's the only thing that matters in life! Such rash, misguided alliances inevitably end in heartbreak and disaster!" She lifted her teacup to her mouth, and Livia could see that her hand was shaking badly.

"Ma'am! Are you quite well?"

"Of course I am! Don't you shortly have a riding lesson? Leave us, if you please, and put on your riding-habit! You may, at least, comfort yourself with the reflection that your mother came from good stock!"

Livia flinched at the harsh tone in the old lady's voice, and swiftly rose to her feet. She dipped a small curtsy and as she left the breakfast-parlor she could hear a soft murmur from Miss Cott, and Mrs. Penhallow saying curtly, "We shan't speak of it, Evangeline! Pray refrain from hovering over me! I can't abide it! Go back to your toast and that repulsive mound of butter you've slathered upon it!"

An hour later, Livia and Gabriel were riding together

through the streets of Bath. Their pace was sedate, little more than an amble, for Livia still sat on Daisy in a distinctly ginger way.

"You're improving, Livia," Gabriel said pleasantly. "However, you might hold the reins a little lower."

Livia complied, looking at him wonderingly. How cool and controlled he was. How baffling to her. Oh, these Penhallows, with their *Et honorem, et gloriam*— their honor and pride! She'd never understand them. "Who is Richard?" she asked suddenly. "Or who *was* he? Someone your grandmother once knew."

"Richard? That was my grandfather's first name."

"He's dead?"

"Yes, he died two years before I was born. Why?"

"Your grandmother mentioned a Richard once— something about Richard and dancing. So she married him, then! Were they happy together?"

"Happy? I have no idea."

"Was it an arranged marriage?"

"I don't know that either. I assume so."

"I'm sure she was a diamond of the first water, too. She's still quite beautiful." Livia rode in silence for a few minutes, then went on: "How many children did they have?"

He gave her a quizzical glance. "Three. My father was the oldest."

"What happened to the children?"

"Two died quite young, from what I understand. And my father died when I was seven, as did my mother."

"A sad story," Livia said, softly. "Losing her husband, and all her children, gone from her. And sad for you, too."

Gabriel only shrugged. "I hardly knew my parents. As is the custom in families such as ours, children lead very separate lives from that of the adults."

"That seems sad to me as well. Do you know if your parents were happy together?"

"Good Lord, who knows, and who cares? You're quite maudlin this morning. Why this odd line of questioning?"

Livia looked at him, thoughtful. "At breakfast, your grandmother spoke a little about the past. Her recollections seemed very painful to her."

He shrugged again. "Yes, well, I don't know her very well either. I went off to school shortly after my parents died, as I would have regardless, and saw her only sporadically after that. However, this sad little story of yours certainly explains Grandmama's determination to see me—us—married and repopulating the dwindling Penhallow stock. Too bad for her."

Livia's mouth thinned. She said nothing, only gazed fixedly ahead, between Daisy's velvety ears.

"I see I have offended your delicate sensibilities! Very missish and ladylike and proper of you, my dear. You've learned your lessons well."

She was ignoring him now, and when Gabriel glanced over at Livia's profile, he saw that her expression was stony. Oh God, he was indeed a stuffy ass. But this engagement was, for some reason, getting harder by the day, not easier as it should have been. And then to be dragged into an uncomfortable conversation about the past, when he spent far too much time dwelling on his strange future—well, a man had his limits.

They'd come to Cheap Street, its cobbled lanes crowded with carriages and carts and gigs, while the pavements flanking it on either side, abutting the shops, were abustle with pedestrians. Livia had to learn how to negotiate streets like this, but nonetheless Gabriel kept a wary eye on Livia's placid horse Daisy, and on Livia, too.

She was still staring straight ahead, but all at once she gasped, stiffened, and then scrambled off Daisy's back with more haste than dignity, providing anyone who happened to be looking a scandalous glimpse of long shapely legs, and once her boots made contact with the ground she darted forward among the press of vehicles, the tail of her riding-habit dragging dangerously behind her.

Christ Almighty, she'd be crushed under a carriage, thought Gabriel, adrenaline roaring through him, and immediately he slid off Primus, praying that both horses would remain safe and calm, and quickly threaded his way toward Livia. A yellow high-perch phaeton was bowling straight toward her, its driver shouting and waving his whip, and Gabriel's heart seemed to stop in his chest. There was no way that he could reach her in time.

"Livia!" he shouted, urgently, desperately.

Hopelessly.

Time slowed down to a horrifying crawl.

He was going to lose her.

No.

Please, God, no.

He could only watch as Livia, with what felt like an excruciating slowness, bent down and picked up something in the street. Then—reminding him, somewhere in the far reaches of his mind, of an exquisitely choreographed dance he had once seen in Spain—she whirled about, grabbed the tail of her gown, and at the very last moment sidestepped the phaeton.

Vaguely Gabriel heard the high-pitched female screams issuing from the pavements on either side of them.

The phaeton's driver abruptly pulled up short, and time resumed its normal pace as Gabriel finally reached

Livia, who stood stock-still, not yet having gained the safety of the pavement, clutching something to her breast.

Fear having spun, in a heartbeat, into relief and then anger, it was in a blind fury that he grabbed her roughly by the shoulders. "You little idiot! What the devil were you doing?" He actually shook Livia, so enraged was he, before he realized that her face was dead white, with ominous undertones of sickly green.

"Oh, good God!" he muttered savagely. Without bothering to see what she was holding in her arms, he quickly turned her around, propelled her to the pavement where he spotted a large wooden crate, and steered her to it; none too gently, he had her sit (she *did* have a propensity for sitting on the oddest things, but it certainly wasn't his problem right now). "Stay!" he ordered her, much as he would a willful dog, then turned back to the street.

Two enterprising jarveys from a nearby hack stand had thrust themselves into the fray. One had already grasped Daisy's dangling reins, but the other was still nervously attempting to approach Primus, who danced a little, clearly taking exception to the overtures of a stranger.

Swiftly Gabriel went to Primus, took hold of his reins, and calmed him with a few soft words; he then led him aside while the other jarvey did the same with Daisy. Gabriel had just thanked them and given them both some coins when he realized that the phaeton's driver, still within easy shouting distance, was continuing to do just that, his profane invective only getting louder and nastier.

In a towering rage Gabriel turned and looked up at the driver, a young man who evidently aspired to the Four Horse Club as he wore a long many-caped greatcoat with enormous mother-of-pearl buttons and his showy bays were outfitted with silver harnesses. Extravagantly waving his whip about, the driver not only denounced Livia's virtue but slandered Gabriel and every one of his antecedents in highly vulgar terms.

Of course, he should have walked away, but instead Gabriel snatched the end of the whip in his gloved hand, pulled it free, contemptuously threw it into the street and proceeded to rip the driver's character to shreds, in such icy, concise, articulate, and well-chosen language—much more effective than any obscenity, the admiring jarveys would later agree among themselves— that within a very few minutes the driver was stammering out abject apologies and on the verge of tears.

With a last look of withering scorn, Gabriel turned to the pavement where Livia still obediently perched on the crate and had, he saw, drawn a crowd that included at least three of his grandmother's aged cronies who stood at a horrified remove, none of them making the least effort to offer assistance to his pale and trembling fiancée. Lovely: more fodder for the Bath tabbies. Still in a red haze of fury he bundled Livia—who was hanging on her mysterious burden—into a hack, then remounted Primus and followed behind, leading Daisy by her reins, now all too aware of the spectacle they had collectively enacted on a public, highly trafficked street.

So much for his vaunted self-control, he thought bitterly. The last time he'd allowed himself to give way to such a violent maelstrom of emotions, he'd ended up kissing a saucy, tempting girl in a garden and within the hour been engaged to her. And here she'd done it once more.

Naturally it would have been too much to hope that Grandmama would have been elsewhere. What with paying off the jarvey, instructing Crenshaw and his footmen to look after the two horses, and helping Livia from the hack and escorting her up the front steps, the commotion was sufficient to bring his grandmother and Miss Cott down the stairs to meet them in the hall.

"Now what?" said Grandmama. "*Another* disastrous riding lesson?"

"That, ma'am, would be putting it mildly," Gabriel answered, his tone matching hers in acerbity. "I begin to seriously question your wisdom in wishing Livia to become a horsewoman."

His grandmother brushed this aside. "What's that you've got?" she demanded of Livia. "Whatever it is, it has the most appalling odor. Crenshaw! Summon one of your footmen."

Just then the smelly object in Livia's arms wiggled and gave a small yelp, and she cuddled it more closely to her (almost as one would an infant! flashed the unwelcome thought in Gabriel's brain).

"It's a dog, ma'am," she explained.

"A dog?" Grandmama echoed, with as much astonishment as if Livia had said she was holding an elephant.

A pair of black, button-shaped eyes peered fearfully out at them from behind dirty fringes of fur that might once have been white but were at present an unappealing shade of brown.

"You risked your life for that?" Gabriel snapped.

She looked up at him. "I had to. It was going to be killed otherwise."

"Do you have any idea how close *you* came to that fate?"

"I'm sorry. I—I didn't think."

"That is painfully obvious." He turned to Grandmama. "You may as well know the whole of it, as I'm quite sure it's already making the rounds in the Pump Room. I'm sorry to say that I—"

His grandmother held up her hand. "Not here! Come up to the drawing-room. Ah! Here is—"

The young footman bowed. "James, ma'am."

"James, take away that miserable creature to which Miss Livia is clinging and dispose of it."

"Dispose of it?" Livia cried. "What does that mean, ma'am?"

"Just what you think. I detest conversing in the hall! Gabriel, give me your arm up these stairs. Evangeline, bring those new drops from Dr. Wendeburgen. Something tells me I'm going to need them when we are regaled with what Gabriel has to say."

After the minutest of hesitations, Gabriel went to her and offered his arm; together they proceeded upstairs, Miss Cott stalwartly bringing up the rear, while Livia turned slowly to James the footman, feeling as though her heart would crack in two. Oh, the old lady was hard, hard. Life, perhaps, had made her so, but still . . .

She looked down at the little black eyes gazing back at her. A small pink tongue darted out and the dog lifted its filthy head, trying feebly to reach up to her. Livia bit her lip and finally, reluctantly, she held out the little dog, which whined and weakly struggled, as if resisting the transfer that spelled its inevitable doom.

Gently, James received it in his gloved hands, and under his breath he said, very low, "Don't worry, Miss Livia. I'll see it's not harmed."

He said no more, and went off toward the kitchen, but Livia was filled with sudden, hopeful happiness. Lightly she went up the stairs and into the drawing-room where she found Mrs. Penhallow accepting from Miss Cott a small, long-stemmed glass filled with a dark liquid that smelled strongly of decaying wood.

Gabriel said: "Grandmama, what *is* that foul stuff?"

"The very latest tonic, direct from Mühlhausen, and

crafted by an ancient order of Ursuline nuns," the old lady replied, and swallowed it down in a single gulp. She choked slightly, gave a slight wheeze, and directed her cold gaze to Livia. "I suppose you expect me to congratulate you for saving that mongrel's life?"

Livia lifted her chin. "No, ma'am."

"Well, I won't! And now we have a new debacle facing us! *Do* sit down, Miss Stuart, you give the distinct impression of hovering, which I can't abide."

Livia thought back to the none-too-clean crate upon which she had sat. "I'd better not, ma'am," she said, and went on in an impulsive rush: "I know my behavior wasn't what it should have been, but I simply had to do it! And Gabriel was splendid! The way he confronted that awful man in the phaeton—oh, ma'am, I wish you could have heard it!"

"Yes," Mrs. Penhallow replied with awful sarcasm, "my grandson practically brawling in the streets of Bath, and you scrambling about in a disgracefully hoydenish manner. I call *that* splendid! Evangeline, more tonic!" When shortly she was fortified with a second dose (followed by a slight gagging noise), she went on acidly:

"I had been used to think you a most ill-assorted couple, but now, after today's exploit, I have changed my mind. You, Gabriel, are capable of the lowest, most boorish behavior, and you, Livia, are obviously the proverbial silk purse. It seems to me you are perfectly suited."

Gabriel said nothing, only gave his grandmother a slight, ironic smile, which she received in fulminating silence, her white hands twisting together in her lap. Miss Cott tactfully kept her eyes fixed upon the needlework on which she was industriously employed.

Livia stood by the mantel and looked thoughtfully at each of them in turn. In the past weeks, she'd exchanged more words with these three people—individually and collectively—than she had with her aunt and uncle at Ealdor Abbey in all her years there.

And she'd come to learn quite a lot about them.

For example, she knew that Gabriel was an excellent dancer, never tugging one about or stepping on one's foot or trying to maneuver too close in an unpleasantly insinuating fashion. And that he liked beef but not venison, and his tea served very hot and without sugar. That he never doused himself in pungent fragrances as so many other men did, but always smelled clean and masculine and exactly like himself. That he was, like her, an orphan. That he spoke courteously to servants. That his teeth were very white and mostly straight but for eyeteeth that were, ever so slightly, crooked, a little flaw which somehow made his smile all the more devastatingly attractive.

She knew that Grandmama was widely read, and had fascinating things to say about literature and poetry (and that she did not in the least care for the *Sturm und Drang* poets such as Wordsworth and Bryon, favoring instead Milton and Dryden and the Augustan poets of the previous century). That she preferred emeralds over diamonds, and although she frequently changed her rings she always wore on her fourth finger an exquisite square emerald, of modest size, in a simple gold setting. That despite her age, she walked and moved with a grace that was unmatched.

As for Miss Cott, Livia was well aware of her dignity and kindness, even when Grandmama was at her most curt and demanding. She'd learned that Miss Cott had the charming first name of Evangeline. And that her gray hair was curly, but she somehow managed to subdue it into a severe chignon. That she was very fond of dessert, although she was scrupulous about partaking of it in a moderate way. And even when one was ignorant, she never made one feel stupid or small.

Yet, Livia mused, the three of them all shared a common characteristic: they seemed to wear—more often than not—what she had, in her own mind, termed the Penhallow Mask, Gabriel and Grandmama most of all, of course.

On the occasions when she'd seen the mask slip, she'd gotten glimpses of them as, well, as human beings, shaken by turbulent emotions, alight with humor, fallible and imperfect and wonderful and *real*.

Yes, in some ways, she knew a great deal about them, but in others, they remained almost as strangers to her.

Wistfully she looked back to Gabriel. In the quiet which had descended upon the drawing-room, he had picked up from the table at his elbow one of the newspapers which lay upon it, and was now unhurriedly leafing through it. He sat with one leg crossed over the other, perfectly at his ease in boots and buckskins and a beautifully cut black coat. He was indeed wearing the Penhallow Mask: his countenance was again cool and impassive. Remote.

On the whole, she liked it better when he was shaking her so hard the charming silk tassels on her bonnet had batted crazily against her cheeks. His topaz-flecked eyes had been sparkling with rage, and his breath came fast between his lips, and she could feel the immense strength in those big, long-fingered hands of his. Even better had it been when she had fainted and fallen off Daisy—not the fainting part, of course, but after, when he had held her against him, the whole length of her pressed against his muscled hardness: she had felt safe and protected and at the same time taken over by a languorous heat that seemed to set her very flesh and bones and blood on fire with the wanting of him.

Even now, standing primly by the fireplace, she could feel that same powerful and galvanic pull, as if some invisible, unnamable force connected her to him, compounded of highly improper but irrepressible curiosity and desire. What would he look like without all those clothes, the buckskins and waistcoat and impeccably tied neckcloth and whatever else it was that men wore underneath all that?

He would be breathtaking. She knew it.

And what would it feel like to run her hands across those broad shoulders, down his chest and along his arms, and to know that his eyes were glittering not with anger but with passion—with desire for *her*? Not in a garden or on a riding path or anyplace where they could be interrupted, but some private realm where they had all the time in the world to . . . explore each other.

Pressing her hands to cheeks that now burned with what was undoubtedly a revealing crimson, Livia tore her gaze away from Gabriel and looked down at the tips of her black and green half-boots, peeping from underneath the soiled hem of her riding-habit.

Here she was, indulging in the most indecent thoughts.

Oh, she would never be a true lady, that much was evident.

They'd been trying to make a silk purse out of her, but she was clearly a sow's ear.

Still, maybe that was good news.

Maybe, deep inside, she was still herself.

So why didn't she feel more cheerful?

There was a soft knock on the door, followed by the dignified entrance of Crenshaw. "The chairs which you requested, to convey you and Miss Cott to the Pump Room, have arrived, ma'am."

Irritably Grandmama waved a hand in dismissal. "I

shan't be going to the Pump Room after all. You may send them away."

"Very well, ma'am. Shall I bring refreshments, or order a nuncheon?"

"No, for we are all dispersing, and the sooner the better!"

Crenshaw bowed and left the room.

"Giving us our *congé* as well, Grandmama?" said Gabriel.

"Yes, for I'm tired, and feel a bout of dyspepsia coming on. Evangeline, prepare me another dose of tonic."

Miss Cott promptly rose, and Gabriel said, with lifted brows, "Are you sure it's not the tonic giving you dyspepsia? The odor alone is enough to make anyone feel ill."

She glared at him. "It disperses excess bile."

"I'm sure it does. Perhaps a little too thoroughly."

"When I am wishful of your further interference in my affairs, be assured I will so inform you." Grandmama took the glass of tonic from Miss Cott and with what had all the appearance of one throwing down the gauntlet she swallowed it at a gulp. Her eyes bulged slightly, but after rapidly blinking her eyes several times she smiled and triumphantly handed the little glass back to Miss Cott.

Livia saw that Gabriel was frowning.

"Grandmama, truly, are you quite well?"

"Spare me your empty words of concern! Exercise your mind instead by concocting a tale with which we might explain away your appalling escapade."

When Gabriel did not reply, and continued to narrowly eye his grandmother, Livia blurted out:

"I *hate* having to make up an explanation! It's so stupid!"

"*You* give the appearance of being stupid with your impertinent comment!" retorted the old lady. "Such is the way of the world, and the sooner you learn it, missy, the better off you shall be."

"Then I think you ought to say that Gabriel was gallantly defending the Penhallow name! Which he *was!*"

"I agree," Grandmama answered, unexpectedly. "And what about *your* role in this mess?"

"Oh, say merely that I'm an idiot! Stupidly trying to save a worthless dog. And that's the truth also."

Grandmama was silent for a moment. "I shall say that you behaved in a heedless but heroic way, bravely disregarding your own safety."

"That last part at least bears some semblance to the truth," remarked Gabriel. "Overall it's an excellent tale, Grandmama, and I quite fancy being portrayed in such a flattering light. I encourage you to staunchly counter any animadversions with it."

"You may be certain I will," she answered tartly. "No doubt you shall, at your own convenience, thank me for my unstinting efforts on your behalf."

"To be sure. Speaking of dogs, I also encourage you to keep on that little beast."

Livia sent him an astonished look and Grandmama demanded, "Why in heaven's name would I do that?"

"It had the look of a ratter, which no kitchen in Bath should be without."

The old lady knitted her silvery brows. "Are you saying there are rats in the house?"

"They are, I'm told, endemic here. And nothing is more efficient than a dog at dispatching them."

"Rats! Nasty, vulgar little things!" She shuddered visibly, then added: "I myself would suggest a cat, but—oh, never mind! Very well! Go and deal with it at once, before James—before he does whatever he had been going to do. And don't come back! I'm going to take my nap. But you are to return at six, to escort us to Maria Tenneson's dinner-party."

"If you're sure you are equal to the exertion?"

"Naturally," was his grandmother's haughty reply. "Go away, do! I'm tired of all of you!"

"I am all obedience." Gabriel stood, bowed politely to the ladies, and left the room.

Livia dipped a quick curtsy in Mrs. Penhallow's general direction and hurried after him, catching up to him when he was halfway down the stairs. She tugged at his arm. "Thank you!" she whispered eagerly. "I think—I believe—James hasn't yet—"

"Drowned it? Yes, I did see that exchange between the two of you. That, and the fact that I watched you nearly exterminate yourself in your haste to snatch it up from certain death, more than convinced me as to your feelings on the matter." Gabriel paused, two steps below her, bringing them to the same height. He looked into her face, and almost immediately began to regret it, for her very nearness once again thrust him into a state of bewildering purposelessness.

With a kind of scornful self-mockery he congratulated himself for his coolness upstairs just now. It was all the more impressive when he'd only recently been awash in irrational fury. And also in—he could at least admit this to himself—complete terror that Livia was going to be killed, right in front of him.

Of course he would hate to see anyone trampled by a runaway carriage, but to think of this happening to Livia—

Livia gone from the world—

A world gone dark, cold, lonely—

The intensity of his own feelings shocked him.

Buck up, old man, nothing happened, he told himself

firmly, *there's no need to torment yourself with imaginary scenarios.*

Still he couldn't erase the sense of horror, only just barely escaped.

And as he stood there struggling to control his emotions, all the while facing her, standing just a little too close, awareness of her beauty, her indelible presence, rushed upon him almost like a physical blow. That beguiling vitality—which he had come to associate with her alone—seemed to emanate from her very pores. In his chaotic state of mind he almost expected to see flames crackling around her body, like some goddess from an ancient, exotic mythology: and how badly he wished to move closer to her, to bury himself within her and be immolated, enfolded in her heat and light.

He looked straight into her wide green eyes, and wanted, in a wild torrent of desire, more than anything to have her pleasure before his own. Not to see her submit to his passion but to allow him to raise her to the heights—

No.

Enough.

He couldn't take it anymore. To her he said, very quietly, with unguarded anger:

"My God, how you spin me about."

He wished that he need never see her again.

No sooner had that thought blazed across his troubled mind came an aching, unwelcome sense of loss.

And then swiftly he reached out his arm, wrapping it around her back, bringing her hard against him and without ceremony he kissed her, so swiftly and so roughly that their teeth clashed painfully. Then her lips parted at the ungentle insistence of his, and for a moment or two he gloried in the sweet, lush welcome of her mouth before, just as roughly, he broke the embrace.

"Don't—" he began. He could see her breast heaving as she swayed slightly on her feet, then grasped the polished bannister to steady herself.

And in the heat of the moment, before he could stop himself he said the worst thing he could think to say:

"That imbroglio in the street today? Don't embarrass us again."

He turned away and went rapidly down the stairs.

He didn't look back.

Chapter 9

Life—rather to Livia's surprise—went smoothly on. She danced with Gabriel in the New Rooms, she sat next to him at the theatre, she strolled with him in the Sydney Gardens, and not once did he betray to her the slightest glimpse of what he might genuinely be thinking or feeling. And after that savage, soul-shaking kiss on the stairs! She wanted to take *him* by his shoulders and shake him, rattle him, arouse him.

But she didn't. In what felt like a defensive, cowardly way, she'd taken on the Penhallow Mask for herself. Pride kept her from grabbing him, pride kept her from taking the risk of revealing her own thoughts and emotions. There was, she'd found, an odd sort of comfort in staying hidden behind this impenetrable mask.

Her single reprieve from this frozen world of rigid decorum was a clandestine visit to the kitchen where, the moment she stepped into it, she was greeted by friendly yips, and a small white dynamo—snowy white and clean-smelling—hurtled joyously toward her.

Livia knelt on the floor and couldn't help but laugh as she petted the little dog whose behind wiggled furiously, his funny curling tail thumping wildly back and forth. He could not be called a handsome creature, with his short skinny legs and oversized paws and pointy ears that looked far too big for his head, but there was something so engaging about those bright black eyes, which seemed to sparkle with alert intelligence, and about his small furry frame which almost vibrated with exuberance.

"There now, Miss Livia," Cook said comfortably, "it's plain as a pikestaff he knows who he's to thank for his deliverance!"

"Oh, Cook, he's adorable. I hope he hasn't been a trouble to you?"

"Not a bit of it! He's ever so smart and obedient."

"I'm so glad! Is he a good ratter?"

Cook looked surprised. "Ratter, Miss Livia? We haven't a rat anywhere in the house, that I can promise you! As for him, I shouldn't think he'd be a ratter, for he's never happier than when he's in someone's lap." She laughed. "Truth be told, there's terrible competition among the staff to grab him up. He's become quite the favorite among us."

"I can see why." So Gabriel, Livia thought, had pulled the wool over Grandmama's eyes! The little dog was trying with great earnestness to scale her knees and establish himself among the folds of her skirt. Livia picked him up and with flattering promptitude he snuggled against her. "Not only does he smell better, Cook, he's quite a bit plumper."

"As to that, miss, so am I—if we're to talk of deliverance!"

Livia looked up and saw with pleasure that Cook had indeed lost her distressing gauntness. "You've Mr. Gabriel to thank for that, and for intervening on behalf of this little fellow, too. Have you given him a name yet?"

"He has a hearty appetite, miss, but he does seem to

favor my muffins, so we've all fallen into the habit of calling him that—Muffin."

"I like it. It suits him." As if in agreement, the little dog vigorously licked her chin.

"Lordy, where are my manners? Can I offer you some muffins, Miss Livia, and a nice cup of tea?"

"I'd like that very much, Cook, but I'm afraid I have to go. Thank you for taking care of Muffin so beautifully." Livia put him down on the floor, where he capered gaily around her feet. "Sit," she told him, and without hesitation he did so, gazing meltingly up at her as if his sole desire in life was to obey her every command, large or small.

With lagging steps Livia left the kitchen and went up to her bedchamber. Soon she'd have to dress for the evening's dinner-party. While she waited for Flye, she sat in an armchair near the window which overlooked the walled garden below; she stared out at the rain that fell in heavy drops, matching her darkening mood completely.

Dogs were so simple. You loved them, and they loved you back. If she could, she'd bring Muffin upstairs and keep him with her. Wouldn't it be wonderful to feel so adored, to bask in such unconditional affection?

It was hard to imagine.

Gabriel acted if he didn't care if she lived or died. And she'd allowed herself to sink into a stupid melancholy.

What a fool she was.

Flye tapped on the door then, and listlessly Livia stood up. Time to get ready for another dull dinner-party.

A few hours later, there she was, sitting next to Sir Edward Brinkley, recently arrived from London. He'd been pointed out to her in the Pump Room as a widower, just out of his blacks, whose wife had died without issue. He'd come to Bath, according to report, for the sake of his sister—a sallow, middle-aged dame with the look about her of a scared rabbit—as well as to cast about for a new wife. No one doubted that he'd have an easy time of it, for Sir Edward had an enormous fortune as well as considerable estates in Lincolnshire.

He was also thought to be exceedingly handsome. He was trim, elegant, with blond hair, neatly arranged *à la Brutus*, and light-blue eyes. Though his expression was pleasant, friendly, there was something about him—something about those rather red and fleshy lips that smiled too frequently—that made Livia wish her hostess had placed her elsewhere.

He drank glass after glass of wine and his urbane flow of polite inanities washed over her; toward her he displayed a kindly cordiality, twice saying, "Why, I'm old enough to be your father, my dear," but more than once did she feel, underneath the table, his knee pressing against hers.

As discreetly as possible, Livia hitched herself away from him. But her stomach seemed to clench itself into an angry knot.

He'd been describing at some length the highlights of their journey from London, and now he said:

"When we paused in Chippenham to change horses, my sister and I came upon a most diverting sight. There was a village green, very quaint, and what do you think we saw there?"

"I can't imagine."

"Crowds of people gathered around a stake. A woman was tied to it and being whipped for a witch." He laughed and reached again for his wineglass. "These provincials! According to the ostler, they were actually going to toss her in a pond, to see if she floated. One felt quite transported back to medieval times."

Livia stared at him. "What did you do?"

"Do? It's absolutely legal, and very likely the woman deserved it. Our wonderfully informative ostler disclosed that she had used evil charms to enchant a man belonging to another woman, and stolen him away." He laughed. "Quite the tale, *n'est-ce pas?* Evidently they were taking bets in the common-parlor as to whether or not she would sink."

"Perhaps," Livia said, striving to keep her tone neutral, "the man in question was at fault."

He smiled at her, and underneath the table his foot groped for hers. "Surely not, my dear Miss Stuart. Well, well, it was all most entertaining. Travel can be so broadening, don't you think?"

The way he said *broadening* made Livia feel slightly ill. He kept his gaze fixed on her, not unlike, it seemed to her, the way a cobra would paralyze its prey. What, she wondered, would a lady do besides covertly slide her foot away from the unwelcome encroachments of a gentleman in the seat next to hers at a grand dinner-party? And what would that paragon of Society, the Honorable Cecily Orr, say in such a situation?

Why, Cecily would smile, and nod, and agree, of course, and (one assumed) continue to covertly shrink away in her chair.

But she was not Cecily. Never again would she be like her.

Livia said, with quiet politeness, "No woman deserves such a treatment. Perhaps if you had intervened, sir, you might have saved her from such dreadful humiliation and danger."

There was a sudden silence all around her, and Sir Edward put down his wineglass a little too quickly: the red wine within slopped onto the white tablecloth. His blue eyes were less friendly as he answered:

"Surely you'll accept the advice of one old enough to

stand in lieu of your father, my dear, and refrain from shaming yourself with such odd pronouncements."

"I'm not ashamed. It was you, sir, who introduced the topic." She was aware that her hands were shaking—with suppressed rage—and very carefully she put down her silver knife and fork, set her linen napkin next to her plate, and stood up. "Pray excuse me. Strangely, my slipper seems to have become soiled and I must attend to it."

She was not in the least bit surprised that later, once more in the drawing-room in Upper Camden Place, she was made to endure a tremendous scold from Grandmama. Gabriel, who had been summoned as well, sat by without saying a word (looking so imperturbable that Livia wished she could throw something at him, hard). Finally, when Grandmama paused to furiously draw breath, Livia said, sitting very straight:

"Sir Edward is detestable. How could anyone talk about that poor woman like he did? Also, for what it's worth, he was—he was *bothering* me under the table with his horrid feet."

At that, Gabriel leaned forward, frowning, and Grandmama said, in a slightly less severe tone, "Oh! Well! Why didn't you say so?"

Livia gave her a small, glinting smile. "It would hardly have been polite to have interrupted you, ma'am."

The old lady scowled. She was quiet for a minute or two, then added, as if the words were being dragged from her: "You were right to withdraw. I confess I'm quite put off by Sir Edward. Very poor *ton*."

"If he troubles you again," said Gabriel, his dark eyes fixed on Livia, "let me know. I'll tend to him."

In his voice was a serious intent, one that did not bode well for Sir Edward Brinkley.

Livia smiled faintly. "Thank you. But I'll take care that he doesn't."

"Well! Let us move on," put in Grandmama irritably, "and hope that tomorrow will be unexceptional! These fireworks of yours are most fatiguing."

Grandmama's hope, alas, was not to be fulfilled. The next evening, at a dress ball in the Upper Rooms, Livia declined, with the utmost refinement, to dance with Mr. Adolphus Olivet, having made up her mind that she could not, would not, bear a full hour of every single sentence being cut off by that worthy gentleman.

Having seen him off with a polite smile, she looked around the crowded room and saw, sitting conspicuously by herself and with vacant chairs around her, a tall, brown-haired lady no longer young, appearing to be, perhaps, thirty-five or forty. She wore a plain gray chemise robe over white satin, a style some three or four years out of fashion, and her white satin slippers had about them the appearance of long use.

An image of herself at the Orrs' ball, very much alone, flashed through Livia's mind, and determinedly she made her way to the brown-haired lady. "May I join you?" she asked.

The lady smiled. "If you dare." She was not pretty, but her hazel eyes were twinkling in a very appealing way.

"It's you who must dare to sit next to me, I fear," Livia said ruefully, settling herself on the adjacent chair. "I'm really a dreadful person. Or so I'm told."

"Oh, I know all about you, Miss Stuart," said the other lady, with calm friendliness. "There are very few secrets in Bath, you know. You are a young lady from the country about to make a brilliant match with a most eligible *parti*, the aloof and captivating Mr. Penhallow."

"Yes, I am quite stepping out of my sphere," responded

Livia, with a frankness that surprised her. But there was something about the lady—an unusual charm which imperfectly concealed a fierce intelligence—that made Livia feel an immediate sense of camaraderie.

"Stepping out of your sphere? How so? You are a gentleman's daughter, and he is a gentleman; therefore are you not equal?"

"Perhaps."

"Not perhaps, but indeed it *must* be so. And for you—I am set on it!—there must be a happy conclusion." She laughed, seeing Livia's puzzled expression. "Do forgive me, my dear! My imagination, I fear, is very rapid, and jumps from fancy to fancy. I have not yet ascertained whether it's a blessing or a curse. Oh, goodness, I'm bewildering you, I perceive. Let me allay your concerns at once as to my sanity, and inquire, as I should have already, as to your opinion of Bath."

Livia smiled. "You seem to me to be one of the sanest people I've yet met here, ma'am! Are you new to town? I've not have the pleasure of meeting you before."

"I'm merely passing through. Business took me to London, and my mother wished to visit former acquaintances and drink the waters prior to our return to East Hampshire."

"She is unwell?"

Livia's new friend gave a gentle, satirical laugh. "She fancies herself to be so. Tell me, do you care to read? Or do you not number that among your accomplishments?"

They proceeded to pass a very enjoyable half hour in conversation before Livia was drawn inexorably away by Lady Enchwood, who hustled her off to the tea-room, clucking all the way there.

"My dear Miss Stuart, I simply *had* to rescue you! I nearly had a spasm when I saw with whom you were sitting!"

It was then that Livia realized in dismay that she had failed to learn the name of her friend. She tried to turn back but her ladyship's hold on her arm was unexpectedly strong for one whose ailments seemed to be so numerous and so daunting. "No, no, Miss Stuart, you must not, I do assure you! She is such a peculiar woman, and occupies quite the lowest fringes of the gentry! A mere country parson's daughter, horribly poor, *and* on the shelf! Not at all the sort with whom you ought to converse! I do wonder at her coming to the ball—who on earth would dance with her? And for you to leave poor Mr. Olivet without a partner! The dear fellow is *such* a delightful conversationalist! Now here is Mrs. Penhallow! I am sure she feels just as I do!"

Sure enough, Livia was roundly chastised for having rejected Mr. Olivet. (And by the time she could escape the old lady and make her way back to the ballroom, her new friend had disappeared.) But it was just the beginning: on the days that followed, she was reprimanded for having been seen walking too fast, swinging her arms in a boisterous way, along Laura Place. For chatting, in a familiar manner, with a beggar outside the Edgar Buildings. ("He was an old soldier, ma'am," Livia returned, her eyes flashing, "and very lame. I had nothing to give him but a few moments of my time.") For laughing loudly with Captain Arbuthnot during the interval at a concert in the New Rooms:

"You give the appearance of being *fast*, Livia," said Grandmama sharply. "I am told you were positively flirting with the captain."

"He was only being friendly, and trying to amuse me," Livia answered, thinking to herself: *Unlike your grandson, who seems to find me repulsive.*

The old lady swung around on Gabriel. "And where were *you?*" she demanded.

"My dear ma'am," he answered coolly, "have you forgotten that I had gone off in search of tea for yourself?"

For a moment Grandmama looked perplexed, and placed a hand to her brow. "Oh! Yes, of course, so you did." Then she seemed to gather herself and now rounded on Livia. "You are making yourself the talk of Bath!"

Livia thought back to a wry comment her mysterious friend at the ball had made, about Bath being a place filled with voluntary spies. Now she only looked at Grandmama and shrugged.

"Evangeline! My drops, if you please." As Miss Cott hurried to comply, the old lady glared at Livia and Gabriel. "It has not escaped my notice that neither one of you has made the slightest inquiry as to your wedding plans. Given the infelicitous nature of your betrothal, I can but suppose you are dreading its inevitability. I, however, have been giving it a great deal of thought."

Wedding plans . . .

This simple phrase made Livia feel as if she had been forcefully pushed from one room into another, a room she had been avoiding. Oh, yes, people—women mostly—had been asking her about the wedding, and with a skill that she found more than a little disturbing, she had lightly put them off.

We're simply enjoying being engaged. It's all so new and exciting. There are so many possibilities I don't even know what to think! I can't wait to start having my gown made. We're in no rush—I declare I'm all in a whirl. The romance of it all! Mr. Penhallow quite swept me off my feet. Am I not the luckiest girl alive?

And then, after trotting out a few of these giddy phrases, she would add:

Pray tell me about your engagement. What did he say? Were you surprised? Where did he propose? I'd love to hear about your wedding. What did you wear? How many came to the breakfast after the ceremony? May I have a closer look at your ring? How beautiful it is! Is it a family heirloom?

Anything to turn attention away from herself. It was a gambit that, to her relief, succeeded brilliantly.

But now, thanks to Grandmama, the trap was abruptly closing in on her. With false bravado she said, "I had thought, perhaps, a long engagement, ma'am? So that Gabriel and I might get to know each other better."

Grandmama smiled without humor. "I am confident that you're sufficiently well acquainted. Besides, I'm tired to death of being asked for details about your nuptials. If we delay any longer we may well expect to be the subject of further gossip, and I won't stand for it! I had originally intended for you to be married this winter at St. George's in Hanover Square, surrounded by some four or five hundred guests—and very likely half a dozen members of the Royal Family—but now I believe it would be best to forego the notion of a London wedding and organize a very small, very private wedding, here in Bath, in a month's time."

"A—a month?" Livia echoed, taken aback.

"Your trousseau can't possibly be made in a shorter interval. Following your wedding I trust you will betake yourselves elsewhere—anywhere!—so that I may look forward to resuming the peaceful course of my life here."

Livia stared at Gabriel, who said only, indifferently: "As you wish, ma'am. I can only apologize for burdening you with our presence for as long as we already have."

"Most tiresome it has been!" retorted Grandmama. "I am all too aware of it."

"Evangeline! What is taking you so long? I'm waiting for you!"

Miss Cott was rapidly sorting through a collection of amber vials set atop a silver tray. "I'm sorry," she murmured, "I want to ensure I have the correct one," and then suddenly one of the vials was knocked to the floor.

"Clumsy!" snapped the old lady as Miss Cott quickly bent to pick it up, apologizing in her soft voice.

Livia looked at each of them in turn, her gaze pausing when her eyes met Gabriel's. He smiled sardonically at her.

"Yes, we're quite the loving family, aren't we. I'm sure you can't wait to become a part of it."

She said nothing, feeling all at once so lonely she wanted to cry, and wanting—more than anything she'd ever longed for in her life—to throw herself against his broad chest and feel safe, sheltered, loved. His face had become as familiar to her as her own, the deep timbre of his voice seeming to resonate in her ear like the echo of something dear; never, even when she was furious with him, did that delicious, magnetic pull wane or falter.

Did he feel that pull, too?

How could she even ask him without sounding more than a little odd?

Her eyes traveled across the strong planes of his countenance, the dark brows, his dark eyes, that ridiculously straight nose and those beautifully molded lips, the firm chin and the strong column of his throat: and she realized with a painful sense of shock that she had come to care for him.

There was more—so much more—to Gabriel than what he so often presented to the world. She had gotten glimpses, tantalizing glimpses, of his humor, kindness, vulnerability, passion.

But it was like standing at the gates to a magnificent castle. One could peer through the bars, view the tiniest bits of the pleasures within, but one could never, ever gain entrance.

Allowing herself to care for Gabriel Penhallow would be condemning herself to a lifetime of excruciating deprivation.

Crumbs at a feast.

A sham marriage, a sham life. All show, without substance, she'd be a player on a stage, saying her lines, gesturing as if from a script. And soon enough would come the shadows, the emptiness, and she'd end up dying a little every day, until, sooner or later, she would be an empty husk, surrounded by all her magnificent *things*.

Her soul, her spirit, seemed to cringe away from the idea.

She simply couldn't do it.

That life wasn't enough.

It may have been for some people, but not for her.

What could she do now?

How could she get out of this horrible mess she'd made?

Life was so complicated, so confusing, and she was all alone; how was she to find her way?

That night Livia dreamed she was in the biggest cathedral in the world, filled with thousands of elegantly dressed people, all standing and facing her, immobile and staring like inquisitors. She was poised at the entrance; before her loomed a wide marble aisle. Panic swamped her. It would take forever to walk along it, to reach her destination at the front, where someone was waiting for her: a man, dressed all in black. Who was it? She couldn't tell from here. She only knew that she *had* to get to him, that her very life depended on it.

In her dream Livia put a foot forward and saw on it an extraordinary slipper made of transparent crystal. It fit her perfectly in a way she did not question in the least. Curious, she pulled back her heavy, jewel-encrusted gown to see what was on her other foot, and was horrified to see that it was bare.

All at once she felt a dreadful slithering sensation around her ankles. Something cold and clammy, and infinitely disgusting, was there, and frantically Livia clawed at the heavy folds of silk and damask, the sapphires and emeralds and diamonds glowing and sparkling and nearly blinding her. At last she pulled up her gown, wretchedly aware that everyone in the church could see what she was doing, and despising her for being such a disgrace, and then she realized that a snake—its coils as big around as her own wrist—was twisting around her feet, and it had tiny beady blue eyes and, horribly, a red human mouth, and it said, very distinctly, in the smooth, patronizing voice of Sir Edward Brinkley:

"And now I'm going to kiss the bride."

Frozen like a little creature of prey, unable to move, Livia screamed.

And woke up, gasping, in the familiar dark quiet of her luxurious room in Upper Camden Place.

Madame Lévêque and her troop of assistants became once again a fixture in the house, with Livia restlessly enduring endless hours of fittings and adjustments. She noticed that Grandmama was less omnipresent than she had formerly been; Dr. Wendeburgen was more frequently in the house, dashing up and down the stairs with his jovial, self-important air—looking, Livia was perturbed to see, plumper, while Grandmama got even thinner.

"Oh, Miss Cott," she confided during a brief private moment together, "I *loathe* that man!"

The older woman sighed. "Yes, so do I. It's very unchristian of me, but I confess I share your feelings. I fear, however, there's nothing to be done, for Mrs. Penhallow greatly values his advice. Come; it's time to depart for the Pump Room. Mrs. Penhallow wishes to drink the waters."

"Again? We were already there this morning."

"Yes, again."

Not long thereafter, Livia stood gloomily at the edges of a group of elderly ladies clustered around Grandmama, wishing heartily she were somewhere—anywhere!—else.

"Why, it's dear little Livia!" gaily said an all too familiar voice, and feeling her jaw drop in astonishment, Livia turned quickly to see the Honorable Cecily Orr advancing upon her, gloriously pretty in a long-sleeved gown of the palest pink, lavishly trimmed with Van Dyke lace at the throat and cuffs. Her shining straw-colored locks were twisted up underneath a handsome Moorish bonnet in the latest mode and she carried a velvet reticule whose golden snap was shaped to look like an eagle's head.

A rather predatory-looking eagle.

"Isn't this jolly?" said Cecily, standing just a little too close. "I vow it's been an age since last we saw each other! We have so much to catch up on!"

Livia pulled herself together. "Not really."

Cecily laughed. "Oh, but you're wrong. So very wrong." She dipped a respectful curtsy to Mrs. Penhallow, then put her arm through Livia's and drew her away.

Livia would have preferred to dig in her heels and remain exactly where she was, but unfortunately there was no purchase for her elegant little half-boots on the too-smooth floor of the Pump Room, nor would she relish the image of herself being tugged along by Cecily Orr as if she were a child's wheeled pull-toy.

So she walked alongside her.

They swept right by Lord and Lady Glanville, Tom Orr (who looked acutely unhappy and more awkward than ever), and a richly dressed, black-haired young lady with a sharp crease between her black brows.

"I'll introduce you to Miss Gillingham another time," Cecily told her. "She and Tom are engaged, by the bye. It was all arranged after you left. She's the daughter of a baronet, you know, and has a dowry of twenty thousand pounds. It's so romantic! Now here at last is a little space in which we can comfortably promenade, and chat without being overheard. No, dear, do allow me to keep my arm tucked through yours. It's so convivial, isn't it? And everyone who sees us will know just how close we are—two longtime friends from Wiltshire, together again."

"Yes, good friends," said Livia sarcastically.

But Cecily only smiled and edged herself yet closer.

"Dear little Livia! How you've changed! Lord, you're a veritable fashion plate, aren't you? Such a charming gown, and that sea-green spencer suits you to perfection."

"How kind of you to say so, Miss Orr. What brings you to Bath?"

"Oh, do call me Cecily! There's no need for formality, after all that we've been through together. How is dear Mr. Penhallow?"

"He is well."

"I'm so happy to hear it. Aren't you the most fortunate

girl in the world. Oh, and you wished to know why we are here in Bath, didn't you." Cecily's breath tickled at Livia's ear in a highly unpleasant way, making the skin on the back of her neck prickle uneasily.

"Well, after you left, Livia dear, I'm sorry to say some horrid rumors began to circulate—all about how Mr. Penhallow didn't like me well enough to propose, and how I'd been upstaged by some poor little country mouse, and how I had failed so pathetically. Oh, there's no need to stare. I know you didn't say anything, nor did Mama or I. But people talk, and servants gossip, too. After a while, Mama thought it best that we travel to some agreeable watering-place until things quieted down at home. She proposed Tunbridge Wells, and Miss Gillingham wanted to go to London, despite its being so thin of company just now."

Cecily squeezed Livia's arm. "But I made them come to Bath. I knew you were still here. And now," she concluded gaily, "now I can make your life just as miserable as you made mine."

Her tightening grip on Livia's arm reminded her vividly, too vividly, of her nightmare with that nasty snake in it. But as the import of Cecily's words sank in, Livia felt a strong impulse to laugh—in a thoroughly cynical manner—in the other girl's face. As if Cecily had the power to make her life even *more* miserable.

Just then someone said:

"Good day, Miss Orr! How—how do you do?"

It was, to say the least, a welcome interruption of this ghastly little *tête-à-tête*. Gratefully Livia pulled herself free from Cecily and turned to face a man in his early thirties, brown hair cropped unfashionably short, clad with neat propriety but not distinction, and otherwise unremarkable save for a pair of fine gray eyes, just now fixed eagerly on Cecily.

"Oh, Mr. Thorland," Cecily answered, without warmth. "I didn't know you were in Bath."

"Yes, I—that is to say, my mother felt she would benefit from a change of scene," he replied with a slight stammer. "She is there, drinking the waters."

In a cursory way Cecily performed an introduction, and Livia learned that Mr. Thorland also lived in Wiltshire, not far from the Orrs' estate. He valiantly attempted to engage Cecily in conversation but without much success; her gaze wandered rudely around the room.

Goodness gracious, he loves her! thought Livia in amazement. *He's followed her here so that he can be with her.*

She looked at him intently. She vaguely remembered, now, seeing him in passing at that fateful ball of the Orrs'. He had the soulful eyes of a poet, all dreamy and soft and lit with adoration of his golden idol. Perhaps he perceived an entirely different Cecily than the shallow, spiteful one that she herself had the dubious pleasure of knowing.

She spared him a few moments of pity—imagine feeling compelled to love Cecily Orr!—before detaching herself, but in the days that followed, it seemed that Cecily was *everywhere*, the very picture of grace and charm. Livia's ears were practically ringing with the continual praise she heard for Cecily's beauty, Cecily's poise, Cecily's good manners. Even Grandmama said— with Livia standing right next to her—in a horribly pointed sort of way: "Now *there's* a proper young lady for you! Never quarrelsome, suitably obedient to her elders, always smiling."

Worse, Grandmama continued to embroider on this theme, alternately commenting bitterly about lost opportunities and wistfully remarking on Cecily's manifold attributes. These Livia managed to shrug off, but in her secret heart she cringed whenever she saw Gabriel standing near Cecily—his own dark good looks seeming to enhance her delicate blonde ones—and when he danced with Cecily, it felt as if she was being ripped to shreds with stupid pointless jealousy. Livia wondered if Gabriel found Cecily desirable; if he wanted to kiss her, and more . . .

Oh, this was awful.

She began to feel not unlike a little bug struggling in a spider's web. And so, defiantly, desperately, Livia openly encouraged the attentions of the dashing Captain Arbuthnot. She knew that he was secure with his income of five thousand a year and in no hurry to be married, and that he dangled after her only to discourage matchmaking mamas.

The atmosphere at Upper Camden Place grew icier by the day.

And then Livia discovered that Cecily did, in fact, have the ability to make things worse.

Gradually she became aware that maliciously insinuating gossip about her was making the rounds of Bath.

Miss Livia Stuart had a dark and mysterious past in India.

Miss Stuart grew up in a crumbling abbey, living as a veritable savage, dressing—most peculiarly—in rags.

Miss Stuart had never had a governess or a chaperone; it had been whispered that she was overly familiar with her uncle's stable-boys.

Miss Stuart's aunt was practically bedridden with an obscure illness, said to have been caused by her distress at Miss Stuart's wild behavior.

Miss Stuart had set her cap in the most overt and vulgar manner at the Honorable Tom Orr. Then she had done the same thing with Mr. Gabriel Penhallow.

And why was it, by the way, that their marriage plans
had been so precipitously advanced?

As she looked at Cecily's innocently benign face, as
bland as an infant's, lines from *Hamlet* floated grimly
through Livia's mind:

That one may smile, and smile, and be a villain.

These rumors were without doubt also reaching the
ears of Grandmama, whose countenance got paler and
her temper shorter.

One morning, Livia woke very early, and thought,
It's time.

Time to end this.

She dressed and slipped out of the house, and resolutely made her way to Milsom Street. There, between a
milliner's shop and Fankhauser & Sons Tobacconists, a
small brass signplate was set in the brick wall adjoining
a stairwell. On it was discreetly engraved:

**POOLE'S EMPLOYMENT AGENCY—
RESPECTABLE DOMESTICS
OF ALL TYPES FOR HIRE.
INQUIRE WITHIN.**

Livia took a deep breath, then went upstairs. Twenty
minutes later, after an extremely discouraging interview during which Mrs. Poole made it painfully clear
that Miss Stuart's unsavory reputation had preceded
her, Livia found herself back on the pavement and staring bleakly at the little brass sign.

The practical difficulties of her situation bore down
upon her. Opportunities for decent employment in
Bath were plainly unlikely. Besides, why would she
even *want* to stay in Bath? With the wedding now
only two weeks away, the Penhallow trap was closing ever tighter about her. She'd have to get away from

Bath—far away—in order to find work. And just how would she go about it?

Of course, it would certainly be easier if she could bring herself to sell some—or many—of the things the Penhallows had given her. But of course she wouldn't. She'd despise herself for all eternity if she did that. Nor would she leave with her old portmanteau filled with her new and exquisite clothing. How fortunate that she'd squirreled away some of the things she'd brought with her from the Abbey.

Yes, how very fortunate she was.

A cool breeze had sprung up, and despite her warm pelisse Livia shivered. A strand of her hair came loose and thoughtfully she took it between her thumb and forefinger. Could she sell her hair? It came nearly to her waist, thick as a horse's mane. How awful to think of it being made into false plaits or a wig, and adorning someone else's head, but this was, she reminded herself sternly, no time to be petty.

For an instant she considered trying to somehow get back to Ealdor Abbey. Then she recalled the exceedingly curt note Uncle Charles had sent, declining the invitation sent to him and Aunt Bella to attend her wedding. Livia was not to expect any gifts, nor would a bride-visit to the Abbey be welcome; and in fact, further communication between them was now to cease forthwith. And if she *did* show up on his doorstep, Uncle Charles was more than capable of slamming the door in her face.

And quite possibly having her thrown bodily off the estate.

The cold hard truth, Livia realized, was that she had nowhere to turn.

"What are you perusing with such seriousness?" said a friendly familiar voice.

Her shoulders tensing with dread, Livia turned to see Cecily—again! Was she *following* her?—beautifully dressed in a white robe of French cambric over which was draped a rose-colored mantle of twilled silk, trimmed with a white lacy ruffle all round. Cecily came up close, and peered at the brass signplate. "Oh! An employment agency." She turned her pretty blue eyes, limpid but uncomfortably searching, to Livia's face.

Livia willed her expression to remain neutral, but she knew, with a sinking feeling, that a hot, red blush was suffusing her entire face. Finally she said, with an attempt at casual speech:

"Yes, I—I am in search of a new dresser."

"And you are visiting an employment agency yourself? How enterprising of you! And how peculiar. But everyone knows, of course, what an unusual young lady you are."

"No thanks to you," Livia said through gritted teeth. And then blurted out something which surprised her. "Those awful things you're saying about me—I don't care about myself, but you're hurting Mrs. Penhallow."

"An hour ago, I would have said that didn't matter to me, but now—" Cecily broke off, looking very thoughtfully at the brass signplate again. "Do you know, Sir Edward Brinkley offered for me yesterday."

Sir Edward! Livia suddenly recalled seeing him quite frequently at Cecily's side these past days, smooth and urbane, but it was only now that she recognized the strange similarity between them, both blond, blue-eyed, polished and elegant and somehow lacking in essential human warmth.

They were, she thought with a sick feeling in her stomach, birds of a feather. Her own problems temporarily forgotten, Livia stared at Cecily, who returned her gaze with a new complacency.

"You look amazed, Livia dear. It's quite a splendid match. Sir Edward is even wealthier than Mr. Penhallow, and I'm afraid I could outshine you in every way."

"*Could?* You didn't accept him?"

"Naturally I said I wasn't certain. His ardor must be increased by maidenly hesitation. Everyone knows that. Sir Edward said he would certainly press his suit. How delighted Mama and Papa are—how very pleased with me. I am quite their golden girl again. And not only would I be surpassing you, I'd put Miss Gillingham in the shade as well. No wonder she's been giving me black looks, poor dear."

Livia now said something else that surprised her. "Cecily, don't do it."

Cecily gave that horrible little tinkling laugh of hers. "Jealous, Livia dear?"

"No. Not in the least. But Sir Edward—he doesn't seem like—like an easy man. Do you truly think he'll be kind to you?"

"I could manage him," replied Cecily confidently. "Why, he's old. Old men are so weak. And that pathetic sister of his! She acts as if she's afraid of her own shadow. Now that I think on it, I might turn her out of the house entirely. Why would I want to look at her wrinkled old face all day? But . . ." Cecily paused, looking thoughtful again. "Money isn't everything, after all. Well! And here you are, with your nuptials nearly upon us. And yet, so much could happen between now and then, I imagine. I *must* think of a way I can be helpful to you. That is, more than I've already been doing."

Revulsion rose within Livia and, sorry she had said anything at all about Sir Edward, she said quickly: "I must go; I have an appointment. Pray excuse me, Miss Orr." And she hurried back to Grandmama's, where she changed her walking-dress for her riding-habit. It was time for another lesson with Gabriel.

The last and final one.

Chapter 10

Gabriel rode silently alongside Livia. A sideways glance showed him that she had a distracted air about her. He noticed, too, that she wore a charming new habit of russet-brown styled *á la militaire*—had her previous one been unalterably dirtied in her mad dash on Cheap Street?—which displayed her admirably rounded figure to great advantage.

Abruptly he looked away.

No. He would *not* gaze at her like some lovesick boy. He was fighting this.

God in heaven, he'd spent years in the Diplomatic Corps expertly managing emotions which got in the way of doing his job. Setting them aside; concealing them. This situation was, when it came right down to it, all of a piece—and besides, his ordeal was nearly over.

Only two weeks remained until his mockery of a wedding.

And then it would be all over. He'd be free again to go his own way. Europe was not an option, of course, due to the war, but why not travel even further afield? Brazil was said to be an interesting place, and it was enormous: it would take him a long, long time to thoroughly explore it.

The sea voyage alone, out of Falmouth, would be a lengthy one.

He had even booked his passage, which gave him a wonderfully solid feeling of certainty, although he could not deny that certain other, logistical issues had arisen.

When exactly would Livia be sent to the Hall? How would he get her there without giving rise to scandal? In what terms would he explain it to Grandmama? Should he let young Hugo Penhallow know he was definitely—definitely—the heir?

He looked at Livia again.

And realized, with an odd kind of shock, that it wasn't only desire which drew him to her.

It was *herself*.

She annoyed him, bothered him, enraged him. Interested him; fascinated him. She made him think, smile, laugh. In so many ways, she was unlike any other woman he'd ever met.

It was going to be harder than he thought, saying goodbye to her.

Then again, nobody ever said the Penhallow way was going to be easy.

He heard again his grandmother's voice in the Orrs' garden, when she had grudgingly consented to his reckless engagement:

Never let it be said that a Penhallow failed to perform a necessary act, no matter how distasteful.

Livia said, jolting him out of his reverie:

"What will happen to Daisy after—after the wedding?"

"I've purchased her. I had thought she would be conveyed to Surmont Hall."

"Yes, good," Livia said, although she didn't, in fact, give the appearance of being particularly pleased. Just then Daisy stumbled slightly over a dip in the gravel path, and Livia wobbled precariously in the saddle.

Immediately Gabriel reached out for her but she leaned away from his hand, managing to right herself on her own.

He felt absurdly hurt, but concern for her safety made him say, "I'm not certain you're quite ready for the ride to Stanton Drew tomorrow. It's all of thirteen miles."

He saw her eyes narrow, and for a moment he would've sworn she was just about to agree with him; but she lifted her chin and replied with familiar, exasperating, endearing stubbornness.

"I have long wanted to see the Druidical monuments."

"Then go in the carriage with Grandmama."

"I won't. She despises me."

He started to disagree, but there was no doubt that relations between Livia and his grandmother had radically deteriorated, especially now that Miss Orr had come to Bath. Lovely, charming, proper Miss Orr, who would have made him the ideal wife; who would never dream of stepping foot in the kitchen, or snatching up a dirty mongrel on a crowded street, or kindly sitting with an obscure spinster at a ball. The safe, perfect, dull Miss Orr who, he remembered, was to be one of the party making their way to Stanton Drew, along with her lump of a brother and his dour fiancée.

Oh, it was going to be a delightful day. He glanced over at Livia, looking as cool and proud and aloof as any Penhallow. Deliberately he said, wanting to ruffle her, "Well, you *have* been making things rather difficult, haven't you."

Livia smiled at him, but mockingly. "Oh, sir, 'twas yer granny who said it first, after all! I'm naught but a pig's ear, don't ye see? Ye can't make a silk purse out o' me, I fear!"

They were riding side by side, but they might have well as been a million miles apart.

Grimly Gabriel set his jaw and did not reply.

There really was nothing else to say.

At the last minute Grandmama changed her mind about going to Stanton Drew. "I'm going to Great Pulteney Street," she announced, "and partake of Dr. Wendeburgen's cold whey baths. I'm in need of fortification, especially with tomorrow's evening-party. We can expect the house to be filled to capacity." She fixed a gimlet eye on Livia. "Maria Tenneson is driving in her landau with a Mrs. Thorland, and so your group shall be properly chaperoned. *Try* to consort yourself suitably."

The weather was pleasantly cool and breezy on the road to Stanton Drew, and the sun alternately showed its face and disappeared behind the banks of clouds massing high in the sky. Livia began the journey riding next to William Thorland who, having tried and failed to accompany Cecily Orr (she blatantly ignored him), allowed his horse to drop back and amble alongside Daisy.

Livia discovered that she'd been correct about his soulful manner: she introduced the topic of poetry and saw his mournful face brighten. While he recited some lines of his own—an epic historical poem after Homer, actually quite interesting but rather long and sprinkled with a number of terms in the original Greek which were unknown to her—Livia's mind began to wander, although she was careful to keep her eyes politely on Mr. Thorland's face.

Last night, after she had dismissed Flye, she'd found her heavy boots and put them on. How ludicrous she looked in the mirror, clad in her frilled cambric nightgown and wearing those incongruous old boots. She had all the appearance of a comic actress in a farcical play. All she needed, she'd thought sardonically, was a chamber pot on her head to complete the stupid picture of herself.

Quickly she had unlaced the boots, tugging her feet free, and hidden them again in her armoire. She supposed she should have been glad to know they were still there, in fact, but instead only a great heaviness filled her.

At least, she'd thought, as slowly she went to her bed and climbed into it, tucking the warm covers securely about her, at least her disappearance would—after the initial, inevitable sensation—relieve the Penhallows of further embarrassment.

Grandmama's life would be quieter and she would be—well, if not happy, *happier.*

And Gabriel?

He would rejoice.

Had she not been a thorn in his side from the moment they met?

Possibly—sooner, later, right away—he'd even marry Cecily Orr. That is, if Cecily managed to put off Sir Edward Brinkley. It had been clear enough, during yesterday's conversation on Milsom Street, that Cecily had put two and two together and was considering again her chances of becoming the Penhallow bride.

It had taken Livia a long time to fall asleep. Over and over in her mind ran a depressing image of Gabriel and Cecily meeting at the front of a church and saying their vows, the minister intoning *You may kiss the bride,* all the while she herself was off in the middle of nowhere, her hair no doubt sheared off, sewing gowns for other people, scrubbing floors and emptying chamber pots.

At least it would be honest work.

Still, this reflection hadn't cheered her much, especially when, meeting up with the others earlier this morning, Gabriel had raised her gloved hand to his lips in what seemed like a perfunctory way, Cecily Orr greeted her with too bright a smile, and her brother Tom tried to say hello but had been quite literally herded away by the black-browed Miss Gillingham who had only given her a cold bow.

There were a handful of other people assembling: acquaintances she had made during her time in Bath. They were certainly civil to her, but at the same time their speculative looks, their curious glances, told Livia they had definitely heard the nasty rumors which Cecily had been so assiduously putting about.

Still, what did it matter?

It would all be over, soon enough.

For she had finally come to a decision: tomorrow night, after Grandmama's evening-party had ended and everyone in the house was asleep, she would go. It would be cruel to do it tonight, and leave Grandmama with the harried awkwardness of having to cancel her party. The old lady had done her best with Livia, and the least *she* could do would be to spare her a fresh tribulation.

Livia felt so heavy with sadness that for a crazy moment she found herself concerned that Daisy could no longer bear her weight.

Gabriel, Gabriel, she thought. It was then she learned that one's heart could actually hurt in a physical way. She put her hand to her breast, as if to hold back the pain, then suddenly realized that Mr. Thorland had stopped speaking. Quickly she said:

"Most enjoyable, sir. Thank you."

He smiled. "You're too kind, Miss Stuart. I'd share with you my ode to my lady's shining golden hair and eyes the color of the Mediterranean Sea, but . . ." His smile faded, and he gave a deep sigh.

"It's so hard when love isn't returned," Livia said gently. Empathetically.

His sad gray eyes strayed to Cecily Orr, far ahead, who sat with consummate skill on her pretty chestnut mare, looking as if she didn't have a care in the world.

Mr. Thorland sighed again, and turned back to Livia. "I've been in love with Miss Orr for years. Absurd, don't you think? Not only does she regard me with complete indifference, my suit must fail for other reasons. I'm merely a simple country squire; my estate is modest. It's folly to think her parents would even consider me. Yet—when I heard she'd gone to Bath, I couldn't help trailing after her. *Sperare semper,* you know."

Livia looked a question, and he translated.

"To hope always."

His mother, mild of face and with soft gray eyes like her son, called to him from her seat in Mrs. Tenneson's landau, and with a courteous word of apology, Mr. Thorland left Livia to edge his horse alongside it.

Livia could hear her inquiring about the plans for luncheon. Her own eyes strayed ahead to Gabriel, tall and straight on Primus; beside him was Tom Orr who was talking eagerly.

To hope always.

Why, what a wonderfully optimistic sentiment. In theory it sounded so uplifting, but in practice—Livia had no hope. Not a particle of it. She could practically hear the clock ticking at her back, the hours before her departure speeding along.

As she stared at Gabriel, she was aware that all her prickly, bristling, hard-edged hostility had drained away. And what was left?

A sudden, desperate longing.

Just to be next to him.

Just to talk. Without fighting.

She felt like a small, hungry bird. Grateful for any crumbs tossed her way.

Miss Gillingham drew close to Tom Orr, and firmly bore him away. And then, as if feeling Livia's gaze upon him, Gabriel turned his head; he looked at her. And Livia watched in great surprise as he guided Primus into a turn.

Toward her.

To her.

When he had brought Primus around so that they were riding side by side, he said nothing, only looked at her again with those fine, brown, topaz-flecked eyes and slightly raised those sleek dark brows.

Livia struggled with emotions that felt beyond her control. This was her last chance to talk with him, *really* talk with him. She wanted to tell him she was leaving, but the words simply wouldn't come. As if she would die if she said them out loud. And so finally she said in an urgent rush:

"Did you like school?"

His eyebrows went higher. "I beg your pardon?"

"I was—I was just wondering. You said that your parents died when you were seven, and after that you went away to school."

His expression was a little questioning, but after a moment he replied, in a neutral tone, "Not at first. I suppose I was still in shock about losing my parents. Although we weren't close, it was very much a loss of stability."

"Yes. Of course. Did you ever come to like it? School, I mean?"

"After a time, yes. I liked learning. I liked the sports. And I made some good friends."

"And then?"

"I went to Oxford."

"Did you like it?"

He smiled a little. "Very much."

"And after that?"

"At Grandmama's urging—by which I mean, of course, at her command—for a few years I obediently went about in Society."

"You enjoyed it?"

"Not particularly. I wanted occupation, something that would utilize my intellect and energies. Instead I was pursued, vigorously, even relentlessly, as an eligible bachelor. I began to feel like an object rather than a man."

Livia nodded. She understood perfectly. But now, when she was so desperate, was no time for irony. "What happened then?"

"I was able to secure a position with the Diplomatic Corps, and traveled throughout Europe promoting England's interests against Napoleon. I spent two years involved in the development of the Fifth Coalition with Austria."

"And this—did you enjoy this?"

"Yes, a great deal."

"Wasn't it dangerous?"

"Sometimes, when traveling in areas hostile to the English."

"You look as if you liked it."

He laughed. "I did."

"How long did you do it?"

"Six years."

"Why did you come back?"

"While I was in Vienna, at the time Austria was being forced to sign the Treaty of Schönbrunn, there were multiple attempts on my life. Apparently some of

Napoleon's agents seemed to find my presence there rather—ah—onerous. Against my protests, the government brought me home, thanked me very graciously, and released me from service."

She looked at him curiously. "You would have stayed on?"

"Yes. But Prime Minister Perceval insisted. I can't prove anything, but I wouldn't be surprised if Grandmama had dropped him a hint. Perceval's an old acquaintance of hers, *and* he has twelve children, so he may well have been sympathetic to her dynastic imperatives."

"Are you angry at her for helping to end your diplomatic career?"

He smiled again. "It's merely suspicion. I devoutly hope it's only that, for otherwise it would put her too close to omnipotence."

Livia smiled back. "She would like that, I think."

"Undoubtedly. On the other hand . . ." Gabriel paused. Then he went on, thoughtfully: "On the other hand, she may have somehow gotten wind of the assassination attempts. I can hardly blame her for wishing me to return home. I am, after all, her only grandchild. Perhaps—perhaps it was selfish of me to place myself at such risk, and to be so far away."

He looked at Livia and said, slowly, as if surprised at himself: "It is, I admit, a new perspective. Grandmama is not—shall we say—the easiest person with whom to get along. During my schooldays I heartily disliked holidays spent with her here in Bath, and as I got older I managed to spend some of them elsewhere with friends. I always used to wonder how Miss Cott could stand it. But I've never once heard her complain."

"Nor have I. She is saintly, I think!"

Gabriel laughed. "Yes, she is. Although she might

be shocked to hear herself described that way. She's a clergyman's daughter, you know."

"I didn't know. She never talks about herself."

"No, she doesn't. I know very little about her either. It occurs to me that we all take her very much for granted."

He was quiet for a few minutes, although it was, Livia thought wonderingly, a rather companionable silence. Then he said: "While we're on the subject of talking about oneself, I've been prosing on very boringly, I'm afraid."

"Not at all. I want to hear more."

Her interest seemed sincere, and Gabriel couldn't help but think how easy it was to talk to her. It was like conversing with—well, with a friend.

Something had changed between them, something positive and unexpected.

And yet . . .

Yet beneath Livia's attentiveness, he sensed—he wasn't sure what he sensed, precisely, but it was like looking at the ocean during a placid interval when, underneath, roiled strong, troubled currents.

They talked all the way to Stanton Drew. She told him about India, about coming to Wiltshire. He told her more about his time at school and in Europe. But when they arrived at the Great Circle, they were separated; little Mrs. Thorland called Livia over, and he was buttonholed by Tom Orr again, accompanied by his fiancée Miss Gillingham who proceeded without pausing to lecture them about the history of the Stones, their geological composition, excavations that had been conducted on the site, and finally concluded by summing up some of the most colorful of the local folktales.

"By Jupiter," said Tom Orr, with patently false enthusiasm, "you're as good as a book! Wonderful things, books, so they say!" He reached into his pocket and pulled out a cloisonné snuff box, refreshing himself with a hearty pinch. He held the box out to Gabriel. "Sir?"

Gabriel refused, and looked about for Livia, but as the party proceeded in due course to the inn where luncheon had been bespoken, he had no opportunity for further private conversation with her; and as they all set out on the return journey to Bath, Cecily Orr brought her mare up to him and said playfully, "We've barely said two words to each other all day! I *must* have you to myself for a while!"

"Certainly," he said absently, casting a quick look up at the sky. The masses of clouds that had been gathering all day now began to have about them a heavy gray look, and the breeze that had been merely sportive had rapidly picked up in strength.

Once again he looked for Livia. There she was, at the end of the cavalcade, just behind the landau of Mrs. Tenneson.

Cecily had demanded his presence; courtesy, in turn, demanded that he obey.

As they rode, he found himself thinking about rules and etiquette and social dictates. He had lived by these codes all his life.

But was it really so dreadful for Livia to walk briskly, or to refuse to dance with a gentleman who was not just dull, but—if one were to be honest—rude? (Yes, he knew Adolphus Olivet.) Or to speak straightforwardly to that cad Sir Edward Brinkley?

Of course not.

Of course it wasn't.

What a revelation.

Vaguely Gabriel was aware that at his side Miss Orr was buzzing in his ear like a pesky gnat, her sweet voice swirling round and round him until he wanted to actually bat her away. He caught phrases about India, Tom Orr, stable-boys, a bedridden aunt, but really—if one were again to be honest—he couldn't have cared less about anything Miss Orr had to say, and mechanically he nodded, said "Indeed" and "I see," and allowed her to think he was actually listening to her.

A strong gust of wind nearly tugged her smart shako hat from her head and, with a sudden petulant frown, she set it straight with one hand. In the next moment she turned a smiling face to Gabriel again. "Heavens, I think we'll get *blown* home! As I was saying, poor little Livia could hardly be expected to know any better, behaving so scandalously, and so I've told simply *everyone.*"

His attention was now caught, and bluntly he said to her, "Have you been gossiping about Miss Stuart?"

She gave an airy little laugh. "Oh—well—discussing, you know. The two of you are such a fascinating couple! Simply everybody thinks so!"

A powerful feeling surged through him. No: more than one. Anger at, disdain for, Miss Orr. Intense distaste at the thought of once again being fodder for the busy Bath rumor mill. And, perhaps most strongly, a surge of protectiveness for Livia. What, he wondered, could he do for her, how could he help her? He couldn't stop people from talking, he couldn't keep Miss Orr's malicious tongue from wagging, but he could at least do this one thing.

He gave a very small, very slight bow and said coldly, "Excuse me." And left her.

The rising wind whipped around the hem of her riding-habit, and caused Daisy's white mane to flutter wildly about her neck. Livia could hear the ladies inside the landau clucking about the weather.

"Oh dear, I *smell* rain," said Mrs. Thorland anxiously. "You and I, dear Mrs. Tenneson, are warm and snug, but as for the others! To be caught in a downpour after such a delightful outing would be a sad end."

"To be sure," agreed Mrs. Tenneson, in a nervous tone. "Only think, what if our roof should begin to leak? Dr. Wendeburgen has told me any number of times I am susceptible to inflammation of the lungs—not to mention putrid sore throat—and that I must avoid situations of dampness at all costs." She then put her head outside the window and beseeched the coachman to pick up his pace.

Livia looked ahead where the group of riders had already begun to string out along the road. A scowling Miss Gillingham chivvied Tom Orr along, and some of the others had urged their horses into a brisk trot. Cecily continued riding next to Gabriel, talking, talking, her countenance as serene and lovely as a flower. And there he was, nodding and responding, in a manner so attentive that Livia felt that she would soon be drowning in her own sorrow and loneliness.

And as if to emphasize just how easily that could be accomplished, several fat little drops of rain pelted her, just like tears, she thought. The ladies in the landau redoubled their anxious twitterings and the coachman nudged his horses again. Overhead there was no more blue sky to be seen; only gray clouds loomed, and the wind blew lustily.

Her horse Daisy, ever placid, seemed unaffected by these portents of the coming storm, and continued to pace sedately along the roadway. Rather than encourage her to go more quickly, Livia only held loosely to the reins and allowed the distance between herself and the others to widen—until, when there was a long curve to the road, she saw that they were completely gone from her view. It was just as well. If not for the knowledge that she couldn't keep Daisy, or take care of her, she would have turned her around, back toward Stanton Drew, and simply kept on going until she had completely disappeared from Gabriel's life forever.

The rain fell more heavily now. She didn't mind, really, because it disguised the fact that she was weeping, with an uncontrolled violence. If a highwayman came along, pointed his pistol at her, and ordered her to stop it, she didn't think she could.

Yes, she who never cried, was doing it now.

Almost as one would who had a broken heart.

Gabriel, Gabriel . . .

Daisy stopped, and twisted her head around to look curiously at Livia with dark liquid eyes. Then, receiving no further commands, she turned her head back around, walked to the side of the road, and began to calmly eat some grass.

Afterwards Livia knew she couldn't have sat there, head bowed, for more than five or ten minutes, but at the time it felt like years. She was dimly aware that she was soaking wet, and starting to shiver.

"Livia," came a deep voice, and she turned to see that Gabriel had ridden up to her. Rain dripped like a wet curtain from the brim of his hat, obscuring his face.

He was here.

Here with her.

But it was all so fleeting . . .

"What is it?" he said, and then:

"Good Lord, you'll catch your death like this. Can you ride on, so that we can catch up to the others?"

"No," she answered, in a little, flat voice.

"We must."

"I can't. I won't. You go on ahead."

"Of course I won't." He peered more closely at her. "You're crying."

"Y-y-yes."

"Why?"

"It's n-n-n-nothing."

"I doubt that. And your teeth are chattering. Are you sure you can't keep riding?"

"Very sure."

"This is a bad place to stop. You'll only get colder."

"I don't care."

"I do." He glanced back toward Stanton Drew. "Will you let me lead Daisy for just a few minutes? I think I saw something back there."

Livia only shrugged, and Gabriel leaned over to take Daisy's reins from her unresisting hands. Then he pressed his heels into Primus's side and, with Daisy following docilely, led them through the torrents of rain that by now had thoroughly drenched them both. In a very few minutes they left the road and into a muddy copse of trees where—very nearly concealed amidst a wild tangle of shrubbery—stood a small, freestanding lean-to.

Around the back was its entrance—a crudely shaped opening—with an overhang made of roped-together boards, supported by four posts and just big enough to shield the horses from the rain.

"Well, here we are," Gabriel said, looking dubiously around. "It's better than nothing, I suppose."

He dismounted, then reached up his hands to quickly help Livia off Daisy. "Go inside," he told her, and began to tie the horses' reins to one of the posts. Primus stamped his hooves, as if protesting the inadequacy of this rackety shelter, and Gabriel soothed him, stroking the proud arch of that glossy neck until he quieted.

As if in a dream—or was it a nightmare?—Livia stood hesitating at the entrance to the lean-to. Through her memory floated a brief image of the old woodsman's cottage all covered in vines, the green canopy that was the roof, the pretty doe and the great stag. She blinked, and focused: she could see, now, in the dimness before her that there was nothing inside; on the earthen floor were only stray lengths of hay, randomly scattered about. While its roof may have, at one time, been reasonably well built, rain dripped through here and there, creating a patchwork of soggy little puddles.

This was, she thought dismally, the sort of place she'd soon be living in. If she was lucky. She stepped inside, sniffed at the mingled scents of sodden dirt and old hay, and, ineffectually repressing a sob, pulled off her gloves and wiped at the wetness on her face, an exercise in futility if ever there were one.

She didn't wish she were dead, but neither was she sure about going on living. Maybe Gabriel could take the two horses and leave her here.

To gently molder into oblivion.

Ducking in order to pass underneath the low-hung entrance, Gabriel came in, big and solid and familiar. He took off his hat, hung it on a rusted nail protruding from one of the boards, then shook his head like a dog, sending raindrops scattering from his hair. Then he looked closely at her.

"My dear girl, are you still crying?"

It was the first time he had called her that without a tone of condescension. Instead she heard concern—genuine concern—and mutely, wonderingly, she nodded.

He went on: "This rain is a nuisance, but the way the wind is blowing, the storm will pass within the hour. We'll be back on the road quite soon, I promise you."

An hour.

Livia knew this was meant to be good news, but it also signaled the very last time she would be alone with Gabriel. Another sob escaped her, and she leaned against the wall, grateful that it—unlike the roof—was sturdily built.

"You're dreadfully uncomfortable, my dear, but as quickly as I can I'll get you back to Upper Camden Place." From a pocket he produced a white linen handkerchief, embroidered in black with his initials. "It's only a little damp," he assured her, then stepped closer and gently dried her cheeks as best he could.

It was his tenderness that undid her.

All the rules, all the dictums she had so painstakingly learned seemed now to dissolve in the rain drumming overhead.

What remained was urgent instinct.

She gripped his greatcoat with shaking hands. "I'm c-c-cold," she said, with perfect truth. "Hold me."

For a moment Gabriel looked startled, even uncertain. "You're cold. Of course." He slid the handkerchief back into his pocket and stepped close to her. He hesitated, then undid the buttons of his greatcoat, spreading its panels. "You'll be warmer this way," he explained, and put his arms around her, slowly, carefully, as awkward as a schoolboy.

Livia could feel the tension in him, *knew* he was trying to remain chivalrous and somehow proper even as their bodies met. She was shivering uncontrollably now. "Tighter," she said.

"What?"

"Hold me tighter."

"Ah. Yes." Gabriel obeyed, but with that same tentativeness.

"No. Like this." Fiercely Livia thrust herself against him, slid her arms around his torso, feeling the taut muscles there, and clung to him as if she would never let go.

Here, she thought, was home.

Home and heaven, both at once.

Everything she had ever wanted was here. In him. *Him*.

"Livia," he said, low. "Livia, I—"

"Don't talk."

Everything had come to this, to this tiny ramshackle shelter, where around them were only swaying trees and whirling wind, rain and mud, primeval. At this moment, they were the only two people in the world and she was in his arms, safe, secure, getting warmer and warmer . . .

Her teeth had stopped chattering, she realized.

But how much time had gone by?

Was it her imagination, or had the storm abated a little?

Livia lifted her head. She looked up; Gabriel was watching her gravely. Nothing mattered but this: she pulled his head down and pressed her mouth against his. It was her turn to be awkward and uncertain. She did it like a child might kiss a maiden aunt. Her lips were compressed and blindly she shoved her face toward his, clumsily, amateurishly, but determined.

She felt him go rigid.

Desperately she gripped his hair—all wet and silky to her touch—and tugged at him. But easily, so easily, did he pull his mouth away.

Even in the murky dimness she could see that in his eyes, so often hard and cold, was a new glow.

Gone was the uncertain schoolboy.

Here was a man, sure and confident.

"No," he said, deliberately echoing her. "Like this."

Chapter 11

Gabriel took a step back.

He stripped off his gloves without haste and put them into a pocket of his greatcoat. Then he untied the silky ribbons of her soggy bonnet before lifting it gently from her head. He tied the ribbons loosely and hung the bonnet over the same nail on which his hat was suspended.

He turned to Livia. Her green, green eyes were wide, and he could see the quick rise and fall of her breast.

A kiss.

There was no harm in it, surely.

They *were* an affianced couple, and they *had* to seek shelter, and the storm *would* soon stop.

It wasn't entirely proper, of course, but she was cold, and the least he could do would be to warm her up.

He was, after all, a gentleman.

Yes indeed, he was fully in control of the situation.

With that same slow deliberation he brought his hands up to her face. His fingers were warm, her cheeks still chilly. He leaned down.

Just a kiss.

It felt so good to be master of himself.

Gabriel touched his lips to Livia's, lightly, teasing,

and then shifted his mouth so that he was kissing, softly, that tender, exquisitely sensitive area just above her upper lip. He heard with satisfaction her sharp intake of breath; her hands crept up again, to convulsively clasp his shoulders.

Slowly he slid his tongue across her upper lip.

Ah, God, it was good.

There was a distinctive taste to her: a faint note of sweetness and the tang of citrus, and from her skin came also an elusive scent of cinnamon, spicy, tantalizing, stirring his senses in a delicious way, rousing him to an appetite, a raging hunger for her mouth, for . . . her.

But no.

Just this only.

There was a foot of space between them, and he intended to keep it that way.

Gently he moved his hands to the back of her head, cradled it in his palms, his fingers caught in the thick silken mass of her hair. Gently he tilted his hands, guided her head so that he could slowly deepen the kiss, his tongue a leisurely caress, hot and damp and sure.

She received him with an unmistakable willingness, her lips, so soft, parting for him. And then—and then her own tongue touched his, sending desire blazing through him, through every part of him, and that space which separated their bodies—her breasts, her hips, her sex, her long legs, his legs, his now-hard shaft, his chest—seemed ridiculous.

Besides, he had promised to keep her warm.

Very sure of himself, sure of his comfortable sense of control, slowly Gabriel drew Livia to him. Just as their lips, their mouths, had intimately met, they now met body to body. Almost were they one; with a hot pulse of awareness he realized that between their nakedness was mere clothing, and he wasn't prepared for his own feverish response. The thrust of his tongue intensifying. A groan being wrenched from him. His hands sliding down her back to her slim waist and then to her hips, gripping them with blatant urgency and pulling her roughly against him.

He was playing with fire, he thought, conscious of a new alarm within him.

They seemed to have suddenly moved well beyond a simple kiss.

And this wasn't part of his plan.

He struggled to remember the plan. It took, in fact, a major effort of will to recall it.

Sternly he reminded himself.

They were getting married in a fortnight, and Livia was going off to the Hall, and he had rooms reserved for himself at a Falmouth inn, and a passage booked to Porto de Galinhas. The sea there was famous for its vivid colors and wide swathes of beaches. The weather this time of year was said to be pleasantly warm.

Which reminded him.

Livia was certainly warm enough by now.

He broke the kiss at last, breathing heavily; stepped back from her, raked his fingers through his hair.

"Well," he said, with what he hoped was an appearance of calm, "I do trust that you . . ."

He trailed off.

What the devil could he say?

He tried again.

"You are, I trust, feeling appreciably more—that is, I trust that that now, after our, uh, interlude, that you are . . . well—I mean—"

Without a word she reached up and stopped his mouth with her own. Only this time, it wasn't a maladroit peck of a kiss. It was warm and moist and confident and infused with so much deliberation that he groaned again, all thoughts of his wonderful plan vanishing in a single beat of his heart.

He'd been just about to put on the Penhallow Mask (even though his hair was disordered in an entirely appealing way), and Livia didn't want it to happen. She hadn't wanted that kiss, that embrace, to end. Kissing him seemed to be the most effective way to achieve both her ends.

He didn't seem to object, either.

His kiss was deep, he had brought her against him without hesitation, and she could feel the hardness of him pressing against her belly. Desire spun them together, and a raw need urged her on: there wasn't time to think, only to feel. Livia put her hand on his shaft, tentatively at first, stroking through the smooth fabric of his buckskins, then more boldly. It pleased him, excited him, she could tell, and it was impossible to know where his pleasure ended and hers began.

But she was greedy.

She wanted more, to feel her fingers upon him, on his flesh. And she began to fumble for an opening.

"No," he said, "wait," and then his hands were on her breasts, sending a giddy spiraling warmth through her even through all the layers of her clothing, and Livia felt her head go back, limply, against the wall. He stroked the full, heavy curves, held them, brought their tips to a hard tautness. She was paralyzed, alight, and in the very center of her blossomed rich sensation, delicious, fiery, urgent—

"Why, I'm . . . I'm wet," she said breathlessly, too caught up to properly guard her words.

That glow, she saw, was in his eyes again.

"Show me," he said to her, and Livia felt her knees go a little shaky.

It was at once an order and the humble request of a man to his woman.

A paradox.

But one that in this moment made complete and total sense.

"Yes," she said.

Without hesitation, without shame she grasped at the long damp train of her riding-habit and lifted up the hem. There was a rush of cold air against her legs and she shivered, partially from the sudden chill, partially from anticipation.

"God, oh God." Gabriel's voice was soft, guttural. He stroked an exposed length of her thigh, then in a single slow movement her sex, and Livia jerked with shock and pleasure, aware that his fingers were wet with her excitement.

She was ready.

She knew she was ready for more; ready for him.

Even as he continued to stroke at her with such sweet and deliberate purpose, she reached again with both hands to the fall of his buckskins. She unbuttoned it, pulled at them, and found him, stiff and hot to her hand. Masculine, primal, wonderful.

He groaned again, deep in his throat, and Livia's heart hammered in her chest with a savage kind of joy; and then, for just a moment, she caught the sound of rain pelting on the roof. Time—time was her enemy. She spoke:

"Now."

Her voice was a little breathless, but also clear, determined.

He stilled, and she hated that.

"Livia," he said, low, "are you sure?"

"Yes. Show me how to do this."

She didn't have to say anything else. He kissed her, hard and roughly. Lifted her, with effortless strength, against the wall, held her poised to receive him, and gladly did she open herself to him.

And then he stopped again.

"Now," she told him.

But he broke the kiss to stare down at her, eyes still gleaming, and she could see a new demand in them. He was toying with her, tantalizing her, she could feel his shaft just at the moist cleft of her, and fiercely she gripped at the hardness of his shoulders, where muscles bunched from the holding of her.

"Now," she repeated. "Hurry."

"No. Say my name."

"What?"

"Say my name."

"It's—it's Gabriel Penhallow."

"No. Just my first name. And say it to me."

"Gabriel," she said softly.

He shifted slightly, closer, and a jolt of exquisite pleasure ran through her like lightning. "Again."

"Gabriel," she said, and this time she pushed herself against him.

"Yes," he answered, "yes, Livia," and slid inside her. She cried out, and again at the abrupt resistance within her. Gabriel paused, a question now in his eyes, and she thought she would lose her mind at the wanting of him.

"Yes, Gabriel," she told him, urgently, and he kissed her again and kept going; and when, in a thrust, the resistance within her was gone, there was only bliss, warm, wet, primeval as he moved, steadily, rhythmically, within her a building joy, and she could not for her life have articulated where *she* ended and *he* began, for it made no difference . . .

She kept her eyes open and he did the same.

It was this locked gaze that made her feel naked, no matter that clothes still shielded much of their bodies.

Naked, wild, free.

Right.

Whole.

And then her whole body was shaking as pure ecstasy shot through her, emanating from her sex and radiating to her limbs, her heart, her soul. Livia gasped; she hadn't known, could never have dreamed this was possible. Again she cried out, loudly, choked out his name, even as he moved quickly within her, then groaned, and she felt a hot liquid warmth inside, spilling from him.

"God, oh God," he said, low, "Livia."

Replete now, suffused with a lovely sort of glow, Livia clasped her arms around Gabriel's neck as slowly, slowly, he withdrew, eased her down until her feet were on the ground again, did up the fall of his buckskins. There was sweat on his face, and Livia smoothed it away, smiling. He was smiling too, looking boyishly young, and he tilted his head to kiss her, lightly but with a lingering sweetness that brought an immediate flush of warmth to her cheeks.

Gabriel shifted his kiss to her jaw, the soft skin of her throat, then nuzzled at her ear. She made a little purring sound and his smile widened. Lord, she was delicious, she was splendid. The way their bodies responded one to the other—it was like nothing he'd known before. As desire stirred within him again, his body already demanding more, an idea was forming in his mind.

It was . . . neat and tidy. It was . . . brilliant, really. And it would solve all their problems at (so to speak) a stroke . . .

Gabriel gathered her to him, relishing the feel of her firm, heavy breasts, and slid his hands around her backside. He was already hard again. Damn all this clothing between them! "I want you again," he murmured. "Let's lie down."

She laughed softly. "In the mud?"

With his tongue he caressed the rim of her ear and he felt her sway a little. "Yes, why not?" he urged her. "I'll lay my coat down for us. To hell with the mud."

Her eyes were sparkling. "You are very persuasive."

"And you are delightful." Gabriel brought his hands up to cup her face. He had to tell her now; his idea had formed more fully and his mind raced with the satisfaction of it. It was as if a complicated puzzle, which had been baffling him, suddenly completed itself, all the pieces fitting together cleanly and neatly. They could still lead those separate Penhallow lives, they would avoid scandal, but could share advantages—mutually beneficial ones!—he hadn't before perceived. The Penhallow way *was* good after all. "Livia, this could work," he said, eager to hear her agreement.

"What could?"

"This marriage. Yes, I know it's a marriage of convenience, not a love match, but why not enjoy the— the physical benefits? Obviously we get along well in that department. And in the natural order of things, you'd produce the heir, and everyone would be happy. What do you say?" He smiled down at her, relieved, confident; the weight of the world was off his shoulders. There was so much to look forward to now.

But . . . why wasn't she looking pleased as well?

He leaned down to kiss her but she was stiff.

"So nothing has changed for you?" she said quietly.

"Livia, everything has changed," he said, but aware that there was a new, coaxing note in his voice. "It's all going to work out. Come; let me have you, my sweet. I want to please you again." He ran his fingers around the curve of her breast. And realized that everything *had* changed between them, for she didn't respond, and it felt like his caress was now a clumsy attempt to seduce her.

She took a breath and stepped away. "No."

A sick feeling of horror twisted in the pit of her stomach. Livia looked around the lean-to as if seeing it for the first time: the dirt, the mud, the squalor. Making love with Gabriel hadn't seemed tawdry while it was happening, it had been the most beautiful thing that had ever happened to her, but now . . .

Now she was sad, so deeply sad.

It was about the *act* for him.

Nothing to do with love.

She wiped her palms along the front of her riding-gown, as if trying to clean them, and took her bonnet from where it had nestled atop his. It had once been such a charming confection, with its extravagantly tall crown and a trio of curling ostrich feathers, dyed an elegant shade of russet, festooning its peaked brim. Now the feathers were wet and limp. They could never be made to look pretty again.

"We need to leave," she said. Quickly she put the bonnet on and tied the ribbons—tight, a little too tight—and went outside onto the crude little porch.

The storm had died down. The wind was now only a mild breeze and the rain had nearly stopped.

"Help me up," she said to Gabriel, who had emerged from the lean-to. With his tousled hair and his bewildered expression, he had about him once again the look of a schoolboy, and for a dangerous moment Livia nearly softened. But she steeled herself against it, and set her mind elsewhere at the physical contact between them when obediently he lifted her up onto Daisy.

As soon as he handed her the reins, she dug her heel into Daisy's side—more forcefully than usual, causing that patient creature to look around at her as if in reproachful surprise—and had her trot toward the road, and set her in the direction back to Bath. Gabriel, on Primus, caught up to her within a minute or two. Without looking at him Livia said:

"We'll say I fell off my horse, and slightly injured myself. I'm a poor enough rider, and with all that wind and rain, it's a likely enough story. We must hurry."

Urging him to hurry was a horrid echo of how, so recently, she had been pressing him on in the most intimate way.

Livia swallowed. She would not, must not, cry. Hadn't she just been given a hard repeat lesson that it never helped anything?

Gabriel said in a tone of deep perplexity, "What is going on? What is happening?"

"Nothing is happening," she said, staring straight ahead. "Nothing at all."

And if to mock her, above them gray clouds parted and the sun peeped out, illuminating the landscape with a warm and cheerful brightness.

As his grandmother had requested—or perhaps "commanded" would have been a better word—Gabriel arrived at her townhouse well before her evening-party was to begin. She met him in the hall, but looked rather distracted. She stopped in the middle of telling Crenshaw to move a large vase of flowers back from one side table to another, and said to Gabriel: "I haven't even dressed yet! Go upstairs into the library. Miss Stuart is there by herself, but I can't spare Evangeline for a chaperone. I trust you'll comport yourself suitably?" she added sharply.

"I'll do my best," Gabriel answered, hoping he was concealing his discomfort.

"See that you do. Crenshaw, what about the champagne? No, those flowers need to go over there—and one of the stems has snapped. Pray remove it. Bettina, I'll be up directly. You've pressed my gloves? Very well—"

As he went up the stairs Gabriel was aware that he was both looking forward to seeing Livia, and dreading what might occur between them. He paused on the threshold to the library, and saw her standing before the fire, and caught his breath in wonderment at her beauty. She wore an elegant snow-white gown, with a demi-train and bronze-colored trimmings; in her hair was woven a twist of pearls and on her arms smoothed long white gloves. In profile her lovely face was thoughtful, somber, as if in her mind she was a thousand miles away.

"Hello," he said.

She snapped out of her reverie at once, and turned to him with a polite smile that didn't reach her eyes. It was a Society smile, and his heart sank to see it.

"Hello," she said, as if yesterday had never happened, as if by some mystical freak of the calendar it had been erased, dissolved, eradicated. "How fine you look. Are you looking forward to the party?"

"Livia."

"Yes?"

"What about us? What about my—suggestion? Have you thought about it at all?"

She wrinkled her brow. "I'm dreadfully sorry, but

I've been so busy. There's been so much to do, you see, helping your grandmother prepare for tonight, that I simply haven't had a moment. In fact, I promised to help Miss Cott look over the drawing-room and I'm afraid I'm already a little late. If you'll excuse me?" She moved toward him. Past him—

"Livia," he said, "wait."

She paused at the doorway, cool, polite. "Yes?"

"It's just that—shouldn't we—I thought that perhaps . . ." He paused; stopped, feeling hopelessly tangled up in his words, his thoughts. And she wasn't helping, either. She was looking at him as if he were interfering with other, more pleasant plans she had. And finally he said:

"Nothing. Never mind."

"Very well," she said, and went away.

To no one's surprise, Mrs. Penhallow's evening-party was a huge success. Receiving a card of invitation to one of her rare, select gatherings conferred a singular honor on the recipient and to refuse was unthinkable—as was arriving late. The townhouse, therefore, went from the quiet bustle of preparation to a nearly immediate crush of guests.

Livia helped Mrs. Penhallow greet them, smiling and nodding, nodding and smiling, all the while thinking that in just a few short hours, she'd be slipping out of the house and beginning a long, tedious journey, on foot and in the deep darkness of the night.

She had made up her mind to go to Portishead, a little village by the sea where, with luck, she could find employment. It was nice living by the sea, so people said, and perhaps she really could become a seamstress.

Or work in the fish trade, which meant that she would reek of fish guts for the rest of her life, but now was no time to be particular.

How odd to think she'd never see Gabriel again.

No, not odd. It was sad, unspeakably sad.

How difficult it had been, being alone with him in the library. She had wanted to stay and she had wanted to go; it had taken everything she had to simply hang on to her composure. Luckily, she was numb now—numb, and polite, and correct, responding to questions and remarks about her forthcoming nuptials as if she would actually be there. It was a joke, but not a funny one.

Grandmama curtly dismissed her from her post, and dutifully Livia circulated among the guests. Despite the old lady's continuing coldness, Livia was determined to make the evening as pleasant as possible for her. Grandmama remained standing at the top of the stairs, erect and handsome in her dove-gray gown, its soft hue setting off to advantage her magnificent ruby necklace and matching aigrette. On her patrician cheekbones burned two bright spots of color. While other women might abet nature by the use of rouge, Livia doubted that Grandmama would stoop to such practices. Or had she tonight made an exception? It would never do to ask, of course.

Livia chatted for a few minutes with Mrs. Thorland, assuring her that she hadn't injured herself in yesterday's supposed fall from her horse, and inquired as to her reaction to the Druidical Stones. She asked Lord Gibbs-Smythe about his gout. From Crenshaw she accepted, with a word of thanks, a goblet of lemonade. Deftly she evaded Sir Edward Brinkley, at his most suave, and instead led his timid sister Miss Brinkley to a comfortable seat next to the fire. At Mrs. Arbuthnot's request, she described in detail the wedding gown—all white and silver and Brussels lace—that Madame Lévêque had created, to which the final, finishing touches of embroidery were being set by her assistants. She even managed to civilly converse (if one could call it that) with Mr. Olivet.

And Gabriel was avoiding her.

Not that she could blame him.

All in all, this was the least enjoyable party she'd ever been to. Then it somehow managed to get even worse. She'd gone over to one of the windows, to see what kind of weather she might expect for her journey, when Cecily Orr came up behind her and said, in a friendly, confidential tone:

"I was just wondering, Livia dear, if you'd visited Miss Poole's Employment Agency again, and if your business there had prospered."

Livia whipped around. "And I was wondering," she said with hostile untruthfulness, "how Sir Edward's suit was progressing."

"Oh! Well! Of course he wishes for an answer, as do Mama and Papa, but I am putting them off as best I can." Cecily spoke airily, but then she gripped Livia's arm with clawlike fingers and leaned closer. "You have not considered my situation, I fear. Every day since that horrible ball at my house, Mama talks about how I let Mr. Penhallow slip away from us. Every day, Livia dear. It's become—shall we say—a little trying."

Livia stared at Cecily. That perfect porcelain face seemed suddenly like a statue which was cracking before her very eyes. "Well," she said, "in all fairness, it wasn't your fault, was it?"

"I don't think Mama is seeing it from your perspective."

"Somehow I'm not surprised. Would you kindly release my arm, Miss Orr? You're hurting me."

"Good," said Cecily, and pulled her hand away, suddenly and unnervingly all smiles again. "If it wasn't my fault, then whose fault is it? I saw you in the garden, Livia dear, with your protests; I saw you at the employment agency. I know what you're up to." In those lovely blue eyes shone the intense gleam of obsession. "I've been thinking about your situation quite a bit. And so I have a gift for you. Something to help you achieve your ambitions." She fumbled in the dainty beaded reticule she carried, pulled from it a small package wrapped in silver paper, and pressed it into Livia's unwilling hand. "Here. I'm helping you. Or am I helping myself? It's hard to know anymore." She added, in a conversational tone:

"You'll never be a *real* lady, you know. Not like me. Poor little Livia. I feel so sorry for you."

"I don't need your pity." Livia tried to shove the little package back, but Cecily turned and took a quick step away and just then there was a sudden excited commotion halfway across the long, crowded room.

"Give her air, give her air!" said a male voice, and a high female voice exclaimed in distress:

"Mrs. Penhallow! Oh, *dear!*"

Reflexively Livia crammed the packet into her own reticule and hurried past Cecily to the knot of people which, she saw in horror, had gathered around the prostrate form of old Mrs. Penhallow. "Pray step aside!" she said, then kneeled down next to the old lady, whose eyes were closed and her thin chest rapidly moving up and down. "What happened?"

"Oh, Miss Stuart, she seemed absolutely fine, but then she seemed to totter, and simply collapsed!" It was Lady Enchwood speaking, but Livia didn't look up, only tucked the rumpled hem of Grandmama's gown over her ankles and then held that fragile, overwarm hand in her own, saying urgently, "Has anyone a vinaigrette? And please find Mr. Penhallow at once!"

Someone gave her a little round vinaigrette which she passed underneath Grandmama's nose; the old lady moaned slightly, to Livia's relief, and then, thank heavens, Gabriel was there.

"We must take her to her bedchamber," she said in a low voice, and silently he nodded, his expression grim, then with great carefulness picked up his grandmother and bore her away.

Time blurred, slowed, as the guests departed, Lady Enchwood the first among them, assuring Livia she would send for a doctor immediately; Livia nodded distractedly, forgot all about it, saw the last lingering people out as politely as possible, spoke to Crenshaw. It must have been an hour before she could finally hasten up the stairs to Grandmama's bedchamber, where she found her prone in her enormous bed, seeming very small in it; Gabriel was there, two maidservants were standing worriedly by, and Miss Cott was bathing the old lady's forehead with lavender water.

"How is she?" Livia asked, going quickly to the bedside.

"She's too warm," replied Miss Cott. "I can't get her to open her eyes."

There was a firm rap on the door, and before anyone could say "Enter," Dr. Wendeburgen strode into the room, his ever-present leather bag—the sight of which Livia had come to detest—in one plump hand.

"What are *you* doing here?" she blurted out in dismay, too upset to be mannerly.

"I was summoned by Lady Enchwood, *liebe* Miss Stuart, on a matter of *der Notstand*—as you English call it, the emergency—and lost no time in coming! Now! Let me see the poor lady." He waved Miss Cott aside and bent over Mrs. Penhallow, studying her intently. He sniffed at her ears, delicately felt at her shins, wiggled his fingers in front of her face. "*Ach!* She obviously stayed too little a time in the baths yesterday! Her kidneys are dangerously swelled with intransitive lipids and this foments *der Fieberzustand!* I must bleed her at once!"

He removed his equipment from his bag and Miss Cott obediently went for the bowl she always held during the procedure. Livia looked over to Gabriel, who stood, frowning, then she watched as Dr. Wendeburgen pulled Grandmama's arm from underneath the bedclothes and efficiently pushed up her sleeve. He took his sharp little knife and all at once, something about the old lady's gaunt, white face and sticklike arm seemed to strike at Livia with the force of a blow.

This was wrong.

She knew it.

Without stopping to think further she snapped, with an authority she didn't know she had:

"Stop that at once!"

He paused, yellow eyebrows lifting. "But Miss Stuart, the lipids must be relieved of pressure!"

"You heard me, I believe. You may leave at once." Livia's whole body was nearly quivering with tension. In a moment she would have to rush over and snatch the knife from his nasty fat hand, and hopefully not sever her own veins doing it.

He was affronted, and said to Gabriel: "Please to tell the young lady I am to continue, *herr* Penhallow."

Gabriel's gaze flicked over to Livia, his eyes briefly meeting hers, and then returned to his grandmother. "No. It is as Miss Stuart says. Leave us."

With an attitude perilously close to petulance, Dr. Wendeburgen put away his instruments and officiously shut his bag. "So! It must be said, sir, *fräulein*, that I cannot take responsibility for the consequences. I only hope that you shall not regret this sad night's work. *Abschied!*" He marched to the door and, with an exaggerated punctiliousness that in other circumstances that Livia would have found funny, closed it behind him.

In the sudden silence she groped for the nearest chair and sank into it. Her rush of fierce protectiveness, having shifted into thankfulness at Gabriel's welcome intervention, gave way to a very real panic.

"Now what?" she said in a small voice. "I know we're better off without that horrible Dr. Wendeburgen, but is there another physician in Bath—one we can trust?"

"There is Dr. Crombie," Miss Cott answered, a little doubtfully. "Mrs. Penhallow consulted him a few times several years ago, but did not care for his recommendations. He said she was perfectly healthy, and would likely remain so if only she would refrain from quacking herself. I'm sorry to say that Mrs. Penhallow—well, she offended him so badly that he said he'd never step foot in the house again."

"Oh, my God, how typical of Grandmama," said Gabriel. "Where does he live? I'll go myself."

Later, Gabriel didn't bother explaining precisely how he managed to persuade Dr. Crombie to come, but within an hour or so there they both were. Short, neatly dressed, stern of face and crisp in manner, Dr. Crombie examined Mrs. Penhallow, asked a lot of questions of Miss Cott, and finally said in his thick Scottish brogue:

"Mrs. Penhallow is badly depleted, plain and simple. 'Tis my opinion she's in desperate need o' nourishment, and relief from the so-called treatments o' that *numptie* Wendeburgen. But first her fever must be brought down."

"Agreed," Gabriel said. "Tell us what to do."

In short order one of the maidservants was dispatched to retrieve additional wood for the fire, the other to alert Cook to prepare barley water at once and to start a batch of bone broth. Clean, soft cloths were sent for, and Dr. Crombie told Miss Cott to put away the bleeding bowl before he kicked it out of the room.

There was no disguising the fact that Grandmama was seriously ill. As the long night passed with agonizing slowness, she roused only to choke and cough on the sips of saline draught and barley water Dr. Crombie held, alternately, to her lips. She showed no other signs of consciousness.

All her personal concerns forgotten, Livia—although urged by both Gabriel and Miss Cott to go to bed—remained in Grandmama's chamber, begging to be allowed to be of some use. Aside from helping to place cool, damp, lavender-infused cloths on the old lady's burning forehead, there was little for her to do. Gabriel paced, sat, paced some more; maidservants slipped in and out with tea and refreshments and various other items.

Dawn found them still at their posts, pale and, inevitably, rumpled. But worse was to come. In the morning hours Grandmama began to toss and turn, flushed, muttering disjointedly. It became more difficult to press upon her a few sips of liquid. Dr. Crombie assured them that this new restiveness was a good sign, but now their roles became less passive as they took turns sitting by the bedside, attempting to soothe Grandmama with quiet words or yet another dampened cloth.

By midday, Miss Cott, less robust than either Livia or Gabriel, looked as if she were about to drop from exhaustion, but it was only with reluctance that she was persuaded to leave the room and lie down in her own bedchamber, where she could sleep for a few hours.

"We *must* take turns," Livia said, "or we'll none of us be helpful at all."

Gabriel agreed, adding, "When Miss Cott returns, Livia, it's your turn next. No arguing, please."

"I won't argue." Livia gazed at the old lady's flushed face and the too-thin outline of her wasted form beneath the bedcovers. She looked so frail, so vulnerable. Livia's heart twisted; there was no room within it for their old rancor, only pity.

Over the next few days it became impossible to differentiate between night and day: it was all the same to Livia, the long, anxious hours by Grandmama's side, the softly spoken conferences with Dr. Crombie, the snatched sleep and hastily eaten meals. Dr. Crombie came and went, servants slipped in and out, even Cook emerged from her kitchen, tiptoeing into the room to personally deliver a new bowl of broth or jug of cool barley water.

Gabriel found himself sometimes eyeing Livia in wonderment. Gone was the exquisitely clad and coiffed girl in her light muslins and gossamer shawls, her dashing bonnets and delicate fans. In her place was a drawn-looking young woman who wore the same simple white gown for many hours on end, her hair in a thick, untidy braid down her back. She never flagged, never faltered, immediately performed whatever tasks were assigned to her; Gabriel realized he had completely accepted her presence in the sick-room. Somehow, subtly and gradually, she had become one of them.

At other times, as he sat next to Grandmama, lightly holding her hand, coaxing her to accept a spoonful of this or that, he realized that despite the old lady's many annoying characteristics—her imperiousness, her impulse to tyrannize everyone around her, her ridiculous certainty that she was always right—that she had, over these weeks in Bath, become a part of his life, that he truly did care for her.

These were startling revelations indeed, but as Grandmama grew more agitated, he had little opportunity to further dwell on them. In a quavering voice she many times called out, pleadingly, for Richard, her long-dead husband; she mistook Gabriel for Henry, her oldest son who had become Gabriel's father.

"Henry!" she cried, "I should not have stayed away! Forgive me!" Sadly, so sadly, did she ask for her other children, Titus and Sophia, gone, both of them, for many years now. Sometimes Gabriel's deep, quiet voice would calm her; at other times only Livia could do that, saying soothingly over and over, "Granny, dear Granny, we are here."

Once, Gabriel thought, he might have objected to Livia calling her that. So long ago did that time seem. Now he could only be grateful that the word, or the fact that it was Livia employing it, had an almost magically consoling effect.

He could not have said when the summons came from Crenshaw—the third day of their ordeal? The fourth?—who one afternoon said, just outside the door to Grandmama's chamber: "Lady Enchwood, sir, most urgently requests your presence in the drawing-room."

Gabriel was just barely managing to get a spoonful of Cook's excellent broth into his grandmother's mouth. "Tell her I'm busy."

Softly Crenshaw cleared his throat. "So I have, sir, but she is insistent."

Gabriel knew that Livia and Miss Cott were both taking much-needed naps. He supposed that Lady Enchwood, one of Grandmama's closest cronies, wished to hear from his own lips just how her friend went on. "Stay here, please, with my grandmother; I'll go down."

He found Lady Enchwood sipping at a cup of tea, a macaroon in the other hand.

"Oh! Mr. Penhallow! I must speak with you!" Hastily she swallowed the last bite of macaroon and restored her cup to its saucer. "I need hardly say how pained I am, but only the *utmost* necessity compels me to bring to your attention that fact that rumors are positively *galloping* through the town! It's said that you have vacated your rooms at the York House and are staying here! In the same house as Miss Stuart! Of course that would be quite shocking, if it were true!"

Gabriel looked at her for a long moment. "I thought," he said coldly, "you had come to inquire after my grandmother's health."

"Oh yes, indeed I have!" she assured him. "But one can't safeguard one's reputation too closely, you know, and after what Miss Orr has been disclosing, I am afraid that Miss Stuart is in a—well, a vulnerable situation, shall we say. And with the wedding date so near! Do you think dear Mrs. Penhallow might be permitted to attend, perhaps in one of those darling wheeled chairs? So comfortable, so snug for an invalid! When I was stricken with the influenza last year, Dr. Wendeburgen told me where I might procure one. It was just the thing, for my legs were like *blancmange*, and I was able to select upholstery in the most modern colors. Such a relief, for I had feared I should have to go about in an old fusty chair, looking dreadfully like a *relic* from a Gothic story! But I am happy to tell you that was not the case at all. So many compliments as I received! I vow and declare it quite turned my head."

A vision of himself picking her ladyship up by the scruff of her fat neck and booting her down the stairs floated agreeably through Gabriel's mind. As much as he had disliked Bath before, it was as nothing to the raw hatred for the place which now suffused him.

"You stare, Mr. Penhallow, and I do not wonder at it! You are amazed at my complete recovery. Why, I am myself! *Many* times was my life despaired of! Dr. Wendeburgen declared it was a miracle."

"I'm sure he did," replied Gabriel, in a voice that had gone from cold to arctic. "Now if you'll excuse me, I must return to my grandmother."

"Wait!" Lady Enchwood said, in throbbing accents. "Is it true, dear Mr. Penhallow, that you have rejected the services of Dr. Wendeburgen? It seems an incredible tale! I have been telling *all* my acquaintance that it must be the rankest, most scurrilous falsehood!"

Before he actually grabbed at her neck and did real violence to her person, Gabriel muttered a word of farewell and left the room, taking the stairs three at a time back to Grandmama's chamber.

"Get rid of that damned tabby," he told Crenshaw, "and don't admit her again."

A faint smile, so subtle as to be almost unnoticeable to the human eye, flickered across the butler's normally immobile countenance. "It shall be as you wish, sir."

There were no more foolish interruptions after that, and a good thing too, as in the evening Grandmama's delirium worsened and it took all their combined efforts to keep her as calm as possible. When Dr. Crombie announced his intention to remain through the night, Gabriel's fears for her deepened and though he said nothing aloud, he could see his concern reflected in the worn, pale faces of Livia and Miss Cott. None of them cared to leave the old lady's bedchamber, and when Cook, stepping into the room around midnight with a little pork jelly in a covered dish, they none of them had the heart to send away the small visitor who crept in at her heels.

It was Muffin, the dog whom Livia had rescued.

Flustered and apologetic, Cook tried to quietly shoo him away, but after briefly wagging his tail—as if offering a general, friendly salute to the others in the room—he trotted over to Grandmama's bed, leaped up onto it, and promptly curled up at her side in a small, white, furry ball and would not be dislodged, even by Cook's coaxing offers of a nice bone or her firmer commands to "Come here, do!" Muffin had made his wishes very clear, and obviously would be removed only by force.

Finally Gabriel said, in a voice roughened by fatigue, "Leave him. He'll do her no harm."

The hours ticked by. Dr. Crombie went back and forth from Grandmama to the wing chair he had commandeered. Grandmama muttered, sighed, cried out, then fell ominously silent. The rest of them took turns at the bedside, dozed in their chairs, listlessly accepted tea and sandwiches, the little dog all the while remaining at his post. It seemed that morning would never come. Yet Gabriel knew they all were afraid what it might bring.

Chapter 12

"What . . . what is this . . . this *thing?*"

A weak voice, whispering.

Livia snapped awake in her chair. For a bewildered few seconds she had no idea where she was, then awareness came upon her in a shivery rush of fear and dread, and she jumped up, hurrying to the great bed in which Grandmama lay.

The old lady was awake, and lucid. And she had turned her head to stare at Muffin, who during the latter part of the night had snuggled comfortably up against her armpit. He lifted his head slightly, looking Grandmama right in the eye, and thumped his curly tail in the most affable manner possible.

The old lady looked so affronted that Livia couldn't help it. She laughed. The sound brought Dr. Crombie, Gabriel, and Miss Cott out of their respective slumbers and hurrying to her side.

Muffin yawned, revealing a curling pink tongue.

"I . . . do not care for dogs," whispered Grandmama, her silvery brows drawn together. "Beastly creatures."

Muffin licked her arm.

Gabriel smiled. "It seems he cares for you, however."

She sniffed, faintly, and considered Muffin. "At the

Hall . . . I always had dogs, though. A . . . a lifetime ago." Then she regarded them, each in turn. "I am appalled by . . . your bedraggled . . . state," she went on in that weak, low voice. "Gabriel, you . . . need a shave, and Livia . . . your gown is . . . shockingly creased . . . And . . . Dr. Crombie . . . I thought never to . . . see your hatchet face again."

"And I yours, madam," he said coolly, placing a professional hand on her forehead.

"Granny," said Livia reproachfully, "Dr. Crombie has been invaluable."

Grandmama stared at her. "Granny," she echoed, frowning. Then, after a long pause, she said, "I've been ill . . . have I not?"

Dr. Crombie stepped back and Gabriel sat next to the old lady, taking her hand in his. "Yes, Grandmama, very ill indeed."

"Yes. I've been a . . . great deal of trouble to you, I am afraid."

He smiled. "Oh yes, a great deal."

"I . . . am . . . I am sorry for that."

"Don't be," he answered.

She sighed, and turned her gaze to Dr. Crombie. "Well? Am I . . . going to live?"

"Aye, madam, as long as you stay away from that *dunderheid* Wendeburgen."

The old lady sighed again, but did not argue. "I . . . I should like a cup of tea."

"Of course." Miss Cott went quickly to ring for a maidservant.

"And . . . and I suppose," Grandmama continued, ungraciously, "something for this . . . this ridiculous-looking dog."

It was reassuring to see that the worst danger to Grandmama was past, but it was also evident that her convalescence was going to be a protracted one. At first she was too weak to be combative, and her unusual quiescence kept them all in a state of alert attendance upon her.

Gradually her appetite began to return, and it was less of a struggle to press upon her the light, nourishing soups and beverages Cook made in quantities sufficient for several invalids. But she remained ensconced in her bed, Muffin always with her (and occasionally did her hand steal over, surreptitiously, to stroke him). She allowed Livia to brush and dress her hair, to turn her pillows and straighten the bedclothes; and when Livia asked if she might be of further service, she said, grudgingly:

"You might . . . read to me."

So Livia did. Grandmama still corrected her occasional errors, and very often fell asleep, drifting into a recuperative doze, during which Livia turned her attention to the pretty bed-jacket she was making for Grandmama. Cocooned in an agreeable state of relief, it was no hardship to spend her time reading, sewing, and helping care for the old lady, who, in fact, grew querulous if Livia was gone for longer than an hour or two, and would repeatedly ask for her until she returned.

To these demands Livia responded without complaint. In fact, she was—why, she was content. She was focused only on the present moment, she permitted herself the luxury of making no plans (resolutely she pushed aside the thought of her old stout boots, a dreadfully long walk, Portishead), and it struck her that Grandmama, in fact, needed her. And how wonderful it was to feel needed by somebody! Aunt Bella, more or less infirm for all the years Livia had known her, certainly hadn't found much use for her and, when it came right down to it, had frequently seemed to find her presence at the Abbey completely insignificant.

And while Grandmama, even in her debilitated state, remained her lofty, arrogant self, there was no question that something had changed within her. There was a new hint of softness which she labored mightily to conceal, but there it was. One only had to see her with Muffin to know *that*.

Late on a sunny afternoon, as Livia sat in a comfortable chair next to Grandmama's bed, reading to her from Pope's philosophical poem, *Essay on Man*, a knock on the door interrupted her, and Gabriel strolled in, immaculate in a mulberry coat, buckskins, and shining topboots. Now that the crisis had passed, he had returned to the York House but spent much of his time here in his grandmother's townhouse.

He smiled. "A little light reading, I perceive?"

"I haven't read the *Essay on Man* in a long time," answered Grandmama thoughtfully. "It's a favorite of Evangeline's, you know. Pope's point is that the universe is fundamentally perfect, and that we should all accept our place within it."

"Not always an easy precept to embrace." Gabriel went and sat at the foot of the bed, accepting Muffin's fawning greeting with equanimity. "Down, you cur," he said pleasantly, and Muffin immediately flattened himself, tail wagging. Gabriel stroked his head. "Don't let me interrupt you. Pray continue."

Livia couldn't help but smile a little as she picked up the book again and complied. Oh, but she *was* content! Here was Gabriel, here was Grandmama . . . and then in came Miss Cott. In her hands she carried a silver tray, and she said, in her gentle manner:

"Cook wonders if you'd care for a little of this chicken *ragoût*."

"Indeed I do not," came the tart reply. "I do wish you would all refrain from ceaselessly trying to fatten me up. I feel like a Christmas goose."

"Shall I take it away?"

"No, set it down. Livia is reading Pope to us. I daresay you would like to hear it too."

Miss Cott obeyed and sat down, listening attentively as Livia continued.

Ten minutes later the old lady said crossly, "Oh, stop sulking, Evangeline! I'll try a little of that *ragoût*."

She tasted it, pronounced it tolerable, and ate two-thirds, giving the rest to Muffin. When Miss Cott had removed the tray, and Livia plumped up her pillows, Gabriel rose to his feet.

"I'll take my leave of you. You'll be wanting to rest, Grandmama."

"Not yet. I have something I want to say to you all."

Gabriel raised his eyebrows, sat down again; Grandmama plucked at the bedcovers, frowning a little. There was a silence in the room, and an anxious little chill snaked down Livia's spine. Something seemed to be weighing heavily on the old lady's mind.

At last she spoke, with uncharacteristic tentativeness.

"I have not forgotten that the date for the wedding is four days hence. I have . . . hesitated to discuss it, but—it is terribly selfish, I know, but I would wish to be there on my own two feet. And—and I do not think I will be capable of it."

Livia hadn't *quite* forgotten about the wedding, but neither had she been making inquiries about it. It was amazing, really, the human capacity for diverting one's thoughts, as if storing them away in different baskets and shoving them into an armoire. She flashed a glance at Gabriel who was, she now discovered, looking at her. On his face was an arrested expression that she couldn't decipher. In a moment he blinked, then turned his gaze again to his grandmother.

"Lady Enchwood thinks you should attend in a wheeled chair," he remarked. "She considers it a— what was the term she used?—a darling vehicle for an invalid."

"An idiotish opinion," responded Grandmama coldly. "To own the truth, I don't know why I've put up with Lady Enchwood for all these years. She is a person entirely without intellect."

Livia felt herself goggling at Grandmama, and saw also the smile quirking at the corners of Gabriel's mouth.

"You needn't grin in that unseemly way," the old lady said sourly, "it is beneath you." She paused again. "If you do not object too strongly, it's my desire to vacate Bath as soon as may be arranged. I'm afraid it means removing you from the parties, Livia, the balls, the concerts, and so on."

"Oh, Granny, I couldn't care less," answered Livia impulsively. "I mean—please don't think I'm not grateful for all that you've done for me, but I am *sick* of Bath!"

"As am I," was the old lady's unexpected reply. "It must also be said that I am aware of the unpleasant rumors about you which are making the rounds, thanks to the insidious efforts of Miss Orr. I cannot think they have made your life very comfortable."

Livia shrugged. "They're nonsensical."

"I know that. However, I allowed myself to resent *you* for them, rather than directing my hostility toward the source. And I am sorry for my mistake."

It was an afternoon of wonders, to be sure. Livia felt tears prickling, and nodded silently.

"Where do you wish to go, Grandmama?" Gabriel asked. "To the sea, perhaps?"

"No. I—well, I should like to go home."

Gabriel stared. "You *are* home."

"You misunderstand me. I want to go home to the Hall."

"The Hall," he echoed, and Miss Cott pressed her hand to her mouth, looking all at once very pale.

His mind seemed to be going in too many directions at once. The wedding abruptly postponed, the dynamics among them shifting too rapidly to be grasped, and now this stunning thunderbolt of a request from Grandmama.

Take her home?

It would be an understatement to say that this wasn't what he wanted—wasn't what he had planned on.

It complicated everything.

Then a troubling idea occurred to him. He eyed Grandmama as she lay in her bed—better, yes, but still thin and weak and wan. She returned his gaze and said, with some of her usual sharpness:

"What is it?"

Well, this was awkward. "Your wanting to go to the Hall—it's rather—it's surprising, Grandmama, to say the least. And given your illness, and how severe it was, I just wonder—that is to say, I hope that—"

The old lady startled him by bursting into laughter.

"You think I want to go home to die, don't you?"

He resisted the urge to shuffle his feet like a defensive ten-year-old. "Your announcement is, you must admit, unexpected."

"I'll grant you that. No, Gabriel, I don't want to go home to die, and God willing it shall be many years before that event occurs. I want to go home to *live*." She played with the emerald ring she wore, slowly turning it round and round her finger. "I've had a great deal of time to think these past days, you see. It's been twenty years since I've been at the Hall. Did you know that I was born there?"

"What? No. I don't understand."

"How could you? You were too young when Henry— when your father died, and I never cared to explain things to you. Yes, Surmont Hall belongs to my line of the Penhallows. Richard—my husband, and your grandfather—was a third cousin of mine, a member of the cadet branch." The old lady laughed again, but softly this time. "*He* didn't care about the difference in our rank, but it certainly did bother my parents." She was silent for a while, evidently lost in her own memories. She smiled, sighed, then went on: "I was the only child and a female, but in our family such cases have never meant that the estate must inevitably pass out of our hands to more distant male relations. Fortunately, the Penhallows are known for their strong women."

Gabriel couldn't resist glancing at Livia.

"Yes," murmured the old lady, meeting his eyes, "strong women. So Richard came to live with me at the Hall, and we knew it would, in time, belong to one of our children and thus stay within the line as it has for centuries."

"It is—quite a heritage, Grandmama."

She nodded, then gave another sudden crack of laughter. "I'll tell you who else was troubled by the difference in rank between Richard and me. Your father Henry! It's my strong suspicion that, had he lived, he would never have told you about it."

"Why, Grandmama?" asked Gabriel, fascinated. His past, which heretofore had felt like a closed book, was all at once feeling more vivid to him than it ever had before. More real.

"Henry was a dear, good boy, always very interested

in knowing what the rules were, always wishing to follow them most minutely. To be sure, he loved his father, my Richard, but when he married that Adelaide of his—well, I've sometimes wondered if her own consequence was the most important thing in the world to her. And her influence over Henry was immense; in time he became more like my own parents than I ever could have dreamed possible. It wasn't long after Henry's wedding that—that Richard died. I'm afraid that I was—oh, I was quite crazed with grief. I'm sure I was a great trouble to Henry and Adelaide."

She looked over at Miss Cott, and a smile briefly flickered on her face. "It was Evangeline, whom I had known from my girlhood, who came to my aid, and it was she who suggested a visit to Bath. So I took my little girl Sophia, who was four, along with me, and Evangeline came too. Adelaide made no secret of the fact that she was glad to see me go. I suppose it was only natural that she wished to assume her rightful place as mistress of the Hall. If only—if only we had—well, I tried hard to love her, but she was not an easy person to love."

Gabriel saw with pain in his own heart that her blue eyes were sparkling with tears. Gently he said: "I had no idea."

Grandmama answered gruffly. "It's my fault entirely you've been ignorant of these things. They've been locked up inside me for all these years. I never wanted to revisit my own suffering. But when one has finally faced one's mortality, priorities can change. And one becomes, perhaps, rather more honest. To say nothing to you would be, I believe, insupportably selfish. However, here I am giving you a rather jaundiced view of your own mother."

"As to that—well, I really don't remember her."

"No, how could you? No doubt she handed you off to servants from very nearly the moment of your birth."

"What was she like, Grandmama? Her personality, her interests?"

"It would be difficult to say. She was very proud, very accomplished, and quite an acknowledged beauty. But she was so self-possessed, so self-contained, that it was impossible to know whether there was more to her than that. And she was so lovely that she could dazzle merely by her own presence, without ever needing to open her mouth. It was, incidentally, my own parents who brought her to Henry's notice, and fostered with enthusiasm the idea of a match between them. I am sure you can appreciate the irony of that."

Gabriel smiled slightly, murmuring, without heat, "Indeed."

"Richard and I were unable to tell if Henry truly cared for Adelaide, or if he was more caught by the idea of her *appropriateness* for him. We asked him, as tactfully as possible, but he was not forthcoming. And he was stubborn. He wanted Adelaide, and she—well, she wanted to be wanted by him." The old lady had a far-away look on her face. "A handsome couple they made. They were married at the Hall, of course. And what a beautiful baby you were! You got your coloring from Henry, you know, but those unusual golden flecks in your eyes are Adelaide's. And you have, I am pleased to say, Richard's nose. I had the impertinence to tell him, not long after we met, that it was positively his best feature."

"Granny, what was Richard like?" asked Livia.

"Oh, my Richard, my Richard was . . ." Grandmama trailed off, dreamily. "He was . . . wonderful." Then her gaze focused again and she looked back and forth between Livia and Gabriel. "I daresay you think I'm quite an old stick, worshipping the god of propriety. You should know that I *did* have my share of adventures as a young lady."

"Grandmama, you shock us," said Gabriel, laughter in his voice. "Tell us."

"Yes, Granny, do!" put in Livia eagerly.

The old lady's eyes were twinkling now. "No, those are tales for another time."

"How unkind of you," said Gabriel reproachfully. "We'll now be forced to imagine risqué stories of you masquerading as a privateer, terrorizing unwary merchant ships, or traveling about the countryside among a troupe of players, mesmerizing one and all with your riveting theatrical performances."

She laughed, and Gabriel, laughing too, was filled with amazement. Never in a thousand years would he ever have imagined sharing a conversation like this with his grandmother. Laughing with her. Seeing her so fully human.

He looked again at Livia, his eyes lingering on her face; she was smiling also. All at once he seemed to feel that rush of energy, a visceral connection pulsing between them, vibrant and powerful and alluring, nearly bewildering him with its strength.

Was it issuing from him or from her? And was it real? Or a fancy of his own creation?

He shook his head a little, as if to clear it.

There were so many unanswered questions between them. He hardly knew what he thought of her, of their situation. Except that . . . right here, right now, he was . . .

He was happy, and happy that she was near him.

That was enough for now.

"Well, I'm tired," Grandmama said, "and I'd like a

nap." And indeed she looked very fatigued. But, he was glad to note, peaceful as well.

"I've stayed too long," he said, contrite.

"By no means. However, we have yet to fix on a plan. Will you take me—take us—to the Hall?"

This, at least, was now an easy question to answer. "Of course I will."

She smiled. "Good. I so look forward to seeing my rose garden again. The head gardener and I had the most ferocious quarrels over the superiority of the China rose over the rose of Provins. Ha! As if there could be any doubt about it! And there was a woman in the village who gave birth to triplets. It was a seven days' wonder, you may be sure. Do you remember that, Evangeline? She named one of the girls after me. She would have given both of the girls my name if I had permitted it, and, I suppose, even the boy, too. I am curious to know what became of them. Oh, and I'll show you what was, as a child, my favorite place in all the world—a carved stone seat by the river. There was the prettiest willow overhanging it."

"I can't wait to see them, Granny." Livia made as if to stand, but the old lady reached out to her.

"Will you come back, when I am awake? And read to me some more?"

Warmly Livia clasped the frail, slender hand in her own. "Of course I shall."

"Very well," said Grandmama. "Perhaps a little Shakespeare next." She closed her eyes, and was swiftly carried off in sleep.

Given Grandmama's still-debilitated state, it would have been too much to say that the townhouse was plunged into a frenzy of activity when it became known that the family was decamping to Surmont Hall. However, a new air of bustle, of oncoming change, permeated the place. Although the old lady still lay in state in her vast bed, she assumed command of the move from there, looking, as Gabriel remarked, very much like a French monarch of the previous century, lacking only a towering powdered wig to complete the illusion. The little dog Muffin remained always at her side, occasionally taking exception to certain visitors—for reasons that nobody could ascertain—and once going so far as to bite one of the footmen, Roger, but as he was one of the two servants who declined the invitation to also remove to the Hall, no attempts were made to introduce friendlier relations between them. The other servant was a scullery maid whose entire family dwelled in Bath and who did not care to place herself at such a distance from them.

Grandmama did deign to receive some of her acquaintance as a kind of extended take-leave ceremony (receiving many compliments on her charming new bed-jacket), although she refused far more requests to call than she accepted. Already, it seemed to Livia, her mind stretched ahead to the Hall, and to the multitude of pleasures that lay ahead; her time in Bath was already beginning to fade into the past.

The old lady spent many happy hours deciding which items she wished to bring, and those she intended to leave behind, poring over lists, writing and rewriting them, changing her mind so frequently that only someone with Crenshaw's superhuman imperturbability could endure it with such fortitude. It fell to him, for better or worse, to superintend the arrangements.

Grandmama also expended considerable thought as to the traveling arrangements.

The majority of the servants would precede the family in rented carriages, accompanied by wagons containing as many of the household goods as could be removed without inconvenience to those remaining behind. Because the pace of the wagons would be so slow, for them it would be a four-day journey. Grandmama intended to complete the family's trip in only two days, spending the night in Wells. She pronounced herself ready to depart immediately, but Gabriel was doubtful as to her capacity to withstand the rigors of travel, even in her enormous, luxuriously fitted coach; they argued about it at length, until finally they reached a compromise which satisfied neither of them.

"Very well! A week it is," said the old lady, in the tone of one compelled to walk across a pile of hot coals.

"And while we're on the subject," Gabriel went on, a slight acid tinge to his voice, "where do you propose to stay in Wells?"

"I always stop over at the Royal Hart. Naturally we shall stay there."

"Because you enjoy the fleas?"

"The Royal Hart doesn't have fleas."

"They did the last time I stayed there."

Grandmama sniffed. "Perhaps it was something about your person which attracted them."

Gabriel scowled, and Livia, sitting in an armchair with Muffin on her lap, brushing his silky white fur, thought how handsome Gabriel looked with his eyes flashing like that. Into her mind came once again an image of a grand empty nursery, and she found herself drifting into a pleasant daydream imagining what the Hall looked like.

It *couldn't* look like Ealdor Abbey, that ill-kempt and hulking medieval pile, always damp, always cold, with stupid thick walls of ancient stone. The only other country house she knew was that of the Orrs, but it was of modern construction, built according to precepts of rigid symmetry. Surmont Hall, much older, surely had quite a different design. One of the first places Livia intended to explore was the Picture Galley. Grandmama had described how, as a little girl, she had run up and down its seemingly endless corridor, and as she had gotten older been fascinated by the dozens of portraits which hung there.

Livia wanted to see if there was a painting of Gabriel as a little boy. Did he have baby fat? Chubby legs, adorable pudgy cheeks? She smiled to herself, and wondered if he had been just as strong-willed when he was small.

"You find the ideas of fleas amusing?" Gabriel said to her rather irritably.

Livia blinked. "I beg your pardon?"

"You seem to be entertained by picturing me covered in flea bites."

"Oh! No, no, I was woolgathering."

"This involves you, so perhaps you ought rather to pay attention."

His surly tone made Livia bristle. "As if *I* have any say in the matter."

"You could speak up in favor of an inn that's free of vermin."

"Well, I don't know any inns in Wells! I've never in my life been there!"

Grandmama jumped again into the fray. "I suppose," she said to Gabriel, "*you* wish to stay at the Swan."

"As it's the only other establishment in Wells where I'd even consider stabling the horses, yes."

"The sheets are always damp."

"And how would you know that? You've just said you exclusively patronize the Royal Hart."

"It is the common report," answered Grandmama coldly.

"Fine! *You* stay at the Royal Hart, and *I'll* stay at the Swan."

"Don't be absurd."

"It's not absurd. It seems to me an eminently practical plan."

"Need I remind you that we travel under your protection?" Grandmama smiled triumphantly, and it was to be seen that she had clinched the argument, for Gabriel glared but added:

"Don't blame me when we all emerge from the Hart infested with fleas."

"We shan't," she answered, with maddening serenity. "I won't allow it. Dear me, you're quite peevish today! Go and ride your horse until your temper cools. That's what Richard always did. Not that he was ever as snappish as you are."

"It grieves me to inform you that it's raining today. Again."

"Have you no other occupation? Surely you have something better to do than badger a helpless old woman."

He visibly ground his teeth, his eyes flashing even more magnificently. "Yes," he said with heavy sarcasm, "extremely helpless."

There was, Livia mused, something vivifying about a good brangle. Grandmama had a nice healthy flush of color in her cheeks. And Gabriel looked so handsome that she wished she could go over and take hold of him in a brazen way and kiss him for a good long time.

"You're smirking at me again," he said to her, frowning.

"I'm not smirking!" Nettled, blushing, she lowered her eyes to Muffin, who sat amiably curled up in her lap, oblivious to the acrimony all around him. He gazed up at her with melting black eyes and squirmed onto his back, plainly inviting her to scratch his little pink belly.

And then she saw it.

"Muffin has a flea."

Grandmama let out a squawk and Gabriel laughed in a very unhelpful sort of way. Miss Cott, seated quietly in a chair with some mending in her lap, was found to be—rather uncharacteristically—in a state of such deep abstraction that Grandmama had to speak to her twice before she could get a response.

Livia saw her start, drop her mending, and distractedly grope for it, and then Miss Cott said, "You would like some muffins? Certainly; I shall ring at once."

Chapter 13

Livia had no time to wonder at Miss Cott's unusual absentmindedness as Grandmama's bedchamber became immediately the scene of frenzied activity. A footman swept Muffin off to be bathed, maidservants dove into armoires and the enormous oak dresser to inspect all of the old lady's garments while others stood by to remove the linens from her bed. Grandmama called for a robe, which Livia wrapped around her; then, to everyone's surprise, she rose to her feet, demanded slippers, and once they were provided, allowed Livia to put her arm around her and took some shaky steps across the room to a chair near the fire, from which vantage point she magisterially observed the servants trooping back and forth, carrying away sheets and quilts and returning with fresh ones.

Gabriel, leaning against the wall with his arms crossed against his chest, murmured something about the healing of Lazarus, which Grandmama pointedly ignored but which set Livia to wondering if the old lady had, in some way, relished her invalid state—enjoyed being cared for with such attentiveness.

Aside from the faithful Miss Cott, who had, over the past twenty years, *really* cared for Grandmama?

She faced the imminent prospect of parting from her circle here in Bath without the least evidence of regret or sorrow, which to Livia seemed significant. It might also help explain why Grandmama had formed such a dependence on that awful Dr. Wendeburgen, who had practically haunted the house, all oily solicitousness and overweening self-assurance. Why not? thought Livia. Wasn't it one of the most basic of all needs: to feel cared for?

She glanced quickly at Gabriel, and then away. No, she wasn't going to think about—things. She would keep such thoughts stuffed away, like her old boots crammed obscurely into the back of her armoire.

In due course Grandmama was reestablished in her bed and propped up on pillows, the now unpolluted Muffin was restored to the room, and they dined *en famille* with trays brought up to them. The old lady's color was still good after her exertions; seeing her tuck into a beautifully broiled pork chop with such enjoyment, one would never have suspected her of being a person who, only a few weeks ago, subsisted primarily on such fare as turnip cakes and oatmeal soup in which sodden shreds of corn husks floated like hopeless castaways on an unappetizing sea.

The mood was cozy and mellow. Gabriel refrained from making sardonic comments, Grandmama from provoking quarrels; their hostility from earlier in the day had evaporated, Gabriel going so far as to kiss his grandmother's hand with old-fashioned courtliness before he departed, earning a warm smile in return.

Was this, Livia wondered, how families were? One could fight and snipe and be irritated and angry, yet still, when all was said and done, be connected by the powerful bonds of shared experience and affection?

Well, she herself wouldn't have a real way of knowing,

she thought with a painful sort of wryness, thinking back to her lonely years at Ealdor Abbey. Her mother, her grandfather, were so far back in the past as to be shadows in her mind and heart—ghosts, really, wispy and insubstantial.

It occurred to her that she wished Gabriel had kissed *her* hand, too.

And on these rather melancholy reflections she went to bed.

The servants in rented carriages at length departed, the big wagons of household goods in tow, leaving only a skeleton crew who would accompany the family a few days hence. But a confluence of unfortunate mishaps halted the train on its second leg. Two of the horses threw shoes, an axle on one of the wagons snapped, a footman sprained his wrist while securing a pile of luggage more firmly, and Cook came down with a touch of the flux which while luckily not bloody was certainly uncomfortable.

Crenshaw explained all this in a detailed missive. Grandmama, reading it, sighed gustily, but accepted the inevitability of the situation.

"I had hoped they would arrive in plenty of time before we did," she said, folding the letter, "but I won't delay our own departure because of it." She cast Gabriel a challenging look, but he only said:

"As you wish. However, the Hall may not be prepared to your liking."

"Why not? I've written to Mrs. Worthing to advise her of our arrival."

"Who?"

"She is the housekeeper at the Hall. A mere village

girl when I took her on as a young bride, but even then I could perceive her potential. I'm happy to say that she proved herself to be exceedingly competent. Among her many gifts is a receipt for furniture polish that is, I feel confident, without equal. I believe she uses the peel of lemon, very finely ground, along with beeswax. At any rate, I'm sure she'll have it all in hand. Will you come tomorrow, to go over the house with me one last time before we depart? I should appreciate your arm on which to lean."

"Certainly." Gabriel was conscious of a flicker of gratification. Really, it wasn't such a bad thing to be needed, especially when he recalled that the many times as a boy spending his school holidays here, he seemed to be little more than a pest to her.

He came the next afternoon, just as what had become to feel like the inevitable rain began to fall. The wind was rising, whipping cool and damp about him; the nip of autumn was in the air. Dreary here, but not so at the Hall, perhaps, he thought as he went lightly up the steps to the stoop. There would soon be hunting, and he could invite friends to come and stay.

A list swiftly formed in his mind: Quigley, Farr, Deakin, Donahoe, close friends from school with whom he had remained in touch. And old Hetherenton, too, and Oxley . . . He'd only had time to briefly see them in London upon his return from Europe, but good Lord, what a jolly lot. How odd to think of welcoming them all to Surmont Hall. Odd, even startling—but he was looking forward to it. And to introducing them to Livia. Intelligent, fiery, lovely: a woman any man would be proud to say was his own.

Grandmama's house had assumed that quiet, shuttered look as such places did during a move, but he was immune to any sense of the gloom so often attendant upon such occasions. Grandmama, too, was in good spirits as he carefully escorted her about. So thorough had her efforts been that she found only two items—thankfully, not cumbersome ones—she wished to bring with them, a small bust of Dante Alighieri and a rather ugly vase which, she said, held sentimental value.

Together they dined a final time in the townhouse, upstairs in Grandmama's bedchamber, on cold meat and sandwiches and cider. The rain had intensified and could be heard drumming against the windows, but here, inside, they were warm and dry. Grandmama, satisfied with the results of her inspection, was positively merry, reminiscing about growing up at the Hall, and describing in glowing detail some of the glittering balls held there in her youth.

Listening, Gabriel found himself caught up in her enthusiasm. For most of his life he hadn't given much thought to the Hall, but now he was interested, curious. What, he now wondered, would he do there once they got there? He would familiarize himself with the house, of course, and the stables. He'd never met the bailiff, Eccles; and so he would get to know him at last, and the tenant farmers. Maybe he'd take up horse-breeding . . .

Livia yawned behind her hand, and he saw that Miss Cott's head was drooping with fatigue. "Forgive me," Livia said, "we've been running up and down the stairs all day."

"It *has* been busy," acknowledged Grandmama graciously. "Do go to bed. You as well, Evangeline. Ring for Bettina, please, as you go. Gabriel, you'll wait with me until she comes?"

"Of course. I'll see myself out after."

"You'll have to," Livia said, yawning again. "There are practically no servants left, and I suspect they're all in bed except for Granny's Bettina. Until tomorrow morning, then. Good night." She smiled sleepily at him, and followed Miss Cott out of the room.

Gabriel spent a convivial fifteen minutes making plans with Grandmama about house parties, balls, and, of course, once they were all established and a few alterations to the house made— "New wallpaper in the chief bedchambers, I daresay, and perhaps some rugs," said the old lady comfortably—a magnificent wedding in the chapel where his parents had been married, where Grandmama had married her Richard, and where had many previous Penhallow couples also said their vows.

"Much better than a hurried event here in Bath, and really, now that I come to think on it, how superior to my original idea of a wedding in London. You shall be married at home."

"Fine," Gabriel answered equably, captivated by a sudden a vision of Livia, dressed for her wedding day, walking toward him as he waited for her by the chancel, waiting for the moment when he might kiss his bride. Here his fantasy became rather vague as he didn't really remember the chapel at all. In truth, he remembered almost nothing about the Hall. He could dimly recollect his bedchamber, a room which sometimes unnerved him by its sheer size, a bed which seemed to his small self to be ten feet high, and a nursery, also a gargantuan room, but sunny and filled with interesting things. Toys and books; a globe that spun, a microscope. There were servants, so many and rather anonymous. But there was someone he addressed as "Nanny": searching his memory brought fragmented images of a white apron, a big round face and kind eyes. She used to give him baked apple pudding so delicious that even now he felt saliva gathering in his mouth at the thought.

Grandmama's dresser Bettina hurried into the room, and Gabriel said his farewells. He stepped into the long, dark hallway and softly closed the door. He passed by a series of closed doors—wondering all over again at the sheer size of the place; how many bedchambers had his grandmother thought she needed?—and came to the juncture where the stairs began.

Ahead of him, further down the hallway, a door opened and Livia emerged, still in her white gown, but he could see that she was barefoot. Something about that simple fact seemed all at once to immobilize him and he stood there staring at her, just as she had stopped, eyes wide, lips parted.

Gabriel thought, suddenly, of Artemis, goddess of the wilderness and of the hunt, and lines from the ancient Greek poet Hesiod floated through his mind as if in a dream:

> Leto bore Apollon and Artemis,
>   delighting in arrows,
> Both of lovely shape like none of
>   the heavenly gods,
> As she joined in love to the Aegis-bearing ruler.

Orion, her hunting companion, was said to have captured the resistant heart of Artemis, and while Gabriel entertained no fancies of himself as one of the Greek gods, there was something about the phrase *joined in love*—both coyly evocative and bluntly carnal—which caught at him so hard that he found himself walking, walking to Livia where she stood in the dimness of the hallway. She looked as if she, like Artemis, might flee at any moment, leaving him far behind. Very gently, then, he said:

"Are you all right?"

"I didn't know you were still here," she answered, a little disjointedly. "It's only that—I thought I could reach all the buttons on my gown, but I can't. I didn't want to wait for Bettina, or wake up one of the other maids, so—so I thought I'd go to Miss Cott."

Oh God, he wanted her, and badly too. It felt as if his entire body was filled with light and lust, with hunger and desire. But he schooled himself to say, still gently, "If you like, I could help you with that."

Livia didn't move, only looked at him long and searchingly.

Finally, as if satisfied with what she had seen, she said, "Come."

She turned away and went softly into her bedchamber without waiting to see whether or not he followed.

But he did.

And went into her room.

And slowly, carefully, he closed the door behind him.

The sound of it, the little click, wood fitting neatly into wood, seemed loud in his own ears.

Livia stood a few feet away, her back to him. In the flickering golden illumination from a small candelabra on her dressing-table he saw that of the twenty or so little buttons on her gown, there were five—he actually counted them—five of them, little and white and reminding him of pearls, located just below her shoulder blades, that remained fastened.

"Are you going to lock the door?" she said, without turning around.

"Yes."

He did, with that same careful deliberation, then came up behind her, close but not touching her with any part of him. He could feel again that galvanic pulse of energy, surging between them, roiling all throughout his body like an elemental storm. He was hard, so hard, but with a sort of wonderful, willful denial he stayed where he was; and saw, with pleasure, that Livia was breathing more quickly, as if she, too, was experiencing the same rush of all-consuming desire.

She swayed a little, and he slid his arms around her, embracing her lightly. Then he pressed his lips to the warm skin of her nape, exposed by hair still upswept, and he breathed in that elusive, spicy, cinnamon-like fragrance which seemed to be uniquely hers.

"Yes," Livia said, "yes, Gabriel," and leaned against him, against his hardness. It was another way to say yes and he smiled, and with his tongue he lazily traced a path along the side of her neck, tasting, exploring. God in heaven, he could eat her up.

From outside the room a strong gust of wind sent raindrops splattering hard against the windows.

"Rain," he whispered into her ear, "again. But this time, perhaps, we might lie down together." He kissed the delicate flesh of her lobe and sent the tip of his tongue, lazy, soft, wet, to the canal of her ear, in a provocative mimicry of that other, more intimate act, that sweet joining of their bodies. A shudder rippled through her, and she pressed herself against him more firmly.

He laughed, gently, and drew back, but only to unfasten those five remaining buttons, and to slide her gown from her shoulders, where it puddled at her bare feet, leaving her in only a white petticoat, white stays, white shift. Only these few, flimsy layers of fabric. Excitement, hot and urgent, gripped him, but still with that same lack of haste he put his hands on her shoulders and turned her around to face him.

She tilted her head to look up at him. Her expression was a mixture of calmness and tension, serenity and passion. Seeing it, understanding her willingness, filled him with a wild exhilaration.

Yet he kept himself in check.

In the far reaches of his mind he marveled at his own

control, when what he really wanted to do was to rip those garments from her, grab her up, naked against him, lay her down—gently or not—onto the bed, and have her, have her until she cried out in ecstasy as she had before, in that ridiculous little shed somewhere on the road between Bath and Stanton Drew.

"You are certain?" he asked.

"Yes."

"We must be quiet."

"I know."

"I hope your bed isn't noisy."

"There's only one way to find out."

"Don't rush me," he said. "Take down your hair."

"You do it."

He slid his hands from her shoulders to lightly encircle her throat. Easily did his big hands span this fragile circumference; at once that mysterious, intoxicating energy radiated between himself and Livia and his palms felt as if they were on fire. "Are you telling me what to do?"

"Yes."

He smiled then, and began pulling out the pins and jeweled clasps that had meticulously been set in her hair. Great thick strands, chestnut, deep red, brown, gold, shining and silky, tumbled free, and he remembered how, standing in the none too clean parlor of the Spotted Hare, he had looked at her mane of hair and wondered, despite himself, what it would feel like against his skin.

And now he was going to find out.

Livia watched Gabriel intent at his task. She stood passive, both relaxed and taut, relishing his closeness and

the intimate feel of his fingers in her hair. A few minutes ago, in the hallway, she had stared up into his face.
She had known that she was in control of what would
happen next, knew that he would accept her decision,
yes or no. When they had made love before, she'd ended
up feeling ashamed, sorry. In the hallway she had asked
herself if this time, it would be different. Had things
changed between them?

She hadn't known for sure. She *hoped* so. But still
she felt as if she were standing on the edge of a very
high cliff, possibly setting herself up for a fall which
would be her undoing.

The risk was enormous.

But she was going to do it anyway.

She was going to dwell in uncertainty.

She was going to reach out and make a grab for her
future—for their future. A lovely, delicious grab.

Gabriel had finished. Her hair was completely un-
bound. It lay about her shoulders, down her back,
upon her breasts, a living mantle. He placed the clasps
and pins in a glittering heap on her dressing-table and
she was mesmerized by how slowly he did it, this tall,
broad-shouldered, muscular man moving with such
leisurely grace that a wave of pure animal lust crashed
over her, through her, and she didn't waste a single
moment denying it or fighting it or trying to think
of it with different words. How could she, when she
felt again that sweet wetness, that obvious yearning
warmth, at the very core of her?

They stood facing each other, with only inches sepa-
rating them, like partners in a dance. Only it was up to
them to choose the figures, the patterns.

Livia waited.

Rain beat hard against the windows. A log in the
fireplace snapped, settled itself.

Then Gabriel sank down on his knees before her.

And for a moment she forgot to breathe.

Still with that wonderful agonizing slowness he slid his hands to the backs of her thighs, to the sensitive skin there. He brought his mouth to her sex; it was concealed by her thin shift and petticoat, but he kissed it, kissed her, and Livia felt, with a shuddering thrill, the heat of his breath and the dampness of his tongue through the fabric.

Quickly she reached down to caress his face, his hair, but he shook his head.

"No," he said, not looking up. "Just—be."

She pulled back.

And he slid up her petticoat, bunching it up around her thighs.

There was now only her shift between them. And then his mouth—his lips, his tongue, sweet and knowing—was upon her again. Her knees began to tremble and part of her wanted to tip back her head, close her eyes, grope for something with which to support herself.

But not for the world would she interrupt this moment, or shut out the sight of Gabriel, the man she . . .

The man she loved.

The realization—the truth of it—blazed across her being, her heart and soul and body, and nearly toppled her over. And for a crazy moment she almost burst out laughing. What a time to comprehend her own feelings. And yet, why not?

Why not when he was giving to her this most exquisite pleasure?

How long had she loved this man, so handsome and clever, so arrogant and exasperating, so . . . so . . . so *good* at what he was doing to her with his mouth and hands?

Here Livia lost the train of her thought, as within her a cascade of glorious sensation built, and built—

But she wanted to wait. To delay her own conflagration, save it for later, savor it with him, together. She grasped at his hair. "Stop."

"No. You're nearly there."

"Stop. Please."

He did, and let go of her thighs as well. He looked up at her, and in the candlelight his eyes were dark pools without limit.

He said, low:

"Do you know how much power you have over me?"

"Power? What on earth are you talking about?"

"Look at me. I'm on my knees. Willingly, I might add."

"Don't be an idiot. This is not about power. Get up."

Without haste he stood up.

He was—magnificent.

Then Livia fell to her knees, caught at the fall of his buckskins, rather more expertly than she had before, and revealed him, hard and ready.

"Oh, God," he groaned.

"Be quiet!" she hissed. She sought him with her mouth but he was too tall, or she was too short: in the giddy excitement of her desire she couldn't figure it out and instead rose quickly to her feet, grasped his hands, backed toward the bed and sat on the edge.

This was better. No, it was perfect. She pulled him closer. Touched her lips to him. He was rigid. Hot. His skin there had a kind of delectable softness. She ran her tongue along him and could tell that he liked it.

Liked it very much.

Tentatively she took him into her mouth and knew that he liked that, too. She wasn't sure exactly what to do, but a kind of primal female instinct helped guide her, although more than once her teeth got in the way;

he flinched a little but didn't pull away from her. She stroked the warm globes beneath and heard him sharply draw in his breath.

Now he did pull away.

Fixed his eyes upon her.

"Clothing," he muttered, frowning. "Always too much clothing."

He ripped off his neckcloth. Gone was the languid slowness: with wonderful efficiency and speed—bordering, in fact, on savage haste—he divested himself of boots, shirt, buckskins, undergarments until he stood naked before her.

Livia stared at him in fascination. She had thought him magnificent before, but to see him like this—the hard planes of his chest, the muscled curves of biceps, his narrow hips, long rock-hard legs, the whorl of dark hair at his groin and from it springing his erect shaft—well, she would have liked to have studied him at her leisure, devoured him with her eyes, but he went to her dressing-table and quickly she said:

"What are you doing?"

"Blowing out the candles."

"Don't."

He looked at her. "No?"

"No. I want to see you."

"I am all obedience," he said, and as he returned to her, with a very purposeful air about him, she knew, vaguely, that it probably would have been more ladylike to consent to the candles being extinguished, but at the moment it was hard to care.

She gave him a small, provocative smile. "You don't look very obedient to me."

"No. It was only a figure of speech. Stand up."

"How masterful you are," she murmured, sweetly, but didn't move.

Without replying he took her arm and brought her, rather roughly, to her feet. With that same savage speed he undid the ties of her petticoat, pulled it down, and ripped her shift up over her head and tossed it aside. Now she, too, was naked.

Livia expected him to look at her in the same hungry way in which she had done to him, study her breasts and waist and hips and her own dark mound of hair at the juncture of her legs, but instead he put his hands on her shoulders and backed her to the bed. Silently he pushed her down; she sat, noticing with a little shock the smoothness of the bedcovers against her bare skin, and then Gabriel was on her: with a greater, far nicer shock she registered the feel of his warm muscled self, heavy, hard, utterly male.

She made a little purring sound in her throat, and allowed him to bring her fully onto the bed, although he stopped before her head reached the pillows, as if he couldn't wait a second more, and then he had parted her legs with his knees and with his shaft poised at her sex he stopped, although Livia had the distinct impression that it took every last ounce of self-control that he had.

A voluptuous anticipation made her feel wonderfully limp. She flung out her arms onto the bed, further emphasizing how completely open she was to him, and arched her back a little, knowing how such a gesture flaunted her breasts, full and heavy with nipples that had a lovely tingling feel to them.

"Do you . . ." she murmured, and paused. Very, very delicately she shifted her hips so that the tip of his shaft just touched the wet, warm opening of her sex. She felt Gabriel jerk a little, in a flatteringly responsive way. "Do you think it will rain tomorrow?"

He stared down at her in the dim, flickering light.

His face was very close to hers; she could see the golden flecks in his eyes. She smiled, ever so slightly.

"You," he said softly, "are a fiend."

He plunged into her and she only just stopped herself from crying out with the joy, the pure hot pleasure of it, of him, of being filled so completely by him. Urgently she grabbed at his head, pulled his mouth to her, kissed him with open lips and a tongue that sought his, all warmth and wetness.

Gabriel kissed her back, hard, not stopping in the thrust of his hips, grinding against her. Tightly she gripped him with her legs, receiving, returning. Oh, this was right, right, right. It was like a little voice within her, singing. Like her body was an instrument which he played with a devastating virtuosity. Or perhaps *he* was the instrument she played.

No, that wasn't the right way to think of it, for they were—simply, absolutely, fully—one.

Right, right, right, sang her body and her heart.

She could not have said how long it went on, this rough exquisite joining, only that they were far beyond words, and that all too soon she shattered, gasping, letting him stop her mouth with his own, and hard upon that, he gave a final thrust, shuddered, and was done.

For a few moments Gabriel lay on top of her, his long form a kind of splendid weight blanketing her. He nuzzled her with his jaw, and she could just feel the beginning growth of dark beard; then he withdrew from her, rolled onto his back, still breathing heavily.

Livia listened to this intimate sound in the darkness of her bed, smiling to herself.

Right, right, right.

Then his deep voice said:

"Livia."

"Yes, Gabriel?"

"Lift up your head for a moment."

She did, without bothering to ask why, and gently Gabriel tugged free a mass of her hair.

"Thank you."

She watched as he lay back and draped the long strands across his throat and chest.

"I was right," he said lazily.

"About what?"

"Your hair *is* like silk."

"Thank you."

"Although it's rather tangled, I regret to say."

"Whose fault is that?"

"Mine."

He looked so contented that Livia felt as if her heart might burst with her own happiness.

Right, right, right.

At length she said: "Well?"

"Well what?"

"Is the bed noisy?"

"I wasn't paying attention. Were you?"

"No," she confessed.

He turned onto his side, facing her. "Let's do it again. Only listen, won't you?"

"I'll try."

They made love, more languorously this time, just as satisfyingly, and after, when they had reluctantly disengaged and lay on their sides again, relaxed, the sweat drying on their naked bodies, she looked at him and said:

"Well?"

"Sorry. You distract me."

"Oh well."

"Let's just assume it's the quietest bed in the world."

"All right."

There was a pause, easy and comfortable. Then:

"Gabriel."

"Yes, Livia?"

"You have the nicest dimple in your chin."

"Thank you. I'm glad it pleases you."

"It does. Very much."

"I'm glad," he repeated drowsily, and in the very next moment he was fast asleep.

Chapter 14

Livia smiled, allowed her own eyelids to drift shut, but just as she was about to surrender herself to sleep as well, was brought sharply awake by a consciousness of what the morning would bring. Daylight. Servants. The need for discretion. A vision of herself and Gabriel, trying to explain to Grandmama his presence in his fiancée's bedchamber, had no redeeming qualities to it whatsoever.

Also, suddenly, she was cold. They were both lying on top of the now-rumpled bedclothes, completely naked.

"Gabriel," she said, then, still in a low voice but more forcefully: "Gabriel!"

He slept peacefully on.

Livia would have gladly sold her soul for the chance to cuddle up to him, wrap them in warm quilts, and spend the night this way, but practical considerations overrode her sybaritic self.

She pinched the skin of his upper arm, even as she admired the hard swell of muscle there. Goodness, but he was sinfully attractive.

Gabriel shifted his arm slightly but otherwise showed no signs of imminent consciousness.

As a last resort, Livia hitched herself on top of him.

This clever stratagem brought a prompt response from Gabriel, although it didn't seem likely to induce a swift departure.

He opened his eyes, smiled, slid his arms around her; within a very short time he was hard, and an answering desire threatened her worthy resolve.

"Again?" he murmured. "This is a nice position, too. If you could just slide down a bit—"

"You need to go."

At that, Gabriel stopped his horribly tempting effort to lure her into making love and glanced quickly toward the windows. "Good God, how long did I sleep?"

He looked so adorably startled that Livia couldn't help herself. She kissed him. It *was* a nice position, with her breasts pressed against his chest, and how exciting to have him, well, pinioned beneath her—even though she knew at any moment he, with his vastly superior strength, could flip her onto her back. That was *also* a nice position . . .

But then she rolled off him and scrambled underneath the covers, pulling them primly up to her neck. "Not long. But you must go, you know."

"You're right, of course." He sighed, then said soulfully: "'Night's candles are burnt out, and jocund day stands tiptoe on the misty mountain tops. I must be gone and live, or stay and die.'"

"Yes, Romeo, because otherwise Granny will kill us."

He laughed. "How right you are."

Livia watched, drinking her fill of him, as he rose, dressed, then came to the bedside where she lay, snugly warm again, under the covers. He leaned down to kiss her lightly, and said:

"'Parting is such—'"

"'—sweet sorrow,'" she finished, twinkling up at him.

"But we'll see each other very soon, after all. Granny wants to leave by nine."

He laughed again. "She *says* that, of course, but I strongly doubt we'll depart before noon. *Adieu*, my sweet."

With that, he went to blow out the last of the guttering candles on her dressing-table, and was gone, softly closing the door behind him.

Livia was so happy that sleep suddenly seemed unimaginable. She stretched luxuriously, listened for the rush of raindrops against the house, revisiting in her memory the events—the delights—of the evening. Joy, sweet joy sang within her. She felt with her hand for the spot where Gabriel had lain, but the warmth of his body was no longer there. She sighed, missing him already; then she curled onto her side and finally, finally, closed her eyes. Her last wisp of consciousness was a line from *Hamlet*.

To sleep, perchance to dream . . .

She hoped Gabriel would be in her dreams tonight.

Silently her lips formed the words, as if sending them through the ether to him:

I love you.

Later, much later, to her sleeping self came an image of a great castle, all turrets and oriels and crenelated battlements. And in the abrupt, yet curiously seamless way of the dreaming mind, she was all at once within the castle and in a long, dim corridor. Ahead of her— perhaps twenty paces away—was Gabriel.

In her dream, he looked at her and smiled, beckoning as if urging her to come to him. But then he turned away, opened a door, went inside, and was gone. She ran after him, but the door was shut; she rattled the doorknob but could not turn it, could not open the door. Frantically she looked around and for the first time realized that the walls of the corridor were filled with portraits—dozens, hundreds of portraits, large and small, all of distinguished-looking people clad elegantly in the costumes of previous centuries, surrounded by gleaming, gilded frames.

Livia knew they were long-dead Penhallows. To her unspeakable horror, as she stood there helpless and alone, the people in the portraits seemed to come alive, and they all were glaring at her.

A thousand voices whispered:

You will never be a real lady. Poor little Livia.

Where, she wondered desperately, was Gabriel?

You will never be a real lady. Poor little Livia.

She screamed out his name, but he did not come.

You will never be a real lady. Poor little Livia.

Over and over they whispered it, gaining in volume, until their voices gathered, rose, and the thundering noise of it brought her to her knees. She pressed her hands to her ears, trying, unsuccessfully, to block out these relentless voices; and finally, just when she was sure she would break into a million pieces, the corridor dissolved.

And the welcome silence of dreamless sleep claimed her.

In the morning came sunlight, blue cloudless skies, and only the lightest whisper of a breeze, cool and friendly. It was perfect traveling weather. As Livia went up and down the stairs, here and there, helping Grandmama with last-minute arrangements, it was easy to push away the eerie remnants of last night's dream, especially when she stepped into the deserted hall just as Gabriel arrived, and he smiled at her, which made her feel as sunny as the sky itself.

"Hello," he said.

Hello, she thought. What a delightful word it was. She'd never noticed that before. "Hello."

"Are you well, Livia?"

"Very well. And yourself?"

"Likewise. More than likewise. What are you doing with that pillow?"

"What?"

"I asked why you're holding that pillow."

"Oh." Livia had completely forgotten she had it in her hands. It was hard to think about pillows when Gabriel stood so close. My, he was handsome, and wasn't it nice to see him smiling at her so warmly. It occurred to her that she could get used to this.

"Livia."

"Yes?"

"The pillow."

"Oh! Granny changed her mind about bringing it. I'm taking it up to her room."

"I'll join you. Let's go this way."

He took her into the backstairs, up two flights, and behind a stairwell, where it was wonderfully dark and private and cozy.

"This," she said, teasing him, "isn't the least bit proper."

"Don't be stuffy."

"Ha!" She deepened her voice and said in an extremely pompous way, "Once given, my word is law."

"Very funny, coming from someone who would rather run away and be a scullery maid than be in proximity to my awful self."

"You know, I don't find you so awful anymore."

"I'm glad. Give me that pillow."

Obediently she handed it to him and he tossed it over his shoulder in a very dashing way. "I want to kiss you."

It was rather magical, she thought, how those five simple words, said in his lovely deep voice, could set her aflame, like a lamp tipped over and burning up everything in sight. She said:

"Well, kiss me then."

"How imperious you are." He smiled, came close, and set his hand gently under her chin. He bent and touched his lips to hers, lightly, sweetly, and it was as if her whole being rushed to meet him in his kiss. It was light, sweet, tender, caressing, demanding, and fiery hot all at once. How did he *do* that? There was absolutely no doubt about it. He was an excellent kisser. She could easily get used to this, too.

"You're too far away," she complained, and then gave a happy squeak when he caught her hard against him, deepening his kiss, and her head began to whirl in a very agreeable way.

He kissed her until she was breathless and her knees all rubbery, and she had to cling to him to keep herself upright. When finally he pulled away, she smiled up at him in the cozy dimness.

"You're so good at it. Kissing, I mean."

He laughed. "Thank you. You're quite good yourself."

"I still have a way to go. And you know what they say—practice makes perfect."

"We'll have to keep practicing at it, then. It's going to be agony to be separated at the inn tonight."

"One night," she said, in her voice a promise, "one night only, and then we'll be at the Hall."

"I can't wait to show it to you, Livia. And there's one place in particular I want you to see."

"What place is that?"

"The chapel," he said, and kissed her again, and by the time Livia returned the pillow to Grandmama's room her hair was only a trifle tousled; although the old lady's silvery brows went up, she said not a word about it, to either Livia or to her grandson, who was looking the tiniest bit rumpled himself.

Ultimately they left Bath at (true to Gabriel's prediction) midday, a cavalcade which included a big rented carriage for the servants, and Gabriel, riding on Primus, alongside Grandmama's massive coach, in which the three ladies were comfortably ensconced. Grandmama, with the faithful Muffin on her lap, was animated and cheerful. She did look a little fatigued, Livia thought, and Miss Cott was still a bit absentminded, but other than these small concerns the journey went smoothly. Livia couldn't help but gaze frequently out the window. Every glance she shared with Gabriel seemed only to set the seal on the happiness bubbling within her.

They arrived in good time at the Royal Hart in Wells, where they were met by the proprietor, Mr. Mundy, who assured them he had personally inspected their rooms to ensure that his high standards had been met. Their private parlor, also passed under his stringent eye, awaited them at their convenience, he declared, and dinner was, of course, bespoken.

Grandmama was at her most gracious, although Muffin took one of his unaccountable dislikes to Mr. Mundy and had to be sharply brought to heel. She pronounced her rooms acceptable, and for the duration of their short stay no one in their party talked about either fleas or damp sheets—although in the morning, after breakfast, Grandmama did, discreetly, ask Livia to thoroughly examine Muffin before they got back in the coach. If Livia found anything, she didn't remark upon it, and Grandmama didn't ask. Thus they embarked on the second, and last, leg of their trip with unruffled relations among them.

Livia stared eagerly out the window. Not just at
Gabriel now—although she could never tire of looking
at him—but at the countryside. Somerset, she thought,
was beautiful, with its rolling hills and vast rich grass-
lands, its winding rivers and towering woodlands. She
saw huge flocks of sheep, and cattle, too, and when they
passed by a flourishing apple orchard, Grandmama
commented nostalgically about the cider of her youth,
the apple pudding, and, best of all, apple snow, a sweet
froth of steamed apples and fine white sugar all whipped
together into soft peaks.

"Mrs. Worthing has a wonderful receipt. Cook will
make us some," she promised Livia.

As the afternoon slowly passed, Grandmama fell
into a doze and Miss Cott also closed her eyes, though
Livia did not think she slept. The gentle rhythmic swaying of the coach had a decidedly soporific effect, but she
herself was too excited to sleep. Soon, they would be at
Surmont Hall.

Great white clouds slowly massed overhead, dim-
ming the bright sunshine, and a brisk wind had picked
up. Livia watched as the clouds cast enormous shifting
shadows on fields and green hills and, feeling a chill
seep into the coach, wrapped her shawl more securely
around her. Muffin left Grandmama's lap and came to
Livia; she gathered him up in her arms.

In the distance she saw a village. Gabriel rode close,
tapped on the window. She opened it and he said:

"The coachman says that's Riverton ahead—the village closest to the Hall. We won't go through it today,
but will take a shorter track home. Only a little while
now."

She smiled and nodded, even as a cool breeze snaked
inside, ruffling their shawls and gowns. Grandmama
woke with a start.

"Oh! Riverton? Excellent! Livia, dear, do shut that window; thank you." She craned her head to better observe the view. "Look, there's the rectory, Evangeline. What was the name of that nice parson? He did give wonderful sermons."

"Mr. Markson," said Miss Cott, very quietly.

"Oh, yes, that's right. And there is the Greenlaws' manor. Dear me, it looks smaller than I remember it. They had little girls just my age when I was growing up, although I wasn't allowed to play with them, which seemed to me dreadfully unfair. Mama considered them beneath us. What *were* their names? Drusilla and . . . and Amanda! And here we come to Penhallow land at last. Do you see that crumbling old stone building, Livia? The remains of an ancient fort, dating back to the Roman era. As a girl I thought the ruins terribly romantic and would ride here frequently. And very often I would leave my groom behind. So naughty of me, and what scolds I received from Mama!"

"Where is the Hall, Granny? I can't see anything but fields and woods."

"Oh, no, we must pass by quite a number of fields before we arrive at the park. And even then it's twenty minutes or so before we reach the Hall. The estate encompasses some fifteen thousand acres of land, you know."

"Fifteen thousand?" It was an unimaginably large figure.

"Yes indeed. I wonder what's growing in these fields. If I didn't know better, I would say that they're fallow. Have you any idea, Evangeline?"

"Perhaps it's something to do with crop rotation," answered Miss Cott, but Livia observed that she looked a little uneasy; and that Grandmama, in her animation, did not seem to register the vagueness of the reply.

At length they reached the entrance to the park, a wide path flanked by thickly clustered woodland. An old stone and brick building stood to their left, of a ponderous Gothic design with its high-peaked gable topped by a complicated finial, and a large bay window supported by elaborately shaped corbels.

"There's the lodge!" said Grandmama. "But why does it look so unkempt? And why does no one come to greet us? Where is Mrs. Allard?"

"It doesn't seem as if anyone is there, Granny. See, one of the footmen has gotten down to knock, but nobody has come."

"Upon my word! This isn't the Penhallow way. I shall have to speak to Mrs. Worthing, I perceive. And Crenshaw must attend to it at once."

Their party moved forward. Livia saw that Grandmama had lost a little of her bright animation, and that Gabriel as he rode along had a slightly puzzled expression. The wide path wound its way among the trees which eventually gave way to open land and there, at last, fronted by immense swaths of grass and gardens and a huge ornamental pond, was the Hall.

"There it is," said the old lady, unnecessarily.

Livia stared.

She didn't know quite what she had expected, but it certainly wasn't this vast, looming, irregular stone structure, with numerous wings built on in a variety of architectural styles that clearly displayed a long span of centuries. Even the Glanville family, with all its wealth, had but one building in which they were housed—a mansion, to be sure, but it was as nothing compared to the sheer size of the Hall. Why, it would take hours simply walking through it. At that moment the sun emerged from behind the clouds, glinting against dozens and dozens of windows, dazzling the eye.

"Well? What do you think?"

"It's beautiful, Granny."

"Yes. I think so too." Then a sharp tone crept into the old lady's voice. "Evangeline, do you see the hedges? Why are they not clipped properly? And why is the grass so long? This is not at all what I expected."

Miss Cott murmured something indistinguishable but Grandmama went on, unheeding: "And the gravel of the carriage-drive unraked! Where are the servants to meet us?"

The coach stopped, steps were let down, the ladies handed out. Muffin, pleased to be released from confinement, frisked gaily about their skirts but was ignored. Uncertainly Livia looked from Grandmama to Gabriel, who had dismounted and stood looking about him, frowning a little. He handed Primus's reins to one of their footmen and went up the short flight of shallow steps to the porch and then to a massive door of some dark knotted wood. Imperatively he rapped the knocker but it was some minutes before his summons was answered.

Slowly the door creaked open and a diminutive woman, elderly, thin, wearing a simple homespun gown and apron and a large, not entirely clean mobcap, stood in the entranceway, dwarfed by its enormous proportions.

"May I help you, sir?" she asked timidly. "Have you come to see the family? But I'm sorry to tell you, sir, that they are not at home."

Gabriel stared down at her, more perturbed than he cared to admit. Why had he thought he'd be instantly recognized as master of the Hall? But, more important, where was the rest of the staff? Why was a feeble old woman left to grapple with the massive door?

"Mrs. Worthing!" Grandmama came forward, half pleased, half angry.

The old woman in the doorway dipped a stiff little curtsy and Gabriel fancied he could hear her knees crackling. "Good day, ma'am. What a pleasure to see you. Pray won't you come inside at once?" She tried to push the door open more widely and quickly Gabriel helped her. She smiled up at him and said:

"Thank you, sir! Oh, if you'll forgive me, sir, you have such a look of Mr. Henry, the master! But he is not at home. Nor is the mistress. I don't know where they've gone, but I'm certain they'll return soon, for there's to be a ball tonight. Please, do come in, and I'll ring for tea."

She led the way inside and, Gabriel, exchanging a deeply troubled look with Grandmama, followed her into the Great Hall. This gargantuan chamber he did recall from childhood, specifically his intense fascination with the suits of armor poised upright on either side of a fireplace so large that cattle could be—and probably had been, in earlier times—roasted in it wholesale, as well as with the impressive display of old weapons set upon the wall, the swords and spears and pikes and daggers and shields, all of them wonderfully lethal-looking and very exciting to the imagination of a little boy who used to pretend he was a knight of the Round Table, or a soldier defending the place against invaders.

Good Lord, he hadn't thought about that in decades. A sudden memory of himself, tearing through the hall, brandishing a large stick and screeching at the top of his lungs, floated across his mind, and he smiled faintly.

"Gabriel!"

He blinked, realized he had been staring absently at the family coat of arms carved into the chimney piece—featuring prominently upon it the words *Et honorem, et gloriam*—and turned to see that his grandmother was now visibly distraught.

He glanced around the Great Hall and it was easy to see why. The dirt, the dust, the disorder was everywhere. Livia, standing as if frozen, looked shocked. He saw that trailing upon the hem of her gown was a clump of gray dust and it was this single detail that sent a jolt of anger blazing through him: this was not how he had envisioned introducing her to his birthplace. What in the devil's name was going on here?

Mrs. Worthing had gone to tug at the shabby bell-pull and cheerfully she said, "Would you care to go into the Little Drawing-room? I'll bring your tea to you in there." Then a look of confusion clouded her face and she added, tentatively, "Or do I mean the Rose Saloon? And it's not I who should be carrying the tray, should I? My, my, where is Mrs. Adelaide to set me straight? Oh, I do hope I haven't made a mistake, I would not like to be reprimanded." Her wandering gaze settled on Livia and swiftly she dipped another creaky curtsy. "Good day, miss! You've come to call on Miss Henrietta? I'm very sorry, miss, but she's gone away to London. She's to make her *début*, you see, and she barely seventeen! The prettiest lass in Somerset, if I may be so bold as to say so!"

"Mrs. Worthing," Grandmama broke in, "did you not receive my letter?"

"Oh! A letter!" The old woman felt at once in the pocket of her apron and pulled out a crumpled paper, the wafer still intact. "Here it is, ma'am," she said proudly, and came forward to hand it over to Grandmama. Then she peered more closely at her and abruptly brightened. "Why, Miss Henrietta, it's you! A young lady came to call on you, miss, while you were gone. Such a pretty young lady, too, with lovely auburn hair, but she ran away before I could get her name."

"Mrs. Worthing, where are the other servants?"

It was clear that his grandmother was trying to speak gently despite her flabbergasted duress, but her whole slender frame was so rigidly taut it seemed as if she might, at any moment, snap in two.

"The servants?" The housekeeper shook her head, as if to clear it. "We haven't many, ma'am, for they've left and gone. Gone, gone, gone."

"Gone? What do you mean?"

"So shall ye sow, so shall ye reap," answered Mrs. Worthing. "That Mrs. Adelaide was a hard, hard mistress. Not like yourself, ma'am." The confused expression came upon her again, and she faltered, "It *is* you, Miss Henrietta, isn't it? Come to set us all straight again? That Mrs. Adelaide—why, she would not let me make broth in the winter for the poor folk! I *told* her it was the Penhallow way, but she said it was wasteful, miss." Then she reached out with gnarled hands, to urgently grasp at Grandmama's gloved ones. "But where is Mr. Richard? He went a-riding, Mrs. Henrietta, went a-riding yesterday and we have not seen him since. His tea is getting cold."

Aghast, her face as white as if a ghost had come upon her, Grandmama tried to step away from Mrs. Worthing, but the housekeeper's grip was so startlingly strong that she was plainly trapped. Then Livia was there, her own hands upon those of Mrs. Worthing, coaxing them away, her voice saying softly:

"You need not worry, Mrs. Worthing, all is well."

Immediately Mrs. Worthing smiled and released Grandmama, who dropped the crumpled letter onto the floor. Mrs. Worthing picked it up and tucked it into her apron. "My letter! I'll be saving that until Mrs. Adelaide comes home."

"Yes, yes, to be sure," said Livia soothingly, then looked sharply at Gabriel, with a little jerk of her chin indicating his grandmother. At once he went to place his arm around her and lead her to the nearest chair, disgracefully dusty, but the old lady sank down upon it without seeming to notice.

He straightened up but she clutched at his arm.

"Gabriel, Gabriel," she said in a low, harsh voice, "what is happening here?" She looked so bewildered, so devastated, that his heart went out to her. He was just as disconcerted as his grandmother and as he swept the cold, dirty, draughty room with a frowning glance, he saw that Miss Cott, for once, seemed at a loss as well, standing as if in a daze, her eyes wide and her hands convulsively gripping the strings of her reticule.

It was Livia who took charge.

She brought in the servants who had accompanied them from Bath, and set them to work: the Rose Saloon to be quickly dusted, Holland covers removed, a fire lit, Grandmama and Miss Cott escorted there, tea prepared—makeshift, skimpy, but better than nothing—and served to them.

Bedchambers were hastily cleaned, linens inspected and shaken, pillows plumped, and fires lit there too.

Meanwhile Livia had Gabriel go off to the stables, where a groom of sorts was found, Little Walter he was called. He was a big, shambling man, a nephew of Mrs. Worthing, slow in faculty but eager to help; provisions were scrambled together for the horses, enough, at least, to see them through till morning.

While Little Walter then obligingly went to the henhouse, to produce and efficiently dispatch a pair of chickens, two of the footmen from Bath were sent to the village for food, as the kitchen larder was nearly empty. When they returned, she reviewed their purchases and found, to her relief, that Mrs. Worthing, though her wits were sadly addled, was still able to cook, and with some of the Bath servants assigned to assist her, Livia was able to leave the kitchen with a degree of assurance that everyone would have a decent meal tonight, and breakfast tomorrow morning.

She ran upstairs to look at the bedchambers, getting badly lost on the way there. She had to make her way through what felt like miles of dim corridors, innumerable staircases both long and short, rooms that led straight through from one to the other; as she hurried she caught glimpses of old-fashioned furniture that had been left uncovered, beds beyond counting, magnificent drapery, chandeliers, little tables, large tables, sofas and chairs, escritoires, ornate chests of drawers, washstands, armoires big enough to hold thirty gowns or more. Once she caught her heel in the ragged hole of a once-beautiful Oriental rug and nearly fell. If she hadn't been so focused on what had to be done, she might have felt keenly the eerie abandoned quality of the house, been unnerved by the labyrinth through which she hastened. It was the look on Gabriel's face, and that of Grandmama and Miss Cott, too, that propelled her into action: they all seemed as if they had been dealt a physical blow.

They were stunned, and they were hurting.

She would do anything to help them.

She wished she could have gone to Gabriel, put her arms around him, smoothed away the deep crease between his brows.

Told him she loved him, and that it would be all right.

They had stumbled, unexpectedly, into a dark mystery here, but she would gladly throw herself, heart and soul, into solving it; resolving it.

She would work day and night if necessary.

Anything to take away that stunned, lost look in Gabriel's eyes.

The bedchambers, she was thankful to see, would do for the night. The fires now burning, warm and bright, in their hearths were already banishing the musty chill, and the bedclothes, while obviously needing a good laundering, at least were sufficient.

Gabriel had, very properly, been given what was clearly the suite of apartments for the Hall's master. His bedroom was immense. Set upon a dais, the bed was contained within four great, carved mahogany posts and a stately canopy above, and was so capacious that Livia stifled a sudden giggle at the thought of herself and Gabriel within it.

A tempting thought occurred to her: to seek him out tonight, if only to offer the comfort of her arms, and nothing more if he wished it.

And if he wanted more?

Why, she would say yes, and joyfully, too.

Their time together in Bath—the day before yesterday—already seemed too far away.

Perhaps, later, she could slip out of her bedchamber and come here, and with her body, her self, make that enormous expanse of bed feel a little smaller, and more intimate?

But no, she dared not.

It was anyone's guess as to how well they would sleep tonight. And what if Grandmama or Miss Cott should need her?

It was a risk she couldn't take.

Livia sighed, and straightened the pillows on Gabriel's bed. Then, with a final glance around, she left his bedchamber and began to retrace her steps.

As she walked quickly through the rooms and along the passageways, up and down the stairs, gradually, quietly, there came to her a feeling for, a sense of Surmont Hall. The possibilities of the place. It was a revelation; an inspiration. Once freed from the neglect of who knew how many years, the dirt and cobwebs cleared away, rugs mended, furniture polished, curtains drawn back . . .

Hedges trimmed, grass cut, the ornamental pond filled again . . .

Why, it would be magnificent.

Not a museum—no, never that.

Not a building intended merely as a display of wealth and culture and generations of inhabitation.

But as a place to live, laugh, love . . .

Livia could not have said how this idea blossomed in her mind.

It was audacious, it was far-fetched; she was a stranger here.

Yet it was almost as if the Hall whispered to her, as if there was some kind of subtle magic to it.

Something that could be felt, if not seen, about its potential.

She just knew.

Knew that here was a place that could be home.

Home.

She rolled the word around in her mind but it found its truest expression in her heart. Perhaps, at last, those long, lonely years could be swept away from her memory, from her spirit, like a cobweb brushed away, making space for—

For something new, something better.

Something to last a lifetime and beyond.

Love, laughter, family, home.

With Gabriel, ever and always, at the center of it all.

Livia hurried her steps, eager to be with him again.

When finally she arrived in the Rose Saloon, she found him there, along with Grandmama and Miss Cott. Gabriel was standing near the fireplace, one arm on the mantel, his eyes, somber and remote, fixed upon the leaping flames. Grandmama still looked stunned; her face was drawn and she seemed desperately tired, and her greeting to Livia was but a brief nod of her head. By her side on the sofa, even Muffin appeared to have caught the mood of the room and lay curled up in a tight ball. Miss Cott, fatigue writ plain upon her, nonetheless was quick to offer Livia some tea.

Gratefully Livia accepted. The tea was weak and stale, and the bread far from fresh, but she was, she now realized, ravenously hungry. The butter, at least, was delicious, and she spread it lavishly upon her bread.

As she ate, she became aware of the silence hanging heavy in the air. It wasn't the normal quiet of fatigued travelers; how could it be, she wondered, gazing at the others. There was no eye contact among them, as if they were isolated, alone, wrapped in individual misery. Gabriel had looked at her once or twice, but without a smile, and his gaze did not linger upon her, only returning to the flames crackling—with incongruous cheerfulness—in the fireplace, radiating warmth into the room.

Finally Grandmama spoke.

"I have, I see, been living in a dream."

No one answered. But it was as if she didn't expect a reply, for she went on, stonily:

"Twenty years have gone by. Mrs. Worthing has passed into her dotage. For all I know, good Mrs. Allard, a most faithful lodgekeeper, lies in her grave. And I am the greatest fool in Christendom. I have stupidly, arrogantly, cherished an idea of the Hall which is false, laughably false—as if time would stop for me while I dallied all those years in Bath. My God! My own stupidity amazes me."

"Granny," said Livia gently, "how could you have known?"

The old lady glared at her. "How could I have known? I should have been here! Instead I traipsed off to Bath, with concern only for myself. Selfish, selfish!"

"Traipsing? Hardly that, Granny! Did not you tell us—you told us about—about Richard—Adelaide—"

"It was selfishness, I see that now. The most arrant, appalling self-indulgence! I am disgusted with myself." Her face was set in rigid lines, and she stared straight ahead, as if looking into her own private version of hell. "I had known Mrs. Allard all my life. The Allards have always lived in the lodge. She had a kind word for everybody, whether great or small. And even though she lost three of her five children as stillbirths—three!—she still made baby clothes for the poorest cottagers."

Another silence fell, broken only when Grandmama said, in that same stony voice:

"If you will be so good, Gabriel, as to help me to my room. I am going to bed."

It was then that Livia saw Grandmama's uneaten slice of bread-and-butter, a teacup still full.

"Granny, are you not hungry? Won't you eat a little something?"

"No."

"Would you like something for dinner, on a tray?"

"No. If that rotted bell-pull still works, you may ring for Bettina, and send her up to me. Thank you," she said coldly, formally, to Gabriel, who assisted her to stand, and Livia watched with concern as the old lady staggered slightly, and then almost seemed to limp out of the room as she clung to Gabriel's arm, apparently having completely forgotten Muffin, who trotted after her, but without his earlier gaiety, his funny little tail wagging with a new tentativeness.

Miss Cott rose to her feet. "If you will excuse me, I shall go with Mrs. Penhallow," she said to Livia.

"Will you come down for dinner?"

"No, thank you."

"May I have a tray sent up?"

"No, I thank you," said the older woman, with the faintest of tired smiles, and hurried after the others.

Alone in the Rose Saloon, Livia helped herself to another slice of bread and butter and poured another cup of tea. As she ate she looked thoughtfully around the room. There was a real, if dated, charm to the wallpaper, a soft muted pink with a repeated motif of roses and pretty little birds, as well as to the chairs and sofas, with upholstery in the same shade of pink—faded, to be sure, but still pleasing to the eye.

It was easy to imagine Grandmama as she then would have been, a youthful, vigorous matron, head over heels in love with her dashing husband, enjoying a cozy tea here with him, perhaps with their young children romping about.

A little tired now, but comfortably warm, Livia leaned back against the plush cushions of the sofa on which she sat, her eyes drifting to the dancing fire, as Gabriel's had done. She slipped without effort into a daydream, her fancy luxuriously fashioning an image of the Rose Saloon, a clean and orderly room again, and she a young matron herself, indubitably a proper lady, presiding gracefully over the tea table.

Gabriel was there, exchanging with her a loving smile. How handsome he was, her—

Yes, her husband.

Husband.

What a beautiful word.

In her fancy she added to his left hand a gold ring.

Then she added one to her own left hand, and admired its elegant gleam as if from afar.

How happy they were together! And . . . there were

children with them. Hers and Gabriel's. They had three children—no, four.

Four would be the perfect number. Two boys and two girls, healthy, happy, clever . . . filling the room with laughter and joy.

With the infinite scope of imagination she brought Granny and Miss Cott into the scene; Muffin, too, and a cat (she made sure they got along), a big, fat striped tabby which purred in a loud contented way.

She dwelled on this vision for some time, dreamily aware that she was waiting for Gabriel to return. They would be alone here in the Rose Saloon. They could shut the door, and snatch a few private moments together. She missed him with an ache that was physical, and only being near him, held in his arms, enveloped, kissed, would answer.

But Gabriel did not come.

Instead, one of the servants from Bath, Sally, came to the door, to let her know that dinner would soon be ready, and how many places would need to be set, and where? And could she take away the tea things?

Livia's mood of relaxed drowsiness had dissipated. "Yes, please do, Sally, thank you," she said, standing up. "As for where dinner is to be served, there's no need to make ready that enormous dining-room. Perhaps the breakfast-parlor? But I'd like to send someone to inquire after Mr. Gabriel. Is James about?"

"Yes, Miss Livia, he's in the kitchen, helping Mrs. Worthing bring down some of her big cooking pots."

"I'll come with you. I'd like to see how Mrs. Worthing does."

In the massive old-fashioned kitchen was well-organized bustle, a small crowd of servants busy at their work and the appetizing smells of broiling chicken and roasted potatoes filling the air. Livia sent James to inquire after Gabriel; he returned in due course to say that Mr. Gabriel wished for a tray to be sent up, and a bottle of brandy too, if one could be found.

Trying not to feel hurt, Livia gave instructions for a tray to be prepared, and also gave James permission to search for the brandy. She inquired after the servants' accommodations, and was satisfied that they, too, would be reasonably comfortable tonight.

Suddenly and sharply assailed by a painful loneliness, Livia would have liked to have lingered in the warm conviviality of the kitchen, even joined the servants at the long wooden table for their meal, but realized that they would be made uneasy by such familiarity.

You'll never be a real lady, you know. Not like me. Poor little Livia. I feel so sorry for you.

The sweet, insidious voice of Cecily Orr snaked through her mind, like a horrid weed that one could pull up, but which would always grow back, and with sinister rapidity.

Poor little Livia.

I feel so sorry for you.

Livia tried to shake off an abrupt feeling of melancholy, and told Sally not to bother setting a place for her in the breakfast-parlor, which would need to be at least cursorily cleaned. She too would take a tray in her room.

Chapter 15

That night, in his room, in a bedchamber fit for a king, Gabriel got a little drunk.

Actually, more than a little.

The footman James had brought him his dinner and a bottle of brandy.

His meal was surprisingly good, given the circumstances, but the brandy was even better.

He sat holding up the heavy rounded glass to the shifting light of the fire, admiring the handsome amber color swirling within. Who among his antecedents, he wondered, had chosen and bought the bottle sitting on a table by his side?

Could it have been his father, the late Henry Penhallow? Or perhaps his grandfather, the late Richard Penhallow? Or Grandmama's father—he had no idea what *his* first name was—the late so-and-so Penhallow?

Late, late, late.

Gabriel swallowed in a gulp what was left in his snifter and refilled it, then leaned back, welcoming the sensation of warm haziness spreading throughout his limbs, worming its way into his tired brain, forcing it to slow, quiet, and, he hoped, cease its rapid bewildered workings.

Late, late, late.

They were late and *he* was late.

How was he any different from Grandmama? Callous young fool that he had been, he had ignored his patrimony, wasted his time in Society, gone gallivanting off with the Diplomatic Corps.

So shall ye sow, so shall ye reap, poor old Mrs. Worthing had said. Very like a character from Shakespeare, Gabriel now thought, a bitter smile twisting his lips. Not one of the Bard's great heroines, to be sure, but a minor role, one in which melancholy prophetical commentary, tinged by a stroke of interesting madness, served to highlight the tragic action of the play.

I have been living in a dream, Grandmama had said, with obvious self-loathing.

Apparently, so had he.

Only a few days ago, while still in Bath, he had entertained himself with idle speculation. Oh, yes, he'd be hosting hunting parties with his friends, and with little else to do he'd take up horse-breeding.

What a joke. *He* was a joke.

Horse-breeding.

He had been to the stables and seen what a deplorable condition they were in. They'd be lucky if the roof didn't collapse and injure the horses. Laborers were needed at once. Tomorrow. His hands clenched and he nearly snapped the stem of the snifter. If it weren't impossible due to the darkness and his own ignorance of where tools and supplies might be, he'd go out there right now and start the repairs himself.

If there were any tools and supplies.

It was all so difficult to understand. There was money aplenty. He himself, upon attaining his majority, had inherited from his mother's estate a very handsome income and he had never once touched monies deriving from Surmont Hall. Vividly did Gabriel recall his brief interview with Mr. Farris, the family's man of business, when he had turned twenty-one. He had sat in Farris's London offices, furnished with discreet good taste betokening the firm's longstanding competence and success. In a dry, precise way, Farris had informed him as to the extent of his income, and how things stood with the Hall's estate. Yes, there was plenty of money—a king's ransom, one might say.

Just that it hadn't, apparently, been spent.

He was late, all right.

Years too late.

An unfamiliar emotion—sharp, unpleasant, as if his heart burned rankly within—gripped him and it took him a few moments to realize that it was shame.

It almost made him glad his father and grandfather were dead, that they were spared the knowledge that Gabriel Penhallow, the illustrious scion of the family, was a fool and a wastrel.

The image of Livia standing in the Great Hall, her face shocked, an ugly clump of dust trailing upon the hem of her gown, came to him again and his shame intensified.

How could she possibly respect him? Especially when he didn't respect himself: who *could* respect a man who had abandoned his responsibilities so grossly?

Tomorrow he'd send for Mr. Farris. And find Eccles the bailiff. And see for himself just how bad things were, both throughout the Hall and on the estate.

Tomorrow was going to be quite a day. Yes indeed.

Gabriel took in a deep breath of air and slowly released it. He looked slowly around the unfamiliar room.

It had been occupied, once, by his father and mother. And by his grandparents. And so on and so forth, generations of Penhallows, stretching back into the mists of time. If he were a fanciful sort, he might conjure the shades of his ancestors, perhaps gathering in this very room, despising him, despairing of him, laughing at him.

Gabriel drank some more brandy.

It was a good thing, he thought wearily, that he wasn't prone to such sick fancies.

Besides, his own disgust with himself was more than enough.

His gaze settled upon the bed.

Good God, what a joke. You could put a whale in there and still have room. Room for Jonah, too, who was, after all, a fool to try and escape what was expected of him.

Gabriel laughed, the sound seeming loud in his own ears; he half-expected a sonorous echo of it bouncing off the walls.

Instead there was only silence again—in its own way a loud, booming sort of silence. It seemed to descend upon him like a heavy weight, intent on crushing him. Abruptly Gabriel stood, took a hasty step toward the door, a rush of blind urgent need propelling him toward Livia.

And then he laughed again.

Sat down again.

Picked up the brandy bottle again.

He didn't even know where Livia's room was.

Given the way he was feeling about himself right now, he didn't think he could even meet her eyes, let alone do what he wanted to do, which was to kiss her, hold her, love her.

I have been living in a dream.

"'A dream itself is but a shadow,'" he muttered out loud, mocking himself with a line from *Hamlet*. How annoyingly apropos was the Bard—that clever, dead old bastard—with an aphorism for every occasion, evidently. Including the one in which a man discovers, much to his surprise, that he is a joke to himself and to the world.

And then Gabriel poured himself another drink.

In the morning Livia was more than a little amazed to realize that she had slept soundly. She had anticipated wakefulness, restlessness—nothing but broken sleep—but the obverse had been true. Perhaps it had been her own exhaustion. She woke not long after dawn, and let consciousness of her surroundings slowly seep in. Here she was at Surmont Hall. Gabriel, her love, was here, not far away. Still asleep, or like herself awake? And, perhaps, thinking of her? She would see him soon.

Soon, soon, soon, sang a happy little voice inside her.

With glad anticipation Livia smiled, stretched luxuriously; then, eagerly, she got out of bed, dressed, and went down to the kitchen, where fresh bustle awaited her. Mrs. Worthing, who had been inspecting a basket of eggs, came cheerfully to greet her.

"Good morning, Miss—Miss—" Her brow furrowed, and she peered closely at Livia. "Are you a guest of the family, miss?"

Sally the maidservant swept by with a large pitcher, then paused. "That's Miss Livia, ma'am," she said, already on good terms with the old housekeeper and obviously conversant with her malady. "She's to marry Mr. Penhallow, you see."

"Mr. Penhallow?" Mrs. Worthing gaped in astonishment at Livia. "But she can't! He is already married, to Mrs. Adelaide!"

"It's Mr. *Gabriel* Penhallow she's to wed, ma'am," Sally explained.

"But . . . but he is only a child of five! I just made a pudding for Nanny to take up with her to the nursery!'"

"Now ma'am, don't get yourself into a fret," coaxed Sally, "he's the grown gentleman who came by for a cup of coffee a little while ago, don't you remember that? That's our Mr. Gabriel."

To Livia's relief Mrs. Worthing's brow cleared and she nodded complacently. "Oh yes, and so handsome! He has quite the look of Mr. Henry, you know. And so you're his wife, Mrs. Livia! What a pleasure it was to see the two of you together at the ball last night! But— but why are you here, Mrs. Livia? Mrs. Adelaide *never* comes into the kitchen, to be sure! Is it Nanny you're looking for? Is she not in the nursery with your little ones? I just made a nice pudding for her to take up. Oh dear, could it be that something is wrong? You should not be here, Mrs. Livia."

Livia hesitated, not wishing to agitate the old woman by her presence. She was thankful when Sally came close and said:

"Oh, ma'am, won't you show me the eggs you'd like to have boiled?"

She drew Mrs. Worthing away, distracting her easily. Thank heavens, thought Livia. When James the footman stepped into the kitchen, bringing with him an armful of wood, she turned to him with relief.

"James," she said, "where is Mr. Gabriel?"

"As to that I don't know, miss," replied James, "except that he gave orders for his horse to be saddled and that nobody should expect him back until late."

"Oh, I see. Thank you." Conscious again of that odd feeling of hurt, Livia made herself shrug it off. Naturally Gabriel wanted to look over the estate. And there certainly was plenty for her to do this morning.

"Will you be wanting breakfast, miss?" asked Sally.

"Breakfast? Yes, thank you, Sally, I'll take it in the breakfast-parlor."

Afterwards, Livia made her way back to the wing in which the family's rooms were located.

She tapped first on the door to Miss Cott's bedchamber. It was promptly opened and Livia saw that the older woman's face was still tired and wan. Quickly she asked:

"Did you not pass a good night?"

Miss Cott shook her head. "Mrs. Penhallow did not, and asked for me."

"I'm so sorry. I would have gladly helped."

"Thank you. But it was myself she asked for," gently answered Miss Cott.

"Oh. Yes. I—I came to see if you and Granny were coming down to breakfast."

"Mrs. Penhallow does not wish to. If you could have trays sent up to us, however, I would so appreciate it. The bell-pulls seem to be broken."

"Of course. But is Granny ill? Did she have a relapse?"

Miss Cott shook her head again. "No. But she doesn't wish to be disturbed."

"Oh. Very well. I won't bother her then." Livia looked into those tired, kind eyes, aware, suddenly, of feeling a new awkwardness, and she had to keep herself from twisting her fingers together like a child. "I'll—I'll go and see about those trays."

She hurried back downstairs and only peeped into the kitchen, careful not to upset Mrs. Worthing, and spoke with Sally, who promised to begin preparing breakfast trays at once.

Her immediate responsibility thus discharged, Livia then focused on her next tasks: organizing meals and deciding what needed most urgently to be cleaned. She went through the Rose Saloon again, then the breakfast-parlor, the dining-parlor, the drawing-room, making lists and notes. She stared around the library, marveling at its faded elegance and at the hundreds—maybe thousands—of books it contained. She went on to the ballroom, the old conservatory, and finally the sunny stillroom, imbued with the pleasant scents of lemon and basil and lavender, where she spent a happy hour looking through, and tidying, receipts, jars of herbs, bottles filled with mysterious liquids, iron pots large and small, a set of handsome wood mortars and pestles.

She was sniffing curiously at one of the bottles, half full of what seemed to be an orange-infused liqueur, when Sally came to the doorway and said:

"There's a gentleman come to call, Miss Livia. Will you see him? I've taken him to that monstrous big drawing-room, and dusted off some chairs, and had a fire lit. I do hope I did right, miss?"

"Yes, I'm sure that's fine, Sally." Livia put down the bottle and corked it again, then stood uncertainly for a moment. There was no one else to receive this caller. "Did he tell you his name?"

"Yes, miss, it's Mr. Markson."

"Thank you, Sally. I'll go directly." Yesterday, driving past the rectory, Grandmama and Miss Cott had mentioned a Mr. Markson. As Livia made her way to the drawing-room, she wondered if this was the same parson, or a different Mr. Markson. Perhaps his son? Everything was so topsy-turvy. Anything seemed possible.

Standing near the window, gazing out at the vista of carriage sweep, pond, neglected gardens, and beyond, was an elderly gentleman of medium height, a little stooped, clad in simple black knee-breeches, stockings, and coat. He turned quickly at the sound of Livia's footsteps, and she saw that he was balding, with a high broad scholar's forehead and the kindest-looking face she had ever seen.

Smilingly he came forward to take her outstretched hand. "How do you do?" he said in a quiet, cultured voice. "I am Arthur Markson, the rector. I heard that the family was in residence and came at once to see if I might be of assistance."

There was something so warmly reassuring about Mr. Markson that she immediately smiled back. "How do you do, sir? I'm Livia Stuart, Gabriel Penhallow's fiancée."

"What wonderful news. May I offer my congratulations, Miss Stuart?"

"Thank you, sir. Won't you be seated? And may I ring for some refreshments?"

He sat when she did, but declined her offer. "I look forward to renewing my acquaintance with Mr. Penhallow. He was a little boy when last I saw him, and we parted under such sad circumstances."

"After his parents died?"

"Yes. Mrs. Penhallow took him away, to Bath. And—Miss Cott accompanied them. If I may be so bold as to inquire, Miss Stuart—I heard that a Miss Cott is one of your party. This is Miss *Evangeline* Cott?"

"Yes, sir. You are acquainted with her, no doubt?" Livia saw that the rector had leaned forward, as if straining to hear her response.

"Yes, we are old—acquaintances. She is well, I hope? And Mrs. Penhallow also, of course?"

"They both are well, although fatigued by travel, and by . . ." Livia hesitated. "They've both suffered a shock, I'm afraid. They were expecting things to be—in a better state than they are."

Mr. Markson sighed. "Yes. I've been an unwilling

witness to the decay, the troubles, of these past years. Unfortunately, the difficulties began even prior to the deaths of Mr. and Mrs. Penhallow. The *current* Mr. Penhallow's parents, you know."

"Did it have something to do with Mrs. Adelaide?" Livia asked, carefully. "Forgive me if I'm jumping to conclusions. Mrs. Worthing mentioned something about her unwillingness to provide soup—broth?—and I wondered—but Mrs. Worthing's memory is—well, it's unreliable."

"I do know. Old age has come hard upon her, the poor soul. As for Mrs. Adelaide Penhallow, it is true about the broth. You are familiar with this custom?"

"No." As if Uncle Charles would spend a penny on charitable endeavors.

"During the winter months, it's long been the custom here that the Hall provides a broth for the poorest folks among us. More a hearty beef stew, really, and quite sustaining if their own stores run low. It was always something they could rely upon."

"Mrs. Adelaide discontinued the custom?"

"I'm afraid so. She was not—well, she was not popular with the people here, the farmers and the villagers, I mean. I don't wish to judge the dead, nor is it my place to comment further. I can only say that in the aftermath of their deaths, and of the many others of those afflicted with typhus, that sentiment here was not positive. The long absence of the Penhallow family has created a good deal of hardship among the people here. I've done what I can, of course, but as rector one can only do so much."

"Yes. I understand."

Their conversation shifted to more general topics, and by the time Mr. Markson left some twenty minutes later, Livia felt she had made a friend. He was so learned, so pleasant and easy to talk to; clearly he cared a great deal about his parishioners. The Hall, and Riverton, were lucky to have him, she thought.

Livia then flitted about the house, stopping briefly into the kitchen, exploring the enormous subterranean room where the laundresses would work, a billiards room, other saloons she hadn't yet seen. She'd have liked to prowl along the Picture Gallery, within a long, long corridor, just as Grandmama had said. But she promised herself the treat when she was less busy and instead went to Miss Cott's room, where she tapped on the door but received no answer.

She waited, uncertainly, looked at Grandmama's door, then went away again. She would send Sally up later, to inquire about meals. At midday she took a solitary nuncheon, wondering where Gabriel was and how he was faring. Just as she was finishing, she heard the sounds of carriages arriving and hurried to the carriage sweep where, at last, the other servants from Bath had arrived—a somewhat bedraggled group, as she quickly discovered, for the flux had spread among them and the footman who had sprained his wrist most unfortunately ending up the one to suffer the worst of it. Even dignified Crenshaw had succumbed.

Luckily there were enough of the able-bodied among them to help the less robust into the Hall and to their accommodations. The unloading of the wagons, filled with household goods, would have to wait, and Livia was fully occupied dealing with the hired drivers and their carriages, showing Cook (thank goodness, fully recovered) to the kitchen and quietly, along the way, explaining the circumstances of Mrs. Worthing. Making arrangements for the ill servants to be nursed. Sending to the village for additional supplies. The hours passed quickly, so quickly that the night came upon her before she knew it, and she was in bed again, very tired, but happy.

A new life was opening up for her. Here was work for her that was interesting, meaningful, valuable.

She was already feeling at home in the Hall.

And tomorrow she would see Gabriel, without fail.

But she didn't see him.

If she hadn't known better, she might have thought he was deliberately avoiding her. That was ridiculous, of course; if he had half as much to do as she did, he had his hands full.

Still, his absence began to feel like a physical thing, like a presence dogging her steps everywhere as she hurried about the house.

A Mr. Farris from London came and went. The ill servants recovered, one by one, and Crenshaw assumed command of the staff. Mr. Markson stopped by with a friendly word. Mrs. Worthing, addled and uncertain, gratefully gave way to Cook's authority in the kitchen.

But Grandmama remained closeted in her room, with Miss Cott in attendance upon her.

And Gabriel was nowhere to be found.

An odd, uncomfortable feeling crept into Livia's heart. It was one she had hoped never to feel again.

Loneliness.

One evening, before getting ready for bed, she took her candle and went quietly along the passageway to Gabriel's bedchamber. She took a deep breath, looked left and right, then knocked softly on Gabriel's door.

Silence.

Unbroken silence, seeming to hang suspended in the air.

Feeling like an intruder, Livia opened the door and slipped inside.

The light of her candle illuminated an empty room.

Gabriel was not in the bed; it was neatly made. There were no books, no brushes, no razors, no trousers or body linen draped across the wooden clothes horse set near the fireplace; the hearth was cold and dead. There were no signs of any occupation whatsoever.

Where was he?

That same chilly, desolate sensation wove its tendrils more tightly about her heart.

Quickly, quietly, Livia went back to her bedroom. She undressed, got into bed, blew out the candle, but it was a long, long time before she slept.

The tumbledown condition of the stables had certainly been an omen of things to come, but it was even worse than Gabriel could have anticipated as he rode, day after day, across the vast estate. *His* estate: fields lying fallow, timber uncut and overgrown, cottages rotting, surly and suspicious villagers whose greetings were, at best, perfunctory. And who could blame them? He was a stranger to them.

On the morning after their arrival he had sought out Eccles, the bailiff, whom he'd found morosely eyeing a herd of cows grazing in a pasture. He was middle-aged, short, round, as tough as shoe leather. At his side was a young man, as alike him as a pea in a pod, although with black hair, untouched by gray; Eccles introduced him as his son, Young Eccles, this moniker doubtless being the one by which he would be known all his life.

When questioned about the state of things, Eccles

was inclined to be defensive. He had done everything he could, using time-honored methods which, he added pugnaciously, were the best—despite the rash attempts of Young Eccles to interfere.

"He's after me to bring in the Rotherham plow!" said Eccles with a contemptuous glance at his son. "Land drains, rotating in turnips and clover, interbreeding the sheep! If I ever heard such rubbish! The old ways suited my pa, and *his* pa before him!"

Young Eccles then broke in with an impassioned speech—peppered with references to the Norfolk System, convertible husbandry, and the critical value of the Dutch mouldboard, none of which Gabriel understood—which his sire ferociously overrode, sparking a loud debate between them, one which might have resulted in actual blows if Gabriel had not hastily intervened.

His interview with his man of business, Mr. Farris, was conducted in more temperate language but wasn't very pleasant either. Gabriel was relieved to learn that the estate's income hadn't dwindled away to nothing, and that there were ample funds with which to repair and improve.

He'd been right. The money had been there all along, but there had been no one to see that it was properly disbursed.

"You remain an exceedingly wealthy gentleman," said Mr. Farris with his dry precision, "and may rest assured that you will continue to rejoice in this status. I trust I may now return to London, having relayed to you the news of your financial situation?"

"Yes. But—" Gabriel glanced around the study which he had appropriated for his own. It had an excellent view to the back of the Hall. If, that is, one enjoyed a panorama of untended shrubberies and gardens, grass as high as one's waist, and old benches that would likely give way if one sat on them. Inside, while the room was now reasonably clean, it still had a distinct and rather melancholy air of disuse. Gabriel went on: "I wish you'd informed me, at any time these past several years, that the estate was suffering in my absence."

"I?" Mr. Farris's eyebrows lifted so high that his forehead was a mass of wrinkles discreetly signifying affront. "My duties extend only to your financial affairs, Mr. Penhallow, and given that they have been satisfactorily conducted, I saw no reason to initiate communication with you. You, of course, could have conferred with me at any time should it have suited you."

Farris was right, of course.

Gabriel's sense of shame, his disgust with himself, only deepened.

There was so much work to be done. To his surprise, he found it challenging and engaging—even satisfying. It was just that he had decades' worth of it to catch up on. Often he stayed up till three or four in the morning, poring over books and papers, studying lists, making notes, and frequently rising before dawn. He'd had his valet bring his things to a smaller bedchamber in a wing far removed from that of the ladies.

He told himself it was for practical reasons, that he wouldn't disturb them with his coming and goings at all hours, but the truth was that for three nights running he had stood at Livia's door, stood there like a fool, wanting more than anything he'd ever desired in his life to go inside. In the end, he had turned and gone away.

In the cold light of day he knew that he removed himself from this agonizing temptation because he didn't know how he could face her.

Inevitably, though, there was a meeting. He was

walking down the main corridor off the Great Hall one morning when he heard Livia saying, "Yes, please, Sally, tell Cook to go ahead and make the fricassee, and do ask Crenshaw what he thinks we can do about the candle-smoke stains in the Rose Saloon. I'm going to start mending the draperies now—" and Sally's voice saying, "Yes, Miss Livia, right away," and then Livia had turned the corner and was coming toward him with a swift, eager step, and her great green eyes filled with such a happy light that he despised himself all the more.

"Gabriel," she said softly, "good morning."

"Good morning." His voice, he knew, was cool, and he watched as some of the light left her eyes. She said:

"Are—are you well? You look tired."

"I'm fine. I'm busy."

"Yes. I understand."

He wanted to thank her for all that she had been doing. He knew that it was because of her efforts that bit by bit, day by day, the Hall was looking better, more loved. But he couldn't force the words from his mouth. It was amazing how shame could turn a person into a caricature of oneself. If she had thought him arrogant and aloof before, it was as nothing compared to how he presented himself now.

"Well," he said out loud, "I must be off. If you'll excuse me."

And now she looked as if he'd reached out his hand and shoved her away. His heart twisted painfully within him and he thought of that line from Corinthians, about seeing things *through a glass, darkly*: it was as if he watched Livia blur and fade within his vision. He was a fool and a failure; how he hated her seeing thus. Seeing him like this. Christ, but he had so much to do, to make things right.

Make things right for the Hall, for the estate and its people. Make things right for her. And for them both.

He dipped his head in a curt farewell and brushed passed her.

Leaving her standing there, with her lovely green eyes shimmering with tears.

Chapter 16

He was wearing the Penhallow Mask once again. And he *had* been avoiding her. That was now quite obvious. Fiercely Livia rubbed her eyes. No crying. No. Instead she went to the Rose Saloon and with tiny neat stitches sewed up an enormous rent in one of the velvet draperies.

Then she went to the kitchen garden, to see if the parsley had revived, and if there were any potatoes that could be dug up.

Then she talked with Little Walter about reinforcing the rotted enclosure circling the poultry yard.

Then she went into the Great Hall, where she found Crenshaw supervising two footmen who were cleaning the armament display. She was asking him whether a fresh supply of candles had arrived from the village when all at once came a patrician voice:

"If the candles in my room are an indication of the quality to be had in the village, I shall have Miss Cott write to our chandler in Bath, until such time as a more conveniently located purveyor can be found."

"Granny!" exclaimed Livia, quickly turning.

There was Grandmama, impeccably dressed in a beautiful blue-gray morning gown and not a silvery curl out of place. Behind her stood Miss Cott, also neat as wax, but still pale and wan.

"I'm so glad to see you!" Livia went on joyfully. "Is there anything you need? I was only inquiring about candles but I can ring for—"

Grandmama came forward, her air of authority so palpable that instinctively Livia took a step back. "Thank you, that will be all," she said to Livia, pleasantly, but in a cool, formal tone. "Now, Crenshaw, I wish to speak with you about engaging additional servants. Also, the rugs in the chief bedchambers are woefully dirty and require a thorough cleaning as soon as can be arranged. Can the chandeliers in the dining-room be polished this week? I would also like to arrange—"

"I beg your pardon, but I did talk to Crenshaw about the chandeliers, Gran—" Livia started to say *Granny,* but suddenly didn't feel as if she had the right.

"There is a particular way that it is done here at the Hall," answered the old lady, still in a pleasant, formal voice. "Naturally you are ignorant of it, through no fault of your own, of course." She looked back to Crenshaw and continued speaking with him, and Livia knew that she had been—why, she had been dismissed. Yes, apparently this *was* going to be the story of her life. She saw Miss Cott give her a sympathetic glance but couldn't bear to acknowledge it.

She went to the library, selected a book almost at random, went back to her bedchamber, curled up in a wing chair. She read her book. It was *Robinson Crusoe,* about a castaway on an obscure island. She paced around the room. She tidied the items on top of her dressing-table although they didn't need it; she was only rearranging, really. She took a nap. She looked out the window.

It must have been late afternoon when Flye tapped

on her door and told her she would be wanted at dinner. The whole family would be there.

"Oh?" said Livia, hope surging, irrepressibly, within her. She chose a gown she hadn't yet worn, white gauze over white silk, with tiny, dainty pink rosebuds adorning the neckline and the hem. And she asked Flye to plait her hair into braids which were twisted into a cunning arrangement high on the back of her head, with a sparkling oval clasp of paste diamonds as an ornament.

She knew she was looking her best, although once seated in the dining-room it didn't take long for her to realize that she might have well have worn sackcloth, for all the recognition she received from Gabriel. He didn't even look at her.

The discussion at dinner was all between him and Mrs. Penhallow—serious, intense, rapid-fire.

"Yes, the harvesting has begun," Gabriel said in response to a question from his grandmother. "There aren't enough laborers this year, but we're doing the best we can."

"And the timber?"

"Yes, of course, some of it will be felled, as soon as we can spare the workmen. It'll be cut, stacked, and stored for the winter in as many intact barns as we can find."

"Do you have someone to oversee it? It's dangerous work. I recall quite a few injuries happening if the men weren't properly supervised."

"Young Eccles will do nicely, I believe. He's to gradually assume full responsibilities as bailiff, by the way."

"I see. How is his father taking this news?"

"It was hard for him at first, but I believe that it's also rather a relief for him. He's not as young as he was, you know."

"Nor are any of us," wryly answered Mrs. Penhallow. "You said 'gradually.' Is he to work in other capacities?"

"Yes, he's asked to. He's agreed to oversee the rebuilding of the cottages. It's a huge undertaking."

She nodded. "Good. By the way, I've ordered a new stove for the kitchen."

"To Cook's joy, no doubt. What does Crenshaw say about the servants' rooms?"

"They're in universally poor condition, he reports. I've given him permission to find workmen as soon as possible to make necessary repairs. Oh, and apparently every single one of the copper tubs in the laundry leaks."

"Hardly a surprise," said Gabriel. "I shouldn't think anybody's been down there in years."

"You're right, I'm afraid. Also, there's an odd smell in one of the saloons off the Great Hall."

"Crenshaw mentioned that to me. He thinks it very likely that a nest of rats died behind the fireplace."

The old lady shuddered. "I brought Muffin into the saloon but the moment I put him down he ran out with his tail between his legs."

"Well, I can't worry about the saloon right now. I've got to get the harvest in."

"Yes, of course," Mrs. Penhallow said. "Quite right. And I've got to find someone who knows about plumbing. Also—"

Livia ate her excellent dinner and said not a word.

And so it went.

Tuesday, Wednesday, Thursday slowly passed.

She finished *Robinson Crusoe* and started on James Thomson's book of poetry *The Seasons*. She began walking through the gardens, and beyond, for hours each day. If the weather was bad, she walked through the house, unseen, like a quiet ghost, up and down the stairs and along the many hallways and passages. It tired her out and helped her to sleep.

By Friday the only words she had exchanged with Gabriel were "Good morning," "Good evening," "The weather is fine today," and "I fear it may rain tomorrow."

There was no talk of a wedding.

On Saturday her woman's time came upon her, answering a question she had pushed to the far corners of her mind; wondering if she and Gabriel had, while in Bath, created a child together. But no. She walked up and down the Picture Gallery, back and forth beyond counting. It turned out there *were* paintings of Gabriel as a little boy, and he was just as adorable as she had, in Bath, imagined he would be. She didn't pause long before them, however, she simply walked, her mind turning, sifting, floating as she moved.

This wasn't how she had envisioned things would go here at the Hall.

Of course, none of them had. And it had to be the hardest upon Gabriel and his grandmother. It was admirable, it was wonderful, how single-mindedly they had both turned to what needed to be done.

Not that she *liked* being excluded. Or enjoyed how Gabriel had put her aside.

But now was the time for her to be strong. To be patient.

To wait, and be steadfast.

It wasn't going to be easy.

Sustaining her, though, was the memory of that wildly exciting, tender interlude she and Gabriel had shared in Bath. It wasn't her imagination; it had been *real*.

She knew what she had to do now.

Trust. Look to the future. Wait. Love.

When finally it seemed she had walked for miles,

Livia went back to her room. She looked around. She
didn't feel like reading or sleeping. She wished, for
a moment, that she had someone she could write to.
Then, with a gladness that also seemed just a little bit
pathetic, she remembered that the string of the reticule
she'd brought down to dinner last night had been fray-
ing slightly.

She could mend it.

Livia went to the big armoire, opened one of the
doors, and slid out a drawer. A dozen reticules, more,
in a variety of styles and colors, lay within; Flye had
evidently been through them because the one Livia had
been thinking about wasn't there. Perhaps Flye had noticed the fray, too.

As Livia tucked the reticules back into neat order
her eyes fell upon a small white one decorated with
shiny little artificial pearls. Her hand lingered upon it.
Something was niggling at her memory, something unpleasant, something unhappy.

*I've been thinking about your situation quite a bit.
And so I have a gift for you. Something to help you
achieve your ambitions.*

Cecily, at the evening-party, just before Mrs. Penhallow had collapsed.

Pressing into Livia's hand a little package.

Now Livia opened the little white reticule and found
Cecily's gift, wrapped in silver paper.

Inside was a fifty-pound note and two golden guineas.

Fifty-two pounds.

Somehow, the guineas were worse—more insulting—
than the note.

Livia stared at them, then, very carefully, wrapped
them up again and put them back into the reticule.

On Sunday there was church. She went with Gabriel
and his grandmother, to hear Mr. Markson's sermon.

Miss Cott stayed at the Hall, with a headache, she said. Livia brought her a feverfew tisane before she left.

On Monday and Tuesday it rained, and on Wednesday, the weather having cleared, Livia decided to walk to the lodge. Repairs there had not yet begun, she saw, and a single peek through a cloudy window into the dirty abandoned interior was enough.

She walked back to the Hall, but instead of going inside she went to the lip of the ornamental pond—still only half-filled—and stood there idly, watching the reflections of clouds drifting by overhead. She wondered what she would do next. It was a long time till the dinner hour. She could walk some more, down to the river, or she could go to her bedchamber, and finish *The Seasons*. It was full of depressing poems. She didn't know why she felt obligated to read it till the end. After all, there were so many other books she could borrow from the Hall's library.

And reading was a very worthy way in which to pass the time.

Waiting, waiting . . .

A sound from behind her, from the wide path that joined up with the carriage sweep, jolted her from her reverie: slow hoofbeats crunching on gravel. Quickly Livia turned. A man on horseback was riding toward her, looking none too steady in the saddle.

She narrowed her eyes, shielding them from the bright sun. She didn't know the man; was he drunk? As he drew closer, she saw that he had a crop of thick hair, the color of gold and cut severely short, and the face of a Greek god—at present frighteningly white and creating a sharp contrast to his eyes which were the vivid blue color of a jay's wing.

She saw one of his ungloved hands pulling a little at the reins, and the other slide beneath his unbuttoned greatcoat, toward his abdomen. A frisson of alarm danced along her spine; could it be that he was reaching for a pistol?

"How do you do," he said, unevenly, but in the unmistakable accents of a gentleman. "I beg your pardon, but is this Surmont Hall?"

"Yes," answered Livia warily.

"That's all right, then. I apologize for the intrusion, but—I'll explain later—that is—" He smiled hazily and swayed from side to side. "Gad, you're pretty. I—oh, damn it to hell, I'm going to—I'm Hugo, you see. Hugo Penhallow. I'm most awfully sorry, but I'm afraid I'm going to pass out."

With that he toppled off his horse and fell with an alarming thud onto the gravel. His horse shied away, and with an exclamation of horror Livia flew to Hugo Penhallow, who lay sprawled and unmoving. His greatcoat had been flung open in his fall, and blooming through the fabric of his waistcoat was a red stain.

Blood.

Horrified, Livia ran to the front door which was already opening. Crenshaw, with the uncanny instincts of the truly great butler, came onto the porch with a pair of footmen in tow.

"Crenshaw!" said Livia, with breathless urgency, "it's Mr. Hugo Penhallow, and he's bleeding horribly." She pressed her hands to her eyes in a moment of blind panic. There was no time to consult with Gabriel or his grandmother. She pulled her hands away and rapidly led them toward the prone figure on the gravel. "Lift him—carefully, please!—and take him to a saloon off the Great Hall. Not the one that smells bad! There's the one with a big wide sofa—let's take him there. Crenshaw, who is the doctor here? Can you send for him immediately?"

Once inside the Hall, Livia saw some of the maidservants, goggling at the unconscious man being carried inside. "We'll need—clean cloths, hot water; Sally, to the kitchen, please! Mary, go find Mr. Gabriel and Mrs. Penhallow immediately. And Miss Cott."

Afterwards Livia would only remember in little fragmented memories what happened next: the quiet competence of Miss Cott, fluttering maids, a horrified Mrs. Penhallow. White cloths turning red with ominous speed, and piling up too quickly in a basin. The still, white, handsome face of the injured man. Dr. Fotherham, square, stocky, grizzled, curt, and unflappable, brushing aside everyone in the room and setting to work at once by ripping open the bloody waistcoat and shirt beneath.

"Wounded, eh?—hmmm, hmmm, looks like a bullet went in, and deeply too—whoever got it out made a hash of it. It's reopened, and infected. Somebody hand me that bottle, and that roll of lint—"

Miss Cott complied, and Livia had to turn away as the doctor began to clean the gaping hole, nausea rising within her. Gabriel came in then, dressed in riding clothes and muddy boots; he flung his hat and gloves onto a table and strode to the sofa.

"Hugo! What the devil!"

"Were you expecting him, Gabriel?" asked his grandmother, sitting very straight in her chair, looking pale and strained.

"Absolutely not. When last I heard from him, he was near Canada somewhere. What's the matter with him?"

"Took a bullet, probably a couple of months ago," said the doctor, packing the wound with a professional briskness that only made Livia feel queasier. "He's sick as a dog now. You say he only just now arrived, eh?"

"Yes, on a horse," Livia said. "He fell off it."

"Remarkable stamina! A lesser man wouldn't have been able to get into a saddle. Good thing he didn't break his neck falling off the horse. I'll just check for broken bones—hmmm, hmmm. See how he flinched just then? Hurt that leg at some point. Not broken now, though, just not perfectly right. Overall he's sturdy as an ox. No—the bones aren't a worry. That's a blessing, to be sure. Well, I'm done. He's going to need a lot of care, day and night. Can you keep him in here? The sofa's a decent enough bed—though I may as well warn you, it's already ruined—and I don't want him moved. He'd likely start bleeding again."

"Yes, of course he'll stay where he is," said Gabriel. "You'll leave us instructions?"

"Yes. Writing them down for you. Here. I'll pop by again in a few hours. He's going to get restless tonight, I'll wager. I'll bring some laudanum and some other things. Make certain you don't leave him alone, or he's likely to fling himself onto the floor. No women! Get the footmen to watch over him. He's a strong 'un."

Dr. Fotherham gathered up his supplies and left as briskly as he had come. Gabriel studied the list of instructions while Miss Cott carefully adjusted Hugo's head; one of the maids squeamishly took away the basin of bloodied cloths. Livia stared at the pale face of Hugo Penhallow, so dreadfully vulnerable-looking.

Hugo. Gabriel's cousin. She remembered, now, that conversation in the Spotted Hare—so long ago, it seemed!—when Gabriel had mentioned him to her. How different the two men were in looks, yet both tall, strong, good-looking.

Gabriel began issuing directives to Crenshaw. When he had finished, she said, "May I help?"

"No. Thank you," Gabriel answered shortly.

She nodded—she had expected no other reply—and quietly went away.

She hoped that Hugo would live. She would wait for that, too.

Hugo Penhallow did survive. Not only that, he made an impressive recovery, so much so that a mere five days later, as Livia was coming along the main corridor from the Great Hall, she heard a robust voice issuing from within the little saloon, through a door left partway open:

"Oh, damn and blast, I've dropped the cursed thing!"

Livia looked up and down the corridor, but there was no one else in sight, so she pushed open the door and inquiringly put her head in.

Hugo Penhallow was on his sofa-bed. He was no longer so ominously pale, although as he twisted his torso, trying to reach something on the carpet, he winced and lay back on his pillows. The blankets had slipped down to reveal enormously broad, muscled shoulders and a great wide barrel of a chest.

"May I help you?" Livia asked shyly from around the doorframe.

Startled, Hugo Penhallow met her gaze and then smiled in a friendly way. "Saw you the other day, didn't I? When I arrived? Gad, I didn't fall on you, did I?"

Livia smiled back. "No, but nearly." She stepped into the saloon. "How do you do? I'm Livia Stuart. I'm Gabriel's fiancée."

"His fiancée?" Hugo looked astonished. "Gabriel's to be leg-shackled at last? He hasn't breathed a word of it, although to be fair I haven't been particularly lucid these past days. Well, well, will wonders never cease? That is—I mean—my felicitations, Miss Stuart!" He smiled again, adding confidingly, "I must apologize for having the manners of an ape. I've been so long away from Society that I'm really not fit to be around a lady. Went straight from school into the Army, you see."

"Well, you certainly needn't stand on ceremony with me." Livia saw a book on the floor near Hugo's sofa and came forward to pick it up. "*The History of the Decline and Fall of the Roman Empire*. Are you enjoying it?"

"Very interesting and all that, but I can't lie around all day reading. That nice little woman—what was her name? Miss Catt?—she walks so softly she might as well *be* a cat, a nice, quiet, gray little kitty."

"Miss Cott."

"Yes, yes, that's it. At any rate, she thought I'd find it of interest—as a soldier. Very kind of her. She frightens me half to death, I must say."

Livia laughed. "She frightens you? You're twice her size."

"Yes, but she's brainy, you see."

"And you are not?"

"Oh, I'm not stupid, and I daresay I'm clever enough in my own way. But I'd rather be up and about, you know—too restless to keep my nose stuck in a book. At school I was the despair of the masters. Despised sitting still. Simply couldn't do it. Sporting-mad, and always one for a lark."

"You've been used to leading a very active life," said Livia, sympathetically. "It must not suit you to be confined as you are."

"Just so. Bored to death, if you must know."

"When does Dr. Fotherham say you might get up?"

"I've been asking him so often he'll probably bleed me just to shut me up. But he promises that if I stay quite still, I can leave this blasted sofa in a few days."

"That's not so long, is it?"

"It seems like a long time when you have nothing to

do." He smiled winningly at her. "I say, won't you stay and talk with me? Do sit down. Unless you're frightfully busy, in which case I wouldn't dream of imposing on you."

"I'm not busy."

"Splendid! Everyone else seems to be. Yes, sit there. The sun makes your hair seem as if it's on fire."

"Is that a compliment?"

"Oh, damn, I've put my foot in again, haven't I? But I've already told you I'm an uncouth ass. Yes indeed, you've got awfully lovely hair. Never seen anything quite like it. And you're nice, too! My cousin's a fortunate man. Oh, splendid, here's somebody with tea. Mary, isn't it? See here, Mary, that all looks very good—yes, you can put it on that table, there's a good girl—but I don't suppose you could have Cook rustle up some cold meat? And if there happen to be any of those fish patties left over from last night's dinner, I'll take three or four, with a little of that excellent sauce. And a mug of ale, too, while you're about it."

"Oh, yes, sir," breathed an obviously dazzled Mary, "right away, sir," but it was to be seen that she lingered for a few moments, plumping a chair cushion with her eyes fixed straitly on Hugo, before leaving the saloon.

"You have an admirer," said Livia, twinkling at him.

Hugo grimaced. "A damned—dashed nuisance it is, too."

"Well, you *are* handsome. You quite remind me of—"

"Don't say it!" he groaned.

"Say what?"

"That I remind you of a Greek god."

"Why, how did you know I was going to say that?"

He groaned again. "Everyone does. The bane of my existence, I assure you."

"Don't you *like* being good-looking?"

"I detest being stared at," he growled. "One feels so conspicuous, like a wild beast on display."

"You *are* a modest fellow!"

"I'm sure *you* are stared at. You're a beauty, you know."

"Hardly. Red hair isn't the least bit fashionable, and slender ladies are all the mode."

"Pooh! Men don't want sticks in bed with them!" he said scornfully, then looked so abashed that Livia had to laugh. "Begging your pardon," he added, meekly.

"Like a proper lady, I'll pretend I didn't hear that, Mr. Penhallow. Or—ought I to call you by your military title?"

"Well, you can if you like, but I think you ought to call me Hugo, for since I can't be making up to you, we're to be the best of friends, and cousins, too."

"Very well then—Hugo. May I offer you a cup of tea, or are you holding out for better things?"

"I'm putting my faith in Mary, and that excellent cook of yours. I must say, I'm frightfully glad you're not one of those haughty, proud Society ladies. Although I'm afraid I must learn to cultivate them."

"Why?"

"Why? I'm now a man without a profession—that bullet in my gut knocked me flat for a good long while back in Canada, and as much as I relished Army life, it simply won't do. I've a widowed mother and three younger brothers and a sister to support. Gabriel was awfully kind to make me an allowance, and to purchase my commission, but that's all over now. It was a splendid lark and I enjoyed every minute of it. Time to face the facts, though. Had plenty of time to think on the voyage here. No property to speak of, and I'm too old to be accepting money from a relative, no matter how generous. So I've decided," he concluded cheerfully, "that I must shamelessly capitalize on my family name and my blasted looks, and marry an heiress. Know any?"

The visages of Cecily Orr and Miss Gillingham flashed across Livia's mind. "The only two I know I wouldn't recommend to you even if they were eligible. They're both young ladies who, I am sure, would make you unhappy."

"I suppose," Hugo said, eyeing her thoughtfully, "you think I am horribly cold-blooded?"

"I'm hardly in a position to be judging you! Besides, you're being realistic, and you're thinking of your family."

"That's it. Percy and Francis must be sent to school as soon as possible, and Bertram in his time. And little Gwendolyn must be provided for, too. Ah! Here you are, Mary! Yes, Miss Livia's making room for your tray, you may put it next to the other one. *That's* more like it. And some of Cook's excellent rolls, too! Thank you very much."

Blushing bright red, Mary bobbed a curtsy and left, and Livia made up a heaping plate for Hugo which she passed to him, and set a little table at his elbow with his brimming tankard of ale. She poured a cup of tea and helped herself to an éclair.

"Mrs. Penhallow could introduce you to the Polite World, Hugo. Everyone knows her, and she knows everyone."

"Oh, Lord, Aunt Henrietta frightens me more than Miss Cott! I met her a couple of times as a schoolboy— could rarely afford to go home during the holidays and Gabriel very kindly brought me along with him to Bath. May I trouble you to spoon a little more sauce on these patties? Thank you. In any event, Aunt Henrietta thought me a horrid little terror, and told me so! Probably will never forgive me for the time I slid backwards down the bannister and broke that ghastly old vase *and* the pedestal it stood on. Worth a king's ransom, no doubt. Well, when I've married my heiress and am rich as a troll I'll buy her another one, even uglier."

Livia laughed and took another éclair. "Still, Hugo, Mrs. Penhallow could be very helpful to you."

"Not to worry, Liv, something will turn up. It always does. The luck is with me, you see."

"Liv." She smiled. "I've never had a nickname before."

"Egad, do you mind? I told you I'm not fit to be around proper people."

"Not at all. I like it very much. But Hugo, do you consider it lucky that you broke your leg and nearly died from an infected bullet wound?"

"To be sure! Brought me here, didn't it?"

"How is that lucky, exactly?" Livia buttered another roll and handed it to him.

"Thanks very much. I'll take another whenever you're ready. Why, I had to sell out because of my injuries, and come home. Needed to do that for my family's sake anyway. And then there was a tremendous storm as we neared the coast, forcing us to divert to Bude, rather than weigh in to Liverpool as we'd planned. Knew I was doing poorly, and thought that rather than frightening my poor mother half to death by dropping on her doorstep like a sack of turnips, I'd come to the Hall. Much closer, you see. So I've been able to meet my pretty new cousin-to-be, and tell Gabriel in person he's to cut me off at once."

Livia thought about that hateful little packet of money lying concealed in her armoire. "Hugo, have you any money to get home?" she asked bluntly. "I have a little bit of my own—"

"Lord bless you, child, I've enough." He laughed. "Just barely. Which reminds me—I need to write to the mater and let her know I'll be back in Whitehaven as soon as I can sit a horse again. Will you bring me pen and paper by and by?"

"Of course," Livia said, and their conversation wound its way, easily and comfortably, to other topics.

In the corridor outside, Gabriel walked by on his way to his study. He heard Livia's voice, and Hugo's deeper one; they both were laughing. He thought, absently, how pleasant it was that Hugo had company; he himself was too busy to be much of a host to the lad. Then he bent his mind once again to the knotty problems confronting him today: a blight afflicting the apple orchards in the northeastern corner of the estate, and a perplexing resistance among some of the laborers to having their old crumbling wattle-and-daub cottages replaced with trim, warm timber structures. It was a mystery.

Chapter 17

Livia left off her solitary rambles and now spent her days with Hugo. He regaled her with amusing stories of his youth, and told her all about his gentle, forbearing mother, his siblings, his brazen exploits as a schoolboy. At her urging he talked about his time as a soldier, too, although he was steadfastly self-effacing about the dangers he faced, choosing instead to highlight his comical misadventures.

It didn't take long for her to realize how much she valued Hugo's easy companionship, the laughter they shared; how badly she needed a friend right now.

In due course Hugo was allowed to get up. He joined the family at meals but Gabriel and Mrs. Penhallow continued to talk, with a single-mindedness that frankly bordered on rudeness, of matters pertaining to the estate and the Hall. With the air of one shrugging good-naturedly, Hugo spoke affably with Livia and tried to coax Miss Cott—who also, Livia had noticed, seemed increasingly shut out of the Penhallow world—into joining their conversation, but with limited success.

Livia and Hugo took to walking outside as his strength returned day by day. His limp, the result of that badly broken leg, was not a severe one, but it did worsen when he was tired. One afternoon, as they strolled slowly among the old overgrown maze of hedges that dated back to Elizabethan times, Hugo asked:

"I say, when is your wedding? Hope to be there for it, but I haven't heard you speak a word about it. Most young ladies, I imagine, would be obsessed by all the planning—the fripperies and the guests and all that."

"I don't know exactly. I think—I hope—that is, Gabriel's had so much to do after his long absence . . ."

"Oh yes, of course. First things first, is it? He always was one to focus. In school he was famous for it, whether it was about books or sports. He'd be studying for exams, and you could bring an eight-piece band into his room and he'd completely ignore it." Hugo laughed. "Once we actually did just that. Never once looked up from his book. Amazing. Of course, he was the one with the top grades. And he was the most fearsome boxer, you know—couldn't count the times I saw him mill down chaps outweighing him by five stone or more. Pure single-minded determination."

Livia pondered this image of Gabriel as Hugo went on, "You're very different—in a good way, mind!—from the sort of young lady I'd have thought Gabriel would choose for his wife. Always supposed he'd end up with one of those dreadfully proud Society females. I tell you, he was a hunted man! I was shocked when he managed to escape by joining the Corps and disappeared to Europe. How did the two of you meet, anyway?"

"Oh, it's a long story," Livia replied a little self-consciously. "At first it was to be a marriage of convenience, but . . . things changed, and—well, it's just that now Gabriel is so busy. I do love him, Hugo, with all my heart and soul."

"I can see that, for you've lit up like a lamp. Well, well, and very happy the two of you will be," said Hugo easily. "I say, Liv, do you think we'll ever get out of this cursed maze? Don't know about you, but I'm ready for a nuncheon."

With the help of Young Eccles Gabriel now had some hope that the apple blight would be vanquished, and they had moved on to the urgently needed repairing of fences. He had persuaded Eccles, senior, to stop haranguing the laborers about the new cottages, convincing him (he hoped) that a gentler tone would be more efficacious; the lodge was finally being renovated, with the late Mrs. Allard's middle-aged son expressing his willingness to reoccupy it, accompanied by his large family, as soon as was feasible. Crenshaw reported positively about improvements in the servants' quarters, and Cook adored her modern new stove.

Yes, progress was being made. But there was still so much yet to do, and he vowed to work even harder. As he came and went from the Hall, Gabriel registered, vaguely, how Livia was always with Hugo. Talking, laughing, strolling, and sometimes arm-in-arm, heads together, very companionably.

Gabriel also realized that Hugo wasn't the lad he'd remembered him as. No, Hugo was a man fully grown and only an idiot would fail to observe how the maidservants fluttered over him—he was obviously a damned attractive fellow. No doubt he'd be settling down now that he'd sold out from the Army and was back in England: find some congenial work, marry and start a family, and so on. Hugo had insisted on repaying him for the cost of his commission, which Gabriel hadn't in the least wished to accept; it was only the understanding that Hugo's pride would be injured that had finally overcome his reluctance.

Gabriel now cast a troubled glance up at sky threatening rain. As soon as he'd seen all the wheat and barley and oats and rye harvested, cut and carted to barns, he thought absently, he'd ask Hugo about his plans, and see if he might provide any other kind of assistance to his young cousin.

Hurry, he told himself, *hurry.*

The next day Gabriel was up before dawn and as the morning sun rose over the fields, promising a bright and beautiful day, he sat on Primus watching the laborers and wagoners work. Young Eccles rode up on his neat cob, and Gabriel nodded a good morning to him.

"It's coming along, sir."

"Yes. The gleaning will commence soon?"

"Or we could keep on harvesting. Up to you, sir."

"No, leave plenty for the womenfolk and the children. Set the men to threshing."

"As you wish, sir. Reckon we'll have a good Harvest Home this year. Nice change, if I may say so, sir."

Gabriel nodded, conscious of feeling both satisfaction and pride. And aware of just how bone-tired he was. And how much he missed Livia. It felt like years since he'd seen her, *really* seen her. Suddenly he turned to Young Eccles and said:

"Can you do without me for a few hours?"

"Of course, sir. All's well here."

"Yes, it is." Gabriel grinned, touched his heels to Primus's sides, and galloped back to the Hall.

After a pleasant walk with Hugo after breakfast, Livia went upstairs to change her half-boots for slippers, then proceeded to the drawing-room where she found Hugo stretched out on one of the sofas, feet propped comfortably on a tufted hassock. He was engrossed in a letter, but looked up when she sat down on the sofa opposite his.

"Good news, Liv! I've just heard from the mater—all's well at home, although Bertram has destroyed two more of the best pots with his latest experiment on conductivity, and Mama's cook is livid—but that's neither here nor there. Seems there's a likely heiress practically on our doorstep."

"Oh! That *is* good news, Hugo!"

Briskly Hugo folded the letter and stood up. "Well, I'm off! That is, if you'll excuse me?"

Livia stared at him. "You're leaving right now?"

"No, I'm going to the stables to make sure my horse is ready for a journey. I'll go tomorrow. No time to waste! Stands to reason these heiresses are snapped up pretty quickly. And it's well over three hundred miles to Whitehaven." He smiled at her affectionately. "Terrible houseguest, aren't I, hotfooting it out of here on a moment's notice? But I've barely exchanged a sentence with Gabriel and Aunt Henrietta—awfully preoccupied, aren't they?—and I daresay they won't even notice that I've gone."

"I will notice, Hugo."

He smiled. "You're a sweet one."

Livia wasn't quite able to return his smile. "Oh, Hugo, I'm so glad for you—glad for your promising matrimonial prospect. You deserve every happiness. But I'm going to miss you so much!" And with that, she burst into noisy tears.

"Oh, I say!" exclaimed Hugo, appalled. He knelt down before her, taking her hands in his own massive ones. "Don't cry, dear Liv, don't cry!"

Livia only sobbed, and when he took her in a brotherly embrace, she leaned against him and gave in to the luxury of a good cry. And when finally she began to feel a little better, he was so warm and comforting that she didn't want to move.

Hugo was awkwardly patting her hair, causing it to tumble down around her shoulders. "Women!" he said wonderingly, "I hope my heiress won't do such unfathomable things," which only made Livia laugh.

Gabriel stood stock-still on the threshold to the drawing-room. His brain wanted very much to reject the evidence of his own eyes.

Livia and Hugo.

Livia in Hugo's arms.

Her beautiful hair loose, wild.

Gabriel knew what that had to mean. He wasn't stupid.

Then he heard her laugh. A happy sound.

Quickly he turned on his heel, went to his study, shut the door, stood there with his back against it as if seeking solidity. He had been in an earthquake once, in Crimea. Dishes had tumbled from shelves and broken, candlesticks toppled, books and little *objets d'art* disarranged as if by the careless hand of an unseen giant. In a heartbeat the world which had seemed so firm, so fixed, had revealed itself to be, quite literally, shaky.

So, too, had all his plans—his hopes and dreams—just now been shattered, as if they were as insubstantial as a little china figurine.

While he had been painstakingly bringing his estate from ruin, Livia and his cousin Hugo had fallen in love.

Really, he thought with a sort of cold, analytical lucidity, could they be faulted? They had been thrown together. He had virtually ignored them. They were both young and attractive. He couldn't even find it within himself to be angry at Hugo, for he was such a handsome, pleasant, easygoing fellow—

"Unlike myself," he muttered out loud, bitterly. No, *he* was a monster of blind selfishness.

But no more.

He knew what he had to do.

He would let her go.

It violated one of the most sacred precepts of Polite Society for a man to renounce his engagement, but it was his very love for Livia that would galvanize him into doing something so unorthodox—so dishonorable.

He loved her and he would set her free.

And he'd do everything in his power to help the young couple begin their lives together happily and comfortably. Money, whatever else they needed, no matter how Hugo might protest.

He would not think of himself.

And he wouldn't waste a moment.

Gabriel looked blankly around his study. Remarkable, how one could be alive and yet feel dead. He turned around and reached for the doorknob.

Hugo gave Livia's hair one final clumsy pat. "It's awfully nice to hug a girl without having to worry about one's intentions being misread—like I'd hug the mater or little Gwendolyn. By the way, I've completely mussed up your hair. I *am* sorry."

Livia pulled away, smiling at him. "It was worth it."

"To be sure!" Hugo replied cheerfully, then jumped to his feet. "Done crying, Liv?"

"Yes. Thank you."

"I'm off to the stables, then. *Adieu,* as those beastly French say."

"Goodbye." Livia watched him go, then stood up and went to the window which overlooked the front of the Hall. Why, there were laborers out there, cleaning the ornamental pool, and gardeners, too, at work. How lovely it would all look, and soon. She stepped back a pace so that she could vaguely see her own reflection in the glass. Quickly she put her hair back into a semblance of proper order.

"Livia."

Gabriel's voice. Cold, stiff, as if he spoke from atop a tall mountain. She turned; summoned up a little smile of greeting.

He said:

"Forgive my brevity, but in such cases as this, it's doubtless for the best. I release you from our engagement. I wish you well. Please know that all possible steps will be taken to see that you're well provisioned." He fell silent. His hands, which had been hanging at his sides, lifted, then dropped.

"Wait," Livia said. Her smile was gone. Surely he hadn't said what she *thought* she heard. "What are you talking about?"

"I'm sorry," he said. "Our engagement is over. As it must be."

Behind her, one of her hands groped for one of the heavy velvet draperies, and clung to it, as if to steady her. She hoped she didn't clutch it so hard it brought the entire long drape down upon her. Although if that did happen, at least she might be buried beneath it, where she could shut out the sight and sound of him looking so cold and saying such awful things.

"I still don't understand you," she said.

"It's over," he repeated. "It's doubtless for the best. I wish you well. And I tender my congratulations. If you'll excuse me?"

He was *congratulating* her?

"Wait," she said again. There was a kind of roaring in her ears as a mad confusion overtook her. "Stop. Just a moment." She let go of the drape, quickly crossed the room, and in a curious reversal of what had happened between them during that fateful evening at the Orrs' ball, she reached up to take him by the shoulders and she tried to kiss him. Anything to make this madness stop. But he pulled away, with horror in his eyes.

"You can't do this. *We* can't do this. I must go."

Livia watched with her own sense of horror as he bowed slightly, formally, and turned to leave the room. All at once a rush of bitter anger swamped her and she cried out, "Go! I couldn't care less! I hope I never see you again, Gabriel Penhallow!"

He paused, turned back for a moment to say, stiffly, "I'm sorry," and then he had turned again, walked away, and left the room.

For a panicky minute or two, Livia was afraid she couldn't breathe. Her hands flew to the bodice of her gown. And fiercely she made herself bring air into her lungs. In, out. In, out.

Then, with a calmness that struck her as slightly ludicrous given the circumstances, she went and sat down again on the sofa.

Well.

That was that, then.

It was really, truly over.

All the conflicts and misunderstandings; all the quarrels and hostilities; all the tenderness and the loving.

Was it possible she had been, on some deep level, expecting this dismissal for some time? Wasn't it, after all, the story of her life?

At least there was a certain, cheerless consistency to it all.

Livia felt like a child's slate which had, at a stroke, been wiped blank.

There was nothing left.

Nothing to strive for, nothing to fight for.

Go talk to him, urged some desperate little voice within her.

And do what? she answered herself. *Beg him to reconsider? Plead with him to love me? Keep waiting and hoping, like the blind fool that I am?*

No.

It was time to take action, to change her own story, to take life into her own hands.

And she knew what she had to do.

It might have been ten minutes or ten years that she sat there, perfectly upright and absolutely still.

"Oh, Miss Stuart! I hope I am not intruding?"

It was Mr. Markson.

"Good day, sir," she said, pleasantly, numbly. "Do come in. Won't you sit down? Shall I ring for some tea?"

"No, please don't bother." Mr. Markson came and sat on the sofa opposite. "I apologize for bursting in on you like this, but I've come to see Mrs. Penhallow and she isn't quite ready for me. Apparently she is in the Green Saloon, interviewing candidates for the housekeeper's position."

"Is she?"

"Yes, Mrs. Worthing is to go and live with her

sister's family—the mother of your Little Walter. Quite contented she seems, and she's to receive a generous pension."

"I'm glad."

"Yes, it is the Penhallow way. I'm so happy to see it reinstituted."

"I too."

There was a moment's silence. Mr. Markson cleared his throat, and said:

"We're starting a school, you see, for the village children. Mrs. Penhallow is to be our benefactress, of course."

"What good news. Won't you tell me more about it?"

Mr. Markson replied at once, and Livia, nodding and smiling, didn't hear a word of it; eventually she realized that he had stopped talking and it was as if he had seen the most wonderful thing in all the world. His plain face had been transfigured into something approaching real handsomeness. She half-turned: there was Miss Cott, her countenance white except for two burning spots of color on her cheeks.

"Oh," said Miss Cott, very quietly, "I didn't know you were here, Arthur. Miss Stuart, I came to ask—but it can wait. Excuse me, please—"

She said no more, but hurriedly left the room.

"I—I must go," said Mr. Markson, himself very pale. "Matters at the Rectory—please extend to Mrs. Penhallow my apologies. I will come again—will send a note first—good day, Miss Stuart."

Swiftly, he too left.

Livia pushed aside all sense of self; her heart was dead but her mind was turning, conjecturing, troubled to see these two gentle souls in such obvious distress. She ran up the stairs and caught up with Miss Cott on the landing. "What's wrong?" she asked softly.

"It's—it's nothing," faltered Miss Cott. "Ancient history only, surely of interest to no one."

"*I* am interested. Please won't you sit? I'm worried for you." There was an alcove nearby, in it an intimate grouping of chairs as well as an old rococo *chaise longue;* Livia drew Miss Cott to this and coaxed her down next to her. She took the older woman's hands in hers, and felt their trembling. "Oh, Miss Cott, you look so sad. Won't you tell me why?"

There was a silence, an indrawn breath, and then, finally, a quiet reply. "There's not much to say. Long ago, when I was a very young lady, I fell in love with Arthur Markson. And I believe he with me. I was happy, Miss Stuart—Livia. So happy."

"And so?"

"You already know, I think, what happened next. My friend Henrietta Penhallow lost the love of *her* life, her Richard, and her collapse was so complete that I feared for her sanity, even for her life. She needed me. How could I fail her in her darkest hour?"

"Of course you couldn't," answered Livia. "But Miss Cott, that hour became much more than that, didn't it? That hour became—years."

"Somehow it did. I don't know how it happened. But I've never stopped worrying about Henrietta."

"You're so *good*, Miss Cott," said Livia, impulsively hugging her. "You're the kindest person I've ever known. Do you still love your Arthur?"

"Yes. How foolish of me, don't you think?" A single tear rolled down Miss Cott's pale cheek and quickly she reached into her reticule for a handkerchief with which to dab it away. Livia had already made up her mind; she said:

"Not foolish at all. You were going to your room? I'll send a maid to you, with some tea, perhaps?"

"Yes, I'd—I'd like that. Thank you. And—thank you for listening."

They parted, and Livia sped downstairs, found a maidservant, then went quickly to the Green Saloon. Mrs. Penhallow was alone, sitting at a gilded escritoire after the style of Louis XIV, looking through some papers. At Livia's knock on the open door she looked up, frowning a little.

"I'm quite busy. Mr. Markson is waiting to see me."

"I'm afraid he had to leave. May I speak with you?"

A little irritably Mrs. Penhallow laid aside her papers. "If you must."

"It's about Miss Cott," said Livia, coming forward, "and Mr. Markson. She loves him, you see, and I believe he loves her."

The old lady's frown deepened. "I don't understand. I don't think Evangeline has even seen Arthur Markson since our arrival here."

As briefly Livia explained, a look of mingled sadness and bitterness came like a shadow upon Mrs. Penhallow.

"I see, once again, how far I am from a true perception of things," she said slowly, when Livia had done. "Of course I'll release Evangeline at once, and *force* her to marry Arthur Markson if I have to."

"Forcing people to marry may not always be the wisest course, ma'am," Livia replied quietly. "I suspect that Miss Cott needs your blessing to the match more than anything. She cares deeply for you, you know."

"I'm not sure why. I'm an overbearing old fool."

Livia felt a sudden rush of sympathy at seeing the indomitable Mrs. Penhallow looking so stricken, so defeated. She couldn't help herself and went to her, embraced her warmly. "I must go. Goodbye."

Mrs. Penhallow looked a little cheered. "You have

disarranged my fichu," she complained, but Livia was not deceived.

She would miss the old lady. Miss them all.

For a moment, standing in the hall outside the Green Saloon, Livia stared blankly at nothing. Then, as if moving beyond her own volition, her steps took her, inexorably, to the Hall's ancient chapel. Here, for centuries, in this sacred space had the Penhallows gathered, worshipped, wed, found solace, mourned the passing of their loved ones. But the neglect of recent years manifested itself in a dank, damp odor; its oaken pews were filthy, the chancel's floorboards rotting.

Livia slowly looked around.

There wouldn't be—couldn't be—a wedding here.

She thought of another wedding, in distant India, before she was born. Her father Jonathan, rejecting the pursuit of money so abhorrent to him, and instead following his true avocation; and in this way finding love and happiness with his Georgiana, Livia's mother. What a joyful wedding that must have been.

And even before that, Georgiana's parents, fleeing England and the separation others were trying to force upon them. How bravely they had fought for their future, settling for nothing less than what was in their hearts. Theirs must have been a joyful wedding, too.

This, Livia thought, was her heritage.

She wouldn't settle for anything else than what was real and true. Surmont Hall no longer held that for her. If it ever had.

She knelt, bowed her head, prayed for the strength she'd need for the dark, lonely days ahead.

Afterwards, Livia felt an odd sense of calm certainty, but even so, she hadn't been quite courageous enough to come down to dinner. She told Flye she had a headache and refused an offer of a tray sent up to her. She'd regret that later, she knew, but for the sake of pretense it was how it had to be.

At midnight she dressed in her oldest gown, and finally—finally—put on the boots she had brought with her from the Abbey. She took a long look at the money Cecily had pressed upon her with such spiteful malice, and tucked it into a pocket bag she had secretly sewed and now tied underneath her petticoat. Who, Livia wondered, would have the last laugh now? Cecily would have the satisfaction of knowing that Gabriel had not married his little country miss; on the other hand, Cecily had given Livia her freedom.

One last thing occurred to her.

Should she leave a note?

Oh, and what could she say?

I'm sorry you don't love me. But it's as Lady Glanville says, life isn't fair. A disagreeable fact, but what can one do?

No, she'd leave no note.

Decisively, she put on her old dark-blue pelisse and buttoned it up to her throat. She doubted she'd be warm enough, but, after all, one couldn't have everything one wanted in life.

And then, observed by not a soul, she left.

Gabriel hadn't been able to bring himself to join the family at dinner. Instead he had gone out to one of the barns, put on a laborer's smock, and helped the other men with the threshing until it had gotten dark. He'd returned to the Hall, bathed, had his meal sent up to him, wondering all the while why doing the right thing also felt like he had cut himself off from all that he cherished in this world.

In the morning, he told himself he would be civil, magnanimous, as kind as humanly possible when encountering the joyful couple. He went down to the breakfast-parlor like a man facing his own execution. But only Hugo was there, making his way through a plate heaped high with ham and sausages and fried potatoes.

"Hullo, coz!" said Hugo cheerfully. "Beautiful day. I say, do have some of this ham. It's excellent. I've left you two slices."

"Thank you." Gabriel tried not to grit his teeth. It would not do to murder his own cousin. He sat, stared at his empty plate as if he had never before in his life seen such a thing. This was going to be harder than he had thought. Surely, he chided himself, it wasn't worse than the time he had outmaneuvered that hostile Prussian count who (sporting an outlandishly greasy set of black mustachios) had laced his conversation with thinly veiled references to an oubliette beneath their feet. Or that evening in Vienna when he'd been forced into a rather nasty fight with a French spy who, without warning, had leaped upon him brandishing a very sharp, very deadly *navaja*.

"May I—" He noticed he had been clenching his fists, and deliberately he relaxed them. "May I offer my congratulations on your upcoming nuptials? I hope you will both be very happy."

"Dashed kind of you, coz. Although you're perhaps a little premature."

Premature? After what he had witnessed yesterday? If Hugo was going to treat Livia with such shocking cavalierism, he *would* murder him. "I assumed," Gabriel said carefully, "that it was settled between the two of you."

Hugo laughed, and Gabriel had to resist the urge to leap across the table and throttle that immense column of a neck.

"Now that *would* be a trick," said Hugo cheerfully, "seeing as how I haven't yet spoken to her."

"You haven't spoken to her?" He knew his face was going a deep red and he could only hope his eyes weren't bulging with fury.

"Why, coz, how could I? I say, if you're not going to eat that ham, I'll have it."

With icy civility Gabriel passed the platter. "If you'll forgive my bluntness, it seems to me that a gentleman would speak to her today."

"I assure you I would if I could," said Hugo amiably. "But I would dearly love to know how you think I might do so given the distance between us."

At this vacuous reply Gabriel finally snapped. "You're under the same roof, man!" he snarled. "Go and talk to her!"

Hugo lowered his fork and stared at Gabriel. "I beg your pardon?"

"Go talk to her! What are you waiting for, you fool?"

"I *am* going, but we're hardly under the same roof. Gad, you haven't been drinking, have you? Because if I may say so, you look like hell."

In his despair and confusion Gabriel grasped the one thread of the conversation that had any connection to reality. "You're going? Going where?"

"Why, home to Whitehaven. That's where my wife-to-be—that is, if she'll have me—lives."

"Your fiancée lives in Whitehaven?"

"Yes, that's what I'm telling you," answered Hugo patiently. He poured Gabriel a cup of coffee and pushed it across the table to him. "Here. Daresay you need this.

Don't take this the wrong way, coz, but you're acting like a horse has kicked you in the head."

Gabriel ignored the coffee. "Let me understand you. You're going to marry some female—for whom I already feel the deepest sympathy—in Whitehaven? *Not* Livia?"

"Livia? You've been drinking *and* a horse has kicked you in the head, because evidently you've forgotten that *you're* engaged to Livia."

"Yes, but—" It was only in the nick of time that Gabriel refrained from spluttering in a completely undignified way. "But I saw you and Livia yesterday— embracing—and I assumed that the two of you were—well, in love."

"In love? With a tame embrace like that? I assure you, coz, that when I'm embracing a girl with amorous intent you'd know it at fifty paces."

Gabriel digested this new information. This new, wonderful, soul-reclaiming information. He could feel himself smiling. Breathing a deep sigh of relief.

"You know," Hugo said reproachfully, "you'd have saved yourself a great deal of trouble if you'd only asked what was going on."

"You're right. You're absolutely right." Gabriel couldn't stop smiling.

And then he remembered.

The smile was wiped from his face.

He pushed back his chair and stood up, toppling it in his haste. "Oh, good Lord, yesterday I broke off our engagement!"

"*You're* the fool," Hugo remarked placidly, reaching for the bowl of potatoes.

Gabriel didn't bother to dispute this slur or even respond to it, for he was already halfway to the door. Impatiently he took the various stairs three steps at a time and when he reached Livia's bedchamber it took all his self-restraint to knock and wait. It would all be all right, it was all going to be fine, everything was wonderful again—

There was no answer and Gabriel went into her room. She wasn't there. The bed was made and the curtains still drawn. Well, perhaps she was . . . where? It was entirely possible, given the convoluted maze of staircases and passageways, that they had bypassed each other and she was, at this very moment, sitting in the breakfast-parlor eating breakfast (if Hugo had left any, that was).

But she wasn't.

A few hours later, every servant in the Hall having been dispatched to help search for her, it seemed pretty clear that Livia was gone.

"My God, I've driven her away," said Gabriel to Hugo, who had just come down the stairs into the Great Hall carrying his neat rucksack. Then he blinked. "You're leaving? Now?"

"Yes, I to my business, you to yours," said Hugo with a breeziness that to Gabriel bordered on callous flippancy. He clapped Gabriel on the shoulder. "Thanks for your hospitality, coz. Much appreciated. She loves you, you know," he added. "Heart and soul. Can't hope for such devotion myself, but I'm glad for you."

With that Hugo was gone, leaving Gabriel to marshal his scattered thoughts. He learned that Livia hadn't taken a horse from the stables, and one sprightly lad reported seeing bootmarks in the path that led toward the lodge. On Primus, Gabriel followed the indentations, which seemed to approximate the size of Livia's feet, all the way to the village where they were lost in the welter of everyday traffic. There he made inquiries about an auburn-haired young lady who might have recently departed on a coach for parts unknown.

Opinions were varied and contradictory, running about half and half for Exeter versus London, and becoming increasingly heated when suddenly silence fell, and a plump old dame stepped forward, very much in the authoritative manner of Moses parting the Red Sea, and accordingly all the other villagers seemed to recede in two separate but equal waves.

"I seen it in my tea leaves this very morning," she pronounced, and by this Gabriel was given to understand that here before him was the acknowledged oracle of Riverton.

"*Not* London, nor Exeter," she said, casting a scornful glance about her. "There was a good bit of tea left in my cup, sir, which means the ocean, of course. And I seen a yellow pitchfork as well. Old John Roger over there—he's my husband, sir—said it was only pieces of straw, but that's rubbish! I seen what I seen. *That's* where you'll find your good lady."

Gabriel felt like *he* was grasping at straws but said to the crowd at large: "Did a coach leave from here toward the ocean?"

"Oh yes, sir," piped up somebody else. "The Bristol diligence passed by just about daybreak."

Gabriel waited no longer. He rode off, hoping he wasn't the stupidest man in existence to place his faith in a village seer with straw in her teacup. Was his love—his dear, noble, infinitely brave love—actually planning on boarding a ship somewhere, and if so, where did she think she would go? For all he knew, she was planning on sailing to Porto de Galinhas, just as he had once thought to.

How long ago that seemed.

Oh God, he hoped she was safe. He hoped she was all right.

He hoped he wasn't too late to tell her what was in his heart.

Chapter 18

She was dreadfully hot and uncomfortable. Her head felt like someone was cruelly beating it with a cudgel—and her throat was raw—and every other part of her felt painfully achy—and she was dying of thirst. Why did no one come to help her? Someone—anyone?

A sudden chill swept over her entire body, as if snow had been dumped upon her. Livia told herself to pull up her blankets. Too weak to even open her eyes, she set her hand groping feebly amongst the bedsheets and touched rough, thin, unfamiliar fabric.

Then it all came back to her: her flight from the Hall, the diversion to the little town of Barrow Gurney which she had thought so clever until, after a tense two days spent hiding and then boarding a coach to Bristol, she discovered that she'd contracted the ague which seemed to have afflicted both her neighbors on the tediously long journey out of Riverton.

She had dragged herself from the coach, took a whiff of the salty sea air, and had just managed to secure for herself a room at the Inn of the Golden Trident before taking to her bed, such as it was.

What day was it? How long had she lain ill like this? For a moment Livia knew a hazy sort of indignation.

She, who never got sick! She had never had the ague in
her life! This brief spurt of vivifying indignation faded
abruptly into miserable self-pity and she wept a little,
tears trickling from the corners of her eyes which she
didn't even feel she had the strength to wipe away, which
only made everything worse. Then she was roastingly
hot again. And shiveringly cold. Eventually she managed to drift into an uneasy sleep in which she dreamed
of endless rides in drafty dirty coaches and suspicious
innkeepers; Surmont Hall, so beautiful and welcoming, and Gabriel, Gabriel, his beloved face above her
own . . .

A big warm hand was lifting her head, and a deep
voice was saying, "Drink this," and the light, pleasant taste of barley water was in her mouth. Eagerly she
gulped at it, felt her head eased back onto the pillows,
and sleep came hard upon her.

Fragments. Being lifted in strong arms, cradled like
an infant. The feel of smooth sheets, warm quilts, a mattress without nasty lumps. A blind, aching exhaustion.
Hot, cold, hot, cold. Her head lifted up and that deep
voice, commanding her to drink, over and over again.
Cool, fragrant cloths on her forehead. Sweet oblivion.

Then, at last, Livia swam up to consciousness and
back into the world of the living. She felt better. In
fact, she felt good. She opened her eyes, to a large, airy
room—a different, nicer room in the inn?—in which—

In which Gabriel himself was there. Oh, how she
hoped this was real, and not a dream. She didn't think
she could bear it otherwise. He was sitting in a chair
next to the bed in which she lay. His long legs in shining boots were stretched out before him, crossed at the
ankle. He wore buff-colored buckskins and a handsome dark-green jacket and his neckcloth was tied very
neatly and attractively.

He *seemed* solid.

Hope—wild, fluttering—leaped into life within her breast.

Gabriel had been reading a book, but as if sensing that she was awake he turned his head and looked at her.

He didn't say anything, which daunted her for a moment, but then she saw that his eyes were warm. So she said, tentatively:

"You came for me."

"Yes."

"And took care of me when I was ill."

"Yes."

"Why?"

"Because I love you."

Without moving a muscle, she let his words sink in. Reverberate. Settle in her bones. Was this much happiness even possible? Joy so great one couldn't even smile?

"Say it again."

"I love you."

"Again."

"I love you, Livia. I've loved you for weeks—for months—quite possibly from the moment I met you. But it's taken me far too long to understand that. Understand myself."

"Can you say it one more time?"

"Yes. I'll be saying it every day for the rest of my life, if you'll let me. I love you."

She sighed, deeply, as if breathing in happiness and exhaling all her misery of those difficult weeks and months.

"Why did you break off our engagement?"

"I saw you in Hugo's arms. And I assumed that you'd fallen in love with him."

"You're an idiot."

"Apparently."

"I didn't mean what I said, Gabriel."

He smiled a little. "Can you be a bit more specific?"

"When I told you the other day that I hoped never to see you again. I was hurt. And angry."

"Naturally you were. I was behaving—ah—idiotically."

"Oh, let's not think about that awful conversation! Tell me instead how you managed to find me."

"On—er—good advice I came to Bristol and searched for you, but you weren't here then, so I went to Severn, Chittening, and Portishead, just in case. Ultimately I came back to this inn because I was looking for a yellow pitchfork."

"A yellow pitchfork?"

"Yes. This is the Inn of the Golden Trident."

She would ask him later to unravel these confusing details. Right now she had more important things on her mind. "Do you know that I love you, too?"

"So Hugo assured me. But I'm glad, Livia—so very glad—to hear it from your own lips."

"I'll never get tired of saying it. Are we going to be married, then?"

"If you'll have me."

"I will. With all my heart. Although—" Livia hesitated, and saw the look of highly gratifying concern on Gabriel's face as he said:

"Although what?"

"I'll never be a proper lady, Gabriel. A *real* lady."

"What does that even mean?"

"Oh, *you* know. Always saying and doing the right thing, keeping my thoughts and opinions to myself. Pretending to be someone I'm not. Being perfect."

"I would never want that."

"You wouldn't want me to be like—oh, Cecily Orr?"

"Never," he said, so fervently that Livia's last, tiny, lingering doubt vanished, never to return.

She smiled then, and reached out a hand which he took in a warm clasp.

"No more running away from me, Livia?"

"No," she promised. "No more."

"Say it again."

"No more running away."

"When I didn't know where you were, I thought I'd lose my mind."

"That's in the past, Gabriel. I am here, with you."

"Yes. Livia, can you feel it?"

"This—energy, pulsing between our hands? Yes. Always."

"An unbroken cord." He was silent for a few moments. Then: "I'm sorry I've been so distant. I've been a beast."

"You've had things on your mind."

"I was so ashamed, so furious with myself, that I couldn't face you. I was afraid."

"I would never have turned away from you, Gabriel."

"I wish I'd known that. I wish I'd talked with you more. Can you forgive me?"

"If you'll forgive me, too." She gave a little sigh. "It's hard, sometimes, to talk, isn't it? In a real and honest way. During all those years at the Abbey, I didn't really have anyone to talk to."

"It *is* hard, Livia. I know that all too well. And now you have me to talk with. I'll do better from now on."

"We both will."

"We already are, I think," he said. "About the Hall—I wanted it to be perfect for you, you know."

"I do know, Gabriel." Thoughtfully, Livia added, "Although it occurs to me that I'm starting to dislike the word 'perfect.'"

"Yes. I too. Let's make a pact to use it very carefully in the future."

"Done."

"Livia," he said.

"Yes, Gabriel?"

"About the Hall. It's going to take a great deal of effort to remedy those years of neglect."

"I'm not afraid of hard work."

"You'll help me?"

"I would love to."

"I suspect the roof leaks in hundreds of places, Crenshaw says they've found more dead rats, and I'm afraid to even go into the cellars."

"I'll go with you."

He smiled. "Thank you. Oh, and Grandmama says we must have cats."

Livia thought about the big striped purring tabby she'd envisioned while daydreaming in the Rose Saloon. *Joy*, sang a little voice in her heart, *joy*. "If Granny says we must have cats, cats we shall have."

"Grandmama was distraught to learn that you'd gone. She's very fond of you—I hope you know that? She wanted to come here and nurse you herself."

"Oh, you wrote to her, then?"

"Of course. But I told her that I claimed the privilege for myself, and that I would bring you home soon."

"Home," echoed Livia dreamily. "Such a lovely, lovely word."

"Yes, I've come to think so too."

Livia smiled at him, then suddenly thought of something and her smile faded. "Oh dear."

"What is it?"

"My stupid reputation—you here at the inn—*your* reputation . . ."

"Oh, you needn't worry. I sent for Flye. She's been

here preserving the proprieties, although I think she's probably been bored out of her mind with so little to do."

Livia stroked his hand, admiring its strength and capableness. "You think of everything," she said approvingly.

"I try. In my letter to Grandmama I asked that Flye bring along some of your clothing as well."

"Thank you, dear heart."

"You're welcome, my love." He paused, then said: "I have something to ask of you. If you feel you cannot do it, however, I would understand."

"What is it?"

"I'd like to invite Grandmama to live with us."

"Of course she must live with us."

"Are you sure? She may try to rule the roost."

"I'm certain she will," said Livia serenely. "But I have a lot to learn from Granny. And, perhaps, she has some things to learn from me. Together, we'll all be a family."

"I don't have much experience at that."

"Neither do I. But I want to try."

"I do too," he said. "Also, there's a good chance I'll occasionally revert back to the Penhallow high-handedness."

"Oh, only occasionally?"

"Old habits are hard to break."

"I know. *I'll* try to keep my temper in check."

"Still, we'll probably quarrel sometimes," he said.

"I have no doubt of it."

"But it will all be worth it."

Livia squeezed his big warm hand. "Yes. We're going to be very happy together."

"I know we will. And while we're on the subject of family," he added, "I'm hoping you'll want children."

"I do. You?"

"Yes. And not for dynastic purposes. I want children for love."

"I'm glad. We're going to have four," Livia told him firmly.

"Four is a good number."

His eyes, she noticed, were sparkling in a very appealing way.

"Shall we begin right now?" he asked.

Livia caught her breath. And smiled a slow smile. "There's no time like the present."

"Wait," he said.

"What?"

"Are you sure you're up for it? That is, you've been ill, and knowing you you're probably hungry. Shall I ring for food? Of course I'm happy to wait until you—"

"Do stop talking and come here." Livia tugged at his hand, and willingly he joined her on the bed where they lay, side by side, looking into each other's eyes.

"You are beautiful," Gabriel said, very softly.

"I'm glad you think so." Livia reached out to pull gently at his neckcloth. "Clothing," she murmured mischievously. "Always too much clothing."

He smiled and kissed her then, and after that—why, after that, there really *was* no more talking. There was no need. That same, familiar, limitless energy connected them, the incandescent heat of desire joined them, and the magic that is love bound them together: warmly, trustingly, forever.

Five days later . . .

The luxurious rented carriage in which Livia and Flye had traveled from Bristol, with Gabriel riding alongside on Primus, pulled up onto the gravel sweep, now beautifully raked. Footmen hurried out to let down the steps and hand Livia down and to take Primus's reins, and through the Hall's open door shot Muffin like a small white cannonball, barking joyfully. He capered about them, doing several speedy laps around their feet, paused for a moment to yap provocatively at the horses, then dashed back to the steps where Grandmama stood, straight and regal and smiling. As Livia approached, she opened her arms wide, and Livia could see that she was crying.

"My darling Livia!" exclaimed Grandmama shakily.

Livia smiled. "Hello, Granny dear," she said, and walked straight into the old lady's embrace, hugging her tightly.

"Can you ever forgive me?"

"For what, Granny dear?"

"For behaving so dreadfully to you."

"There's nothing to forgive, I promise you. That's all behind us now."

Grandmama looked searchingly into Livia's face. "If you're quite certain?"

"Quite certain, Granny."

The troubled tension left the old lady's face, and she pulled a dainty handkerchief from her reticule with which to dry her tears. "Well then, come inside," she said briskly. "We've so much to do! Your wedding, and Evangeline's, to plan. Yes, Arthur Markson has proposed and been accepted! Also, there are two particularly capable candidates for the housekeeper's position—I want to tell you all about them, and arrange for you to meet them. Oh, and I'd like your opinion about new wallpaper for the breakfast-parlor. Come see the samples! Crenshaw, tea, please, in the Rose Saloon. Cook has made your favorite muffins, Livia dear, and she expects you to eat at least three of them. That is—"

She lifted silver brows inquiringly. "Unless you'd rather go to your room, and rest a while?"

Livia laughed. "No. I'm well again. Tea sounds lovely."

Gabriel bent to kiss Grandmama's cheek. "What, no word of welcome for me?" he said reproachfully. "And I like muffins, too."

His grandmother twinkled up at him. "As do I. In fact, I may have three of them myself. Cook made a vast quantity in honor of your return."

"Excellent." Gabriel ushered the ladies inside, and glanced with pleasure around the Great Hall, clean and dusted and orderly once more. He looked at Livia, smiling, remembering their interlude together at the Inn of the Golden Trident, and then wondered if their children would find the armament display as fascinating as he had when he was little. He suspected they would. Many spirited and noisy reenactments of the Knights of the Round Table would take place here someday. Aloud he said: "You've all been busy, I see! How splendid it looks. Thank you! It's wonderful to be home."

And it was.

Two weeks after that . . .

They had done miracles with the chapel. Rotted wood had been replaced with new; the pews stood gleaming in the warm glow of many candelabra. Ancient wall hangings had been lovingly, carefully, cleaned and restored. It was a place entirely different from the one in which Livia had stood in her heartbreak and despair. Now it was filled with light, love, joy.

She stood next to Gabriel, wearing not the elaborate

gown of silver and lace that Madame Lévêque had created back in Bath, but instead a simple dress of deep forest green which had been made for her by Alice Simpkin, the Riverton seamstress. Not only had Grandmama graciously applauded Livia's decision, but she had also offered some very helpful suggestions regarding the design which Alice had received with great willingness.

Livia's hair was twisted low at the nape of her neck in an elegant knot, and she wore a pretty diamond aigrette that had once belonged to Gabriel's mother; around her neck was a diamond necklace which Grandmama had given her. It had, she explained, been in the Penhallow family for generations, and been presented to her upon the occasion of her own wedding. She smiled, sighed, smiled again, saying, *How my Richard would have loved you as I do.*

Now Livia glanced over at Gabriel, tall, broadshouldered, and so very handsome. He wore a coat of deepest mahogany, an exquisitely embroidered waistcoat, and tawny pantaloons, the color of which reminded her of the magnificent stag she had seen—so long ago, it seemed—in the moments before she had met Gabriel for the very first time. Never could she have dreamed that with this man she would find such happiness. Work to share, goals to accomplish together; companionship, laughter, the deepest pleasure, too.

As if feeling her glance, Gabriel turned his head, met her eyes, and smiled down at her.

Right, right, right, sang a little voice within her.

She smiled back at him, then they both looked ahead to where Arthur Markson, with quiet dignity, was conducting the ceremony.

Afterwards, Gabriel had kissed her and she had kissed him, and the guests in the chapel had broken out in spontaneous applause. Then, as husband and wife, master and mistress of Surmont Hall, they joined the Harvest Home celebration in the village where, many times over, their health was toasted, and bonds with the Riverton folk began to heal and grow anew. Grandmama, to her delighted surprise, discovered among the guests the Greenlaw girls—with whom she had decades ago been forbidden to play—no longer girls, no longer Greenlaws, but elderly widows returned to their manor, and just as amiable as she had imagined them to be. Within minutes she, Drusilla, and Amanda had found comfortable seats and, their gray and white heads close together, were talking, smiling, busily making up for lost time.

A month after that . . .

In the Rose Saloon, where a cheerful fire crackled cozily in the hearth, Livia set aside her teacup and opened a letter.

> *My dear Livia,*
> *Mama mentioned that she saw in the papers the announcement of your wedding to Mr. Penhallow, and I must send you my felicitations. You've gotten what you wanted after all. Naturally I was curious (as I'm sure everyone is!) as to why you were married privately and with so little in the way of proper celebration, but I'm certain you had your reasons.*
> *As for myself, you may not have heard—inured in the countryside as you are, and perhaps the papers do not reach you?—that I am betrothed to Sir Edward Brinkley. We are shortly to be*

*married in London, with four hundred guests,
and are to make a bridal tour of the Lakes and
Scotland which is, of course, what the most fashionable couples do. Mama said there was nothing
about your own bridal tour and I suppose Mr.
Penhallow didn't care to take you anywhere.*

A loud purring noise interrupted her. Livia looked
up from the letter, smiled to herself, then reached out
a hand (on which a lovely gold and diamond ring spar-
kled) to stroke the yellow-and-orange-striped tabby
that lay curled up at her side, its furry face looking both
supremely contented and impossibly smug, as only the
happiest of cats can.

*Sir Edward and I will then return to London
for the Season. He has quite a large mansion in
Grosvenor Square, and only think of the balls
and assemblies and rout parties I'll be attending! How unfortunate that you'll have to miss
them. Mama says that I shall be quite the Toast of
Society, given (dare I say it? but I am only quot-
ing her, after all) my looks, my connections, my
fortune and, naturally, my brilliant marriage.*

*How I wish you could attend the wedding. My
gown cost very nearly two hundred pounds.*

> I remain,
> Yours, etc.,
> Cecily

Thoughtfully, Livia folded the letter and put it next
to her teacup. It was strange, but it was to Cecily that
she owed all her happiness. If Gabriel hadn't come into

Wiltshire in order to propose to the Honorable Cecily Orr . . .

It would not do, Livia knew, to thank her. Instead she wrote a brief, impersonal, but courteous note congratulating Cecily upon her engagement, and forgot all about her.

Three months after that . . .

Evangeline Cott and Arthur Markson, both glowing with a happiness that made them look years younger, were married in the Riverton church. In attendance were Mr. and Mrs. Gabriel Penhallow, Mrs. Henrietta Penhallow, the two former Misses Greenlaw, and as many of the villagers as could cram inside.

Afterwards, during the festive wedding-breakfast, quite a few people told Livia that she was glowing, too. One plump old dame, Mrs. Roger, said, nodding wisely, "Two and two, that's four, madam, I seen it in my tea leaves this very morning," and when pressed for an explanation by her fellows would only smile cryptically, with a pleased, faraway sort of quality, as if looking into a future of which she highly approved.

A month after that . . .

> *Dear Livia,*
> *Thank you for your note. As no doubt you have heard, my wedding was quite the event of the Season. The Duke of Clarence himself came toward*

the very end of the ceremony which was, I assure you, a signal honor. Mama said that she has never seen anyone with such an air of royal dignity.

Sir Edward did not, after all, care for a bridal tour, and although it goes without saying he was sorry to forego the pleasures of the London Season, he thought that perhaps it would be best for us to go directly to his home in Lincolnshire. It is enormous—mentioned in all the guidebooks—and extremely historical. Queen Elizabeth is said to have had dinner here and been very complimentary as to the stewed rabbit. Speaking of which, Sir Edward is very fond of hunting and so we often enjoy a variety of rabbit dishes. The wine cellars here are the talk of the county—they are extensive and also very historical. Sir Edward knows a vast deal about wine and I am learning more about it every day. You would be amazed at my knowledge, I am sure.

Sir Edward's dear sister Cassandra and I have become great friends, and spend many hours together. She has taught me some very clever stitches and Sir Edward says he has never seen such superior altar cloths.

Well, I suppose you are terribly bored by life in the countryside. I myself find it wondrous agreeable, with so many diversions that it would take me an hour to write them all down for you. The days simply fly by.

> *I remain, etc.,*
> *The Honorable Lady Brinkley*

Nearly one year to the day after she and Gabriel were married, Livia gave birth to their first child.

Sitting up in bed against a bank of pillows, she held the baby, wrapped in the softest of blankets, in her arms and stared in wonder at the small, perfect face. Gabriel sat next to her, his arm snugly around her shoulders, staring too.

"She's beautiful, just like her mother," said Gabriel, softly. "Well done, Mrs. Penhallow."

Livia smiled. "You played a role in this, too."

"A modest, but enjoyable one. I believe she's going to have auburn hair."

"Dear me, do you think so? I hope she'll be blonde, like Granny was. And look! Your dimple on her chin. I'm so glad about that. What shall we call her?"

Gabriel pressed a gentle kiss onto the top of Livia's head. "When I met you in the woods that day, I almost thought you to be a pixie, a sylph of the forest. What if we were to name our little girl Titania, the queen of the fairies?"

"Shakespeare's Titania," said Livia, musingly. "It reminds me of Titus as well—Granny's son. What a wonderful way to remember him. I like it. But only if Granny does also."

And when shortly Grandmama came to meet her first great-grandchild, her opinion was sought, and she liked it, too. So the baby was called Titania, after her great-uncle Titus, and Georgiana, after Livia's mother, and Elizabeth, after Grandmama's mother, and Johanna, after Livia's father Jonathan.

"Titania Georgiana Elizabeth Johanna Penhallow," Livia said, "you have a very nice name. Welcome to the family, little one."

The baby opened her eyes, and it was as if a kind of sweet eldritch smile passed across her tiny face, as if she was seeing the pleased countenances of her predecessors, Stuarts and Penhallows and Espensons and more, stretching back into the distant mists of time immemorial. Then she opened her rosebud mouth and in a very imperious way demanded something to eat.

"Good Lord," said Gabriel, in comical dismay. "She already has your appetite, my love."

Smiling, Livia put their babe to her breast. "Why, so she does," she said placidly. "And speaking of which, please could you ring for a nuncheon? I'm *starving*."

Don't miss the next
Penhallow Dynasty novel

THE LAIRD TAKES A BRIDE

Coming Fall 2017
from Avon Books

The stronghold of clan Douglass
Near Wick Bay, Scotland
1811

It was Fiona Douglass's seventy-first wedding.

To be precise, it was her seventy-first time *attending* a wedding.

When you belonged to a large and thriving clan, there were naturally a lot of weddings to go to and the total number was bound to be high, especially if you weren't a giddy girl any longer, but—to put it politely—a lady of considerable maturity.

So: seventy-one weddings for Fiona.

The details had long begun to blur, of course, but there were certain ceremonies that stood out in her mind.

Today would be memorable because her youngest sister, Rossalyn, was getting married.

Two years ago, in this very church, a spectacular brawl had erupted at the altar when the bridegroom's twin brother (already roaring drunk) had lunged forward, seized the hapless bride, and tried to carry her off. A wild melee had ensued as several other men (also already drunk) had, with joyful shouts, joined in. Forty-five minutes later, the combatants subdued by brute force and the bride's veil hastily repaired, the ceremony had proceeded without further incident, the chastened, bloodied twin the very first to warmly shake his brother's hand.

It was also in this church that three years ago Fiona had attended the wedding of her younger sister Dallis.

Seven years ago, old Mrs. Gibbs, aged ninety-eight and heartily disliked by nearly everyone in the entire clan, had loudly expired just before the vows were spoken. The general agreement was that she'd done it deliberately in a last triumphant bid for attention, and that she was likely chuckling up in heaven (or down below in the other place) because afterwards, as her corpse was being removed, her pet ferret had crawled out from a pocket in her skirt and dashed up the towering headdress of a haughty dowager from Glasgow, from which vantage point it had leaped gracefully onto the shoulder of Fiona's own mother, who had screamed and then fainted, sending the bride into hysterics and several small boys into paroxysms of noisy laughter, thereby provoking Fiona's father, the mighty chieftain of clan Douglass, into a fury so awful that the wedding was quietly called off and no one dared to partake of the gargantuan feast laid out in the Great Hall, resulting, of course, in a great deal of secret rejoicing in the servants' hall for at least three days after that. The ferret was never seen again.

Eight years ago, it had rained so hard during the wedding of Fiona's cousin Christie that the church had begun to leak in (Fiona had counted) fourteen places and quite a few hats had been ruined.

And nine years ago—why, nine years ago Fiona had

watched as her younger sister Nairna had married the love of her life.

The love of *Fiona's* life.

Fiona had never told Nairna that. She knew that seventeen-year-old Nairna was madly in love with Logan Munro, and as for Logan, who could fault him for preferring sweet Nairna Douglass, as soft and playful as a kitten, petite and rounded in all the right places and with masses of dark curls that framed her piquant little face most fetchingly? Who *wouldn't* prefer Nairna to Fiona, at eighteen painfully thin and gawky and oversensitive, who blurted things out and tripped over her own feet? Especially since, at that moment in time, Nairna's dowry had been substantially greater than Fiona's.

It all made total sense.

Even back then, in the darkest period of her devastation, Fiona hadn't been able to summon resentment or hostility toward Nairna, whom she had loved—still loved—with the fierce, protective devotion of an oldest sister for her younger siblings.

To be sure, there was a secret part of her, a sad and cowardly part, that would have driven her far from home on this lovely summer's day, where she wouldn't be forced to look upon Logan Munro's handsome face, but to this desire she hadn't succumbed; wild horses couldn't have kept her from attending Rosslyn's wedding. She had, though, slid inconspicuously into the very last pew. She did this also as a kindness to her fellow guests. Even with her hair twisted into smooth braids, all coiled together and set low on her nape, she was so tall that she could easily block the view of others behind her. Nonetheless, and thanks to her accursed height, she could plainly see Logan where he sat, several pews away, next to Nairna.

Logan's hair was still black as a raven's wing, still

thick. His shoulders were still broad and heavily muscled beneath the fine mulberry-colored fabric of his
fashionable coat.

And, Fiona realized, a heart could still physically
hurt, could ache painfully within one's breast, even
after nine long years.

She made herself look away from Logan.

Instead she gazed down at her hands, loosely clasped
in her lap. Hands that weren't white as they ought to
be, fingers that were a little coarsened by riding without
gloves, by long hours working in her garden.

Around her slim—the less charitable might even
have said bony—wrist was looped the silken cord of
her reticule.

Surreptitiously Fiona loosened the opening of the
reticule and pulled out a small piece of paper, quietly
unfolding it. On it she had written her latest list.

Ask Dallis—when new baby due?
Avoid Logan
5 sheep with bloody scours, 2 with rupturing
    blisters—why?
Help Aunt Bethia find her spectacles
    (bedchamber? solarium?)
Avoid Logan
Avoid Cousin Isobel, too
Mother's birthday next Saturday
Tell Burns—STOP cutting roses too early
Avoid Logan
Avoid Logan

Fiona withdrew a small pencil from her reticule and
added another item.

Stop thinking about Logan

She also wrote:

*Make sure maid packed Rossalyn's warmest
    wraps & tartans
Northern cow pasture—fence fixed?
Osla Tod—toothache—better or worse?
Stop thinking about Logan*

Then she carefully folded the little piece of paper in
two, slid it and her pencil back into her reticule, and
looked toward the front of the church, ensuring that her
gaze was firmly fixed on Rossalyn and her bridegroom,
Jamie MacComhainn.

How exquisite was Rossalyn's gown, all shimmery
silk and delicate lace, and how beautiful she looked in
it. Jamie, in his turn, was a bonny young man. Fiona
eyed him—the back of him—speculatively. Perhaps
even a little bit suspiciously. He was amiable and intelligent, and from a good family. Father had approved
his suit readily enough and had even, in a sentimental
spasm, doubled Rossalyn's dowry, and so here she was,
not quite seventeen, a bride.

Fiona watched as Rossalyn and Jamie turned to each
other and smiled. Oh, she hoped that all would be well.
She wished that she knew Jamie better, that she trusted
him more.

But thanks to handsome, charming, winsome Logan
Munro, Fiona tended to view men with a certain
skepticism.

A certain reserve.

She thought back to that dark time when she was
eighteen, when Logan had come to Wick Bay to visit.
Nothing formal had been declared between them, but
enough had transpired, previously, in Edinburgh, to
make Fiona feel confident that she'd soon be engaged.

Instead, with stunning speed Logan had trans-
ferred his affections to Nairna, gone to Father to request her hand in marriage, and been—to everyone's
amazement—accepted on the spot, quite possibly because Nairna, among all her sisters, held the softest
spot in the hard and erratic heart of Bruce Douglass.

Even though Fiona had confided in her mother about
her hopes, Mother had, without missing a beat, continued to smile and flutter around Logan, petting and
praising her future son-in-law. Fiona had long considered her mother—warm and affectionate, plump and
still pretty in middle age—as soft and yielding and altogether as comfortable as a child's stuffed toy, but still,
her behavior did seem a trifle callous.

Privately, Fiona had said to her, hating the little
tremble in her voice:

"Mother, why are you so *friendly* toward Logan?
After what he did to me?"

"Oh, my darling child, I know how hard it is for
you, truly I do," said her mother, her large dark eyes
filling with tears. "I remember how dreadful I felt when
I discovered that your father had married me for my
fortune—I really had thought it was a love match. It
all happened during that terrible famine of the eighties,
and people were starving. I was an heiress, you know.
And only seventeen, like dear Nairna! But," she had
added, smiling through her tears, "I was considered
quite beautiful in my day! Even your father said so! And
he used my dowry so cleverly—within a few years he
brought the clan back into prosperity!"

Earnestly Mother had leaned forward to pat Fiona's
hand. "Thanks to your father we all live so comfortably, Fiona dear! Our gowns and jewels! Everything of
the finest quality! So you see, everything always works
out for the best. I'm sure that Nairna and Logan will

be very happy together—such a *handsome* couple, and he simply *dotes* upon her!—and that another suitor will come along for you—someone you'll like even better."

Fiona had brushed that aside. "You don't regret marrying Father?"

"Regret?" Mother's dark eyes had shown nothing but bewilderment. "What a foolish notion, Fiona, to be sure! Besides, by the time I met your father I had, luckily, very nearly recovered from my stupid infatuation for my second cousin Ludovic—or was he my *third* cousin? So confusing!—it would never have done, you know, for the very next year he went to America and was killed. And your father so tall and so strong, and so *handsome!* Like a Viking warrior, everyone said!" Mother had fidgeted with the soft fringe of her shawl, then smiled again and with every appearance of sincerity went on: "I've been very happy these twenty years. Your father has taken such good care of us, and I'm just sorry that I haven't been able to do my duty by him."

She meant, Fiona knew, that she had not been able to produce a living son, despite miscarriages (the full number of which she didn't divulge), two stillbirths, and four healthy baby girls. Of this sad fact everyone in the Douglass keep was fully aware, for periodically Father would erupt into one of his angry outbursts, quite often in the Great Hall with dozens of people present.

You've failed me, madam! he would roar, pounding his silver goblet on the table, denting it badly. *Other men have ten sons—a dozen sons—and I have none!*

Or: *I had my pick of maidens, and 'twas my misfortune to choose you, madam. They told me you were fertile! Fertile for sons, that is,* he might add, with a contemptuous glance toward his daughters.

Or: *I've managed to save this clan from extinction, and what have you done all these years? Nothing!*

Mother would sit quietly, passively, but Fiona—watchful, observant, even as a child—would see the quiver of her tender mouth, the quick rise and fall of her chest as she gave a deep silent sigh, her shoulders held tensely high.

And then Father might fling his tankard out into the Hall, striking an unwary soul, or abruptly stand up and shove back his chair, toppling it, or stalk off, aiming kicks at the dogs who, fortunately, had learned to be preternaturally nimble when their master's voice was raised. Fiona would look around and see the tears in Mother's eyes, and in her sisters' eyes, too. Not hers, though: her eyes were dry and her heart would feel all stony and angry.

"Mother," she would hiss, "he's *awful.*"

And then Mother would pull herself together, and drop her shoulders, and smile. "Oh no, Fiona dear, it's just that he's had so much on his mind. Didn't you hear him say there's a wolf after his sheep, and the Talbots are feuding again and setting fires? It's not easy being chieftain, you know. Here—won't you have another slice of mutton? I vow, you've somehow gotten thinner since breakfast!"

And grumblingly Fiona would accept the mutton, being, in fact, still hungry.

The human storm that was Father would just as easily shift into good humor, and then there was no one in the world more delightful to be around. But you could never trust that he'd *stay* cheerful. His expression could darken in an instant, his fists would clench, and things might fly across the room. You always felt a little wary around Bruce Douglass.

Eventually, he seemed to accept his fate as the father of only daughters. There was, at least, a crumb of comfort for him in this unfortunate debacle: the wealth he'd amassed made the Douglass girls highly desirable matrimonial quarry.

Father had therefore had quite a bit of fun by decreasing his daughters' dowries on a whim, or suddenly increasing them to astronomical sums, thus keeping his lawyers in a continual anxious flurry of documents destroyed and rewritten. Fiona's case was a little different. When, in his opinion, she'd been particularly annoying by—for example—forcefully challenging something he'd said, or disappearing all day on her horse, Father would retaliate by eliminating her dowry entirely. But not forever. The sun would shine, Father would change his mind, and eventually restore it, quite possibly to a radically different amount.

Over the years, suitors for the Douglass girls came and went, thronged and melted away, and Father watched, welcomed, interrogated, feinted, scorned, rejected, laughed, and allowed himself to be shamelessly flattered by them all. One by one, his daughters wed.

All except Fiona, who had never, somehow, found someone she liked enough to accept, and Father, rather surprisingly, had only nine or ten times threatened to lock her in her room until she said yes.

And so the time had passed, on the whole not unpleasantly. Fiona had kept herself busy. There was always so much to do.

But weddings tend to resurrect old issues, old emotions; new ideas, new possibilities.

As if on cue, Fiona was distracted from gazing steadfastly (if a little absently) at Rossalyn and Jamie when, from his seat four pews away, Niall Birk turned and smiled at her, showing all his teeth and this, in the context of a rather long face with large damp eyes, reminding Fiona forcibly of a horse.

Niall Birk hadn't given her the time of day for a quite

a while, which probably meant that Father had, in a last-ditch effort to get his remaining daughter off his hands, taken advantage of the massive clan gathering at the keep to make it known that Fiona was not only dowered again, but—judging by the breadth of Niall Birk's grin—very generously as well.

Fiona's suspicion was confirmed when, as soon as the ceremony was over, not only was she swiftly approached by Niall, but Ross Stratton and Walraig Tevis came crowding up around her, eagerly soliciting her hand for the dancing that was to follow the enormous meal awaiting them in the Great Hall.

Fiona looked at them thoughtfully. She was twenty-seven. Since Logan, she'd never met a man who had caught her interest, or made her laugh, or inspired her blood to run a little hotter.

Perhaps that was all behind her now.

Perhaps she was incapable of falling in love again.

Still, marriage had its benefits, didn't it? She would be mistress of her own household. Maybe there would be children. And she'd no longer be subject to the unpredictable, tempestuous swings of Father's moods—that in itself was appealing.

Walraig Tevis, a great lumbering fellow nearly as wide as he was tall, pushed spindly Ross Stratton to one side. "You're daft, Stratton, to think you've got a chance with Fiona," he said, his heavy face alight with malicious humor. "Eh, she's a full head over you, you wee mousie, you'd be the laughingstock of the clan!" He jabbed a beefy elbow into Ross's chest with such force that the smaller man reeled backwards and nearly fell over, but with surprising dexterity he whipped from his boot a nasty-looking dagger and only the quick intervention of the scandalized minister prevented what promised to be a vicious altercation, and possibly a murder or two, from occurring a mere twenty paces from the church.

Yes, as a married woman she'd be free of Father, Fiona thought, but she'd also be putting herself in the power of a husband who would have the indisputable right to do anything he liked with her.

To her.

And yet . . . and yet if *any* of them had given the slightest sign that they really liked her, she might be tempted to seize the opportunity provided her by Father's momentary generosity. Niall, for example, wasn't bad-looking (especially since she liked horses). He wasn't completely stupid. And he had a decent estate not far from where Rossalyn would be living with her husband Jamie MacComhainn; she could visit them often.

Experimentally, Fiona stepped a little closer to Niall. She caught a whiff of stale sweat, alcohol, onions, and even—her nose wrinkled—a faint, flat, rank scent of blood. She flashed a quick glance over him and saw a reddish clump of matted hair near one temple.

He grinned. "Bad, eh? You should see Dougal Gow. Poor lad couldn't rise from his bed to come to the wedding. He'll miss the feast *and* the dancing. So, you'll give me the first two reels, lass?"

Fiona had a sudden image of Niall, stinking of blood and onions, saying casually to Rossalyn at some future festive gathering: *Fiona couldn't come, for the poor lass is in bed—fell down the stairs and she's all black and blue.*

She took a step back, abruptly reminded of something that happened during last year's sheep-shearing festival, when she had allowed Niall to kiss her behind a shed (she'd had a dowry then). Pressing his mouth on hers, he'd bent her neck back too far, while at the same time he squeezed her breast so roughly she'd thought for a bad, a very bad moment she would pass out.

She answered coolly: "No. I'm not dancing."

"Your loss."

"I'll try to bear it."

His arm shot out and he took a hard grip on her upper arm. "I don't care for your tone. You're to be a good girl and choose a husband from among the three of us. It's your father's decree."

"A fine way to woo, Niall Birk, grabbing at a woman and scowling at her. Let go of me."

His fingers tightened painfully for a moment before he released her. "You're thinking I'm a bad bargain, no doubt, but at least I'm not a great lump like Walraig Tevis, who'd crush you under him like a bug, or Ross Stratton, who'd as soon garrote you as kiss you."

A cold chill shivered up Fiona's spine, but she only said, lightly, "You may be right. Would you excuse me, please? My mother needs me." And she flitted off to where Mother did, in fact, require help untangling herself from the enormous plaid shawl she had wound about herself in so convoluted a fashion she was in danger of—curiously enough—falling down the church steps.

"Oh, thank you, dear!" Mother said breathlessly. "It was a lovely ceremony, wasn't it? I cried just like a baby! But I always do at weddings. I cried at my own! Isn't our Rossalyn the bonniest bride you've ever seen? Although Dallis, of course, was *just* as pretty, and so was Nairna! Your Aunt Bethia quite agrees with me! And oh! Bethia shared with me the most astounding piece of news! She had it from her sister-in-law Sorcha who is, I'm sure, *most* reliable. Apparently Alasdair Penhallow has been scandalizing the Eight Clans for years with his disgraceful behavior, and not just on special occasions but every day! Consuming spirits to excess, presiding over debaucheries, and so on! A monster of irresponsibility! And he the great laird of Castle Tadgh!"

"Well, Mother, so what? Besides, if he's been doing this sort of thing for years, it's hardly news," said Fiona, guiding her overexcited parent down the uneven stone steps and at the same time keeping a sharp eye out for Logan Munro.

"No, no, you mistake me! According to Bethia, Alasdair Penhallow, on a dare, recently rode his horse all throughout his castle, and without a stitch of clothes on!"

"Did the horse have a saddle?" inquired Fiona, now a little interested.

"Bethia didn't say. I'll have to ask her. But isn't it an atrocious tale?" Mother made a tsk-tsk sound, but whether it was because of the enormous pile of dog manure blocking her path or her feelings about the shocking Alasdair Penhallow, Fiona didn't bother to ask. Her flicker of interest had already waned. And she had more important things to think about.

Nairna—is she expecting too??
Make plan: must get rid of Niall, Walraig,
    & Ross
STOP THINKING ABOUT
    LOGAN MUNRO

Throughout the feast, Fiona was irritated to find that her three would-be suitors had decided to all sit next to her, two on one side and one on the other, altogether giving her a disagreeable sense of claustrophobia. It quite took away one's own appetite, which made her even more resentful.

Nonetheless, as the evening wore on, seemingly interminably, she not only managed to avoid the dancing, she also went here and there and got quite a lot accomplished.

She found Aunt Bethia's spectacles, which were, in fact, in the stillroom, although they had inexplicably been placed in the bowl of a large wooden mortar otherwise used for crushing herbs.

She dashed up to Rossalyn's room, spoke with her maid, approved the packing of the trunks.

She neatly avoided speaking with Cousin Isobel, against whom she still bore a grudge after nine long years, for her role in the Logan Munro disaster—

But no. She *wasn't* thinking about him.

She went on.

She learned that her sister Dallis, three years married and with a little one at home just taking his first wobbly steps, was looking forward to the birth of her second child in six months or so.

She enjoyed a fascinating and productive discussion with old Clyde Keddy about rupturing blisters and the various possibilities for treatment, although he confessed he was stumped about the bloody scours.

She drew Nairna aside, into a private alcove, and clasped her hands in her own. She looked down into her sister's lovely heart-shaped face; it was thinner and paler than she remembered, although Nairna looked decidedly plumper in her midsection. "Are you quite well, my dearie?"

Nairna smiled radiantly. "I've never been happier! Oh, Fiona, it's happened at last!"

"You're increasing?"

"Yes! Finally!"

"I'm so glad for you!" said Fiona, meaning it, and warmly hugged Nairna, already thinking, in the back of her mind, about sewing some adorable little garments for the baby in addition to the ones she'd already planned for Dallis's.

"Logan's been so patient all these years," Nairna said, blushing. "It's not been for lack of trying. But three months ago, my courses ceased, and I'm already showing! And it's all thanks to Tavia Craig!"

"Who is that, my dearie?"

"She's a wisewoman, and so awfully kind! She cured Logan's mother of the warts on her hands—they've been plaguing her for *months*—and knew exactly what to do to make his sister's cough go away!"

"Yes, but—" Fiona hesitated. Wasn't there a vast difference between warts and coughs, and difficulty in conceiving a baby? "What does Mother say?"

"Mother said she wished *she'd* consulted a wise-woman, for very likely she would have had boys instead of girls."

Fiona refrained from commenting that Mother's regret implied a desire to negate her daughters' very existence, then immediately was ashamed of this sour thought, for she knew that Mother loved them all. "Well, it's wonderful news to be sure, my dearie!" she said instead.

"Yes, and Tavia is *certain* it's a boy! Logan is so excited!"

"So excited about what?" came a familiar voice, and at the sound of it Fiona felt as if her stomach dropped like a boulder to her toes. She took a breath, and tilted her head toward Logan Munro. She was considered very tall for a woman, but Logan was even taller. Once upon a time, she had loved that about him, loved gazing *up* into his deep, dark eyes.

"Excited about the baby, Logan!" said Nairna breathlessly, her pretty face lighting up as it always did when she saw him. "I've just been telling Fiona all about it—about *him!*"

"Yes," Logan replied, smiling, "it's wonderful news, my beautiful one."

Nairna blushed all over again, then said, "Oh! I have another question for Dallis about the lying-in! Stay,

368 LISA BERNE

darling, and talk to Fiona! Doesn't she look lovely in that blue gown?"

"Indeed she does." Logan watched as his wife hurried away.

With that crest of thick black hair and juttingly straight nose, his profile was magnificent. And how often, how very often, had he called her, Fiona, *my beautiful one* . . . Fiona tamped down a treacherous rush of sweet memories as Logan turned to her again. Behind them, along the stone corridor, tramped a raucous horde of guests, singing "At the Auld Trysting Tree" at the top of their lungs and banging—God in heaven, where had they gotten pots and pans?—on the walls. Yet Logan never took his eyes from her. It was another one of his attractions: He always made her feel as if she was the only one in any room, at any gathering . . .

Fiona almost felt as if she was melting in the delicious warmth of Logan's proximity. The years seemed to suddenly dissolve between them—she was once again a romantic, dazzled eighteen-year-old, and she found herself leaning a little closer to him, her lips parting expectantly, her limbs all at once feeling wonderfully heavy. Then, with an inner gasp, she thought in horror: *You fool! Nairna! Your sister!*

She drew herself up to her full height, said coolly, "My congratulations to you both," and briskly walked past Logan Munro, away from him, ignoring the fact that in his expression, his half-smile, was a sympathetic sort of understanding, as if a little secret bond, unshakable, unbreakable, drew them together.

A night and a day later, the celebrations were finally over. Her sisters had all left with their husbands. Nearly all the guests had gone, too, and the weary servants were hard at work cleaning up the keep—no small task given the broken dishes, the spilled food, the toppled bottles of spirits, the rushes in the common areas sodden and bad-smelling, and everywhere discarded items of clothing which made Fiona frown as she made her way up to the solarium where Mother spent much of her time. Here, at least, was order and cleanliness. Well, actually, to be honest there was more cleanliness than order, for Mother, as dear and delightful as she was, wasn't known for her organizational abilities.

Still, as afternoon sunlight poured in through the long bank of narrow windows that had once served as arrow-loops, the solarium was a pleasant chamber, with the scattered piles of fabric, the great loom in the corner, Mother's harp, old copies of *La Belle Assemblée,* shawls and ribbons and colorful spools of thread all combining in a scene of familiar and cheerful disarray.

"Hello," said Fiona cautiously, standing at the threshold.

Mother looked up from the escritoire at which she sat and put aside her quill, her face brightening in welcome, then promptly clouding. "Oh, Fiona *dear,*" she said uneasily.

Fiona came in, and threw herself into a chair by the fire, stretching out her long legs to warm her toes in their tall boots. "What's done is done, Mother," she replied, unable to keep a slight note of defiance from her voice.

"Yes, but to challenge Niall Birk and Walraig Tevis to an arm-wrestling match?" said Mother with plaintive dismay. "And then to beat them both!"

"I can't brag about it, Mother, for they were both so drunk they could hardly sit up."

"Brag about it? Oh my goodness, why would you?

So unmaidenly! And then to dare Ross Stratton to compete with you in a footrace!"

"It wasn't a fair match either. He was drunk *and* for some reason he had on someone else's shoes, and they were far too small for him."

Mother gave a little moan. "Oh, Fiona, this is dreadful!"

"Yes, but Mother, I *had* to get rid of them, don't you see? Everyone mocked them so badly that they left before dawn, without trying to propose to me again. And now Father can't pressure me into accepting them. Wasn't it clever of me?"

"Well, yes, of course it was, darling, you've always been so terribly clever, but now . . ." Mother looked nervously toward the doorway. She lowered her voice and went on: "But now your father is *furious* with you, and he's completely taken away your dowry again."

"I don't care about the dowry, but—" Fiona felt a frisson of anxiety on Mother's behalf. "—he's not angry at you, is he?"

"Oh no, dear, it's all you, I'm afraid. But without a dowry, and for who knows how long, what is going to happen to you? Who will want to marry you?"

Fiona knew that Mother didn't mean to be hurtful. But still it did hurt, a little, in some obscure, unprotected area of her heart. "Why, I'll go on living here forever," she said lightly. "When Father isn't angry at me, he finds me quite useful to have around. In fact, when he's in a pleasant state of mind, or is a little inebriated, he's often said I'm nearly as good as a son—such a way as I have with the crops and the animals."

Mother brightened again. "That's true. And you're *such* a help in the keep! Speaking of which, Cousin Isobel would like to switch bedchambers. She's worried her room is overlarge and requires too much wood to keep warm. I've tried to dissuade her—we've wood enough for an army!—but she insists! Please could you talk to Mrs. Abercrombie about it?"

"Cousin Isobel is still here? Ugh. Why?"

"Yes, dear, she's come for a nice long visit. You ought not to scowl so. You'll get wrinkles before your time, and that won't help matters! I invited her to stay on because she's suffered some financial reverses. She's had to give up her house in Edinburgh, you know, the poor thing. Where are you going?" Mother added, as her firstborn stood and shook out her skirts.

"Riding." Fiona glanced down at Mother's cluttered escritoire. "Your quill needs mending. Would you like me to do that?"

"No, thank you, darling, I've quite finished my letters. *Six* thank-you notes, and I even managed to write to Henrietta Penhallow—I've owed her a letter for these many ages."

Penhallow. That name again. How odd. "Who is she, Mother?"

"A distant connection in England, whom I met in London many years ago."

"Oh," said Fiona, losing interest. Not only did she want to avoid Cousin Isobel, she'd prefer to get out of the keep without encountering Father if possible, while his temper was running high. "Well, I'm off to see Osla Tod, and bring her a tincture for her toothache. You know she lives beyond the bogs, so don't expect me for dinner."

"Oh dear, *must* you stay out past sunset? You'll take a groom, won't you?"

"No." Mother knew she'd left off having a groom accompany her on her rides for many years now, but still she faithfully asked, in the same sweet and hopeful way. Fiona dropped a kiss on Mother's smooth white forehead and quickly left the solarium, her boot heels clicking sharply on the cold flagstone flooring. She spoke with the housekeeper Mrs. Abercrombie about accommodating Cousin Isobel's request, and it was with relief that some half an hour later she was on her stallion Gealag and riding fast—away from the keep, away from Father, away from them all. Sleep had not come to her last night and now she was fatigued to her very bones, but at least she could, for these few snatched hours, be free.

She loved the feel of the cool afternoon air ruffling her hair and her skirts, loved the vibrant green of summer all around her and the great blue sky above. Loved gripping the leather reins in her bare hands and how willingly her big white horse carried her along. It was almost like flying. Her tired mind calmed, quieted; slowly, slowly, almost without realizing it, she drifted into a pleasant daydream.

Herself. In a lovely blue gown. Dancing, swirling circles on a polished wood floor, her lacy hem fluttering around her ankles. Held in strong arms. Her heart beating hard. Looking up. Looking up into dark eyes, alight with passion . . .

No.

Fiona snapped out of it. Gripped Gealag's reins more tightly. And fiercely summoned a new image into her mind.

A small piece of paper.

Rheumatism—Mrs. Ambercrombie—
    chamomile? Cat's claw?
Order new parcel of books
Sheep & rupturing blisters—research.
    Cause, treatment?
Visit northern cow pasture tomorrow

Gift for Mother's birthday?
Start sewing baby things
Gealag—to be shoed next week
NEW RUSHES brought in tomorrow
   WITHOUT FAIL

And so it went. Today she would visit old Osla Tod. Tomorrow she would cross off as many items as she could from her list. The next day, she would do the same. And the day after that as well. There was, after all, a kind of comfort in knowing what the weeks and months ahead would bring.

But Fiona was wrong.

Five days later, the letter came—the letter that would change everything.

THE SMYTHE-SMITH QUARTET BY #1 *NEW YORK TIMES* BESTSELLING AUTHOR

JULIA QUINN

JUST LIKE HEAVEN
978-0-06-149190-0

Honoria Smythe-Smith is to play the violin (badly) in the annual musicale performed by the Smythe-Smith quartet. But first she's determined to marry by the end of the season. When her advances are spurned, can Marcus Holroyd, her brother Daniel's best friend, swoop in and steal her heart in time for the musicale?

A NIGHT LIKE THIS
978-0-06-207290-0

Anne Wynter is not who she says she is, but she's managing quite well as a governess to three highborn young ladies. Daniel Smythe-Smith might be in mortal danger, but that's not going to stop the young earl from falling in love. And when he spies a mysterious woman at his family's annual musicale, he vows to pursue her.

THE SUM OF ALL KISSES
978-0-06-207292-4

Hugh Prentice has never had patience for dramatic females, and Lady Sarah Pleinsworth has never been acquainted with the words *shy* or *retiring*. Besides, a reckless duel has left Hugh with a ruined leg, and now he could never court a woman like Sarah, much less dream of marrying her.

THE SECRETS OF SIR RICHARD KENWORTHY
978-0-06-207294-8

Sir Richard Kenworthy has less than a month to find a bride, and when he sees Iris Smythe-Smith hiding behind her cello at her family's infamous musicale, he thinks he might have struck gold. Iris is used to blending into the background, so when Richard courts her, she can't quite believe it's true.

JQ4 0916

At Avon Books, we know your passion for romance—once you finish one of our novels, you find yourself wanting more.

May we tempt you with . . .

- **Excerpts** from our upcoming releases.

- Entertaining **extras**, including authors' personal photo albums and book lists.

- Behind-the-scenes **scoop** on your favorite characters and series.

- **Sweepstakes** for the chance to win free books, romantic getaways, and other fun prizes.

- Writing **tips** from our authors and editors.

- **Blog** with our authors and find out why they love to write romance.

- **Exclusive content** that's not contained within the pages of our novels.

Join us at
www.avonbooks.com

AVON

An Imprint of HarperCollins*Publishers*
www.avonromance.com

Available wherever books are sold or please call 1-800-331-3761 to order.

FTH 1013

*G*ive in to your Impulses!

These unforgettable stories only take a second
to buy and give you hours of reading pleasure!

Go to *www.AvonImpulse.com* and see what we
have to offer.

Available wherever e-books are sold.

AVONIMPULSE

IMP 0811